MIDNIGHT TRAIN TO PRAGUE

ALSO BY CAROL WINDLEY

❧

Home Schooling
Breathing Under Water
Visible Light

MIDNIGHT TRAIN TO PRAGUE

A Novel

CAROL WINDLEY

HarperCollins *Publishers Ltd*

Published by HarperCollins Publishers Ltd

First Canadian edition

HarperCollins books may be purchased for educational, business
or sales promotional use through our Special Markets Department.

HarperCollins Publishers Ltd
Bay Adelaide Centre, East Tower
22 Adelaide Street West, 41st Floor
Toronto, Ontario, Canada
M5H 4E3

www.harpercollins.ca

Library and Archives Canada Cataloguing in Publication

Title: Midnight train to Prague : a novel / Carol Windley.
Names: Windley, Carol, 1947- author.
Identifiers: Canadiana (print) 20200173200 | Canadiana (ebook) 20200173251 |
ISBN 9781443461023 (softcover) | ISBN 9781443461030 (ebook)
Classification: LCC PS8595.I5926 M54 2020 | DDC C813/.54—dc23

Printed and bound in the United States of America

LSC/H 9 8 7 6 5 4 3 2 1

For Robert

MIDNIGHT TRAIN TO PRAGUE

PART
ONE

——

In rivers, the water that you touch
is the last of what has passed and the first
of that which is to come; so with present time.
—LEONARDO DA VINCI

CHAPTER ONE

One day, she would return to her villa in the Palermo district of Buenos Aires, her mother said, speaking as much to a photograph on the wall in their Charlottenburg apartment as to Natalia. The photograph was printed on albumen paper. It was fragile, irreplaceable, and to her mother an object of veneration. Sometimes Natalia heard her speaking to it in Spanish, as if it had ears. The villa in the photograph had curved iron balconies, tall windows, and was set in a lush, subtropical garden with a marble fountain and peach trees espaliered against a stone wall. Although her mother hadn't returned to Buenos Aires in something like twenty years, she had never sold the villa. She paid the taxes and the upkeep and the wages of a caretaker and his wife, who had the use of three rooms on the ground floor. On the globe in the living room, her mother traced a finger from the port of Hamburg across the Atlantic to the mouth of the Río de la Plata. In Buenos Aires, she said, she would walk to the Avenida de la Mayo and find a tram to Palermo, and she'd go in the door of her *casa perdida*, the lost house, and maybe she'd never leave again. What did Berlin hold for Beatriz

3

Faber, a widow with no family to speak of? Not even her friends would notice she was gone. She gave the globe a push, setting it spinning crazily on its axis.

In this house, in Charlottenburg, it was a late summer's evening; a fire crackled in the grate, and Hildegard, in the kitchen, was cooking dinner. The table was set with good china and crystal goblets. This is my home, Natalia thought, and I am happy here.

"Don't look so sad, *Liebchen*," her mother said, her silk dress rustling as she knelt beside Natalia. "I would never go anywhere without you. You know that, don't you?"

In 1916, when she was six, Natalia began school at an Ursuline convent in Munich, where her mother said she'd be safer than in Berlin. But was anywhere safe, in a war? That summer, English and French planes dropped bombs on a circus tent in the town of Karlsruhe, killing seventy-one children as they innocently watched acrobats and lion tamers. In November, a French aviator bombed the Munich train station, damaging the stationhouse and a length of track, so that for weeks Natalia's mother could not visit her at the convent. When the nuns told Natalia this, she was afraid it was a lie and that her mother had died in the war and was now a beautiful ghost in her stupid empty *casa perdida*. But her mother was well. She came to the convent and took Natalia home for Christmas. Natalia remembered lighting candles on the tree, going to Mass to pray for peace, and Hildegard cooking an enormous roast goose Natalia's mother had procured on the black market.

At school she wore a dark blue tunic, a white blouse, itchy black stockings, black shoes, a double-breasted wool coat with

4

brass buttons. There were eighty-seven pupils from the age of six to eighteen. That first year, Natalia was teased when she didn't always understand the other girls' Bavarian German, and someone stole her blue Teddy-Hermann bear from the pillow on her bed. Without him to comfort her, she couldn't sleep at night or speak in class, which infuriated one of the nuns, who struck her across the knuckles with a ruler. A pair of gloves Hildegard had knitted for her disappeared, and outdoors, when playing in the snow, her hands turned blue with cold. A girl called Claudia lent her a pair of gloves lined with sheep's wool. Natalia and Claudia became best friends, although the nuns decried their exclusivity and forbade them to sit together in class, where they had a lamentable tendency to giggle and whisper, Sister Johanna said, like chimpanzees.

Claudia's mother was English; her father, a glassware merchant in Rothenburg, had gone to war with the Royal Bavarian Army. In October 1918 he fell in action in France. Claudia went home for the funeral and stayed with her mother and brother for two months, returning with a black mourning band on her coat sleeve and a cough that turned out to be the start of the Spanish influenza. The illness swept through the convent, afflicting the nuns and older girls first and working its way down to Natalia's class. She was one of the last to become sick and was put to bed in the infirmary, where she heard a nursing sister say, This one is very ill. When the fever at last broke, she opened her eyes and saw her mother leaning over her with a glass of water. Just a sip, Natusya, she said, just a sip. Natusya was a pet name Natalia's Papa, who had been half Russian, had given her.

Every morning her mother came to the convent from the *Gasthaus* where she'd rented a room. She carried trays of soup and dry toast from the kitchen up to the dormitories and the infirmary, changed bedsheets, administered alcohol baths to reduce fever, tenderly held girls racked by coughing. When the invalids began to recover, Natalia's mother amused them by recounting the adventures of a girl whose name was Beatriz and who lived in Buenos Aires in a mansion with rose-colored walls and a southern aspect, near a park and a racetrack and a tennis court. This girl, Beatriz, had a governess, who often traveled with her by train to Montevideo or Rosario, where they had tea and went into shops, pretending to be locals. The governess, who came from Swabia, and was only a girl herself, liked to take long walks with Beatriz into the wilderness. They were not afraid of poisonous frogs or stinging insects or even of jaguars or of getting lost. The governess carried a pocket compass that indicated true north, even in the southern hemisphere, where the stars at night were not the stars of Europe. What happy times they had, those two, Natalia's mother said, playing with a necklace of small blue beads around her throat. She sat up a little straighter in her chair and said that, sadly, an idyll cannot last. For some unspecified dereliction of her duties, Beatriz's parents sent the governess home to Swabia, and those paradisiacal days came abruptly to an end.

The girls said: Is that all? Tell us more, Frau Faber.

They wanted to know: What happened to Beatriz? Where was Beatriz now?

In those days, her mother said, it was customary for Europeans living in Argentina to send their children home to be educated, and that was what Beatriz's parents did. They sent her to her mother's brother and his wife, in Berlin. Onkel Fritz and Tante Liesel, a childless couple in late middle age, adored Beatriz. They called her their *Schatzi*, their darling *Mausbärchen*, and showered her with gifts. They took her on vacations to the Côte d'Azur and Monte Carlo, to Vienna in winter, Paris or Budapest in spring.

She learned to appreciate foreign travel, almost to crave it. But then, she told the girls, an exile was always searching for what had been lost.

Frau Faber had the face of an angel, the girls said to Natalia. The face of a Madonna. They asked Natalia: When is she coming to see us again? Never, Natalia said firmly. Why should she share her mother with these girls? It was true, her mother had the face of an angel. People on the street saw her beauty; they smiled, they stared after her. But Natalia thought some of the convent girls were mean and didn't deserve to have her mother wiping their noses and feeding them from a tray. Besides, it seemed wrong to her that her mother was pretending to be two people at once, the real Beatriz and the one who lived in that country on the globe of the earth in a villa that no matter how glorious it had once been, was nothing special, just an old image, susceptible to damage, erosion.

In November 1918, the war ended. Germany was defeated, the Hohenzollern dynasty vanished, and Kaiser Wilhelm II abdicated and was granted asylum in the Netherlands. The Bavarian House of Wittelsbach and the Austrian House of Habsburg-Lorraine both collapsed—the latter like a house of cards, people said, and the vast Austro-Hungarian Empire simply ceased to exist. In the cities of Berlin, Hamburg, Weimar, and Munich, revolutionaries and paramilitaries battled in the streets. In Munich, the Bavarian prime minister, Kurt Eisner, was assassinated on a street not far from the convent. For a time, Munich became a Soviet Socialist Republic and took its orders from Moscow. The girls returning to the convent from visits home repeated what their parents had said. The British navy's blockade of ships bringing food to German ports continued even months after the war ended. People were rioting in the streets over food shortages; children were dying of malnutrition. Then, in 1919, at Versailles, the Allied nations demanded Germany pay war reparations amounting to three billion gold marks a year. The Reichsbank was printing money like it was nothing, and it *was* nothing; three years after the war, the mark was worth less than zero. It was true, what their parents said, the girls all agreed: in Germany, the peace was worse than the war.

The nuns grew vegetables in the convent garden and kept chickens and gave every scrap, every crumb they could spare, to those in need. Natalia saw men begging on the street, lining up at church doors for a bowl of soup. Soldiers in filthy, torn uniforms, disfigured, sightless, missing limbs. Don't stare, the nuns said, don't pity them; they are brave men, they are heroes.

In Natalia's history class, Sister Maria-Clare said God lived and moved in history; they were not alone in their suffering. As Germany's future wives and mothers, they must have faith that life would improve. Natalia's mother said something like this, in a very different way, when she spread documents out on the dining room table in Charlottenburg: land deeds, certificates of shares, stocks and bonds, passbooks to German bank accounts, statements from foreign banks. In 1914, weeks before war broke out, her mother's friend Erich Saltzman, a senior official at the Reichsbank, arranged for a large part of her wealth to be sent out of the country, to Switzerland and then to "safe havens" in America and England. When the situation stabilized in Germany, as it would eventually, her assets would make the return journey, like a flock of migrating geese fattened up from a season in the sun.

It was not impossible to make money during a war, she told Natalia. Far from it. Property could be cheaply acquired; investments in armaments and coal and steel paid off handsomely. War was costly, she said, and as in most of life, the cost was borne by those who could least afford it. Not that she was any sort of Communist.

In 1924, on the advice of Erich Saltzman, Beatriz bought land in the new western Berlin suburb of Zehlendorf and hired an architect to design a villa for her. The house ended up being larger than she'd planned, too much for Hildegard to manage alone, and Beatriz found a Polish girl to help her. Trudy was young, skinny, wore a starched apron over ankle-length black skirts, spoke with a Polish accent, and adored Natalia's mother. Hildegard and Trudy had their own rooms near the kitchen, looking out on the kitchen garden, where Trudy planted carrots, peas, and tomatoes. Hildegard brought home a black-and-white kitten. Natalia named him Benno and missed him desperately when she went back to school. But she liked school now that she was older, and Claudia was there, and she had more good friends as well. She enjoyed learning and worked hard, imagined doing something worthwhile with her life, and wondered, at times, whether she had a religious vocation and would enter a novitiate.

Then, on a dark March morning, snow falling outside the classroom windows, her mother arrived unannounced at the convent. In Sister Mary Ignace's office, Natalia listened in disbelief as Beatriz said Natalia must pack her clothes; a taxi was waiting to take them to the train station. Sister Mary Ignace tried to convince Beatriz to give Natalia a chance to finish the term and write her final exams. A place at a university was assured; she could look forward to a rewarding career in one of the professions. Beatriz smiled. Her daughter, she said, would never need to work for a living. Anyway, she had plans; they were going to travel, do lots of interesting things. Surely Sister Mary Ignace would agree that seeing firsthand the world's great cultural capitals equaled or surpassed whatever dry bit of information could be found in the pages of a book?

Beatriz, in a long crimson wool coat, like a prince of the church, was an incongruous, febrile splash of color in the principal's austere office. She made Natalia's eyes water. Later, when they were at home in Zehlendorf, her mother said they lived in modern times. Girls didn't live sequestered behind stone walls anymore. And why even have a sixteen-year-old daughter if she couldn't enjoy her company? They were going to have such fun. Did Natalia remember their vacation last summer?

Yes, she remembered, and it had been nice, the two of them together for a week at a resort on the North Sea. They walked great distances on the sand and went swimming when the water wasn't too cold. In the afternoons they sat on the hotel veranda, watching seabirds skim the waves while fishing boats and freighters sailed past, far out at sea. By ten every night, Natalia retired to her room to read and was asleep before midnight, only to be awakened a short time later by Beatriz, throwing herself down on the bed beside her. She talked about the sore losers at cards, the handsome pianist who stared at her while he played Schubert, the young man with the eyes of a poet, who in fact was a poet and recited his sonnets to her from memory. The poet had spent some time in Buenos Aires and was thrilled to hear she'd been born there. She'd told him, and now she had to tell Natalia all over again, how her parents had emigrated to Argentina in 1879. They'd arrived in a new country with nothing and had built up a prosperous exporting business, working twelve-, sixteen-hour days, which hadn't left much time for their daughter. Her father would say, Where is the little nuisance, and her mother would say she hadn't seen her, even though Beatriz was right there, in front of her.

"You know, Natalia, that I never saw my mother and father again, after coming to Germany? Your grandparents Dorothea and Einhard März died in a cholera epidemic and are buried in the Recoleta cemetery in Palermo, which is like a city unto itself, a vast, strange, and rather ugly city of tombs. One day the residents of the Recoleta will arise, and they will all be reunited in Paradise. Isn't that how it goes?"

"That is our hope, Mama. Were you and my father married, when your parents passed away?"

"I think so. Yes, I'm sure we were."

"Tell me about my father."

"I'm too sleepy, my darling."

"Just one thing."

"Your father was born in Königsberg."

"Yes, I know. But I'd like to hear something new."

"Oh, you are a little nuisance too." Beatriz sighed. Alfred's father and grandfather were cabinetmakers, she said. Their furniture was of such a high quality, it was coveted by Europe's royal houses. A grand duke of Mecklenburg-Schwerin commissioned a four-poster bed of such immensity a team of six horses was required to transport it to his castle. "One day, and this would have been around 1885, Alfred's father cut his hand on a saw, or an adze, some implement, anyway, and within forty-eight hours he was dead of blood poisoning. The factory, the family home, and all the money went to Alfred's uncle, while Alfred and his mother were left with nothing, not even, ironically, a stick of furniture."

But Alfred made a new life for himself. He became an importer of specialty goods from Eastern Europe: bolts of silk, furs, tinned caviar, Russian firearms, oranges from the Crimea, spices. He knew what people liked. He brought these commodities into Germany and sold them at a substantial profit. Truly he was a self-made man. She and Alfred were struck from the same mold; they didn't let anyone get the better of them.

"What was my father like as a person?"

"As a person? Well, he skied in Thuringia in winter, and in summer he sailed on Grosser Wannsee. He smoked a pipe. In general, he found people disappointing and claimed to have no great expectation of anyone. He insisted on having his meals served on time. He was fond of his dog, Rufus. He liked the opera. Not the dog, I don't mean. What kind of music the dog liked, I wouldn't know. Alfred loved listening to Brahms, Chopin, Tchaikovsky. Sad music. Look on the bright side, I would say, and he'd say, Why must there be a bright side? He inherited his melancholia from his Russian family, not that I ever met any of them. They didn't acknowledge your birth with a word of congratulations, let alone a gift. Natalia, I'm exhausted. I'm going to my room now."

Natalia, unable to fall back asleep, listened to the sea rushing in along the shore and thought of the three photographs of Alfred Faber her mother kept in an embossed leather album in her desk. Three only. In one, taken in 1910, the year of Natalia's birth, Alfred Faber stood in the Tiergarten, beside a perambulator, only the scalloped edge of a shawl visible, no sign of the infant within. In another, he stood outside the Adlon Hotel on Unter den Linden, a slight figure in a hat, gloves, a cane hooked over his arm. Then he was on the deck of a river steamer, at the ship's rail, his face turned slightly away. She stared at these photographs, but what did she see? Not him, not really. She could not see the Russian in him, the music lover, the owner of a faithful dog, could not hear his "Natusya" or know if he loved her, if he'd had time before he died to feel anything for her. But always she gave the impassive face of Alfred a kiss. One kiss for each image.

After leaving the North Sea resort, she and Beatriz went to Bad Schandau, where they met Beatriz's friend Sophie Brecht. A week later, Sophie drove them through Bavaria in her open Daimler-Benz. At restaurants along the way they compensated for the spa's meager diet with *Spätzle* and lamb chops, roast beef with sauerkraut, strudel, potatoes in cream, brioche, custard-filled pastries, while men in lederhosen and women in dirndls sang folk tunes and played the zither and the hurdy-gurdy. In the evenings, in their rooms at a *Gasthaus* or a hotel, Sophie, who had three sons, liked to comb out Natalia's braids. So fine, so silky, she said, scrunching Natalia's hair into bunches on either side of her head and calling Beatriz to look. "See how pretty she looks with short hair? It emphasizes her eyes and her delicate bone structure, don't you think?"

"What are you doing to my daughter?" Beatriz said. "You're making her grow up too fast."

"She will grow up," Sophie said. "Whether you like it or not."

"Don't tell me," Beatriz said.

The next day, her mother and Sophie took her to a beauty salon. Natalia saw her severed braids coiled on a glass tray and almost wept, but then, when her hair was shampooed, dried, and brushed, she began to like it, the way it fell against her face, the lightness.

Since March, she and Beatriz had been to Paris, where it rained every day, and to Vienna, and last month they'd gone on a walking tour to the Harz Mountains that had almost ended in disaster. Natalia learned to book hotel rooms, exchange foreign currency, rinse out clothes in hotel handbasins. Beatriz traveled with an extensive wardrobe. For her, every trip began at the exclusive little dress shops on Kurfürstendamm and Leipziger Strasse, where salesclerks greeted them effusively and said what everyone said: Frau Faber, how is it possible you have a grown daughter? They were invited to sit on Louis Quinze chairs while models paraded past in gowns with airy handkerchief hems, bias-cut jersey afternoon dresses, afternoon dresses in Chinese silk, cobweb-fine lace shawls. The models were disdainful and thin as paper dolls from living on nothing but black coffee and cigarettes. A form of penance? More a necessity of survival, Natalia imagined. The nuns at the convent fasted on holy days and sometimes in class felt faint and weak, and once Sister Monica had fainted while writing on the chalkboard, and a nursing sister had come with the cook's helper and carried her out of the room. In the season of Lent, Natalia too had skipped lunch and had eaten only a little soup for supper. Alone in the dormitory washroom, she had bitten her arm hard enough to leave teeth marks but not hard enough to draw blood. The pain, although slight, brought her closer to the saints, she believed. It interested her for a short time, this practice, and then she gave it up, just as she'd given up the sour little candies that she remembered the nuns doling out as a treat on Sunday afternoons.

Today they were departing for Lake Hévíz, in Hungary, where Beatriz would undergo treatments at a health spa, after which she hoped to spend a few days in Budapest before heading south to the Dalmatian coast. Benno had been taken to Erich Saltzman's apartment in Grunewald. Hildegard and Trudy had prepared the villa for their absence, closing the shutters on the downstairs windows, draping the sofas in dust sheets, and disposing of all the perishable food in the kitchen. Yesterday Hildegard had taken the train to Hamburg, where she was to stay with a sister, and Trudy was already in Poland, visiting family. No one remained to press Natalia against a starched apron front and say: *Auf Wiedersehen, viel Glück!*

Beatriz came downstairs and went to the mirror over the Biedermeier console table. She adjusted her cloche hat on her pale blond hair. She was wearing a new lilac traveling suit and a blouse with a jabot at the neck. Was the blouse too fussy for a train journey? she asked Natalia. What did she think? The jabot was perfect, Natalia said. Yes, her mother's medications were in her purse, and no, she had not forgotten their passports or money for incidental expenses. Precisely at eight, as he had promised, Herr Saltzman arrived to drive them to the Anhalter Bahnhof. Natalia helped him carry their suitcases out to his car. In the night, a rainstorm had flooded parts of Berlin, and traffic was congested. Herr Saltzman, although a new and rather nervous driver, managed to get them to the station early, with plenty of time, he said, to cross the street to the Hotel Excelsior for coffee and a bite to eat.

"Oh, Erich, that's a lovely idea," Beatriz said. "But you know me. I like to settle in at the station before boarding the train."

On the pavement a violinist was playing Beethoven's "Ode an die Freude." Beatriz held her hat against a sudden gust of wind and sang: *Diesen Kuss der ganzen Welt!* This kiss is for the whole world!

"Write to me, Beatriz," Erich Saltzman said, tipping the porter who came to take the luggage from him. "Write every day. Do you promise?"

"Yes, Erich, not every day, but I'll drop you a line when I can."

Erich Saltzman, his eyes moist, said, "Natalia, you're a sensible girl; take good care of your mother for me, won't you?"

Yes, she would, she promised. Uncle Erich, she had been taught to say, when she was younger. Be good to Benno, Natalia wanted to remind him, but he had turned away and was walking, very stolid and upright, back to his automobile.

On any given day, a newspaper had once enthusiastically reported, half of Europe moved through the Anhalter Bahnhof, and every six minutes a train departed from the glass-roofed train shed in a cloud of black smoke. Beatriz stood inside the station, entranced, watching as people greeted friends or relatives, or bid them farewell, sometimes tearfully. Parents could be heard chiding fractious children. Luggage got lost and reclaimed; the heels of clerks and porters rang with authority on the marble floors. Then there was the drawing-room elegance of the Anhalter: oil paintings, potted palms, crystal chandeliers. Beatriz impulsively bought a sprig of lily of the valley from a flower seller and asked Natalia to pin it to her lapel, and somehow, between that moment and the next, Beatriz vanished. Natalia couldn't go looking for her, in case they missed each other. When at last her mother emerged out of the crowds, she explained breathlessly that she'd seen someone she knew, but it turned out to be someone else, a stranger. But then, she said, people en masse always tended to resemble other people, didn't they? The scent of lily of the valley was giving her a headache, she said, and Natalia unpinned the flower from her mother's collar and dropped it in a waste bin. Their train was delayed by an hour, and then they had to search through several coaches before finding a compartment with two empty seats. A young man stood and offered his window seat to Beatriz. She thanked him with such a radiant smile he blushed. He sat beside Beatriz and read, or pretended to read, while glancing surreptitiously at her. Not unaware of this attention, Beatriz slowly removed her gloves and hat and ran her fingers rather sensuously through her hair.

Natalia sat across from the young man, between a stout woman in a mustard-colored wool-flannel dress and a gentleman who was reading the *Berliner Morgenpost*. The front page, she could see, was devoted to coverage of Commander Byrd's arrival in Paris, where he had been honored by the president of the Third Republic, whose name she couldn't remember. There it was, beneath his photograph: Gaston Doumergue. He had a nice smile, she thought. Charles Lindbergh had won the transatlantic race in May, flying the *Spirit of St. Louis* solo from New York City to Paris in thirty hours. His rival Commander Byrd ran out of petrol and had to ditch his aircraft in the sea off the coast of France. He and his crew were fished out of the water, the newspapers said, by the villagers of Ver-sur-Mer.

Near Leipzig, Natalia caught sight of an open motorcar racing along on the road beside the tracks. Sunlight glinted off the dazzling paintwork and silver wheel spokes. The car was as blue as the blue sky over the green fields of Saxony. She leaned forward for a better look. The driver wore a tan jacket and a blue shirt. He steered with one hand and rested an arm casually on the door. The passenger, a woman, turned to him, laughing, her scarf fluttering in the wind like a banner. How happy they looked, those two!

The motorcar disappeared behind a hedgerow. She sat back, feeling as if it had taken part of her away with it. She understood why aviators risked their lives crossing an ocean in a flimsy aircraft. Imagine the freedom up there, alone in the clouds. Or here on earth, in a motorcar like that one.

The train rattled on, past fields in which pools of water left by the storm reflected the summer sky. Villages, house roofs, groves of trees.

"It's very close in here," the man beside her grumbled. He folded his newspaper and got up and opened the window as far as it would go. Before he sat down again, he managed to step not only on her neighbor's foot but on Natalia's as well. Her mother looked amused. She traveled second-class on principle, having been tipped off by Herr Saltzman that the Reichsbahn overpriced first-class tickets and underpriced second-class.

Soon after departing from Dresden the train came to a stop at a station near Pirna. Not a breath of air came in the open window. Have patience, the assistant conductor advised, when he poked his head in the compartment to announce that they were waiting for debris to be cleared from a branch line up ahead. Beatriz said she was going to walk in the corridor to try to get a breath of air. Time passed, and she didn't return. The young man across from Natalia left the compartment and came back a few minutes later to inform her that her mother was unwell. "You should go to her, I think," he said.

Beatriz was in the next carriage, leaning against a window. Her eyes were dark; she looked very pale and complained of feeling faint. Natalia guided her to a lavatory and ran cold water on her wrists, which did nothing, Beatriz said, except get her sleeves wet. Later, in the corridor, she spoke of unexpectedly encountering an old and very dear friend, someone she hadn't seen for a long time. She thought she'd seen him at the Anhalter, and now here he was, on the train. It was a shock; her heart was still racing like mad. Natalia suggested going to their compartment, where Beatriz could rest and perhaps take one of the tablets the doctor had prescribed. "No, everyone will stare at me," Beatriz said. "And it's too hot in there. I think a good strong cup of coffee would settle my nerves better than anything. Shall we go and see if the dining car is open?"

CHAPTER TWO

This, for Miklós, Count Andorján, was the inaugural run of his Bugatti Grand Sport Type 43, shipped to him three weeks earlier from Automobiles E. Bugatti in Molsheim, Alsace. The 2.3-liter in-line eight-cylinder engine generated 120 horsepower. Zero to ninety-seven kilometers per hour in twelve seconds. The fields and pine forests of Saxony slipped past. Somewhere between Leipzig and Dresden he opened it up, racing a train to a crossing, winning easily, with a little room to spare.

"What are you trying to do, kill us?" Zita said, laughing. The wind caught her scarf; it floated away, snagging on a tree at the edge of a field. Should he turn back? No, she said; what was gone, was gone.

The Bugatti's wheels spun, slipped, gripped the road. Already his investment had yielded a good return; he felt young again, and happy.

→·←

Earlier, he'd called at his office on Kochstrasse, where he'd glanced at reports coming in on the teletype: overnight a cloud-burst high in the Erzgebirge had sent torrents of water roaring down the Gottleuba and Müglitz Rivers, inundating villages, sweeping homes right off their foundations. You can't go, the news chief, Paul Eisner, said, when Miklós reminded him he was leaving on vacation. He had one correspondent in Vienna, Eisner said, another in Palestine; he had sent a reporter to Spain to write something on Primo de Rivera's reforms. In a few weeks, the damned Nazis were staging a rally in Nuremburg, and he'd have to send someone to cover it. What else? Half of Berlin was underwater, and transportation was at a standstill; distribution of the day's papers threatened to turn into a nightmare.

Miklós offered to detour into the Erzgebirge on his way to Prague and send back a story. Eisner's secretary came in with the news that the Tempelhof airfield, near the building hous-ing the new Ullstein printing press, was underwater. "You could sail a boat on it," she said. Eisner looked at Miklós and said, "All right, yes, go there, send me a report." Meaning a report from the Erzgebirge, Miklós understood, not from the flooded airfield.

→·←

As they neared Pirna, he and Zita noticed signs warning that the macadamized road running along the Gottleuba and Müglitz Rivers had been washed out. Miklós took his foot off the accel-erator pedal, letting the car slow. He was undecided: Should he turn back, since they would be unable to get to the scene of the disaster by motorcar, or should he keep his promise to Eisner? They came to a village, and he parked the Bugatti in front of the *Rathaus*. Children were running around, shrieking, kicking a ball back and forth. As soon as his back was turned, he knew, they'd be all over his car with their dirty feet and sticky hands. "It's only a machine," Zita said, and he said, yes, but it was new and didn't have a mark on it. She licked her thumb and wiped it across the hood. "Now it has a mark," she said. "Do you feel better?"

"Not much," he said, and laughed.

A dog barked; the *Rathaus* clock struck the hour; a goat tethered on a patch of grass lifted its head and stared at them. He got his camera case and his jacket out of the Bugatti, and after asking directions from a woman sweeping her garden path, he and Zita set off on a trail leading up through a pine forest. It was a steady uphill march in the heat. Zita wiped sweat off her forehead and said, "Miklós, are we lost?" He thought it possible. "Listen," she said. Somewhere up ahead, quite close, there were motorized vehicles, and when they walked out of the forest, they were passed by a convoy of army trucks en route to the disaster. Miklós flagged down the last truck, showed his press card to a Reichswehr corporal, and they were invited to hop in. They sat on a bench in the back of the truck with two young soldiers and piles of sandbags, tarpaulins, and shovels. They stopped at a village on the banks of the Gottleuba River, a peaceful mountain stream transformed overnight into a torrent that had inundated the village. The saturated air had a green tinge, and the roar of water was deafening. The floodwater carried along house doors, window shutters, furniture, an overturned farm wagon, uprooted trees. The carcass of a cow. An infant's cradle. Soldiers were carrying the bodies of drowning victims on stretchers from the river to higher ground. A young woman's arm had been torn off at the shoulder, exposing a knob of bone and gristle. A man appeared to have been flayed alive. A little girl of about three, hair streaming water, feet bare beneath the hem of her nightgown, seemed carved of wax. Zita took a step back. Miklós could see that she was shaken. And this was Zita, who liked to think she could maintain an almost inhuman coolness and reserve in any emergency. He put his arm around her. Everything seemed unstable, shifting, in a way that reminded him of the war, when he had seen villages reduced to rubble, people displaced from their homes. She shook her head, her eyes filled with tears. "I'm going to see what I can do to help," she said.

He changed the lens on his camera, framed the scene, pressed the shutter, advanced the film. A man in a plaid jacket and a peaked cap came over and introduced himself as Richard Houghton, a journalist with the *New York Times*. He was working on a feature on the Erzgebirge region of Saxony for the travel section of his paper. Yesterday he'd photographed centuries-old stone houses, and in the night those houses had been swept off their foundations. This morning he'd talked to a man whose five daughters had been asleep in their beds when the water rose, flooding the first floor of their house. "Not one of his daughters survived. What do you say to a man who tells you something like that?"

Richard tried to light a damp cigarette with wet hands. Miklós offered him one of his and lit it for him. Zita had been helping clear debris off the high street and when she saw Miklós talking to Richard Houghton she came over, wiping her hands on her skirt, and introduced herself. As they began talking, they had to stand aside to let members of a paramilitary organization, der Stahlhelm, pass. They were young recruits, arrogant, loud. Other paramilitary organizations were in evidence, Miklós could see, but it was the Stahlhelm, an armed unit attached to a right-wing political party, that Zita despised. "They have no shame," she said. "What are they doing here, in any case? They are exploiting a disaster. Don't you think so, Miklós? This is nothing but an opportunity to rehabilitate their unsavory reputation for shoot-ing unarmed factory workers in the back and beating up Jews on the streets of Berlin." She stared at them. "I've seen it," she said. "I've seen them in action." She went back to helping the villagers clear the street, and Richard Houghton said he was going to talk to a Reichswehr corporal about getting a ride back to Pirna. The flood had cut communications with the rest of the country, and he needed to file a report to his paper.

A woman in a nightgown and muddy boots, her hair loose down her back, asked Miklós if he had seen her husband. Herr Eck, she said. He had gone out in the night, and where was he now? A man took the woman's arm. "Put the damned camera away, would you?" he said to Miklós. Had he no respect for people? After the man had led the woman away, Miklós got a shot of two small chil-dren crouched together on the cobblestones. They were barefoot, drenched, lost. A woman stopped and knelt and spoke to them comfortingly. He took a picture. He was familiar with the anger people felt at the sight of a photographer at a disaster scene. But the photographs formed an important part of the historical record. Images touched people, left an impression. And that was why he was doing his job. He photographed an uprooted tree lodged in a doorway, sunlight trembling in the leaves.

Later, he and Zita went with Richard Houghton to the *Gasthof*, where the innkeeper was serving coffee. Richard had been able to arrange a ride down the mountain in a Wehrmacht truck and was going to collect his belongings from his room, having spent two nights at the *Gasthof*. In 1918, he said, he'd been a young, inexperienced war correspondent in France. One of his inten-tions in taking an assignment in Germany was to make peace with his memories.

"And have you?" Zita said. "Have you succeeded?"

"When a country has been your enemy, it's not easy to change how you feel, but yes, I think I've had a certain success." He looked at Zita and said, "You're Russian, aren't you?"

"I was born in Saint Petersburg. That is, Leningrad. My father and I lived for a time in Moscow. We left in 1922."

"It is in my mind to see Russia, if possible."

"It isn't very possible at all," Zita said.

"I would go as a tourist, not a newspaperman. I'd like to see the Russia of Dostoyevsky, Gogol, Tolstoy."

"We knew Maxim Gorky, didn't we, Miklós? Have you read Gorky, Mr. Houghton? The founder of Socialist Realism, they say of him."

"I read *The Mother*," Richard Houghton said.

"It is the great Russian revolutionary novel, and what's interesting is that Gorky wrote it when he was living in the Adirondacks," Zita said. "The Bolsheviks sent him to America to raise money for the revolution. Lenin respected Gorky; they were friends, even when Lenin had no friends, just enemies. My father used to say that if Lenin had a tenth of Gorky's human- ity, the revolution would have retained its integrity. *Bitter*, that is what the name Gorky means. He chose it for himself, his *nom de plume*: the Bitter One." She asked Miklós for a cigarette. "Count Andorján is a writer," she said. "He writes lovely novels."

"*Trivialliteratur*," Miklós said.

"They are not trivial," Zita said. She held the cigarette, watch- ing the smoke.

He would make a point of reading the count's books, Richard Houghton said. He hoped reading German would improve his facility with the language.

"Your German is good," Zita said.

"Well, thanks. It's getting there. My landlady in Pirna has to ask me to repeat everything I say three times, and even then she looks bewildered."

Miklós said that, yes, he and Zita would like to take a ride down the mountain with him, if possible. Before he left, though, he wanted to have a word with the village's mayor, a Herr Schirrmeister. Miklós found him near the river, directing cleanup operations. His brother lived in Glashütte, the mayor told Miklós, where the scale of the disaster was beyond comprehension. A passenger train had been swept off the station siding into the river; its coaches became uncoupled and were washed up onto the Hauptstrasse, severely injuring a number of people, killing several. Every fifty or hundred years a catastrophic flood occurred, he said, and this was because of the region's geology: narrow, rocky waterways could not contain the water generated by these summer cloudbursts. In twenty-four hours, more than three hundred millimeters of rain could fall. And this was the result. He broke off. "Look, over there. A woman has fallen in. She was helping another woman, and now she's gone in herself."

The woman was Zita. Herr Schirrmeister picked up a plank of wood and handed it to Miklós, who held it out. Zita grabbed it and was able to pull herself out of the water. But right away she slipped in the mud and went back into the river, and this time the current carried her away. Miklós threw his jacket on the ground and waded into the water. His old adversary, floodwater. Rivers choked with ice, the land a wide sea darkening, spilling out across the pastures to the forest's edge. Every spring the river that cut through his land in Hungary flooded. In 1912, he remembered, it rose to new heights, flooding tenants' cottages, chicken coops, hay wagons, pigpens, stranding cows on islands of dry ground. The child of one of the estate's workers was swept into the water. Miklós and his brother, László, had swum out to her. He reached the little girl first, and then the water closed over his head, and László had to rescue him as well as the child. But they were too late. László had carried her body out of the water to her mother, whose cry of anguish Miklós would never forget.

When the flood receded, he had seen how the river had carved out a new path for itself. It was no longer the river he had known as a boy.

But this was a mountain stream in a village in Saxon Switzerland in summer, and he couldn't let Zita drown in it. He held her head above the water, and somehow they were on solid ground, if mud could be termed solid. Zita bent over, her hands on her knees, and coughed up some water.

"Good, that's good," he said, smoothing her wet hair away from her face.

"I lost my shoes," she said.

"Shoes can be replaced," a woman said. "We must get you into dry clothes. Look how you are shivering." Her name was Frau Kappel. Because her house was flooded, more with mud than with water, she took Miklós and Zita and Richard Houghton to the home of her husband's parents, a distance above the village. Frau Kappel's father-in-law showed Miklós to an outbuilding behind the house, where he was able to shower off the mud from the river. He got dressed in clean pants, a shirt, socks, and sandals loaned to him by Herr Kappel. In the house, Frau Kappel invited him to sit, to sit and rest. You and the Fräulein were heroes today, she said. She told him the Fräulein was upstairs, having a nice hot bath. The older Frau Kappel had set the table with bread, sausage, and cheese from their dairy, which Miklós was urged to taste. It was very good, he said. Zita came downstairs, dressed in a blouse with gathered sleeves, a skirt cinched in at the waist with a leather belt. He sat beside her at the table.

He wanted to embrace her, and in lieu of this he kept turning to regard her with the greatest pleasure. If anything had happened to her, if she had drowned, he could not have gone on living. What madness in him, what idiocy had allowed him to bring her here in the first place?

When they'd finished eating, Richard Houghton stood and, in his Berlitz School German, gave a speech, thanking the Kappel family for their hospitality and wishing them well, wishing the village a quick recovery from the disaster. Miklós promised to return the borrowed clothes by mail. Frau Kappel's father-in-law said they must keep them. If they called at his house on their way back to Berlin, he said, their own clothes would be laundered and pressed and ready for them.

In the truck, on the way down the mountain, Richard produced a flask of rum, which they shared with a young soldier in a mud-splattered uniform. Richard got off at Pirna. Miklós and Zita said they should try to meet again. Yes, we must keep in touch, Richard Houghton said, and produced a business card on which he'd written the phone number of his boardinghouse in Pirna.

Miklós and Zita rode as far as the village where they'd left the Bugatti, which was completely unharmed, as Zita had predicted it would be. Look at it, thought Miklós, waiting patiently, like a horse with its nose in a feedbag. He saw that everything in the village square had changed. The shadows were longer, the light richer, more forgiving. The goat had gone; the woman sweeping her garden path had vanished. And he and Zita were no longer the same people they'd been that morning. They had been so close to death, they had witnessed grievous loss and raw pain, and yet here they were. It made him catch his breath. He stopped, his hand on the car door, and the strange notion came to him that the river at full flood had swept them out of one life into another. It was like a second baptism. He felt weak, almost, with gratitude and humility. He got Zita settled in the Bugatti and spread a plaid rug over her knees. He sat behind the wheel, started the motor, and engaged the gears. Within ninety minutes, they were in Prague.

CHAPTER THREE

G*nädige Frauen.*" The young man from their compartment was standing beside the table in the dining car where Natalia and her mother were sitting. He nodded deferentially and cleared his throat and said to Beatriz that the others in their compartment had been most concerned about her. It was the heat; everyone was affected. Had she recovered? Could he be of any help? Natalia looked from the young man to her mother, who smiled and invited him to join them. "Are you sure?" he said. "Yes," Beatriz said, glancing in amusement at Natalia. He sat beside Natalia and set the book he had brought with him on the table and then transferred it to the floor at his feet. His name was Becker, he said, Martin Becker. He was a law student, living in Berlin.

"Frau Faber," Beatriz said. "And this is my daughter. So, Herr Becker, you are reading Spengler, I noticed."

"Yes, and I can tell you, Frau Faber, it's true, what they say: Spengler stimulates the mind. Almost overstimulates. As you read, new ideas take possession of you, one after another, like that." He snapped his fingers. "Spengler's thesis is that history is not linear but an endless cycle of birth and death. Decay and renewal. We Germans, Spengler proposes, are a Faustian race, striving toward a perfection we cannot attain. Every thousand years we enter a tragic twilight, a gradual dimming of energy and vigor. Then, as the end threatens to close in on us, a cataclysmic event occurs, restoring our native vitality, and the cycle begins anew. Spengler believes that national character is formed in those times when people are tested and tried by adversity."

"Only by adversity? Surely a song will do the same, don't you think?" Beatriz said. "A song everyone sings, a tune everyone whistles, a book everyone reads. I suspect that these days even films and radio programs contribute to the making of national character. Wouldn't you agree?"

"Frau Faber, you are very perceptive. If you haven't yet read Spengler, I highly recommend him, if only for his poetry. If I may?" He retrieved the book. He flipped through the pages and read aloud: "'Regard the flowers at eventide as, one after the other, they close to the setting sun.' And this: 'Strange is the feeling that then presses in upon you—a feeling of enigmatic fear in the presence of this blind dreamlike earthbound existence.' But I apologize. I proselytize unnecessarily, I'm sure. I'm afraid I've taken to heart Thomas Mann's dictum that we must all become, in his words, 'soldiers of ideas.'"

Natalia thought Herr Becker was not much older than she was. His mustache looked soft, drab, like a moth's wings, and yet, in contrast, his cheeks were red, his eyes bright blue. He told them he had just completed a year's clerkship at a law firm in Berlin and was on his way to Prague, where his maternal grandparents owned a jewelry shop in the Staré Mesto, or Old Town. His grandfather, a goldsmith, designed and made jewelry, Herr Becker informed them, holding out his right hand to show

Beatriz the garnet ring his grandfather had given him on his twenty-first birthday.

"Your grandfather is an artist," Beatriz said.

"He has a wonderful eye for design, doesn't he? Frau Faber, I'd consider it an honor if you'd allow me to introduce you to my grandparents and show you and Fräulein Faber around Prague."

"How kind of you, Herr Becker, but we're leaving Prague early tomorrow morning. Another time, perhaps? Natalia, do you think we should order lunch? Will you have something too, Herr Becker?"

"Yes, why not? A good suggestion, Frau Faber."

Beatriz ordered toast and liver pâté, Natalia had a salad, and Herr Becker talked while eating his soup. His father, like Spengler's father, was a mining engineer. His parents and his brother lived in Blankenburg, another Spengler connection.

"Natalia and I stayed in Blankenburg this spring," Beatriz said. "We were on our way to the Harz Mountains on a walking holiday. Except—in the Harz Mountains, I got lost and was alone up there all night, in the cold and dark."

"Even in fine weather the mountains can be deadly. You were fortunate, Frau Faber."

The train began to move; everyone cheered and then groaned in unison as it halted. Natalia and her mother, accompanied by Herr Becker, returned to their compartment. Natalia's seatmate lit his pipe. She tolerated the fumes for as long as she could and then went out to the corridor, where, honestly, the air seemed no fresher. "Why in God's name is this taking so long?" she overheard a man saying. "It can't have anything to do with the floods, because the Elbe is not flooded. It doesn't make sense to me."

"The railway, not the weather, is to blame for this. We'd arrive in Prague faster if we walked."

"Or crawled on our hands and knees," someone said.

"In my day," a man said, "there was a sense of obligation to people. There was courtesy, and there was efficiency."

Natalia bumped into someone. "Excuse me," she said. "The pleasure is all mine, Fräulein," the man said, grinning. She hated him and everyone else on the train, without exception, including Herr Becker, who, mopping his face with a handkerchief, appeared at her side. "This is a beautiful area, is it not?" he said, looking at the spindly trees beside the track. Years ago, his father took him and his brother hiking somewhere near the Pravice Gate, on the border between Germany and Czechoslovakia. "As a boy I was overwhelmed by the Elbe Sandstone Mountains. Those monumental, towering rock formations! Once I saw an immense stone figure lean forward, as it were, and beckon to me with a giant hand. I have never told this to another soul, Fräulein Faber. Did you know that a hundred million years ago, those mountains were under a saltwater sea? Eons ago the action of water on sandstone sculpted those stones into the fascinating and terrifying shapes you see now. Can you think of anything stranger?"

"No, indeed not," Natalia said, now amused by Herr Becker's enthusiasm and his flushed, eager expression. She could hear the assistant conductor, who had just entered the coach, asking if anyone present was a doctor. We have a matter of some urgency, he repeated several times, standing on tiptoe, scanning the crowd. A man volunteered to fetch his wife, a trained nurse, and two men began to argue, one believing a certain passenger was a medical doctor, while the other maintained the man in question was a professor and an entomologist, and the study of insects had few, if any, similarities with that of human physiology. A young woman holding a small boy by the hand made her way to the assistant conductor. She was a doctor, she said. Her name was Dr. Schaefferová. "You said it was urgent?"

Natalia saw the assistant conductor's confusion. The doctor was very young. She wore a pearl-gray suit and a white blouse with an oval enamel brooch at the collar; her blond hair was arranged in a gleaming coronet of braids. Everyone was looking at the doctor and the assistant conductor, who wiped his round red face with a handkerchief, put it in his pocket, and said there was a situation in which a passenger had experienced some difficulty getting his breath. He had then seemed to fall asleep, but he couldn't be roused, and his breathing was labored. Likely a simple case of heat prostration, the assistant conductor said, wouldn't you think, Frau Doktor?

"Perhaps," Dr. Schaefferová said. Her husband was several coaches away. Could anyone keep an eye on her son for her? Natalia said she would be pleased to do that. "This is Franz," Dr. Schaefferová said. "I am Natalia," Natalia said, smiling at Franz, who clung to his mother's hand. His lower lip trembled. Natalia told him they would follow along behind his mother.

In the first-class coach, a porter had remained with the patient, who was slumped over in his seat, his hands limp at his sides, his hunter-green jacket buttoned almost to his chin. His brown leather shoes looked new, scarcely worn, Natalia noticed. His book and eyeglasses and a cellophane bag of peppermints had been set on the seat beside him. Dr. Schaefferová felt for a pulse in the man's wrist and neck. Natalia hesitated. But she must remove the little boy from this distressing scene. She walked with him to the end of the coach, which had been emptied of passengers. She chatted to Franz about the speed the train would go once it started moving again—as it would soon, she said. He looked hot in his long-sleeved smock. She picked him up, so that he could feel the slight breeze at an open window, and he placed his arm around her neck.

"Do you see the ducks on the riverbank," she said. "They're eating grass, aren't they? And do you see the boats on the river? There's a paddle steamer. It's pretty isn't it?"

He frowned; paddle steamers were not pretty, he said; they were boats. Where he lived, there was a river full of fish. It had so many fish they almost jumped out of the water into his father's fishing basket. At home, Sora cut off the heads with a knife. The fish were completely dead, he said, and Sora put the heads and tails on a plate for their cat. Natalia said she had a cat called Benno, and he, also, was crazy about fish. She set Franz down on his feet.

"Where's my mother?" he said.

"She's helping someone. Do you see how, at times, the river appears higher than the road? It's an optical illusion, I suppose. Isn't that funny?"

"Yes," Franz said. "It is funny." He had been to Heidelberg, to visit his grandparents. In Heidelberg there was a river called the Neckar, and this river was called the Elbe. His river, the one he and his father fished in, was the Vltava. In German, it was called the Moldau. He hoped one day to fish out at sea in a big boat. He would put a net in the water and catch the most enormous fish in the sea. "Is the train broken?" he asked.

"No, it will start again soon," she said.

"My mother is a doctor. She makes people well."

"You're very lucky to have her for a mother," Natalia said.

"Yes, I am," he said.

Dr. Schaefferová stepped out into the corridor. She shook her head slightly. "There was nothing we could do, I'm afraid," she said. She smoothed Franz's hair and asked if he'd been a good boy. He glanced shyly at Natalia and nodded. Natalia hated to part with him. How wonderful, she thought, to have a child of your own, a little boy like Franz. But it was unseemly—wasn't it?—to anticipate the future in the presence of death, even if the deceased had nothing to do with her. So she thought, and would have continued to think, had Beatriz not entered the coach at that moment. She was with Herr Becker. As soon as he had told her about a passenger falling ill, she had started to worry that it was someone she knew and had decided there was only one way to put her mind at rest. Before the assistant conductor could stop her, she slid open the compartment door, went in, and knelt and took the man's hands in hers. "It's all right, my dear, I am here," she said, as if he could hear her. She looked at Dr. Schaefferová. "He's not sleeping, is he?" she said.

"No, he's not sleeping," the doctor said.

"Only an hour or so ago we were talking, and he was fine, in good health, he said so himself. He did complain of some discomfort, right here, in his chest—something he ate went down the wrong way. He was never sick, never. Isn't there something you can give him? An injection? A stimulant?"

"It was very quick, Frau. I'm certain Herr Faber won't have suffered."

"Herr Faber?" Natalia said.

"I will bring you a glass of water, Frau," said the assistant conductor.

"We can't leave him, like this, alone. I will stay with him."

"Are you a relative, Frau?" the assistant conductor asked.

"No, not a relative. But we are very close, very dear friends. He would want me to stay with him," Beatriz said. She requested that the assistant conductor send for a priest. "Alfred would want a priest," she said.

CHAPTER FOUR

July 9, 1927. Flash floods following a cloudburst in the Erzgebirge transformed the tranquil Müglitz and Gottleuba rivers into furious torrents during the night, inflicting severe damage on homes, shops, factories, and farms. Train travel in the immediate area has been indefinitely suspended. There is no word on when telephone and telegraph communication will be restored. Herr Manfred Schirrmeister, mayor of B___, on the banks of the Gottleuba, estimated the death toll there alone at thirty, and this could rise, as there are people still unaccounted for. Had he not gone door-to-door at midnight raising the alarm, Herr Schirrmeister said, the number of fatalities would have been higher. The Reichswehr and local police forces continue to carry out rescue operations. They have set up temporary shelters and are providing hot meals to the villagers. By early afternoon, the floodwaters began to recede. No further storms have been forecast for the region in the coming days.

From a telephone kiosk in the hotel lobby, Miklós dictated this report to the night desk at the newspaper and then went to the dining room, where Zita was waiting for him. They ordered dinner but were too tired and overwrought to eat. He lit a thin Egyptian cigarette. Zita was wearing an embroidered Chinese silk jacket with wide sleeves. She told him that when she went under the water, she'd had a sort of vision, like a film projected on her mind. She was transported back to a day in 1917, when Aleksandr Kerensky had become prime minister and was giving her and her father a private tour of the Winter Palace. "Kerensky wanted to show us that the Romanovs' exclusive property now belonged to the people, to the peasants and soldiers and even, I suppose, to me and my father. But mostly, we could see, it belonged to Aleksandr Kerensky, who was conducting the affairs of the provisional government at the desk of Alexander the Second and sleeping in Tsar Nicholas's bed and eating off the tsar's fine china. Some called Kerensky 'our new emperor.' Alexander the Fourth, they said of him, and the epithet was not unwarranted. Still, he had my respect. My father and I truly believed he could save Russia. Poor Kerensky. Poor everyone, in fact. Russian soldiers were fighting Germany and the Austro-Hungarian Empire, and they were dying, thousands had died that winter. In Petrograd, malnourished children and women were fighting over a moldy onion, a scrap of bread. And there I was, a proper little grand duchess, drinking coffee in the Malachite Room with the head of the provisional government. I was willing to die for Kerensky. I had no fear of death. But today, I was afraid. I told myself, well, Zita Kuznetsova, you've had a good life; who needs to live forever? But drowning—that is not the death I would have chosen."

He would not have let her drown, Miklós said.

"So many drowned," she said. "That poor child. I can't stop seeing her. She was just a baby."

He added a splash of brandy to their coffee.

"If we leave now," Zita said, "we can be in Berlin in three hours."

"In the morning you might feel differently."

"I won't," she said. "A vacation, what a crazy, bourgeois idea. What an indulgence. I dislike vacations intensely."

"Yes, we both do, don't we?" Miklós said, and Zita drew back and said she didn't know what he liked or disliked. A young man came into the dining room, went to the piano, and began playing one of Liszt's Hungarian Rhapsodies. Rippling notes, highly emotive crescendos.

Zita narrowed her eyes. "I can't take Liszt tonight. I'm exhausted. I have to get to sleep."

They said good night at the door to Zita's room. Miklós went down the hall to his own room, where he stood at the window watching stars appearing in the sky over Prague. He could not stop seeing Zita carried away in the floodwater. He had nearly lost her once; today he could have lost her forever, and it would have been his fault. A drowning victim saw scenes from the past, visions that made death seem inevitable, desirable, consolatory. Aleksandr Kerensky, the Winter Palace, the war: he hadn't known her then. They had met for the first time two years later, in March 1919, at the Eighth Congress of the Russian Communist Party.

He had arrived at the Finland Station in Petrograd suffering what he thought was typhus but turned out to be food poisoning. It had taken him days to recover his strength, and then he'd had to make his way to Moscow. The temperature never went above zero degrees Celsius, and the Hotel Lux, on Tverskaya Street, where the foreign press was quartered, was unheated except for two hours in the evening. From his hotel, it was a short walk to the Hotel Metropol, which had been nationalized by the Bolsheviks and renamed the Second House of Soviets. There, in the great hall, he had seen Bolsheviks with earnest, furrowed brows and threadbare garments the color of dust milling around like, well, he didn't know what they were like. Industrious ants, maybe. In the crowd he'd seen the philosopher Peter Kropotkin; the English writer Arthur Ransome; the recently installed president of the Hungarian Soviet Republic, Béla Kun; Maxim Gorky; Joseph Stalin; Nicolay Bukharin, editor of *Pravda*; Vyacheslav Molotov; Feliks Dzerzhinsky, chief of the newly formed security police, the Cheka. He saw Vladimir Ilich Ulyanov, by then known as Lenin, with his entourage. As Lenin made his way to the front of the hall the crowd shifted, allowing Miklós to see a young woman seated at a table in an area reserved for the party's inner circle. She smiled and gestured to him, and he crossed the floor. She held out her hand and said, "Comrade Kuznetsova. Zita Kuznetsova."

She invited him to sit with her. The astrakhan collar of her coat framed her face, which was heart-shaped, delicate. Her almond-shaped eyes were violet blue. She kept taking out the tortoise-shell combs in her hair and replacing them more securely. She asked: Where was he from, what paper did he represent? Had he known Professor Rosa Luxemburg and Karl Liebknecht?

He had, in fact, once interviewed Karl Liebknecht; apart from that, no, he did not know them.

They were murdered in cold blood, she said. The German president, Friedrich Ebert, ordered their execution. "Socialists killing Communists, it was an atrocity," she said. "I adored Professor Luxemburg. My dream was to meet her." She placed a hand on her breast, smiling wryly, as if to simultaneously confess and renounce this sentiment.

There were 301 registered voting delegates at the Eighth Congress and 100 nonvoting; she was a nonvoting delegate. She took a small green tablet from her coat pocket and, after picking off the lint, swallowed it, grimacing. For pain, she said; she had a toothache and a bit of fever. He offered to help her find a dentist. To be honest, she said, she preferred toothache to dentistry. "You don't need to suffer," he said. She smiled, her gaze warm, confiding, and he was lost. He heard indistinctly, as in an echo chamber, the speech of Vladimir Lenin, which began with the mantra of the revolution: *Peace, Bread, and Land*. Russia was shipping grain to Germany, Lenin announced, to feed unemployed German workers and their families. Worldwide Communism, a solidarity of workers, an end to the exploitation of the working class by capitalists and landowners: this Lenin predicted.

Miklós took notes in his self-taught version of Gabelsberger shorthand. Zita watched, amused. She moved her chair closer to his in order to observe more closely. She supplemented his rudimentary Russian, translating key points of Lenin's speech. Lenin began identifying people in the hall for special recognition. He identified the chief of police, Dzerzhinsky, while, Miklós noticed, avoiding any mention of the newly formed Cheka, with its power to arrest, imprison, and carry out executions. Miklós had heard credible reports of torture, hanging, people being thrown into pits and buried alive. Even as the Eighth Congress convened, these horrors were being unleashed. In March, in Kharkov, a thousand people had been executed.

Lenin said: You have to crack a few eggs to make an omelet.

The next speaker, the commissar for education and enlightenment, spoke about an increase in the number of free libraries in Moscow from thirteen to eighty. Cultural opportunities previously reserved for the ruling classes were being made available at no cost to all comrades. Institutions of higher learning had been ordered to open their doors to factory workers and peasants.

43

Zita nudged his arm. "He is my father. The commissar is my father. Leonid Kuznetsov."

Impossible, Miklós thought, that this dry stick of a man was Zita's father. She, however, regarded the man fondly and kept looking at Miklós and once even nudged his arm to make sure he was appreciating Commissar Kuznetsov's brilliance. Russia could no longer rely on foreign trade for essential commodities, Commissar Kuznetsov pronounced. Russia must ensure a reliable domestic supply of coal for power generation and trains, turf for hearth fires, gold for monetary stability, sulfur for matches. Salt, a substance vital to life, from now on would be mined by Russian workers in quantities sufficient to meet the needs of the Soviet Republic.

To hell with Russia's enemies, he said. Russia needs no one.

He received a standing ovation. He stood with his head bowed, and then he composed himself, this thin, plain, unremarkable-looking man, and made his way to the table where his daughter was sitting. He gave Miklós a cold, incurious stare. Zita said how nice it had been to meet Miklós. She gathered up her things and went with her father to the hotel lobby. Miklós followed behind them, discreetly, and watched as they went out onto the pavement and got into a waiting limousine. In Moscow there was no gas for streetlamps, supplies of coal and wood were in short supply, and yet the Kuznetsovs traveled in a chauffeur-driven German car.

At the Hotel Lux, Miklós asked around: Could anyone tell him where he might find Commissar Kuznetsov and Comrade Kuznetsova? Everyone warned him to stay away from the Kuznetsovs, who had a reputation for being one day this kind of socialist, the next another kind of socialist altogether. The pair of them, *père et fille*, could fall into a Moscow latrine and come up smelling of attar of roses. Anyway, if it was the daughter he was interested in, he was told, Kuznetsov allowed no one near her.

At the First House of Soviets—in the temporarily repurposed National Hotel, the seat of government while the Kremlin was under repair from damage sustained in the war—he presented his press card. He would like an appointment to interview Commissar Kuznetsov. This was denied. He walked on Prechistensky Bulvar, where, he'd heard, Kuznetsov had an apartment, hoping he'd see Zita. But nothing, no sign of them. Had they left Moscow? Should he look for Zita in Petrograd? Then, when he had reached a fever-ish pitch of longing to see her, even from a distance, just to know that she was all right, she came into the lobby of the Hotel Lux. She was wearing the astrakhan coat and carried a satchel over her shoulder, and her head was uncovered, the tips of her ears red from the cold. He had been talking to another journalist and broke off in the middle of a sentence when he saw her. She told him her father had taken her to a dentist, who had yanked out the rotten tooth with pliers. It was not pleasant, but here she was. She had two tickets to a performance of *King Lear* at the Moscow Art Theater, and since her father had been called to an emergency meeting of the war cabinet, she wondered if Comrade Andorján would care to accompany her.

That evening they joined an audience of factory workers, schoolteachers, and minor bureaucrats, all smoking cheap tobacco and reeking of damp wool and unwashed flesh. Even if not everyone in the audience was familiar with Shakespeare's play, they recognized the brutality, enmity, intrigue. When Gloucester was blinded, Zita reached for Miklós's hand.

He thought: I will live in Moscow, to be near her. Or I will bring her with me to Berlin.

But the cold, gray light, the darkness, the shifting late-winter ice on the Moskva River seemed purposively manufac-tured by the Bolsheviks to conceal and confound. Again, Zita

45

disappeared. His temporary visa was running out; he could not get an extension and had no choice but to return to Berlin, where he wrote to her at the First House of Soviets. His letters went undelivered, were lost in the mail, or Zita Kuznetsova chose not to reply.

Three years later, in March 1922, he saw her on Unter den Linden. He knew her at once and sprinted across the street to speak to her before she disappeared, as she had in Moscow. Her face was wet with rain; her shoes were soaked. "Fräulein Kuznetsova," he said. "Do you not remember me?" "Should I?" she said, staring at him. "I wrote to you," he said. "You didn't get my letters?" She shrugged slightly. "I got them," she said. He tried to hide his dismay at her pallor, the shadows under her eyes, her thinness. She let him take her satchel, heavy with books, and agreed to have coffee with him. He took her to a café where a faulty coal stove was poisoning the air with fumes. He ordered strudel filled with meat and potato. She finished everything on the plate. "How long have you been in Berlin?" he asked.

"Not long. Five months."

"You left Russia?" he said.

"Yes, obviously, since I'm here," she said. "No one is in Russia if they can help it. Lenin's 'transitional phase' of pure capitalism is killing Russia. Gangsterism is rampant, and the black market flourishes; people are burning chairs and tables to keep warm. You know Lenin requisitioned the entire grain harvest for export? The last time my father and I saw a play at the Moscow Art Theater, the actors were so weak from malnutrition they could only whisper their lines. My father said, 'Commissar Lenin, you need to understand something. People require a thousand calories every day to stay alive and more if you want to get any work out of them.' No response from the great man. The next day, Lenin had my father detained at the Butyrka prison—not the worst prison in Russia; he was allowed books, paper and ink, medical attention. When he was released, Lenin embraced him like a brother. Lenin," she said, and paused. "Lenin has grown paranoid, unpredictable," she said. "Do you know what the great man says, these days? He says intellectuals are shit, the nation's excrement. Can you imagine?"

They were living, Zita and her father, in a district of Berlin where thousands of Russian émigrés had settled: Mensheviks, Bolsheviks, Whites, Leninists, Trotskyites, all of whom had brought the old animosities and grievances with them. It was worse than Moscow, she said. Her father had wanted to settle in Paris, in Russian Montparnasse, where he planned to contact Aleksandr Kerensky, but then he remembered Kerensky despised him, and instead they had remained in Berlin. She told Miklós she was finishing a degree at the Berlin University. She had written a monograph on Rosa Luxemburg, published in a socialist magazine. "Did I tell you I want to write her biography one day? I am beginning work on it. It is to be factual and poetic at the same time." She picked up crumbs from the table and licked them off her fingers. He got a waiter to bring her a piece of raisin cake. She wrapped it in a handkerchief to take to her father. He gazed at her bent head, his eyes filling with tears. How could he part with her? He longed to take her in his arms. He wanted to see her to her apartment, but she said it was not far and he must have other things to do. No, he said, nothing. Dear, immovable, stubborn Zita Kuznetsova. But he, too, could be stubborn. He waited with her at a tram stop. She told him she was going to England, to study at Oxford. It meant leaving her father, and she worried about him; he was frail, he had a heart condition. Would Miklós look in on him while she was away?

That summer, Miklós shopped for Commissar Kuznetsov, prepared meals for him, played chess with him. They began using first names. Leo would seem to be drowsing at the chessboard, and then he'd snap awake, raise his eyes, and with thin trembling fingers capture a bishop, a knight. Checkmate, he would say, with satisfaction, making a slight clicking noise with his teeth. He'd been born in Saint Petersburg, he told Miklós. His parents were middle class; there were three sisters; he was the youngest child; he'd studied law; his career began in the legal department of the imperial railway. His political awakening came late, as he began to see how wealth defied gravity and flowed ever uphill into the hands of the banks and moneylenders, into the already fat purses of the monarchy. Never into the hands of those who needed it simply to sustain life. He began to think: Why not a liberal democracy? Then: Why not Bolshevism? In 1917 he gave his support to Kerensky. But Kerensky kept fucking up. He, Leonid Kuznetsov, advised Kerensky to cease Russia's participation in the war, bring the Russian army home, and do something meaningful for the people. Put food in their stomachs, give them hope. What did Kerensky do? Nothing. He seemed paralyzed with fear of the generals. When Lenin came back to Russia—brimming with energy, bullheaded, not eloquent, exactly, but forceful in his speeches—he made people believe in him. Kuznetsov saw that Lenin was the future. Lenin did what Kerensky had been incapable of doing and brought the soldiers home from the front. Leo said he had seen what he must do and had collaborated with Lenin on the drawing up of a new constitution. He accepted responsibility for culture, for libraries and free universities. Exhausting work but good. He wouldn't go through it again. His political beliefs had narrowed. Or had they grown wider? He believed government had one obligation—

to ensure that the citizens in a democracy could live in peace, read a newspaper at a café, stroll in a park, go home to a pleasant meal, raise a family: selfless love. Like in Dostoyevsky.

"Some would call that revolutionary," Miklós said.

"Yes. First you would need to eliminate the egoists and the ideologues."

One year, he said, when Zita was small, he had taken her on vacation to the Crimea. They walked in a citrus grove at dawn. He picked oranges off a tree for her. He cooked fish over an open flame on the beach in front of their dacha. He read Russian folktales to her.

His hair lay in a damp fringe around his face, which had a coppery, masklike sheen. He quoted Solan, the Athenian, who had said: "No one can be called happy till he is dead and buried." The hour of his own death was known to him, Leo told Miklós, and he named a date. He was nearly right, almost to the day.

Miklós found him in his bed, as if asleep. His reaction surprised him; he fell to his knees, tears came to his eyes. He bowed his head and remained like that, as if waiting for Leo to awaken, his dark eyes glittering, and say, What, did you think I was dead?

It was evening. Zita was not at the number she'd given him. He asked the long-distance operator to keep trying. He sat beside Leo's bed. What was he to do about the body? In the morning, he at last spoke to Zita. She returned immediately from Oxford. On the phone, her grief had seemed restrained, but she broke down completely when she saw him. He didn't know how to comfort her. Without her father she had no one, she kept saying. Manifestly untrue, Miklós had said. He was there, he would take care of her. "I'm not a child," she retorted. "I'm not an invalid." Then she said, "Miklós, please hold me."

49

Several months passed before he broached the subject of marriage, which seemed to him an obvious solution and a very happy one. Zita said marriage was an institution devised by the state to keep women silent and subservient. Marriage was a linchpin—was that the word she wanted?—in the capitalist system. It would be more honest, she said, if they lived together. She moved into his third-floor apartment in the Tiergarten borough. It was a small apartment, *gemütlich*, cozy. They owned one desk, a table, two typewriters, many books. Two editions of *Das Kapital*; two of *The Communist Manifesto*; duplicates of Emma Goldman's *My Disillusionment in Russia*; and *Ten Days That Shook the World*, by John Reed. Several copies of Dostoyevsky's *Crime and Punishment*. Maxim Gorky. Gogol. Pushkin. Turgenev. Several books on Russian civil and criminal law, the property of Leo Kuznetsov, with his annotations in the margins. Zita's leather-bound set of Dickens's novels, which she requested to have buried with her, saying that at least in the grave she would be able to read in peace. At night Miklós stayed up late working on a novel. The clatter of typewriter keys disturbed Zita; his cigarette smoke made her throat raw. He tidied up, took the sheets and pillowcases to a laundry, cooked supper; he became proficient at housewifery and enjoyed it. You could clean and think, cook and be at peace with yourself. Zita propped a book on a loaf of bread and read while she ate. She was a mistress of abstraction; she had the émigré's permanent sadness. Even when she was beside him, in bed, he sometimes felt she was far away, in Russia, in a birch forest, a pale being in eternally falling snow. He trudged after her, in the bitter cold, calling her name.

Zita was employed at Ullstein Verlag. She was editing a book on domestic life in Prussia at the time of the 1870 Franco-Prussian war. Later, when the book had gone to press, she told

Miklós she and the author, a professor of history at the University of Cologne, had become lovers. That was not the right word, she said, because she did not love him. She liked him, respected his erudition. She spoke earnestly, choosing her words with obvious care, with intent, as if Miklós were deficient in understanding. Which, in fact, he was, since he at first refused to believe her and then thought he was going mad. He remembered how they'd argued and how, one night, Zita had run outside in her nightgown, and he had run after her and had brought her back to the apartment so that they could go on fighting, throwing things, smashing plates. Zita took an apartment near Alexanderplatz. He moved to the Adlon. There were other women. He felt something for them, some affection, perhaps, but they were not Zita. He ordered the Bugatti: another distraction. Back in Berlin, he saw Zita at the newspaper. She gravely handed him a note, in which she'd written, "You must know that what happened had nothing to do with you and me. I was fond of that professor from Cologne, he's a good man, a fine person. I love you, Miklós. Do you get it?"

She quoted Lenin, who had written to his lover, Inessa Armand, "Fleeting intimacy and passion, too, may be dirty and may be clean."

What was that supposed to mean?

He and Zita met, by custom and happenstance, at work, at restaurants, at the theater, alone and in the company of others. Zita remained his editor at Ullstein Verlag.

Then, in June, she came to his rooms at the Adlon and presented him with a brochure from Ullstein's in-house travel bureau. She had been working too much; she couldn't endure another summer in Berlin, and there was this place in Hungary, beside a thermal lake, in serene countryside.

Miklós knew the Hotel Meunier. He had stayed there as a child, with his brother and their parents. Always in winter, when his parents were not occupied with running the estate. He remembered sleigh rides, snow melting on the surface of the lake, which was always warm, always thirty-five degrees Celsius. Swans floating in clouds of mist. The scenes in the brochure were all of summer. On a pier outside the hotel, men and women, radiant in white, stood gazing at crimson water lilies floating on cerulean-blue water.

Zita worried that she wouldn't fit in, a woman alone. Who would she talk to? What would she do all day? "Come with me. We would travel as friends, naturally, book separate rooms, share expenses."

How long would that last, he and Zita as nothing more than friends? Her use of the plural pronoun disarmed him: We would travel. We would go on vacation.

He had said: "I will drive you there, in my motorcar. I'd like a chance to take it for a longish run."

And they had set out, on a clear summer day, after a night of floods and storms, and there had been that moment when he had understood clearly that everything had changed, they had changed. A second chance.

He could not sleep. He got his jacket, his cigarettes and lighter, and opened the door. There, in the hall, was Zita, in a long white nightgown and bare feet. She'd had a bad dream, she said, and went past him and lay down on the bed and appeared to fall asleep. Or perhaps she had never woken properly. Tenderly, he covered her with a blanket. He left a lamp on and went out, walking as far as the Charles Bridge, where he stood staring down at the Vltava, its surface mottled, iridescent, like the skin of a fish. The statue of Saint John of Nepomuk regarded him with beneficence. The saint had been martyred by drowning in this river. As children, he and his brother, László, had believed they could see John of Nepomuk's crown of stars glimmering in the water. László was devout, as a boy and as a man; he loved the church, his country, his family, and the Andorján land. It was what he was born to. And yet he'd encouraged Miklós to pursue his dream of working as a journalist, because, he'd said, life was too precious to be wasted.

László, his beloved brother, dead in a Serbian field hospital hours after the cessation of hostilities in 1918. He had to lean against the balustrade. He felt on the edge of breaking down. Tomorrow he could be back in Berlin, things still unresolved between him and Zita. He looked at the Vltava shining in the dawn light and saw the other river, swollen, bursting its banks. He saw Zita, her hair streaming water, pale and shaking, coughing up water. The dead laid out on the village high street.

People were crossing the bridge; the day was beginning.

He returned to the hotel, trying to enter the room without a sound, but Zita was awake. Where had he been, she wanted to know. And what was the time?

"I went for a walk. It's early, half six. Did you sleep well?"

"Yes, I think so," she said. "At first, when I woke up, I didn't know where I was."

He sat on the edge of the bed. She looked at him for a long moment. Then she put her arms around his neck and drew him to her and kissed him. "You're cold," she said, her hand on the side of his face. "Here, lie down."

He hesitated. He lay down. She rested her head on his chest. She slid a hand inside his shirt. He buried his face in her warm hair, tucked a strand behind her ear, so that he could see her eyes, her lovely eyes. I love you, he began to say, and she placed

53

her hand over his mouth. I belong to you, he wanted to say. An hour, two hours later, she retrieved her nightgown from the floor and slipped it over her head. He held out his hand; she smiled and went away. When he woke, she was standing beside the bed, dressed in Frau Kappel's blouse and skirt. She showed him the borrowed clogs on her feet and said they gave her a nice sense of sobriety and stability. That morning they had breakfast at a café in the Old Town. Zita no longer had any desire to return to Berlin. "Once you have set your mind on something," she said, "it is better to see it through, isn't it?" This, he said, was also his belief.

They finished breakfast and went to the Bugatti. Zita put on dark glasses and a wide-brimmed hat she tied under her chin. Somewhere, she said, she must try to find a scarf to replace the one she'd lost on the road near Leipzig.

CHAPTER FIVE

atalia wrung out a towel in the handbasin in Beatriz's hotel room and placed it on her mother's forehead. She shook a tablet from a vial and held it out on her palm. Beatriz swallowed, grimaced, and said it left a bad taste in her mouth. Natalia got her a glass of water. She moved a chair beside the bed and sat down where Beatriz could see her. She said, after a moment, that she would like to hear the truth about the man on the train.

"Natalia, wanting to be happy is not a sin. As for the truth, I have been honest with you. Alfred Faber is not 'the man on the train.' He is your father. We met when I was seventeen and Alfred was in his late twenties. He came to my uncle Fritz's house early in the morning along with several other men, friends of my uncle's, who were leaving to hunt chamois in the Austrian Littoral. I remember how, when we were introduced, Alfred and I simply stood there staring at one another. Love can happen like that, and when it does, it's the most profound experience. Nothing equals it. Alfred wasn't handsome; he wasn't the man I'd imagined falling in love with. He had the kind of fair complexion that ages prematurely, and he was nervous. He kept smoothing his hair, touching his mouth, adjusting his necktie, as if to reassure himself of his own existence. Weeks after we met, I received a note from him suggesting we lunch together at the Imperial Hotel. Soon, we began to see each other regularly, whenever he was in Berlin. He happened to be in the same business as my parents, which gave us something to talk about. He admired my knowledge of finance and trade. After a few weeks, we went to his apartment, because, he said, he wanted to avoid chance encounters with my aunt and uncle. I told him I didn't give a damn who saw us together. Alfred promised we would announce our engagement on my eighteenth birthday. When that day arrived, he poured a glass of brandy, told me to drink it down, and then bluntly informed me he had a wife and three sons, one of whom was an invalid. How could he leave his wife, Klara, who had dedicated her life to caring for this boy?

"I told him I had news for him, too: I was going to have a child. I was angry, frightened, and he kept saying he would divorce Klara—he would petition the church for an annulment; he would take whatever measures were necessary. Don't cry, he said, like an idiot, because I wasn't crying, I never cry. When, inevitably, my aunt noticed my condition, she was furious, and Onkel Fritz had a sort of seizure that affected his speech, and Tante Liesel blamed me and ordered me out of her house. I stayed at Alfred's apartment until you were a year old. You were the most beautiful baby, Natalia. Alfred adored you. As you got older, he chose to keep his distance; I think it hurt him too much to part from you. Whenever I met him, he would ask, 'Is the child in good health? Is she doing well at school?' Every year I had your portrait taken for him, and he gave me gifts for you: Byzantine icons, Russian nesting dolls, books, a fur muff. Sometimes I let you have these gifts, sometimes not. How could I say: Here is a little something from the father you don't have? The situation was unfeasible—you can see that, I think—and yet it went on. Then, this year, in March, I met Alfred at the Café Kranzler. We were sitting outside. It started to rain lightly, and the air smelled of violets. I said you had left the convent. He was annoyed and said your education was important. I was lonely, I told him, and needed to have my daughter near me. He placed his hand on mine and said, Things cannot go on like this any longer. He intended to begin divorce proceedings. And what about Klara? I said. His wife would be well taken care of, the boys were devoted to their mother. He was under no illusions; it would be difficult for all of them at first. Perhaps, he said, with a sideways glance, we could start again in Buenos Aires, as a family, with our daughter. With you, Natalia. I thought this such a reasonable proposal, such a courageous and obvious solution to our problems, that I agreed at once."

She sat up against her pillows and gazed out the window.

"What are their names?" Natalia said.

"Who?"

"His sons. What are their names?"

"They are grown men now. Leopold, the eldest, is an optician. Roland is a dentist, I believe. The youngest, Richard, lives at home, and Klara still looks after him by herself, and I know she must be a lovely person. I've never wished her ill." After a moment she said, "I suppose the nuns taught you to despise people like me?"

The nuns had taught her to be virtuous, Natalia said.

Beatriz laughed. "You are a funny little thing, Natalia. God help you, you have his nose and his eyes and his temperament." She sat up, holding the compress to her head. "The last time I saw him, before today, was in June, in the Harz Mountains. Does that surprise you?"

"I'm afraid it does not," Natalia said in a sharp tone she almost didn't recognize as her own. At the time, she remembered, she'd thought her mother's sudden passion for hiking in the Harz Mountains had been motivated only by a desire to outfit herself and Natalia in feathered Alpine hats and snug braided jackets and hiking shoes of gleaming leather. Natalia's shoes had rubbed her heels raw the first time she wore them. A woman in the *Wanderverein* gave her sticking plasters, which helped, but still she couldn't keep up with Beatriz, who seemed indefatigable. On the third morning, a cold, wet fog descended on the mountain, and all but the most determined and hardy walkers turned back. By six o'clock everyone had returned to the *Gasthaus* except for Beatriz. At eight, the guests sat down to eat without her. At ten, the police were notified, and a search party was organized.

"I wasn't lost," Beatriz said. "Alfred had sent me a map, showing where I was to wait for him on a path beside a small waterfall. From then on, nothing went as I had hoped. Alfred arrived late, complained about the damp, unseasonable weather, and was silent for most of the walk to the inn where he was staying. The landlady had set a table for us. Alfred drank a glass of schnapps and then told me he could not proceed with a divorce. Klara's health was precarious, her nerves weak, and his son Leopold and his wife were expecting a child. A first grandchild. His life was complicated, he said.

"'For a coward like you,' I said, 'everything is complicated.' I reached across the table and slapped his face, and the landlady bustled over and said, 'We can't have this, Frau, you must leave.' I informed her the bread was stale, the meat pies rancid—was she trying to poison her guests? I made sure everyone in the dining room heard me. Then I ran outside and began to walk back down the mountain. Any other man, I told myself, any decent man, would have seen me at least halfway back safely, but not Alfred. The fog was closing in again, and night falls early in the mountains. I went around in circles, unsure of my direction or what path I was on. At last, I reached the waterfall and sat on a rock to rest. Out of the mist a figure emerged. A rescuer? No. Do you know that word for the light just before dawn, when the darkness is speckled and uneven? There's a word for it: *Eigengrau*. The gray light of the mind. Out of this light a figure appeared. My childhood governess, Fräulein Hoffman. She walked three times around the rock I sat on. 'Now you know,' she said, 'what it feels like to lose the person dearest to you in all the world. The pain makes you want to die, doesn't it?' Her eyes glowed; her hair hung in rat's tails. She had been so pretty, and death had made her repulsive. I thought: I should at least feel pity for her.

"I got up and ran down the mountain path. The sky began to grow light, and I heard voices. The searchers. They carried me to the inn on a stretcher. Do you remember, Natalia?"

Yes, she remembered the landlady running a hot bath for Beatriz, and she remembered helping her mother to put on her nightgown and get into bed. Beatriz slept for a day and a night and woke the next morning seemingly unaffected by her ordeal. Then, back home in Zehlendorf, she began to say that her fingers hurt, her wrists ached, and the migraines she'd suffered all her life became more frequent, more severe. Natalia learned to prepare hot compresses—but not too hot, in case they scalded—to apply to Beatriz's painful, swollen joints. Hildegard cooked easily digestible meals to tempt her appetite: coddled eggs; thin, dry toast; clear soup. There were liniments to rub on the skin, herbal infusions, tablets for sleeping, tablets for pain. Beatriz went back and forth from being an invalid to being well. It was, she said, the nature of the malady, whatever the malady was. Her doctors recommended a rest cure at a health spa.

Now, at the hotel in Prague, Beatriz said: Was she intrinsically unlovable? Unworthy? Alfred had loved his family in Leipzig more than he'd loved her. Her parents had scarcely acknowledged her existence. Fritz and Liesel had never forgiven her, but she hadn't forgiven them, either. Perhaps Fräulein Hoffman had loved her. Perhaps she had.

"A ghost in the mountains, Mother? Is that what you call the truth? When you told the girls at the convent about your governess, I remember, you said she had gone home to Swabia."

"A happy ending, I gave poor Fräulein. But no, she did not go home to Swabia. That wasn't what happened. For two years she was my governess. We were always together. Inga Hoffman had the palest eyes, translucent eyelashes, blond hair pulled back in a governessy bun. Her pedagogical methods were unusual. Eccentric. I thrived under her tutelage. I couldn't sit still for two minutes, and Fräulein Hoffman had only disdain for desks and books. It was true, what I told you and the other girls. We did go on the train to Montevideo and Rosario, and we did trek out into wild places, where, I came to believe, not even Amerigo Vespucci and Pedro de Mendoza had ventured. We brought specimens home with us to a laboratory Fräulein Hoffman had set up in the library. She anesthetized the frogs and lizards with something— chloral hydrate. If not quite dead, they at least seemed mercifully unconscious when she picked up a scalpel and made the first incision. 'Do you know, Natalia, that after excision a lizard's heart continues to beat, or appears to beat?' Fräulein Hoffman showed me small white scars on her fingertips, where she had burned herself on the hearts of those poor dismembered amphibians.

"I called her a witch. She slapped my face. 'Behave like a

witch and you are one,' I said. It was true. She bewitched every-one, even my father, who blushed like a boy when he saw her. We were happy, my governess and I, and then she met someone at the German Friendship Club in Buenos Aires. His name was Johannes Winkler. He came with us when we went on our ram-bles. When he was with us, Fräulein Hoffman would send me off alone to search for specimens. I couldn't wait to show her what I'd found. I ran back with a leaf, a snail still chewing on it, and there was Herr Winkler kneeling on the ground, kissing my gov-erness's bare legs—she'd thrown her stockings on the grass—and she was standing with her head thrown back, her eyes closed in ecstasy. I ran away. I waited and returned and found them on the grass, in the open, carrying on. I knew what they were doing. I had seen bulls mounting cows. I had seen dogs copulating in the street. I ran at them, shouting, 'Get up, get up!' My governess pushed Herr Winkler off and scrambled to her feet. Her small breasts looked like apricots blanched in boiling water. Her pale hair was slipping out of its pins. I kicked her and hit her with my fists and screamed: 'Adulteress! Slut! Whore!' Words I'd heard the cook and maids using, gossiping among themselves, when they thought I wasn't listening."

She saw Herr Winkler naked; she saw everything and laughed, pointing, and said she was going to tell her parents, and Fräulein Hoffman would be dismissed, and no one would employ her as a governess. Fräulein Hoffman pleaded with her, begged on her knees, and finally Beatriz relented and said she would keep quiet if Fräulein Hoffman promised never to see Herr Winkler again. Fräulein Hoffman wept, her eyes and nose streamed, she made herself pitiable. A lady would not be so blatant in her sor-row, Beatriz had thought coldly. Her father had asked: What has happened to upset your governess, Beatriz? Nothing, she said.

Fräulein Hoffman grew thinner and, if possible, paler. She lost interest in collecting specimens, and sometimes fell asleep while teaching Latin or reading *Faust* to her. *Faust!*

Fräulein Hoffman never saw her homeland again. She did not return to Swabia, as Beatriz had told the girls at the convent. No, Inga Hoffman contracted yellow fever and died, at age twenty-four. At the graveside, Beatriz's father gave her a handful of dirt to throw on the coffin, and the dry rattle of small stones on the wood made her stomach rise into her throat. But her governess was not in the coffin; she was in heaven, with the angels. The God who created beetles and lizards and frogs must Himself be very mysterious and, well—radical. He would not condemn Fräulein Hoffman for loving Johannes Winkler. Still, Beatriz felt no remorse. In her mind, Fräulein Hoffman had betrayed her and deserved to be punished.

Beatriz refused to have another governess or to attend school. She occupied her time drawing beautiful women in sumptuous gowns. She read her way through her parents' library of travelogues from the 1800s, tedious memoirs of Wilhelmine childhoods, the lives of the saints. At thirteen, she was browsing bookshops for more stimulating material: romance novels, adventure stories, practical guides on astronomy, beekeeping, and bookkeeping, which fascinated her. She taught herself double-entry bookkeeping and began helping in the office of her parents' exporting and wholesale business. Numbers existed as inky symbols on a page and at the same time as actual commodities mined from the earth or grown in the soil or taken to a slaughterhouse and butchered, packed in tins, and shipped across the ocean to Europe. As these commodities increased in value on the open market, the figures in her ledgers grew correspondingly bold and fat, like the biblical ears of corn. It was possible to predict how the numbers were likely to behave in the future, both on the page and in the world, she explained to her parents, who ran their fingers down the immaculate columns in the ledgers and demanded: Who taught you this? How did you come to know this?

She thought she'd made herself indispensable to them, and yet they shipped her off to Berlin, to Fritz and Liesel.

"Why are you telling me this?" Natalia said.

Did Natalia not understand? Beatriz demanded. The truth, the whole truth, was that Alfred was the only one who had ever loved her—imperfectly, but still, he had loved her. And now he was gone.

She got off the bed, letting the wet compress fall onto the rug. Natalia picked it up and took it to the sink, and when she turned, her mother came and pressed her damp cheek to Natalia's and said she wouldn't change anything, because she had Natalia, they had each other.

Natalia moved away.

She ran a hot bath for her mother and unpacked her nightgown, robe, and slippers, her toiletries; she remade the bed, smoothing the pillows and folding down the covers. She closed the shutters on the windows. Then she went to her own room and did not sleep all night.

Lake Hévíz, circular, sapphire blue, ringed by green lawns and birch groves, delighted Beatriz. Her room at the Hotel Magnolia had a view of the lake, a bed with a firm mattress, a bathtub she could soak in, and a vanity table that held her makeup and hairbrushes and the mask she wore at night over her eyes. There was a connecting door Natalia tried to keep closed, but Beatriz threw it open so they could talk to each other as she got dressed in the morning. She told Natalia her schedule: at nine o'clock every morning she had an appointment at the spa's hydrotherapy pool, followed by a session with a Polish masseuse, and then, at eleven, she and the other spa patients sat on the pier and waiters rolled out tea trolleys and served herbal infusions and mineral water— stimulants like coffee and tea weren't exactly forbidden, but they were discouraged. After lunch, she could dabble in watercolors or weave a straw basket at the craft house, if she had the patience, which she did not. She preferred to take a dip in the lake, although she was allowed only ten minutes in the water. Then she had to shower and dry off with one of the spa's fluffy white towels. These precautions were due to the lake's radioactive properties, which, while therapeutic, carried a minuscule risk of harm. The Vienna-trained spa doctor, Joachim Heilbronn, told her he had not personally seen any ill effects from bathing in the lake; it would do her nothing but good. Dr. Heilbronn recommended that she practice Émile Coué's method of auto-suggestion, silently repeating, at fixed intervals, *Every day, in every way, I'm getting better and better*. A surprisingly effective nostrum, Beatriz said. Her nerves were steadier, the headaches less severe, and she was sleeping for eight or nine hours every night. When she spoke to anyone, she referred to herself as a widow.

In the dining room at the Hotel Magnolia, Natalia and her mother shared a table with a young woman from Berlin, Frau Brüning, who wore her hair in an Eton bob and was only a few years older than Natalia. She said her doctors in Berlin had diagnosed a shadow on her lung and had ordered a rest cure of at least twelve months at a Swiss sanatorium. But how could she endure a year away from home? And then there was the expense to consider. Her husband, Herr Brüning, owned a stationery store in Berlin, on Unter den Linden, and when one of his customers recommended Dr. Heilbronn's clinic at Lake Hévíz, her husband had arranged everything, and here she was. "I'm determined to get well, for his sake, but every day the nurse weighs me, and I don't seem to have gained an ounce."

"You could try eating your breakfast," Beatriz said, pointing her fork at Frau Brüning's potato pancakes and sausages. "In thirty minutes," she went on, "I have an appointment at the hydrotherapy pool, for my *subaqualis tractis* treatment. They suspend you in warm water, to relieve the pressure on your spine. It makes you a tiny bit taller, they tell me, although I'm as tall as I want to be. Too much height in a woman can be a detriment. Tomorrow afternoon I'm booked for a mud bath. They slather mud from the lake on you from head to toe and wrap you in wet cloths and you sit, immobilized and sweating like a pig, for forty minutes. There are also . . . ," Beatriz said, leaning closer to Frau Brüning, "there are also *internal* mud treatments. They put the mud you-know-where. For gynecological purposes."

"Oh my goodness," Frau Brüning said.

"So far I, myself, haven't had this . . . application—but it might be interesting to try."

Frau Brüning stared at her uneaten breakfast for a moment. She asked whether Frau Faber and Fräulein Faber would like to walk with her one day. It would have to be in the morning, before it got hot, though, she added, and Beatriz said she also found the heat debilitating and suggested Frau Brüning might enjoy swimming. "The water would do you good, even if you just splashed around. Although I seem to spend all my time in water, and it's very hard on the hands."

"I've been told swimming would be too strenuous," Frau

Brüning said. "And my husband, Herr Brüning, made me promise not to exert myself."

"Natalia goes for a walk every day while I'm having my treatments. Why don't you two go together?"

"I would like that," Frau Brüning said. "Perhaps tomorrow?"

Several days passed before Frau Brüning felt well enough to join Natalia on a stroll along a flower-lined path, past the rear of the Hotel Meunier, where they saw a man unloading wooden crates from a horse-drawn van, while a cook in an apron stood with his hands on his hips and shouted at him to watch what he was doing, four dozen cracked eggs were of no use to him. Natalia looked at Frau Brüning, and they laughed. Frau Brüning linked her arm with Natalia's as they crossed the road to a footpath that led to a tennis court, where a fast, competitive game was going on between a man and a woman. The woman was a better player than the man, Frau Brüning said. He kept having to retrieve the ball when he missed a serve, and the woman stood with one hand on her hip, waiting for him to throw the ball back to her side of the court. Frau Brüning said he reminded her of someone, but she couldn't think whom. When they resumed their walk, she suddenly began to run. She stopped and bent over, pressing a hand to her ribs, and said she had a pain that came and went and meant nothing but was a nuisance while it lasted. "You would never believe it," she said, "but I used to be good at sports, especially tennis. I loved tennis."

"You will play tennis again, Frau Brüning," Natalia said. "I'm sure of it. But for now, let's get out of the sun." She could see the Hotel Meunier through the trees and suggested they have tea at the restaurant.

They were given a table beside the glass wall of a conservatory filled with lush green plants and darting, brightly colored birds.

Frau Brüning shivered and said she did not like to see birds in captivity. Her grandmother had kept cats and caged birds in the same household, and as a child she had lived in terror of seeing a murder take place. This had never occurred, or if it had, she had not witnessed it, but she still couldn't bear to be in an enclosed space with a bird. Even a little bird, a budgerigar. Her father was a Lutheran pastor, her mother taught piano, and she had an older brother, a schoolteacher in Charlottenburg. She and Heinrich lived near her family. When she was seven, she said, her parents had given her a puppy that had a bad habit of chewing on the furniture. Her father had said, let the little rascal eat the table, if it makes him happy; of what importance is a table, in the scheme of things? Her husband, Heinrich, was a good man, but as far as he was concerned, if a dog chewed the furniture, the dog would have to go. She and Heinrich had been married for two years. They wanted a family. Heinrich had borrowed money to finance her stay at Lake Hévíz; the loan would have to be repaid, whether her health improved or not. Sometimes she thought it would be better for everyone if she just wasn't here.

"You mustn't say that." Natalia touched her hand.

"I can't help thinking it, though." She smiled. "Tell me about your family," she said. "Did you have a grandmother who kept birds?"

"No, I never had a grandmother who kept birds, Frau Brüning," Natalia said.

"Call me Julia, won't you?"

"Julia." Natalia smiled. She could see that two people had entered the conservatory and were wandering around amid the plants. The tennis players. The woman tried to entice a bird to perch on her finger. Her dark hair hung down her back in a long braid. Her companion placed a hand on the side of her face; she leaned against him and smiled up at him. This tender scene was visible to everyone in the dining room, which made Natalia blush for them.

A waiter served Natalia and Julia with iced water, tea, and croissants filled with chocolate. Julia squeezed lemon into her tea. Just when she'd felt despondent and homesick, alone at Lake Hévíz, she said, Frau Faber and her daughter had arrived. She smiled. They had done more to lift her spirits than all the doctors and nurses put together. "I'm glad," Natalia said, and when she saw Julia's eyes brim with tears, she said she must try the croissant. "They are deliciously chocolaty inside," she said. "And messy." She licked a finger and then sat up straighter. It had not occurred to her until this moment that, since she hadn't expected to need money on the walk, she had left her purse on the bureau in her hotel room. "A calamity," Julia said, and put her hands in her dress pockets and said she didn't have so much as a pfennig on her. "Will we have to wash dishes until our debt is discharged?" she said, laughing, but seeing the look on Natalia's face, she added, "I'm sorry, but it is funny, isn't it?"

Natalia went to find their waiter, who looked at her coldly and summoned his superior, a stout man with oiled hair and a gold tooth, like a villain in the movie *Dr. Mabuse the Gambler*. "Oh, you young ladies," he said. "You never think, do you?" This once, but only this once, tea was on the house, he said.

In the lobby, as they were leaving, she and Julia encountered the tennis players, who had just come out of the conservatory. Julia stopped and said, "Oh, but I do know you, don't I? What a wonderful coincidence. You remember me, don't you? I'm Frau Brüning. My husband owns the stationery store on Unter den Linden." She turned to Natalia and said, "Natalia, I'd like you to meet two of my husband's most loyal customers, Fräulein

Kuznetsova and Count Andorján. This is Fräulein Faber, who is also from Berlin."

Count Andorján smiled and bowed. Fräulein Kuznetsova said, "Miklós, did you leave the conservatory door open? Because, look, a bird has got out."

"You were the last to leave," Count Andorján said.

"No, it was you." The bird flew frantically around the lobby and then perched on a picture frame before flying into the dining room. Fräulein Kuznetsova remained with Julia in the lobby, while Natalia followed the count into the dining room. He stood on a chair, trying to reach the bird. The restaurant's manager gave Natalia a disapproving look, as if to say: "What? You again?" The bird fluttered around the blades of a ceiling fan before flinging itself at a high window and tumbling to the floor at Natalia's feet. She bent and gently held it in her hands. Two people got up from their tables to examine the bird and give advice. Take it outside, it will recover in the warm sun, said one, and the other said it had broken bones and no doubt internal injuries, better to dispatch it mercifully. Fräulein Kuznetsova came in from the lobby, stroked the bird's head, and said it was a sweet little thing, but was that a speck of blood on its beak? Natalia carried it in her cupped hands to the conservatory. She could feel the warmth of the bird's body, and then the small weight became limp. She opened her hands. "If I'd caught it before it flew into the window," Count Andorján said, coming in and shutting the door behind him, "it might have had a chance."

"It's a finch," Natalia said. "Isn't it?"

"Yes, a finch," the count said. "A linnet."

The count took the bird from her while she dug a small cavity in a fig tree's clay pot. When they'd buried the bird, the count brushed dirt from her fingers. "I'm sorry that happened," he said.

She took her hand back and wiped it on her dress. They stood in silence for a moment. She was aware of the exotic foliage exuding pungent vapors, the smell of damp earth, sunlight falling through the glass roof. The count said, "Rest in peace, little bird." They went out to the lobby, where Fräulein Kuznetsova and Julia were seated on a couch near a potted palm. Fräulein Kuznetsova stood and said, "It didn't survive? Songbirds like that, their hearts are not strong." She said how nice it was to have met Frau Brüning and Fräulein. The count said, yes, it had been a pleasure. He shook Frau Brüning's hand and asked that she remember him to Herr Brüning. They all wished one another well, spoke of perhaps meeting again, and Natalia and Julia walked out of the hotel into a day languid with heat, dazzling with light.

→··←

Natalia asked her mother if they could, in any way, help Julia.

"We can pray for her," Beatriz said absently, not looking up from the postcard she was addressing to Herr Saltzman.

"We could give her money for a rest cure at a sanatorium."

"Natalia, here's the thing. Money isn't like eggs, where you can give your neighbor three out of your dozen, so she can bake a cake. It is more like the Eiffel Tower, which can rise a long way into the air only because of a solid foundation. If the last few years have taught me anything, it is to build a carefully structured edifice out of secure investments and then leave it alone."

"How is money real," Natalia said, "if it can't be made use of?"

"Believe me, it's real." Beatriz handed Natalia the postcard and asked her to run it downstairs to the front desk. "In any case, you're helping Julia by going for walks with her, and I helped her by arranging a consultation with Dr. Heilbronn. He listened to her chest and took an X-ray. 'It is not asthma or bronchitis,' he said. 'It is pulmonary tuberculosis, at a more advanced stage than the doctors in Berlin led you to believe, Frau Brüning.' He said a year at a sanatorium at Davos or somewhere like that was indeed the best treatment, but whether Julia takes his advice or not is, frankly, up to her. She and her husband are not destitute. It is a matter of priorities, isn't it?"

"What about our priorities?" Natalia said. Beatriz did not reply. On her way through the lobby, Natalia gave the clerk at the front desk the postcard and a letter she'd written to Margot Brückner, who was her closest, and perhaps only, friend in Zehlendorf. As soon as she was outside, walking beside the lake, she wanted to go back and retrieve the letter from the clerk. *Lake Hévíz is lovely*, she had written,

> but to be honest, I wish I were spending the summer at home and going sailing with you and Hermann on the Grosser Wannsee. It is beautiful here, but everyone seems to be convalescing from some nervous or physical disorder and taking life very slow. I have made friends with someone, but she is quite ill with consumption and needs to rest a lot. Margot, something strange has happened to me. I saw my father on the train to Prague. I mean, I really did see him, after believing he'd died when I was an infant. He passed away on the train, of a heart attack, I believe. The kind of thing that happens only on the screen or in novels happened to me in real life. I'm still trying to understand, but I will never understand. Margot, you will have to keep this news to yourself. I hope you're well. I miss you and I am sending you my blessings and also please give my regards to your parents and your brother.

71

She walked as far as a birch grove and threw the sweater she'd brought with her on the grass and kicked off her shoes. She was Odette, in *Swan Lake*, dancing beside a lake formed by her mother's tears; she was Odile, the witch, pirouetting, which was not easy on uneven ground. Someone was standing on the lake-shore, maybe thirty-five meters away. He was watching her. Even in the indistinct light she recognized Count Andorján. A match flared as he lit a cigarette. She stepped back, into the trees. Had he seen her? Like a detective in one of Beatriz's favorite mystery novels, she had put two and two together and had come up with a not implausible theory. First, Count Andorján was the owner of a motorcar. This was not mere speculation. She had seen him parking it on the road behind the Hotel Meunier. It was blue, low-slung, with racy lines, tall silver wheels, and identical to the one she'd glimpsed from the train, near Leipzig. The second clue was that the count and Fräulein Kuznetsova very much resembled the car's occupants. Why should she be surprised? Natalia thought. Since leaving Berlin, nothing in her life seemed to make sense.

The count was smoking a cigarette and contemplating the path of moonlight on the water. She gathered up her shoes and sweater and ran to the hotel and up to her room, where she flung open the window and leaned out, the air cool on her face. She could hear the orchestra members in the pavilion talking as they gathered up their instruments.

The girls at the convent would think Count Andorján hand-some; they would have crushes on him. He was handsome, undeniably, but he looked as if he never slept, his hair strag-gled over his collar, and his teeth were stained from smoking. Still, he had such a nice nose, a beautiful mouth, and when they were alone in the conservatory, she had seen lovely, mysterious glints of gold in his brown eyes. His gaze was warm, sympathetic.

He wrote novels, and wrote for newspapers and knew everything that was going in the world. Perhaps he was as famous as Joseph Roth, whose feuilletons she had read in the *Neue Berliner Zeitung* and in the *Frankfurter Zeitung*, when she came across that paper. Last year she'd read a feuilleton by Joseph Roth in which he'd captured a newspaper reader's personality completely by describing his eyes as being, for a moment, shy and mouselike. She had never forgotten that. Count Andorján was nearly as well-known as Joseph Roth; he was an intellectual and would not have taken any notice of her dancing beside the lake, and if he had, he'd think nothing of it. Anyway, she told herself, it was unlikely they'd meet again, at Lake Hévíz or anywhere else.

Then, several days later, on a Sunday morning, after she and her mother had been to an early Mass in Hévíz, Beatriz mentioned having sent Count Andorján and Fräulein Kuznetsova an invitation to dinner at their hotel next Friday evening.

"We don't know them," Natalia protested.

"You've met them, Julia knows them, and Herr Doktor Heilbronn says he's read every one of Count Andorján's books. Besides, they are the most interesting people here, and I would like to meet them."

That afternoon, Fräulein Kuznetsova left a telephone message at the front desk, saying she and Count Andorján would be delighted to join Frau Faber and her daughter at dinner.

Beatriz reserved a table near a window and ordered fresh flowers for the centerpiece. When the evening arrived, she sat for ages at the dressing table in her room, trying to fix a Cartier bandeau to her hair to her satisfaction, and they were late going down to the lobby, where Fräulein Kuznetsova and Count Andorján were waiting. Natalia introduced her mother to the count and Fräulein Kuznetsova, who kissed Beatriz's cheek and said, "What

a pleasure to meet you, and what a delectable gown, Frau Faber."
"Coco Chanel," Beatriz said, turning around to demonstrate the
genius of a gown composed of two panels of light blue silk falling
straight from her shoulders. Fräulein Kuznetsova's dress, a wisp
of ecru-colored silk, had rows of smocking on the elbow-length
sleeves. Her dark hair was piled up on her head; her only jewelry
was small crystal earrings. Natalia hated her childish pink silk
nothing of a dress, which had a wide silk sash that kept coming
untied. In the dining room, Fräulein Kuznetsova suggested they
dispense with Teutonic formality and use first names. Beatriz
agreed happily. The waiter filled their wine glasses. Beatriz and
Count Andorján decided on the roasted game hen; Fräulein
Kuznetsova chose a mushroom pilaf, and Natalia asked for
chicken with asparagus.

Miklós was teaching her to drive, Zita said. "Men want you to
believe it's difficult, driving a car, but it's not. I'm learning fast,
aren't I, Miklós? Every woman should learn."

"As long as there are trains, and they can take me where I
want to go, I am happy to travel on them," Beatriz said. "I read in
a newspaper that an English airliner now serves a complete dinner to its passengers. A strong stomach would be an asset, if not
a prerequisite, don't you think? And they're predicting that in a
few years' time there will be regular commercial flights between
Europe and America. It really is a new age, isn't it?"

"It is, but haven't we always dreamt of taking to the skies?
When I was a child," Zita said, "I saw paintings with an unusual
perspective, as if the artist were sitting on a cloud. Fields of
flowering flax, the tips of Siberian spruce, rivers winding
through the steppe, tiny babushkas in headscarves holding children by their hands, children with their mouths hanging open,
every detail miniaturized and yet precisely captured. These

paintings were the work of a monk whose spirit left his body and flew around the sky. When he returned to his body, he painted what he'd seen on small blocks of wood. To possess one of his paintings brought happiness and a long life. So it was believed."

"An enchanting story," Beatriz said.

"In Russia—this is another Russian story, also concerning levitation," the count said. "In Russia, animals and inanimate objects were so infected with revolutionary fervor they became unanchored from the ground. Entire buildings, churches, factories, apartment blocks. You could see them hovering above the frozen Moskva River. Empty overcoats and walking sticks and pet dogs flew about like birds. This phenomenon lasted for months, throughout the winter of 1917 and well into the spring of 1918."

"It had nothing to do with the tsar's liberated wine cellars, I'm sure," Beatriz said, laughing.

Natalia said, "The revolution wasn't really like that, though, was it? Not for everyone. People suffered, didn't they? The tsar and tsarina and their children were murdered."

"Yes," Count Andorján said. "The murders were an act of brutality."

"The revolution was ruthless," Zita said. "But it was necessary. It was mandated by history."

"My late husband's family was Russian, on his mother's side," Beatriz said. "I was born in the Argentine and one day, it is my hope, I will return there. As I get older, I believe more and more that it's important to rediscover your origins, in order to know who you are."

"I can never go back to Petrograd," Zita said. "Stalin would have me thrown into a labor camp."

Later, in her room, Beatriz removed her Cartier bandeau and rubbed at the mark it had left on her forehead. Count Andorján

75

obviously adored Zita Kuznetsova, but she did not feel the same way about him, she said. "What makes you think that?" Natalia said. "People give themselves away," Beatriz said. "The expression in the eyes, the way the mouth is held, the shoulders, the hands, everything reveals a person's true inner thoughts."

CHAPTER SIX

On a narrow dirt road south of Hévíz, Miklós stopped the Bugatti and changed places with Zita. He cautioned her that the engine was powerful, and the car had a tendency to oversteer. This, he said, is the speedometer, this is the oil pressure gauge, this adjusts the idling speed, this is for the carburetor jets. She waved him away, saying that a child could manage this machine. "I have found my métier, Miklós," she said. "I want never to stop driving. Like Puck in *A Midsummer Night's Dream*, we'll girdle the earth in forty minutes. What do you say, Miklós?"

"I say, keep your eyes on the road." If he asked her to slow down, she sped up. If he said turn right, she veered left. He gripped the passenger-side door and held on. The wind brought tears to his eyes; the Bugatti's motor coughed and missed a beat or two, then settled down. They passed a roadside religious shrine and a scattering of cottages. Three boys ran out of a yard and began throwing rocks at the Bugatti. Miklós half-stood and shouted at them. "This is not the time to slow down," he said to Zita. She stepped on the accelerator. "No harm done, Miklós, they're just boys. It's a game to them, nothing personal. Sit down, would you, before you get hurt."

A few kilometers on, she stopped the car and pulled over to the side of the road. This, she said, was where they would have lunch, in this pretty place, so pristine, the sky a silk canopy. She laughed. "I'm joking, it's just a field some landowner has forgotten he owns and let go wild."

They climbed down a shallow embankment, and he trampled the grass smooth before spreading out the plaid rug he'd brought from the car. Zita knelt and undid the leather straps on the picnic hamper the hotel kitchen had prepared for them. She took out plates, utensils, vacuum jars of cold chicken and cucumber in sour cream, chilled butter, olives, a loaf of bread. He uncorked the wine. "To vacations," Zita said, raising her glass.

He had returned late the previous night from two days spent with his mother. Within an hour of his arrival, he told Zita, his mother had ordered two horses saddled up, so that they could ride around the estate. She had pointed out recent improvements, including a new artesian well, an expansion to the vineyard, a refurbished horse barn. From memory she gave him the annual net proceeds from the sale of milk and butter, mutton, field crops, grapes, and the sale of two of her prize Andalusian horses. She reminded him that the estate was not a trivial enterprise; it required constant oversight. At her age, she couldn't carry on alone indefinitely. Did he want his land to fall into disrepair, end up on the auction block? Not only the people they employed, but the entire village, depended on him, she had said, jabbing his arm with the handle of her riding crop.

"She is blackmailing you," Zita said.

"No, no, she's entitled to think of me as a disappointment."

His mother had prepared his favorite meal for dinner: spicy

gulyás, and fogas, which the fishmonger in the village had guaranteed had been caught that morning in Lake Balaton. With the fish, they had noodles, floury potato scones, asparagus in cheese sauce. And after, dessert: *mákos guba*, bread pudding with crème anglaise and poppy seeds. Every ingredient, with the exception of the poppy seeds, which were supplied by the greengrocer in the village, and the Lake Balaton fogas, had been grown or produced on their land, his mother emphasized, as she refilled their wineglasses with wine made from grapes picked in their own vineyard. She uncorked a new bottle. When it was empty, she produced a decanter of plum brandy. She outdrank him and remained lucid and sober. At this, Zita laughed. He did not repeat the exchange that had followed between him and his mother, who had said, "You are still with that Russian woman?"

"Her name is Zita," he had replied.

"I know her name. She has the same name as our Empress Zita. That should mean something to her."

"I'm not sure it does."

"Nevertheless," his mother said, "I will pray for her."

The kitchen had smelled of beeswax, wild thyme, and something else. Vanilla beans, dried rosemary. The scents of his childhood.

Before he went to bed that night, his mother had asked him to look at a damp patch on the wall in the second-floor hall. "What I can't understand is why the dampness should be here and not nearer the floor or the ceiling. It's odd, isn't it?" She had pressed her fingers to the wall. "Feel it yourself. It's soft, like clay."

He had scratched the spot with his thumbnail and had felt something, or nothing. He would hire a carpenter to come in and inspect it, he said, and she had demanded to know when that would be. Soon, he said. This summer, his mother said, before the harvest. And you will need to be here, she said. You cannot hire a carpenter and oversee the work from Berlin.

"That was what she said, then, and later, when I was getting ready to leave."

"You are a journalist, not a house builder," Zita said.

He closed his eyes and saw an afterimage of brilliant green sky and red grass. He dug his fingers into the soil, the soil of Hungary.

In 1925, he remembered, he had taken Zita to meet his mother for the first and, as it turned out, the only time. It was autumn, the days clear and cold. His mother had arranged a hunt, inviting the village doctor and his wife to take part, along with Vladimír, his mother's groom, and a count and countess who lived in Budapest but were also local landowners. On the hunt Zita had shot an eight-point stag that stood transfixed as she took aim, as if it understood the inevitability of its demise. The stag was removed from the forest on a pallet pulled by a team of dogs. That was how his mother did things: in the manner of her father and his father before him. The village butcher arrived on horseback, bringing his knives and whetstones. On the last night they had dined on venison. In the dining hall, the table lit by tall white candles in ornate silver and pewter candelabra, Zita and his mother discussed horses and farming and village life. Then his mother said, So, Miss Kuznetsova, I understand you are a Communist. And are you also an atheist? Zita had replied that she remained committed to reform. Radical reform, she had added, smiling sweetly. As an infant she had been baptized in the Orthodox Church, she said, although it was some time since her last confession. He had hoped his lover and his mother would like each other. But there was something between them—not just a lack of sympathy but outright antipathy. A mismatch of personalities. He had told himself this would change, and if not, if he had to make a choice between them, it would be Zita. What he hadn't realized then, was that Zita would never ask him to choose.

When they had finished lunch, Zita dusted crumbs off her hands, took a last swallow of wine, and said she'd read the manuscript of his new novel, which she had brought with her to Lake Hévíz. "It's very autobiographical, isn't it?"

"Not at all," he said. "It is entirely fictitious."

"Well, whatever it is, it will do. Every woman will see herself as the heroine, Inessa. Did you name her for Lenin's lover, Inessa Armand?"

"No. I don't think so. Does it matter?" He loosened his collar. While he was at the castle, Zita had had her hair cut. It fell in glossy curls around her face. The new look suited her—it made her eyes seem even more extraordinarily blue and lively. But he missed her messy chignon and the tortoiseshell combs that kept it precariously in place. He loved this woman. He loved her; he adored her mind, body and spirit. He delighted in her presence. He moved to embrace her; she drew away. "Wait, Miklós," she said. "I'm talking. In your novel, a Hungarian nobleman goes to Russia in 1919, meets a Russian girl, a comrade, and kidnaps her, with minimal resistance on her part. This girl, Inessa, gets taken by the nobleman to his castle in Hungary, where he imprisons her in a crypt, an ossuary filled with the bones of the dead. Frightened, alone, with only one candle for light, she believes the skulls are gabbling to her in their diverse languages. After a few days and nights of this, she fears for her sanity. Her jailer brings her food and water. Why is she being so difficult? he keeps asking, when she know he wants only to marry her and make her happy. Meanwhile, his archrival, a young Hungarian Communist who, correct me if I'm wrong, bears a strong resemblance to

Comrade Béla Kun, has tracked him down and challenged him to a duel, as a result of which our hero suffers a flesh wound in his arm. Weakened by blood loss, he is helped to the castle by his opponent, who, having salvaged his pride, rides off on his horse. Inessa, released from the dungeon, bandages our hero's arm with a poultice of dock leaves and mustard. When he recovers, he sees her not as an obstinate girl who must be subdued but as his equal. And his life appears to him as less durable and robust than he had believed, but precious and of great value. And there is a wedding. Isn't that how it goes?"

"Yes, more or less. None of it is in the least true, or not very true."

"She is me, though, isn't she? Inessa is me. There I am, languishing in your ossuary with one candle—one miserable candle—to keep the ghosts and rats at bay. The ossuary is real, I saw it myself. Your mother took me down to the cellars beneath the castle and trapped us both in that charnel house with one little candle and the grinning skulls and the stench of rats. It was a cruel thing for your mother to do. But never mind, she did free me, in the end. Miklós, look over there, at those sunflowers. Look at the size of them! They are like scrawny, big-headed people, all nodding in our direction, beseeching us."

"Beseeching us for what, do you think?"

"Who knows," Zita said. "For a kind word, maybe, or a smile."

The sunflowers resembled a small, hopeful tribe of people, he thought. They would live like that, rooted to their scrap of earth, until the autumn frosts came along and demolished them.

He yearned to hold Zita. He wanted to know that their lovemaking in Prague had been the beginning of a reconciliation and more: marriage, a life together. He needed to say this to her. But once again the moment seemed to slip away. They gathered up

the picnic hamper and rug and clambered back up the embankment to the Bugatti.

→··←

In the hotel's dining room he breakfasted on coffee and toast
while reading *The Castle*. How strangely Kafka's story reson-
ated with him: the absent nobleman, who had absconded out
of apathy or fear or negligence, or all three, leaving his castle
exposed to the malign curiosity of the villagers. Not that the villagers of Némétújvár were malign, or not generally so, but they
were certainly curious. He knew that. The unspoken question he
got from them was: How long do we have to put up with an absent
aristocrat, a useless, do-nothing Count Westwest like you?

Zita came into the dining room. "Don't get up," she said. His
car was parked in the way of a delivery van; if he gave her the
ignition key, she'd move it. "It's only a matter of a few meters,"
she said. He handed her the key and went back to reading. A
waiter refilled his cup with coffee. On a shelf above a fireplace, a
row of sailing ships constructed of seashells from the Adriatic,
or so the hotel manager had told him, seemed to sail through
the air around him. He thought: How could the Bugatti be in the
way of anything? He had parked nowhere near the hotel's service entrance. He signed the chit for his breakfast and went out a
side door to the street. His car was nowhere in evidence. What a
clever trick. Zita had absconded with his car. He thought of acci-
dents, breakdowns, the car running out of petrol. Rock-throwing
youths. A woman alone, lost. He lit a cigarette. He watched the
empty road, willing the Bugatti to appear.

Fräulein Faber was walking toward him. "Frau Brüning is ill,"
she said. "She is very ill and has asked to see my mother, but at

the spa I was told my mother keeps missing her appointments. I thought perhaps I'd find her here, with Fräulein Kuznetsova."

"I'm sorry, I haven't seen your mother. Is Frau Brüning alone?"

"Dr. Heilbronn sent a nurse to her."

"Good. And has anyone contacted Herr Brüning?"

"No. Not yet, but Dr. Heilbronn will telephone him today."

"Frau Faber may have gone on a drive with Zita," he said. "But perhaps she is somewhere here. Shall we walk around the hotel grounds and see if we can spot her? First, if you wouldn't mind, I'd like to run this book up to my room."

Not once on the way up the stairs did it occur to him that it was inappropriate to take the Fräulein to his room, nor did he realize, until he'd opened the door, that he had left his suitcase open on the floor, its contents spilling out on the rug, and had piled books and newspapers on the coffee table. The little desk he was working at was covered with folded newspapers and writing paper. He saw Fräulein Faber looking at the typewriter and asked whether she knew how to type. No, she did not, she said, but she would like to learn one day. "It's an excellent skill to have. Here, come and sit down," he said. He wound a sheet of paper onto the platen and showed her how to position her fingers on the keys. Just type your name, he said. Tentatively, she depressed a key. "Don't worry," he said, "you can't damage it."

She made a single error, changing *Natalia* to *Natalie*. He rubbed it out with a little eraser on a wheel and brushed the paper clean. She corrected the mistake and said it looked strange, her name on a page like that.

"It does indeed. Seeing my own name on the page never fails to alarm me."

"But at least it is your name," she said. He looked at her, mystified. He asked her what she liked to read. She thought a moment before saying she had just finished reading a story by Thomas Mann called "A Man and His Dog."

"I know the story. Mann is good. He has a devilish turn of phrase, doesn't he? I'm reading Franz Kafka, a Czech writer, not yet well known. It's only in the last two years that his books have been published in Germany. He's unlike anyone else. Here, try this and tell me what you think." He pulled his copy of *The Trial* out of the pile on the corner of the desk and gave it to her. My God, he thought, what are you doing, Miklós? Was *The Trial* suitable read-ing material for a girl of seventeen or eighteen? But if she read Thomas Mann, she should be quite at ease with Franz Kafka.

They rode the lift to the lobby and walked across the lawn to the lake. On the pier, a man was playing a *tárogató*. Miklós and his brother used to play a *tárogató*. They took lessons from the wife of a worker on the estate but never learned how to make real music, only noise that gave their mother a headache. "She was always threatening to run away with the queen of the Gypsies. She meant her friend, a wealthy Sinti woman who lived part of the year on the estate. We were gullible children; we believed her," he told Natalia.

"When I was a child," he went on, "my family stayed here in winter. The lake never freezes. No matter how bitter the weather, the water is warm enough for bathing. I remember sleigh rides in the snow and white swans on the water, in clouds of mist. I asked my mother if the swans were real. She said they were real enough to make a good dinner."

Natalia laughed. "Zita said your home is not far from here."

"Not far. I was there recently, two days ago, in fact." He asked if she would like an iced drink. From the hotel veranda they'd have a good view of the pier and the hotel grounds. They could watch for her mother.

"Thank you, but I don't think my mother is here. And thank you for lending me this book. I can read it while I sit with Frau Brüning."

He watched her walking away in her blue dress and white hat. Then he wandered across the lawn, found a vacant bench from which he could see the road behind the hotel, and sat down. He opened his notebook and wrote:

Here at Lake Hévíz, you drink six or seven glasses of eau fraiche a day. You dine on steamed trout and stewed prunes, take an evening constitutional, and in the morning exercise, play tennis, swim in the therapeutically radioactive water. You see people nervously checking their pulse, and at dinner you overhear these same people discussing their digestion and other bodily functions you'd prefer to know nothing about. You are not like them. Not yet, anyway. You close your eyes against the light of the sun, which shines with more intensity in Hungary than anywhere else in all of Europe, and what you see, in a dazzling afterimage, is a beautiful girl dancing at the water's edge, at dusk, in a cloud of fireflies.

CHAPTER SEVEN

Dr. Heilbronn had diagnosed a hemoptysis, a slight coughing up of blood that could have many causes, some quite benign. "He was trying to ease my mind," Julia said. "Everyone is so good to me. Do you know, your mother gave me a charm to say: 'Every day, in every way, I'm getting better and better.' *Tous les jours, à tous points de vue, je vais mieux en mieux.* In French it sounds less dogmatic, don't you think? Or more so?"

Natalia refilled Julia's glass with water from a pitcher on her bedside table and smoothed her pillows. She bent to kiss her good night. Julia averted her face. "I don't mind about germs," Natalia said, holding Julia's hand. "Go," Julia said, laughing. "Go and enjoy the rest of the evening."

She sat on the grass near the lake and opened the book the count had lent her. *Someone must have been telling lies about Josef K., he knew he had done nothing wrong but, one morning, he was arrested.* The pages smelled of the count's tobacco. After the sun had set, and there was not enough light for reading, she went up to her room. Just after midnight Beatriz summoned her by tapping on the wall between their rooms. When Natalia opened the connecting door, Beatriz was sitting on the edge of her bed, a long filmy scarf, a new scarf, around her neck. She was stroking it as if it were alive, and indeed, it clung to her hands like a treasured pet, a fragile, radiant creature of amethyst, gold, and silver.

"Natalia, I have had such a wonderful day. First, we drove to Lake Balaton, but it was windy, and we'd seen all the shops, so we came back to Héviz. We bought peaches at a greengrocery and ate them in a park. While we were rinsing peach juice off our hands at a village pump, Zita spotted a house with a sign in the window, and when we got closer, we saw that the sign advertised handmade garments. A woman let us in and showed us her handiwork: dresses, skirts, blouses, men's shirts, Hungarian national costume, hats. I bought Zita a skirt and a blouse, to repay her for the petrol we'd used, and we each picked out a scarf. Zita's is like mine but rose-colored and embroidered with astrological symbols. The proprietor, Olga, invited us to her kitchen and served us dishes of raspberries with cream and cake, a surfeit after the peaches, but today everything was a surfeit. Olga has fourteen children. Her husband is a cabinetmaker. My God, such lives people have! Why do we get only one life? It isn't fair, is it?"

"Mother, Julia is not well," Natalia said. "Dr. Heilbronn is very concerned. He sent a nurse to be with her."

"Dr. Heilbronn will know what's best, I'm sure. Hand me my robe, darling. And be an angel and run me a bath, would you?"

"Isn't it too late for a bath?"

"No. And add some bath crystals, would you, please," she said.

Watching the tub fill, Natalia wondered if it was possible to very much dislike your own mother. She didn't add bath crystals to the water. In her own room she lay awake and then slept and dreamed of being in the count's car, in the back seat, behind Zita and her mother. They were traveling along a country road.

Mirages appeared in the sky. Phantom villages, little wooden houses painted in bright primary colors. Masses of flowers colonized the sky. Ghost horses galloped over the plains. The image reversed itself and became like a reflection in water, a phenomenon observed, it was said, only in high summer and only in Hungary. The dream must have been trying to tell her something. In the morning, she went to her mother's room and found the bed not slept in, the wardrobe empty, except for a satin peignoir with marabou trim. In her mother's steamer trunk were a mohair sweater-coat and a pair of shoes with a broken strap. She checked with the hotel desk, but Beatriz had left no messages, and none arrived during the day. Should she telephone Herr Saltzman or Sophie Brecht? Ask the hotel to call the police? But wasn't this the same as Beatriz's disappearance in the Harz Mountains? Beatriz could take care of herself. And at least she wasn't alone, she was with Zita Kuznetsova. In the end, Natalia did nothing.

That evening, when she was in the dining room, the count came to her table with a telegram. It read: ON PILGRIMAGE TO ANCIENT CITY OF RAGUSA NOW DUBROVNIK ON THE COAST OF DAL-MATIA WITH FRAU FABER YOUR MOTORCAR UNHARMED ALBEIT FUEL DEPLETED AT THIS ADDRESS IN KESZTHELY NATALIA TO RETURN HOME REGARDS ZITA.

"What does it mean?" she said.

"I suppose it means what it says." He took the telegram back and folded it in half. As soon as he got the telegram, he'd gone to Keszthely and located the garage, paid the owner for storing the Bugatti overnight, filled the petrol tank, and driven the car back to Lake Hévíz.

"Why would my mother want me to go home to Berlin?" He ran his hand through his hair. "You can't stay here alone," he said. "I'm surrounded by people," she said. "And Frau Brüning would be alone if I left. She needs me." "It's not good for you to be with her too much," he said. "There is a risk of contagion, isn't there? No, you must do as your mother says and take the train." He would drive her to Berlin, he said, but tomorrow he intended to drive south to Dubrovnik and look for Frau Faber and Zita. If Natalia liked, he said, he could see her to the train station in Keszthely. The train for Prague left every morning at ten o'clock. From Prague, she could board a train to Berlin. "Can you be ready by half past eight?"

"Yes," she said.

The desk clerk told her Frau Faber had settled the bill and had given instructions for her trunk to be shipped to Berlin.

Before she went to bed, Natalia packed a suitcase, unpacked it, and then put everything she'd taken out in again. Beneath the window, in the pavilion, the orchestra was tuning up. They began to play something beautiful, plangent, sorrowful, and Natalia went to the window to listen. Why should she obey a directive from a woman she scarcely knew? She was free, wasn't she? Free to do whatever she wanted. She could stay at Lake Héviz, return to Zehlendorf, get a job in an office, do anything. The problem was that freedom and indecision began to feel very much alike.

To her surprise she slept well and woke early. She bathed, washed and dried her hair, dressed in the blue skirt and lawn blouse she'd worn on the trip to Prague, and wished she did not look quite so much like a schoolgirl. A bellhop came to collect her suitcase. She went to Julia's room on the second floor and slipped a note under the door, letting her know she'd had to leave unexpectedly.

In the lobby, while she waited for the count, she picked up a Berlin newspaper and read that the floods in the Erzgebirge on July 9 had claimed more than two hundred lives, and property losses had exceeded seventy million marks. Commander Byrd, returning to the coastal village of Ver-sur-Mer in France, had been greeted as a hero. The villagers had presented him with charts and flight records recovered from his plane. He had kissed every baby in the village, as well as one woman in her eighties. Natalia flipped over the newspaper and saw an article with the byline *Miklós Andorján*, a story about Russian Jewish émigré families that had settled in Kreuzberg after the revolution. The count came in, and she placed the newspaper on a coffee table. He carried her suitcase to the car and held the door for her. At the train station in Keszthely, he handed her a list of telephone numbers where he could be reached and asked her to let him know when she'd arrived in Zehlendorf. She boarded the train and sat near a window. The coach was hot and smelled of coal dust and stale tobacco and perspiration from countless travelers. Beatriz had told her the trains in Hungary were relics of the Austro-Hungarian Empire. The once-luxurious velvet seats and curtains and the braided-gold pull cords were worn and dusty, the gilt trim tarnished, the opulence spoiled and forgotten. She waited, feeling hot and uncertain. She wiped the palms of her hands on her skirt. If the train didn't start to move soon, she would get off. If it didn't start in thirty seconds, twenty seconds, ten seconds, she would leave, and she did; she got out and went to where the count was standing on the platform.

"My mother would want me to wait for her," she said. They both knew this wasn't true. Count Andorján asked the station-master to retrieve Natalia's suitcase from the train. Then they got into the car and he drove to a café not far from Lake Balaton with a view of the water and sailboats with their sails furled. The count asked for coffee and biscuits filled with bacon and cheese. Natalia hadn't eaten breakfast and realized she was actually ravenous. She spread lashings of sweet butter on a warm biscuit. The coffee was phenomenally strong; it made her ears ring. The count lit a cigarette and leaned back in his chair. He tore a leaf off a spindly lime tree in a terra-cotta pot beside the table and twisted it by the stem, let it fall to the ground.

"I should have stayed on the train," she said.

"There are always more trains," he said

A woman was walking past. She bore a superficial resemblance to Beatriz—blond, wavy hair, slender figure, pretty but nothing as pretty as Beatriz. Tears came to Natalia's eyes. The count looked at her. "It's nothing, a little grit from the wind," she said.

"I blame myself," he said. "I knew, or should have, that Zita suffered some residual effects from what happened in the Erzgebirge. Did she tell you? She nearly drowned, you know, and one does not easily recover from an event like that."

She had not known. The floods in the Erzgebirge happened on July 9 and 10; she and Beatriz had left Berlin on July 10. So Zita Kuznetsova had almost drowned on the same day that Alfred had died. Perhaps at the same hour. She looked at the lake, narrowing her eyes at its brilliance in the sunlight, and thought it was as if fate had caught them all in a net and pulled the threads tight.

"I could stay here tonight and take the train to Prague in the morning," she said.

"You could, if that's what you want. I have an alternative idea. Why not stay at my home, as my mother's guest, while I drive to Dubrovnik. Chances are, I'll track Zita and Frau Faber down within a day or so. Then you and your mother can travel home together. But the decision is yours."

"I don't want to impose on your mother."

"She would be delighted." He placed a few coins on the table.

As they walked to the car, she thought: Maybe fate is what happens when you cease to resist, when you make up your mind to trust life.

→··←

That was how it came true: her dream of driving very fast in an open car. Not all that fast, though, because once they left the paved streets in Keszthely, the dirt roads and dust prohibited speed. Natalia's hat wouldn't stay on her head, so she held it on her lap and let the wind blow her hair around. After a while, the count asked how she was doing. She smiled, not trusting herself to speak. She felt the kind of happiness that had dark edges and slipped too easily out of her grasp and was instantly replaced by the fear that she had no right to it. She was glad when the count stopped at a village, where they spent a pleasant hour at a tearoom and then strolled around, stretching their legs. In a small park she stood at his side while he paid his respects to a bronzed statue of a Hungarian poet, a native son who had, according to the inscription the count read to her, married, fathered eight children, and died in this village a quarter of a century earlier, in 1902. Count Andorján said while the poet had never traveled, and his education had consisted of a few years at a small seminary, his writing conveyed a profound understanding of human nature, and his themes were universal.

They got back into the car, and an hour or so later the count slowed and pointed out Kastély Andorján in the distance. She thought it resembled a French château or one of the grand villas on the Grosser Wannsee more than a castle, with turrets and spires and drawbridges, like Schloss Neuschwanstein, for example. It did, however, dominate the landscape, up there on its hill, and it had, on one side, a tower with a circular copper roof that glinted

93

fiercely in the sun. She clasped her hands tightly in her lap. The count did not speak again until he slowed the car as they entered the village of Németújvár. His father, he said, had sworn that the village, with a population of two hundred souls, was the geographical center of Europe, which annoyed his mother, who claimed that her village, in the northwest, had that distinction. "Neither of them was correct," he said.

Németújvár resembled all the villages they'd driven through that day, and yet, because it was the count's village, Natalia thought, it seemed to have something the others lacked. The houses glowed in the strong sunlight; chickens scrabbled in the dirt; washing billowed on clotheslines. There were a few shops, a store with a gas pump, a restaurant. The count waved as he passed some people on the road, but he did not stop. Beyond the village he turned left onto a long and narrow drive bordered on either side by linden trees. He drove over a stone bridge and came to a circular gravel drive in front of the castle. A woman stood in the portico. A servant, Natalia assumed by her dress. Her iron-gray hair hung in a thin, whiplike braid over one shoulder. But the count went directly to this woman and bent to kiss her cheek. Natalia, standing beside the car, heard her say, "Two visits in one month. I am honored. You've brought someone with you, I see."

"Mother," the count said. "I'd like you to meet Fräulein Faber, from Berlin. She'll be our guest for a few days, while her mother is in Dubrovnik."

"Fräulein Faber," the countess said. "Come here, let me look at you." She held Natalia's hands firmly for a moment. Then they went through the open doorway into a vast hall. Natalia had an impression of crossed swords and heraldic plaques high on the walls. Mounted stags' heads. Oil portraits in gilded frames. Sunlight streamed down from a clerestory window, but the air held an arctic chill. The countess said, "Do you ride, Fräulein Faber? Do you hunt? The Russian girl my son brought here could hunt, I'll say that for her."

"No, I don't hunt," Natalia said. "I don't ride, I'm afraid."

"You can learn," the countess said, linking arms with her. "I will teach you."

They proceeded down a long hall with closed doors on either side and came at last to a kitchen. Freshly baked loaves of bread were cooling on wire racks; bunches of dried herbs hung from the ceiling, scenting the air. "Katya, put the kettle on," the countess said to a girl standing at a worktable peeling potatoes.

"This is Fräulein—what is it? Fräulein Faber, from Berlin," the countess said. "She is to be our guest." Katya wiped her hands and curtsied. The countess continued her interrogation: Fräulein Faber lived in Berlin? She was very young; had she finished school? She didn't look seventeen. The countess pinched Natalia's arm. "Skinny," she said. "We will put some meat on your bones." Then she asked: Was she Roman Catholic?

"Mother," the count said. "There's no need to grill our guest."

"I'm interested," the countess said. "It is unusual for us to have such a lovely young guest, isn't it, Katya?" The countess touched Natalia's arm and gazed at her hungrily. Natalia lowered her eyes. She felt almost faint under the intensity of the countess's gaze. When the countess learned her first name she wanted to know if she could address her as Natalia. "We are not formal here, are we, Miklós?" she said.

She turned to her son and said, "You know that Trajan has been lame for some time now? Vladimír insists it's not serious, but I know horses. I know Trajan, and I suspect Vladimír is keeping something from me. Miklós, are you listening to me? I want you to have a word with Vladimír."

95

"Today?"

"Yes, when else?" the countess said. To Natalia she said, "Vladimír is my groom. He is a Sinti, and like many Sinti, he has a sixth sense with horses, but even so, he is not infallible. He'll listen to you, Miklós. Go now, while Vladimír is in the stables." Then she said, "Don't gulp your coffee, you'll get heartburn."

The count emptied his cup in the sink and went out the kitchen door.

"So, your mother is in Dubrovnik?" Countess Andorján said to Natalia. "Years ago, my late husband owned a part interest in a stone quarry in Dubrovnik. I would go with him when he had meetings with the other investors. It was a good enterprise, profitable, and then my husband sold his share of the business, and we had no reason to make those trips to Dubrovnik. Tonight, my child, we will put you in the Green Room. It faces west; the morning sun will not wake you. If, in the night, you need anything, knock on my door. I am a light sleeper, and my room is across the hall."

One night in this castle, one night, and in the morning, I will leave, Natalia thought.

"Throw that pest outside," the countess said, when an orange cat strolled in through the open door and stretched out on the floor. Katya gave him a saucer of milk. The count returned, stepped over the cat, and stood leaning against a sideboard, arms crossed. He said that he and Vladimír had agreed that by any measurement of time you cared to use, horse years, human years, Trajan was a good age and he wasn't going to recover from an injury as quickly as he had when young. The horse would come to no harm if they waited and watched.

"I hope you and Vladimír are right," the countess said. "I am still worried. No one feels what that horse feels. But I do."

—>··<—

In the morning, when Natalia walked into the kitchen, the count was again immersed in the pages of a Berlin newspaper. He looked up and asked if she'd slept well, and she said, yes, she had. She was being polite. In truth, she'd lain awake for hours, listening to wolves howling in the distance, dogs barking, clocks striking the hours from somewhere deep within the castle. In the moonlight the furniture had cast malevolent shapes on the walls, and these shapes had seemed to move, had moved, she was convinced, and for a time she'd thought she heard footsteps pausing outside her door. She had fallen asleep only after she made a promise to herself that she would leave the castle with the count in the morning.

Now, in the kitchen, she knelt and petted the cat. She tickled him under his chin, and he rolled over so that she could scratch his tummy. His name, the count told her, was Monte.

A woman came in, tying an apron around her waist. "Magdolna," said the count. "This is Fräulein Faber."

Magdolna smiled. "Would you like porridge? And watch that cat. He bites."

A few minutes later the countess came in from outside and hung her sweater on a hook by the door and said she had been to the horse barn. Perhaps Vladimír was right and Trajan was on the mend. Later, she would see that the horse had some gentle exercise. She flicked a finger against the newspaper her son was reading. "Are you listening to me? You're very inhospitable, burying your face in a newspaper. What will our guest think of you?"

The count looked at Natalia and smiled. Magdolna placed a bowl of porridge and a poached egg on toast in front of her.

The countess poured herself coffee, sat at the table beside Natalia, and asked her son: Should she hire more workers for the harvest?

"If they're needed, then certainly hire them," the count said.

"My brother tells me that he employs seasonal workers from Slovenia. They are good laborers, reliable, steady, and will work for nothing, for beans."

"You must pay your workers a decent wage, Mother." He turned a page in the newspaper and laughed and said, "Here's something. Aleksandr Kerensky is in New York on a lecture tour. He has pronounced the Russian Revolution an abject failure. Communism, he says, will occur on Mars before it does in America."

"You call that news?" the countess said, spooning marmalade on her toast. Magdolna wanted to know if there was something wrong with the porridge. Had it gone cold? Would Natalia like more milk? "No, thank you, everything is lovely," Natalia said, placing her spoon in the bowl. The countess tapped a finger on the table. "You eat that," she said. "A young girl needs nourishment."

Katya had arrived. She nodded in the direction of the table and tied an apron around her waist before refilling the count's coffee cup. He thanked her; she stood for a moment, smiling at him, and asked if she could get him anything else. "No, thank you," he said. How fine he looked this morning, Natalia thought, with his rumpled hair and his newspaper and blue serge shirt open at the neck.

When, after breakfast, she encountered him in the hall, she said she appreciated the countess's hospitality, but she would like to go to Dubrovnik. "It occurred to me," she said, "that while you drive, I could watch for my mother and Fräulein Kuznetsova. Even in a crowd I'd be able to pick my mother out. And I know the sort of hotels where she'd be likely to stay and the shops and restaurants that would appeal to her."

"Thank you, Fräulein Faber. But this will be a rushed, unpleasant trip. You'll be better off here. As soon as I locate your mother and Zita, I'll telephone or send a wire."

She nodded, said she understood, but couldn't hide her disappointment. He went on to say something about the car not having room on the return journey, with suitcases and so on, and then he said there would be the matter of hotels and traveling without a chaperone. At first, she didn't understand why there was a need for a chaperone, and then she did and refused to blush. Did he think she was afraid to be alone with him? It was his mother she feared. The countess was a Medusa, a Gorgon, with her dark, probing looks and personal questions. If the count wouldn't take her with him, she'd find a way home to Zehlendorf by herself. In the village there would be a telegraph office. She'd send a wire to Hildegard, who by now should be back from Hamburg, to say she was coming home. Later, she asked Katya if there was a bank in the village. The Hungarian National Bank had a small branch beside the shoemaker's, Katya said, but the manager was a little potentate who opened the doors when it suited him. Natalia nodded; she would walk to the village and stand outside the bank all day, if necessary, waiting for the potentate-manager. There was, Katya said, a telegraph operator in the post office who kept more reliable hours than the bank official.

Katya gave her bread and honey and strawberries for lunch. The bread was fresh, the butter sweet, and the tea flavored with cardamom. She finished everything and rinsed the plate and teacup at the sink. Katya told her the countess always ate lunch in her room and then slept for an hour. In the Green Room, Natalia combed her hair and put on the jacket she'd worn on the train from Berlin. If she left the house now, no one would see her going. She walked down the hall to the grand staircase and descended to the central hall, where only a day ago she had met the countess. Time passed very slowly in this place, it seemed. Instead of going outside, she turned left and walked along a wide corridor. Only a houseguest with terrible manners and no sense of decorum would do what she was about to do, but she thought she had a right to know something of this place where she had been abandoned. She turned away from the hall that led to the kitchen and went down a wide corridor to the left. At random she opened doors and looked in at rooms with high paneled walls and gilded plaster trim. The rooms were furnished in what she thought a rococo style, with ornate trim and heavy carved chests against the walls and desks and tables and chairs upholstered in white satin and pink velvet. In the bedrooms the beds had satin coverlets and lots of pillows with fancy covers. A shame, she thought, that no one occupied these rooms. She turned and walked back toward the central hall. On the way, she stopped to open tall double doors painted glossy white, the kind of doors that were hinged in the middle and could be folded out of the way against the walls to accommodate large gatherings. This room, she realized, was the library. It was both very grand and very inviting. She went in and sat on a tufted oxblood leather chair and then tried a red velvet sofa, where she sat facing an immense stone fireplace with a black wrought-iron grill and brass fireplace tools on a stand beside it. Kindling had been set on the hearth, ready for a fire. She got up and opened the glass doors of a tall bookcase and ran her fingers over the gilt lettering on the spines of leather-bound volumes in German, Hungarian, and Latin. Then she went to the windows, which were symmetrically placed along one wall. She looked out at the gravel drive, hoping she would see the count driving up in his car, having decided that Natalia could travel with him to Dubrovnik. But he would not come back; she would go home alone to Berlin as soon as she got her hands on some money and could purchase a train ticket.

She could see sunlight glinting on the surface of the river. Across the river was the village, where, Katya had told her, her uncle owned a restaurant. Her father worked on the count's estate. Magdolna's family raised cattle, as they had for generations.

She picked up a framed photograph of two small boys in blouses and short pants, shoes with buckles. They stood on either side of a man in a hunting cap, with a rifle under his arm and a spaniel at his side. The younger boy had a fringe of dark hair, a mischievous smile. His older brother was taller and fairer. The boys looked like their father, not their mother, but then it was impossible for Natalia to picture the countess as a young mother and wife.

That evening at dinner, however, she found herself gazing at a portrait on the wall of a young woman with small white flowers scattered like stars in her upswept hair. The young woman's skin was luminous. She wore a gown with a filmy, gossamer overlay that pooled around her feet, mimicking the rosy hints of color in low clouds in an otherwise blue sky. The woman's dark eyes shone with candor, happiness, intelligence. She was beautiful, formidable, intelligent, Natalia thought, and then realized with a small start that the young woman was the countess.

"You look surprised," the countess said. "I was a beauty, wasn't I? My husband commissioned the portrait in the first year of our marriage. I was eighteen. My father said I was too young to marry, too young to leave home. I was right not to listen to him. It is true, what the poets say about time. It passes too quickly."

She was born, she said, in the county of Veszprém, to the

north of Lake Balaton. Her father, Zoltan, Count Nemeskurty, grew the finest grapes in the region; his ancestral home was much grander than Kastély Andorján and had a more illustrious history. Her mother, the daughter of a Polish prince, gave birth to eleven children, ten of whom survived, and those children now had children and grandchildren and, in the case of the countess's oldest sister, a great-grandchild. And what did she have? One son remaining to her. One son, whose responsibility it was to carry on the family name. And did Natalia know what this son told her? He said he couldn't live in Hungary under Miklós Horthy.

"I tell him the regent of the Kingdom of Hungary is unlikely to trouble us in our backwater. I say to him, give me a gentleman like Horthy any day over a rascal like Béla Kun, who would have carved my land up like a leg of lamb and distributed it to the people. I would like to know: Who are the people? I will tell you: I am the people."

She passed Natalia a serving dish of potatoes whipped in heavy cream. She said, "How did it come about that your mother has flown the coop with Zita Kuznetsova?"

"She likes traveling."

"*Mehetnék. Vándorlasi kedv.* Wanderlust, itchy feet. I am not one of the afflicted. I have always been happiest here, at home." She put down her fork and sat back. "If you were my daughter," she said, "I would not leave you. Not for all the tea in China."

She rang a bell for Katya to clear away the first course and serve the fish course, and after that came bread pudding with raisins and ginger sauce, and Natalia wished there was a dog under the table eager for a few scraps.

→··←

On the third morning of her stay at Kastély Andorján, Natalia found the countess in the kitchen, dressed in a smock buttoned to her throat, the sleeves rolled up, with a meat cleaver in her hand and two freshly skinned and eviscerated rabbits on the table in front of her. She'd gone hunting, she said, with evident relish, and look what she'd bagged. She wrapped the entrails in newspaper and dropped them in a bucket near the door. She would, she said, teach Natalia to make rabbit stew in the proper Hungarian fashion. Katya wiped the table clean with vinegar and water and set a place for Natalia. She managed a spoonful of oatmeal and gave up and wiped her mouth on her napkin. The rabbit meat, browned in hot oil and tipped into a stockpot, exuded the feral smell of itself alive. The stew must be simmered gently for three days, the countess said. No less, no more. Salt, pepper, caraway, sweet paprika were to be added at intervals sparingly, so as not to overwhelm the flavor of the meat. "Too much attention can be worse than not enough." Then she said, "Magdolna, I am taking Natalia to the paddock, to see the horses."

The horses were descendants of purebred Carthusians, the noblest of the Spanish Andalusians, the countess told Natalia. "I'll tell you what. Just look into their eyes. Look at this one's eyes, so pale, like water. See the depth of his chest, his height. This is Trajan's son. It pains me to think it, but this stallion will be Trajan's last progeny."

People paid whatever she asked for her horses. In the stables, she had an office where she interviewed prospective buyers. She had them fill out a form and provide character references. She turned down as many applicants as she approved.

In the horse barn, Natalia was introduced to Vladimír, the groom, and Herkus, one of the stable boys. The countess dug an apple slice out of her pocket for Natalia to feed Trajan. "He likes you," the countess said, stroking the horse's nose and whispering endearments in Hungarian. When they left the stables, Vladimír's dogs padded after them, two jet-black hunters, lean, sinuous, one named Dani, the other Mokány. The countess shouted at them to go back; they paid no attention and walked at Natalia's side as far as the kitchen door, and then they turned and trotted away.

The count returned from Dubrovnik late at night, and Natalia didn't see him until morning, when she climbed the circular staircase to the tower room with a cup of coffee. One hundred forty-seven steps, winding up and up to the sun-struck copper roof that was, Natalia imagined, like a beacon, a fabulous glinting light the villagers would look to as if for guidance. When she reached the count's study, he took the coffee cup from her. The room, with its curved stark white walls, looked out in all four directions of the compass, a dizzying prospect that made her feel as if she were about to take flight. She remembered Zita's story of the monk who left his body and drifted among the clouds like an angel. Between the windows were rough plank bookshelves filled with books, books piled on books, sheaves of papers, manila folders leaning haphazardly against books.

"Didn't you bring coffee for yourself?" the count said, clearing newspapers from a chair for her. A breeze came in the window and ruffled the edges of papers on the desk. The sunlight in the room was very bright and constant. She saw a cot with a rumpled blanket on it and a table with a tray left on it from a meal. The count was trying to give her his cup of coffee.

"Thank you, but no," she said. "It's for you."

"Next time, be sure to bring one for yourself."

"Yes, thank you," she said.

He apologized for not having better news. "Believe me, I

searched. I inquired not only at hotels and pensions but at hospitals and police stations, where I was assured it was a case of no news being good news. They counseled me to go home and wait. I keep reminding myself that Zita is very capable, and while I can't say she is being sensible, I know she wouldn't let any harm come to your mother. In a week, I'm going to the International Press Conference in Geneva, but I'll be heading first to Berlin. I can take you home then. Is that all right? You were comfortable here, I hope?"

"The countess is teaching me to make rabbit stew."

He laughed. He was writing an article for a Budapest newspaper having to do with the end, this month, of seven years of military rule over Hungary by the Entente powers. "Good news, on the face of it, but the fact is, the Treaty of Trianon robbed Hungary of its only port city and its industrial base and good portions of its land, and how can a country go forward with an economy based only on agriculture? Rabbit stew notwithstanding."

On the morning Natalia was to leave for Berlin, the countess went out riding in a rainstorm. Her riding boots were wet, and on her return she slipped and fell on the flagstones outside the kitchen door. Katya went to her and then ran up to the tower room to get the count, who came down and carried his mother to her bedroom. Natalia and Katya helped her out of her wet riding habit and into a nightgown. Dr. Urbán was summoned; he examined the countess and diagnosed a strained back and bruised ribs. The countess would need time to recover, but fortunately nothing was broken. He turned to Miklós and said the countess should not be alone at night. The count said he would hire a girl from the village to sleep at the castle when he was away. The countess objected. Katya would stay, she said. Or Fräulein Faber. Yes, she said; Natalia would stay. God sent Natalia to her for a reason, and she would remain a while longer, out of the kindness of her heart. Isn't that so, my child? She pressed a hand to her ribs. Pleurisy, she said; she knew the signs.

"You don't have pleurisy, you have bruised ribs," the count reminded her.

Clearly, Natalia could not leave the countess in this state. She promised to stay at least another week.

"You're so good to me," the countess murmured. "You are like a daughter to me."

Natalia remained at the castle with the countess not one week but two weeks. At the end of that time, the count returned. He came into the kitchen and took a postcard out of his pocket and put it on the table, where Natalia could see it. She picked it up. It was postmarked *August 2, Dubrovnik*. She read the message on the back. Zita and Beatriz were guests at a former leprosarium overlooking the Neretva Valley, a hundred kilometers from Dubrovnik. The leprosarium, constructed in 1905, at a time when the dread disease appeared in Croatia before disappearing back to wherever it came from, now offered hospitality to wayfarers like her and Beatriz. So Zita wrote, in very small handwriting. A Franciscan priest cooked for them, and they dined on a terrace overlooking the valley. *Miklós, do you remember the sunflowers? Beatriz and I are like that, clinging to the good earth, the seasons. We are like moss on a stone in the shadow of a sheltering tree.*

A leprosarium, Natalia thought. How like Beatriz to choose for herself the rarest, most unusual experience available. "At least they're alive," she said, and put the postcard on the table, beside a dollop of honey in which a satiated housefly crawled.

The count swatted the fly with a rolled-up newspaper. Natalia asked him if Zita had given a telephone number or address where she and Beatriz could be reached. "No, that would be much too considerate," he said.

This was how it was: She would be in the kitchen with Magdolna and Katya, and she would hear the Bugatti on the gravel drive and act as if she hadn't heard it, or had but without any particular interest. "Ah, Natalia, there you are," he would say, coming in with an armload of books and newspapers. She would be stirring soup, sweeping the floor, or petting the cat, as she was on this occasion. She sneezed. "Look at the fur flying around," the count said. "That cat is making you allergic."

"I'm not allergic to cats," she said.

"Perhaps it's dust on the floor," he said.

"It's certainly not dust," Magdolna said.

One day, and this was in September, Natalia walked with the count on the path beside the river. Leaves like gold coins littered the path; the air smelled of woodsmoke. Geese flew in a long, straggling V overhead. An egret stood sunning itself at the edge of the marsh. How beautiful everything is, she said. Even as a boy, he said, after a moment, he'd wondered why his family possessed acres of arable land, forests full of roe deer and quail, a river teeming with carp and trout, while so many lived in sometimes quite desperate poverty. It had to change, he said. It couldn't go on.

Even his guilt felt selfish to him, he said.

She wanted to tell him about her mother, whose parents had emigrated to Argentina, built up an exporting business, instilled in their only child respect for work and money, or at least for money. Would the poor benefit if Beatriz gave up her wealth? Would anyone benefit if the count did not own this land?

Vladimír's dogs bounded through the trees toward them. Mokány—or was this Dani?—jumped up with its muddy paws on her skirt. Miklós threw a stick into the woods and Dani retrieved it and trotted back with it in his mouth. "Good dog," she said, laughing, and held her hand flat, to indicate he was to sit, and he obeyed, surprising her and the dog equally, she thought.

Miklós—she was to call him Miklós, he said—told her to make use of his study while he was away. The books, the typewriter were hers. She would have a few moments to herself up there, he said.

After several false starts, in which she got halfway up the tower stairs and then turned back, afraid that, no matter what Miklós had said, she would be trespassing on his privacy, she made it all the way to his study. She stood in the center of the room, taking a moment to acclimate herself to the altitude and the sensation of being airborne. She didn't know what she was supposed to do here. She went to the bookshelves and selected a copy of *The Communist Manifesto*, by Karl Marx and Friedrich Engels. It was the German edition published in 1892. "A Communist Confession of Faith" took the form of the Catholic catechism, which disconcerted her at the start. She read a phrase here and there. *Private property ought to be eliminated. Individuals had the right to strive for happiness. The proletariat owned no asset other than their capacity for work, but this was everything, since it was by their labor that wealth was created. The proletariat must join forces in revolution to bring about a classless society.* She couldn't disagree, although at the same time she found it difficult to envision such a society.

She read a few pages of Louise Bryant's *Six Red Months in Russia*. John Reed's *Ten Days That Shook the World. Suddenly, by common impulse, we found ourselves on our feet, beginning in smooth lifting unison the* Internationale.

Zita would understand these books. She had been in Russia when the revolution began. Zita, in a fur-trimmed coat, like Anna Karenina, her hands concealed in a fur muff, stepping up into a troika, giving orders to the driver. Natalia was imagining this; she did not know where Zita had been in 1917. But she suspected that when the dust had settled, when the Bolsheviks had ousted the established order of generals and landowners, and the counterrevolutionaries and insurgents had gone to wage war in the east, Zita would have reappeared to help build a new society, a new order.

How wonderful, if everything could work out for the best, for everyone. Natalia pictured the countess's workers cooking communal meals in the castle's spotless kitchen. Children scampering up and down the halls. Sinti families roasting wild boar on spits in the fireplaces, singing exuberantly. The countess would be scandalized, although perhaps less so than Beatriz, if she were forced to share her immaculate villa in Zehlendorf with anyone, high or low born.

In a corner of the tower room there was the narrow, rumpled bed where Miklós slept if he worked late. She smoothed the blankets and picked up the pillow and buried her face in it and then put it on the bed. She sat at the desk and surveyed the four-cornered world outside the windows. In order to practice typing, she had started writing about her days at the castle, helping the countess with the school, learning to cook complicated dishes that involved a great deal of butchering. The countess wanted to teach her to use a gun. She refused to hunt; she couldn't kill anything. From the desk she could see clouds racing past in the sky and wet, messy snow falling with the rain. Winter, and she was still here.

Miklós had left his copy of *The Castle* on the desk. Natalia opened it. A piece of paper fluttered out, and when she unfolded it, she read her own name, as she'd typed it at the Hotel Meunier. She could see, faintly, where Miklós had erased the error she'd made, changing her name from Natalia to Natalie. She slipped the paper into the book and placed the book on a shelf.

CHAPTER EIGHT

In the village the countess had the shoemaker measure Natalia's foot for riding boots and a pair of what she called serviceable walking shoes. A few doors away, the tailor was sewing a riding habit of fawn-colored jodhpurs and a dark brown fitted jacket with a velvet collar. She went behind a screen to try it on, and then the tailor stabbed pins into it, and the countess pulled at the waistband and said Natalia was like a willow wand, and it would have to be taken in again. Later, in the café across the street, the countess told her the tailor had been a Communist, a supporter of Béla Kun, and she had refused to speak to him for years. The shoemaker had three marriages to his name, each wife having succumbed to some insignificant illness—delicate as flowers, he liked them.

"Countess, I want to reimburse you for the boots and shoes and the riding habit," Natalia said. The countess waved a hand in the air; it was a pleasure to do this for Natalia. She and Vladimír had chosen a mare for her. Ilka was a docile, pretty horse, but she would be insulted if Natalia didn't have the proper accoutrements for riding. The countess eyed the plate of *petits gâteaux* and chose a confection of chocolate and almond paste. "Have one," she said. "They're very nice." Two women came in and greeted the countess, who introduced Natalia as a distant relative visiting from Berlin. When the women had gone, she said, "Those old gossips. They don't need to know everything."

→··←

In the fall, the countess opened her nursery school in an untenanted worker's cottage near the river. It was a single room, heated with a round tiled stove. On the wall there was an enormous portrait of the wedding of the last king of Hungary, Karl IV, and his consort, Queen Zita. Every morning, before prayers, the countess instructed the children to bow their heads to this portrait. As many as fifteen children attended, sometimes only five or six, depending on the weather and how many Sinti children arrived at the door accompanied by a parent or grandparent. Natalia hung the children's coats on a row of hooks and handed out slates and chalk. She taught the children to count, using dried beans from the kitchen and chestnuts and acorns she collected from beneath the trees. *Eins*, *zwei*, *drei*, she said, in German, and the children made her repeat it in Hungarian: *egy*, *kettő*, *három*. The countess arranged beans on a sheet of white paper in the shape of a face with two eyes and an upturned mouth and said, This is me, and the children became giddy with delight. At eleven o'clock, Katya came to the door with buttered bread or cookies and a flask of milk for the children. While the children ate, Natalia made up stories, or retold old stories, to amuse them.

Once there was a farmer who had a chicken that laid golden eggs, so that he wanted for nothing. But a robber began stealing these golden eggs, and no matter how early the farmer got up, or how late into the night he kept watch, he could not catch the thief. Then one day a stranger came and said, if the farmer gave him three golden eggs, the thievery would cease at once. And it did stop. The stranger took his booty and ran away and was seen no more. Once again, the farmer found golden eggs nestled among the brown eggs in the henhouse, and he and his wife prospered all their long lives.

Or, a young wife who desired a child of her own sewed a cloth doll with button eyes, and a witch came to the open window of her workroom and said she could cast a spell to turn the doll into a real, living infant. But there was a price to pay: this infant would vanish unless the wife promised never again to speak a word. The wife agreed to the witch's terms, and at once the doll became a rosy-cheeked infant with eyes as black and merry as the doll's button eyes. The young wife tricked the witch by singing to her child in a voice of such purity that the witch, secretly listening, was beguiled and undid her evil spell. The infant grew to be a fine young man and often said his mother's voice was the sweetest sound in the world.

The countess, who tried not to let the children see her using a cane, held on to Natalia's arm as they walked from the school back to the castle. She said it would please her to be called by her given name, Rozalia. "Since my husband died, no one uses my name, and it's a pretty name, it means rose. The rose that blooms in summer and when autumn comes is devoured by worms." She laughed. "Natalia, tell me, is there a young man, a sweetheart, waiting for you in Berlin?"

"No," she said. "No one is waiting."

"Good," the countess said. "You have no reason to hurry home, then." Frankly, she had never cared for Berlin. Munich she could tolerate, it had substance, a distinct flavor, like a robust stew, and

Dresden was cultured, refined. But as for Berlin—Berliners took themselves too seriously; Germans she thought emotional and easily offended. "Hungarians, thanks be to God, have a native sense of propriety tempered with good humor. You will not find a Hungarian who does not enjoy his own society."

"I am German," Natalia pointed out.

"Ah, Natalia," she said. "All young girls belong to their own glorious principality."

→·←

The first castle built on the estate had burned to the ground a century ago, leaving only a cellar of unknown provenance, Rozalia told Natalia. It was, she said, impossible to describe and Natalia must see it for herself. When they had descended a narrow and steep flight of stone steps and had arrived, via a long corridor, at a cellar with an uneven stone floor and fire-blackened oak beams, Rozalia gave Natalia a candle to hold and removed an iron key from a hook in the wall. She unlocked a low, arched door that swung open on creaking hinges, exactly like a prop in a Fritz Lang film. Rozalia made Natalia go in ahead of her. Natalia knew what she was seeing, and yet it shocked her to know the castle's foundations contained human remains. Arm bones; finger bones that seemed to move, to beckon; skulls with gaping mouths and dark eyeholes. She stood with her back to the wall, near the door. The candle sputtered. To be left in darkness, Natalia thought. She would die. Perhaps the countess wanted that. Wanted to inter her with the bones. She breathed through her mouth, trying not to smell the rats, the decay.

Rozalia brushed dust off her hands and said she had discovered the ossuary when she first came to the castle as a bride. Her husband had been furious. It was the first time he was angry with her, and the last. Can't you keep out of anything? he'd said. Must you go looking for trouble? He'd wanted to have the skeletons taken away and buried in a communal grave dug in the forest, but Rozalia said the dead were the spirits of the house and had a right to rest in peace.

"They don't seem dead, do they? You can hear their breathing, if you listen. Some died in the days of the great Magyar ruler King Árpád, or at the time of the blessed Sanctus Stephanus. They died in the civil war and in the Ottoman invasions, when half the population of Hungary perished. They died here, on our land. It says in the Bible, 'Thy nobles shall dwell in the dust; thy people is scattered upon the mountain, and no man gathereth them.' But my husband's ancestors gathered up the bones. Magyar, Turk, Greek, Frenchman, and Italian alike. Men, women, and children. Christian, Jew, and Muslim."

The candlelight made something macabre of the countess's face. Natalia looked away. She saw an inscription in Greek on the wall and asked what it meant. The countess interpreted: "*The gods cannot count and know nothing of arithmetic.* Aristotle. It means you are on your own. You have to be stronger than your enemies. Do what you have to do, because life doesn't wait around for you.

"I brought that Russian girl, Zita, here," the countess went on. "Godless though she believed herself to be, she was trembling; she had to lean against the wall, and it was cold and damp, and that unnerved her still more. I said to her, don't people die in Russia? Don't Bolsheviks die? She and I did not get along. I will tell you this: if my son thinks she will marry him, he is mistaken."

They went out of the ossuary. Rozalia turned the key in the lock and hung it on its hook. In the wine cellar she chose wine for dinner and gave the bottle to Natalia to carry up to the kitchen.

When Magdolna took the wine from her, she berated the countess for taking Natalia to the ossuary. "Yes, but she wasn't frightened, were you, Natalia?" the countess said. "She's a brave girl. Tomorrow I will show her something nice, to atone."

Atonement took the form of a room along a corridor from the kitchen. A room with white walls and windows that looked out on a garden of neglected topiary and stone urns. At one end of a long pine table there was a stack of accounting ledgers, and against another wall there were three filing cabinets and an escritoire. Rozalia opened a drawer in the escritoire, took out a sandalwood box, set it on the table, and lifted the lid. She removed a deck of cards wrapped in a square of green silk. "Sit," she said. "I will read the tarot for you."

Natalia was the querent, she said, and must ask a question of the cards.

Natalia said she was Catholic; she didn't believe in superstition.

"I am Catholic," Rozalia said, "and I am superstitious.

"The priest at Saint Stephen's, Father István, would come every week to visit me. He would consume my plum brandy as if it was spring water, and then he'd fidget a while before asking, as he invariably did, to see the tarot deck. He pretended to have an anthropological or antiquarian interest, but I could see, from the way his hands trembled, that he believed in the cards. You will believe too, Natalia. You were brave in the ossuary; you can't be frightened of a deck of cards, can you? These cards are agreeable, they wish you well." She laughed and began placing them on the table in the shape of a cross.

"But it is necromancy," Natalia protested.

"The tarot is not necromancy," the countess said. "It is not communicating with the dead. That's something else altogether. I am very fond of these cards and I will tell you why."

She was silent and then said, "When he was still a young man, my husband broke his back in a riding accident. All his life he had been an active man, he'd done everything: he'd hunted, worked in the fields, swum in the river, climbed mountains; never was he still for a minute. Then, after the accident, he was confined to a bed or a chair. He did some painting in oils, he listened to music, he read books, but what made life possible for him were his friends, who came here and played *tarocchi* with him. With this deck of cards. I would sometimes go and stand outside the library doors, just to hear them cursing and laughing, arguing politics, grumbling about a downturn in grain prices. In the end, not even these diversions helped my husband. I have faith that I will see him again; death won't separate us forever. The tarot assures me of this, and the church holds it as dogma; it must be true. Goethe believed electrical and magnetic impulses reside within each of us. He said the soul puts out feelers and receives signals, like a radio set. And for lovers, Goethe said, these forces are especially acute. One day, Natalia, you'll know it yourself."

In July, Miklós came home, intending to remain while repairs were carried out on the castle. He hired a carpenter, a man named Guido, who came originally from Milan. The countess approved of him. He had given her letters of recommendation, one from an Esterhazy, which impressed her. Guido was of small stature, thin, with long, graying hair he tied back with a shoelace. He didn't look strong, yet with one hammer blow he smashed a hole in the second-floor wall and after a brief examination told the countess he could see signs of dry rot, mold, rodent infestation.

These maladies would not be confined to this one place, he said. By now, they would certainly have infiltrated almost the entire structure. He looked at the countess's stricken face and said perhaps he was mistaken. In his experience, these Hungarian palaces were built to the exacting standards of gifted Viennese and Italian architects and would be habitable long after their occupants were dust. Rozalia blanched. Miklós took Guido up to the attics, and the carpenter climbed out a window onto the roof and came back to report cracked and missing slate tiles and crumbling mortar in the chimneys, which allowed rain and melting snow to seep down through the walls. They were fortunate the damage was not worse. Still, the work of restoration would be more than one person could handle. He would need to hire plasterers, plumbers, brick masons.

The countess said to her son, "This should have been attended to years ago. You and your newspapers. Do you think you are Joseph Pulitzer, for God's sake?" She turned to Guido. "Give me your estimates and when you get to work, bring me the receipts," she said. "I will handle this."

The sounds of sawing and hammering filled the castle, and the air became gray with plaster dust. Katya and Natalia had to keep wiping the kitchen table with water and white vinegar. Rozalia had taken it upon herself to provide Guido and his crew with a midday meal. Dishes of noodles with caraway seeds and sour cream, roasted chicken, squash mashed with butter, thin pancakes filled with spiced beef, poppy-seed rolls. Viennese pastries, chocolate tarts, and glazed strawberry torte from the bakery in the village. These meals were served in the kitchen. Whatever was left over, Magdolna set aside for the evening meal. Natalia and Miklós and Rozalia ate in the kitchen, and then Rozalia liked to retire to the library for wine or brandy. One evening, she poured out three glasses of herbal liqueur the color of moss. "Drink it," she said to Miklós. "It will help you sleep." To Natalia she said, "You too, Natalia. It will make your blood strong."

The liqueur tasted of angelica, fennel, mint, aniseed, something chocolaty, something bitter. At first it was vile, but Natalia found the taste improved with each sip. Miklós went to the liquor cabinet and poured whiskey into a tumbler. He stood at the window, his back to the room.

"The work is proceeding smoothly, wouldn't you say, Miklós?" Rozalia said. "Are you listening to me? I think László would be pleased. The castle meant everything to him, as it did to his father. László was the image of his father, Natalia. You can see it in that photograph over there, on the table. Weren't they alike, Miklós, even in character?"

"Yes, they were," he said.

Rozalia began to reminisce about vacations they'd taken years before, in Karlsbad, in Prague, in Vienna. Snowshoeing in winter, fishing in summer. Winter sleigh rides at Lake Hévíz. Did Miklós remember?

Miklós turned and smiled at his mother. He said he had been thinking the other day of how he and László used to take their father's Royal Enfield motorcycle, without permission, and ride through the village.

"Yes, I remember. Hellions, you were. They roared through the countryside, Natalia, like brigands, outlaws. I didn't know them in those years. It was a shame, because as infants they were good-natured, lovely boys, but they grew into demons. They played the *tárogatá* out on the terrace at such a volume, and with such gross ineptitude, that they curdled the cows' milk in the pasture. I threatened to run away with the Queen of the Gypsies. Do you remember, Miklós? László knew I was bluffing, but you,

Miklós, were a credulous child. If I claimed the sky was saffron yellow, you would run outside to look."

"Sometimes before a storm the sky was yellow," he said.

"Me, you mean; I was the storm," the countess said. "But you were the ones who went away. You went away." She set her glass on a table. Her head nodded. Natalia looked at Miklós. "Come, Mother, before you fall asleep," Miklós said. He gave Rozalia his hand, helping her out of the chair, and Natalia held her other arm, and the three of them went upstairs. In her room, Rozalia fell asleep on the bed in her clothes, and Natalia covered her with a quilt. In the hall, she and Miklós said good night.

In the kitchen the next morning, Natalia, helping with the preparations for lunch, let the knife slip as she sliced into a yellow onion and cut herself. Rozalia plunged her hand into a bowl of soapy water. The wound bled; the water turned pink and then red, and Rozalia said she would need stitches to close it. No, she kept saying; she didn't need stitches. Did she want her hand to turn septic? Miklós said, when he came into the kitchen. He took her to the doctor's house in the village, where they waited an hour for Dr. Urbán to return from what he described as a difficult confinement, but mother and twin sons were doing well, he said. He put five stitches in Natalia's hand and told her to keep it elevated and out of water. In a week, the stitches could come out.

Miklós took her to the café and ordered tea, which he said would be better than coffee for shock.

"I'm not in shock," she said.

"Still, it will calm you," he said.

"I am calm," she said. Beneath the calmness, though, she felt shivery and also mortified at having been careless at such a simple task.

The waitress brought two large pieces of chocolate-lavender cake. "Why are you even working in the kitchen?" Miklós said. "You're our guest. My mother is taking advantage of you."

"No, she is wonderful to me, truly."

In a few days, he said, he had to make a trip to Budapest to pick up an order at a bookshop. Would she like to go with him?

Yes, she would like that very much, she said, and she took a forkful of lavender cake and said it did, indeed, taste delicious.

Three days later, they were in Pest, on the Chain Bridge, looking down at the Danube and the upturned faces of passengers on the deck of a riverboat. It was high summer; people were in a festive mood. She and Miklós walked back across the bridge to a stationery store in Pest, where Miklós bought a bottle of Pelikan Tinte ink and a typewriter ribbon in a round Pelikan tin, and she bought chalk and paper for the school. Then, at the bookshop, Miklós picked up his order: the first German translation, in three volumes, of *Ulysses*, by James Joyce. Also Margherita Sarfatti's biography of Benito Mussolini. He remembered that she had been reading Thomas Mann and bought her *Buddenbrooks*. They lunched at the Café Gerbeaud on thin crêpes filled with meat and mushrooms. She thought they looked very well together, Miklós in a light linen jacket, and she in a blue voile dress with a low waist and slightly flared skirt, which had been sewn for her by the village tailor. It was her favorite dress at this moment. Her bandaged hand made it difficult to eat (Katya had helped her get dressed that morning), and Miklós cut her crêpe into smaller pieces. Later, in a shopping arcade, Natalia went into a jeweler's shop and chose a small crystal horse for Rozalia and, impulsively, a tiepin set with a tiny garnet for Miklós. At vendors' stalls in the arcade, she found an embroidered tablecloth for Magdolna and a doll in Hungarian costume for Katya. They drove across the Chain Bridge to Buda and rode the funicular up to Buda Castle and the Royal Palace. They could see the city of Pest across the Danube and in the distance the Great Hungarian Plain. At the Fisherman's Bastion, a man offered to take their picture. "Put your arm around your sweetheart," he said. "It's good," he said, handing the camera back to Miklós. "Someday I would like to own a Leica."

They walked in a park, watched children feeding bread crumbs to ducks on a pond, and then sought refuge from the heat in an art salon exhibiting the work of avant-garde artists from 1900 to the present. Natalia studied a group of three paintings, three scenes of people at sidewalk cafés. Men in fedoras and double-breasted summer suits, patent leather shoes, wide gold rings on slender hands; women in pastel dresses, their faces long and narrow, big-eyed, with pointed chins. Their smiles seemed contemptuous. Or distrustful. Vigilant. Interspersed, a few misfits: dour characters; crafty, suspicious eyes, hands that seemed to grasp at the air. The artist's name, printed on a card pinned to the wall, was Julius Schaeffer. He had studied at the École des Beaux-Arts in Paris and at an academy in Prague, where he'd lived since 1919. A coincidence? Could the artist Julius Schaeffer be related to Dr. Schaefferová and the little boy, Franz, on the train?

They had lemonade at a café and then sat on the steps of Saint Matthias Church, and Miklós told her about living in Budapest when he and his brother, László, were students at the university, and how before that, when they were children, they had come to Budapest with their parents and had stayed at the New York Palace Hotel. Even as a child he had loved hotels, while László had always wanted to know how long until they were going home. Once, while their parents lingered over dinner, he and László had run races in the corridor, and he, trying desperately to beat his older brother, had run headlong into a marble pillar and knocked himself out. When he opened his eyes, he believed for a moment that he had killed himself and was in heaven, which had long, gleaming corridors, gilded ceilings, and lavish chandeliers, just like the New York Palace Hotel. But, he said, that beautiful establishment had been damaged in the war and was closed for repairs. Instead, they went to his second-favorite café in Budapest, where there were red tablecloths on the tables and waiters in short black jackets and a piano player wearing a flesh-colored sequined gown and ballet slippers. They ate steamed Lake Balaton trout and a creamy risotto with parsley and mushrooms, followed by coffee, dark chocolate, sugared almonds, and fresh fruit. While they were talking, Miklós reached over and wiped chocolate from the corner of her mouth with his napkin.

They left Budapest after sunset, as stars were appearing in a sky of mauve, violet, and indigo. The air smelled of warm, freshly tilled earth and summer foliage. Natalia took off her hat and let the wind blow her hair around. Miklós stopped for a farmer herding sheep across the road with his dog. "What kind of dog is that?" Natalia said. "It looks more sheeplike than the sheep."

It was a puli, Miklós said, a Hungarian sheepdog. He and László had once had a puli named Georg, a ferocious animal with an aggressive streak. It had savaged a man's dog in the village and had had to be put down. After that, he and his brother had not wanted another dog.

Something was wrong with the motorcar; steam was pouring

123

out from under the hood. Miklós pulled over. He got out and walked once around the car. He opened the hood. Then he said it was a blown head gasket or a faulty radiator hose. He would walk into the village and borrow a pail of water. "Don't go anywhere," he said. When he got back, he started the Bugatti and instructed her to keep her foot on the gas pedal while he poured water into the radiator. He was no mechanic, he said, but they would hope for the best. It was almost two in the morning by the time they reached Kastély Andorján. They sat in the car, listening to the overheated engine ticking as it cooled down. She started to open the door, when Miklós put his hand on her shoulder. She turned, he kissed her. His hand brushed her cheek, he smiled, kissed her again and then drew back and said he was sorry, he shouldn't have done that. In reply, she kissed his mouth. A long kiss. Should she then apologize? Would it go on like that, first a kiss and then an apology? She would like that.

When she got to the portico, she remembered the parcels in the car. He would bring them to the kitchen. Go inside, out of the cold, he said. Everything will be different now, she thought, everything will be changed, and she did not sleep, thinking of him and how she loved him and how it was all right, now, to admit this to herself. But in the morning, when she went to the kitchen, he scarcely looked up from his newspaper, except to say good morning. "Good morning," she said. He excused himself, saying he had work to attend to, and took the newspaper and a cup of coffee up to the tower room. The next day, he arranged for the Bugatti to be shipped to a garage in Budapest. Then he sat outside reading Sarfatti's biography of the Italian Fascist dictator, in preparation for an upcoming trip to Italy, where he had been granted an interview with Mussolini. Margherita Sarfatti was certainly not an unbiased biographer, he said to Natalia when she came out to tell him dinner was being served. Sarfatti, he said, was Mussolini's closest adviser and friend, his publicist and propagandist.

→ ·· ←

Mr. Petrus, the veterinary surgeon, stood in the kitchen, eating Magdolna's still-warm plum cake from a plate he held in his hand, while informing the countess that his earlier diagnosis was confirmed: Trajan had congestive heart failure and fatal locomotor disease. These were serious, irreversible conditions, he said.

Naturally, Rozalia said, health declined in a horse Trajan's age. One expected it. But Trajan was fundamentally sound, his lameness sporadic, the pain treatable.

"If it was my horse, I know what I'd do," Mr. Petrus said.

"Perhaps we need a second opinion, Mr. Petrus."

"By all means, if that's what you want. But soon, Countess, or your horse will go on suffering."

"Very well," Rozalia said after a moment. "If that is how it is." She asked Natalia for her walking stick, saying, "I suppose I am next to be put down for lameness."

Vladimír had settled Trajan on a bed of clean straw. Rozalia knelt beside the horse. Trajan raised his head, straining to see her face, and at that Natalia turned away. She saw the vet filling a syringe and wanted to cry out: No, what if the countess is right and you're making a mistake? She covered her eyes and then felt ashamed at her weakness. But she was not alone in her distress. Miklós walked out a moment after Mr. Petrus gave the injection and Trajan's breathing became more labored. And then there was silence. The familiar smell of leather, straw, and oats, the slanted, heavy light, the stillness of the horse, his dignity and strength in surrender, brought tears to Natalia's eyes. She and Vladimír helped Rozalia to her feet. The countess was controlled, dignified; she held herself stiffly and said Natalia should go to Ilka. "Horses sense these things. Let her know you are thinking of her."

As soon as Natalia reached the paddock fence, Ilka trotted over and took a sugar cube from her hand. She stroked the mare's nose and assured her that all was well, all would be well, and they would go for a ride soon. She loved Ilka, she thought, and was afraid she was going to cry for Trajan and that once the tears came, they would be unstoppable, not only because of the horse but because of everything. Miklós walked over and stood beside her. He was wearing a soft, much-laundered collarless shirt, and it was charming on him, that shirt. She stared at his hands on the fence rail.

"Before he was my mother's horse, my brother rode him," he said. "In the country, you see animals dying, it's inevitable, but I hate it."

"I know. The animals have a good life here, though."

"Yes. My mother sees to it that even the cows and sheep are happy."

"I have to go home," she said.

"Let me take you," he said.

"I'm not sure when I'm going, it will depend on the countess."

"Natalia, I owe you an apology. I allowed myself to forget, for one thing, that you are our guest, and for another—I am almost old enough to be your father. I am, in any case, old enough to know better. I hope you can forgive me."

"There is nothing to forgive," she said.

They walked down to the castle and at the kitchen door met Guido, who was on his way to offer condolences to the countess.

Magdolna made espresso and sliced the remains of the plum cake. Miklós poured cognac into glasses and offered Guido a cigarette. The countess returned from the stables. She sat at the table and said she would like a cigarette too; she felt the need of a stimulant. She said her horse had not succumbed to disease, as the vet said. Out of courtesy, Trajan had gone ahead of her to the next life, and he would wait for her there. "You get older, life gets smaller and smaller," she said. "Any loss wears you out." She looked at Guido, her eyes half-closed, holding the cigarette close to her face.

Miklós told Guido he had an appointment in a few days' time in Rome to interview Mussolini. The Fascist leader had destroyed the free press in Italy but paradoxically courted the foreign press. "In return, he expects encomiums and favorable comparisons to Garibaldi, Napoleon, Bismarck. Which he can whistle for, as far as I'm concerned." He asked Guido what his family in Italy thought of Mussolini. It went like this, Guido said: one-third of his family believed Mussolini to be a man of heroic dimensions, capable of restoring Italy's economy and standing in the world; one-third detested Mussolini and called him a murderer and a phony; one-third never gave a thought to politics. Miklós asked in which third Guido placed himself. "Ah, that would be telling," Guido said. He got up and pushed in his chair. "Again, my sincere condolences, dear lady," he said, kissing Rozalia's hand.

Before she left, Natalia gave Rozalia the small crystal horse she had bought at the arcade in Pest. Rozalia held it in the palm of her hand. It captured Trajan's gallant and sprightly nature, particularly in his salad days, she said, and then gave Natalia a long look from beneath her waxen eyelids. "Why are you going, my dear child? Will you be back for the harvest? Promise me you'll return in time for the opening of the school, or the children will think you don't like them. What am I to do without you? I will be alone at night, and you know my heart can't take it. If you stay, I'll have the Green Room repainted. You can choose another color, anything you like. Is the bed too hard? I'll replace it."

CHAPTER NINE

As soon as she arrived home, Natalia saw that Zita not only had moved into the villa in Zehlendorf but also had commandeered almost every bit of space. Her books and papers littered every available surface and were piled on the floor beside her favorite chair in the living room. A photograph of her father had a prominent position on the mantelpiece, beside the ormolu clock, and her typewriter seemed a permanent fixture at one end of the dining room table, so that meals were often taken in its august presence. Worse, Benno now slept on Zita's bed. "I enticed him, I'm afraid," Zita said. "My feet get cold at night, a symptom of a vitamin deficiency, from Russia, in the revolution. And he is such a nice, plush cat, aren't you, my darling?" She nestled her face in Benno's fur and the cat purred. Traitor, Natalia thought. When she woke early in the morning, she went into Zita's room and carried Benno back to her own bed. On many mornings, Zita was not in her bed at all, but had crossed the hall to Beatriz's room, and the two of them were sitting up against the pillows and talking. Then Zita would exclaim that she was going to be late, and she'd rush around getting ready to catch the train to work.

In the evenings, Beatriz and Zita hired a taxi to Berlin, where they saw films at the cinema or had tickets to the *Opernhaus* or to the *Philharmonie*. They loved cabarets, singers, any form of entertainment, and liked to frequent a new transvestite bar that was all the rage. In the morning, they recalled gags they'd heard, repeated off-color jokes, and like wayward schoolgirls fell about in fits of giggles. On the last day of August, Natalia went with them to the opening night of *The Threepenny Opera* at the Theater am Schiffbauerdamm. Zita bought the sheet music, and she and Natalia learned the lyrics to the Bertholt Brecht and Kurt Weill songs "Mack the Knife" and "Pirate Jenny." Music to commit revolution by, Zita said.

> *And they'll see me as I stand beside the window and*
> *They'll say: what has she got to smile about?*
> *And a ship with eight sails and*
> *All its fifty guns loaded*
> *Will lay siege to the harbor.*

Beatriz applauded. She said, "Natalia, listen to you, how you sing, and look at you dancing. I would never have guessed my quiet girl was such an actress."

Beatriz gave dinner parties, inviting actors, filmmakers, writers, as well as her good friends Herr Saltzman, Sophie Brecht and her husband, Gustav, a professor of art history at the Berlin University. Everyone an authority, a connoisseur; everyone with an opinion. The conversation, generally lively and stimulating, could become contentious, as on the evening Zita emphatically denounced the disparity between rich and poor. Some of the guests agreed; others argued that society, any society, naturally evolved toward complexity, some won, some lost; how could it be otherwise? The utopian ideal did not exist; surely Zita would agree? No, she didn't agree, Zita said. Like any machine, society required skilled engineering and oversight in order to work. It hurt her when, walking down any street in Berlin, she saw paupers on one side, tycoons on the other. "Inevitably there will be a crisis," she said. "And when it comes, it will be cataclysmic. It will pull us all down."

"A cataclysm? I hardly think it will come to that. Isn't it the responsibility of those who have, to look after the less fortunate?" Sophie Brecht said, a chocolate bonbon halfway to her lips.

"Charity," Zita said. "Charity is poison."

"If everyone thought like that, we would indeed have a crisis. A moral crisis," Sophie said.

"Hungry people need food, not sermons," Zita said.

"Did I say anything about sermons?" Sophie ate the bonbon, wiped her mouth on a napkin.

"I'll tell you what I don't like," Beatriz interjected. "I don't like that the central bank has raised interest rates to eight percent. I wrote to Hjalmar Schacht. I told him straight that tightening the money supply will have a disastrous effect on the country's economy. I let him know I'd already pruned my German stock holdings to almost nothing. He might be the head of the Reichsbank, I said, but I could do a better job blindfolded."

"Bravo!" Herr Saltzman cried. "Although I fear your intervention will get you precisely nowhere." He smiled at Beatriz. Zita got up to refill Beatriz's wineglass and offer her the silver tray of cheese and grapes. Beatriz took a grape. Zita murmured a few words in her ear. Beatriz laughed.

A day later a letter came for Natalia's mother in an envelope bearing violet-colored República Argentina stamps. It was from the law firm that managed her legal affairs in Buenos Aires, informing her that the caretakers at her villa were retiring in October. A new caretaker would have to be hired. Her lawyers would be pleased to act on her behalf, or she could attend to the matter in person, if she preferred. Beatriz kept changing her mind: Was it worth the time and money to travel to Buenos Aires? She stared at the photograph of her childhood home and said, after twenty-two years she owed it a visit, didn't she? One evening, she came into the living room, where Zita and Natalia were reading, and perched on the edge of a chair and announced that she had decided: they would all go. On the mantel above her the ormolu clock shone, as if emitting light, but Natalia thought it was Beatriz; she was the one shedding radiance, from her eyes, from the pores of her skin. "If we leave in late November," she said, "we will arrive in Buenos Aires when the jacaranda trees are in bloom, the gardens in flower. Zita, you'll love it."

"I can't afford to take six months away from work, Beatriz. I would lose my job. Besides, I get seasick, I'm not good around water."

"Well, try not to fall overboard."

The passenger lists on Hamburg-Süd's new luxury liner, the *Cap Arcona*, reputed to be the fastest ship on the South Atlantic, were almost filled, Beatriz discovered. She wouldn't contemplate sailing on any other ship and paid a deposit on the last two first-class tickets, which immediately created a predicament: Who would take the second ticket, Natalia or Zita?

"Natalia must go with you, Beatriz. She's your daughter."

"Yes," Beatriz said.

"One day, I would like to see Buenos Aires," Natalia said. However, she had been away, and now she would like to stay at home. Zita arranged to hand a project over to another editor. Her boss agreed to her going, if she took on the job of contacting an

Argentine writer whose novels Ullstein Verlag wanted to publish in translation.

In November, Herr Saltzman drove Natalia and her mother and Zita to Hamburg. They all stayed overnight at a hotel, so that Herr Saltzman and Natalia could be at the pier as Beatriz and Zita, heads bent against the rain and wind, boarded the *Cap Arcona*. How seaworthy was this new *Cap Arcona*? How safe was Buenos Aires for two women alone? Herr Saltzman would like to know.

This, he said, was the leitmotif of his life. How many times had he said goodbye to Beatriz, not knowing when or if he would see her again? In the past, she had relied on his advice, his friendship; she had allowed him to believe their friendship would grow into something more. But he was tired of waiting; he could not endure it; he could not compete with Zita Kuznetsova, he said flatly. He gave Natalia his umbrella and walked bareheaded, rain pouring down his face, to his car.

Natalia invited Herr Saltzman to dinner on Christmas Eve. Hildegard prepared roast goose, sausages, potatoes with herbs, carrots in butter. They listened to Christmas music on the radio. At nine, Herr Saltzman had a long-distance operator place a call to Buenos Aires, where it was four o'clock in the afternoon. Beatriz came on the line, excitedly telling Natalia that nothing had changed in her villa. It was just as she remembered. Not a stick of furniture was out of place. She could walk through the rooms with her eyes closed and not bump into anything. She kept hearing her parents saying, "*Mein Gott*, what do we have here? Is this the little nuisance?"

Natalia passed the receiver to Herr Saltzman, and when the phone call ended, he beamed and said, "Doesn't she sound well?"

➤∙◄

Natalia and Margot Brückner made appointments at the beauty salon at Kaufhaus des Westens for manicures and haircuts. They walked along Tauentzienstrasse, looking in shop windows. A street photographer took a picture of Natalia and gave her his card. Margot said Natalia must go to his studio to buy the photograph—which she did, two weeks later, and it surprised her. Was this her? She saw a tallish girl, eyes shining, a slight smile on her lips. Her coat came to her knees and showed off her actually very nice legs.

"Look at you," Margot said. "You're beautiful."

Natalia laughed, but the photograph gave her confidence, in a way. The confidence to go about alone, to do things on her own, whatever she pleased, because why should she care what anyone thought of her? She sat in a café on Potsdamer Platz nursing a cup of coffee and reading a book and writing replies to letters from her mother and Rozalia. In her letters Rozalia sounded despondent, querulous, saying the weather had kept her imprisoned without a soul to talk to except Katya and Magdolna, and many days they were late coming to light the kitchen stove in the morning. Late with breakfast and the cooking they were but very prompt in leaving. Many nights she had nearly frozen to death in her bed, but thanks be to God, she was alive. *When are you coming to see me? Don't leave it too long, will you? Katya is going to give the Green Room, now referred to as Natalia's room, a good cleaning and airing in readiness. I await your reply, my dear girl.*

Rozalia's letters made her smile, whereas Beatriz's letters often provoked her. Beatriz too complained of being confined indoors, in her case in her lawyer's chambers, where she was signing endless papers finalizing the sale of properties, some of which she had not known she owned. *My parents were compulsive investors, there was nothing they didn't want to possess, it seems. Vast*

tracts of pampas and ranchland, wheat and sugarcane plantations,
as well as commercial space in the city and warehouses near the river.
Some properties generate an income it's true, but expenditures have to
be set against profits, and my time has value, as well.

Beatriz wrote that she and Zita had traveled on the charming
British-owned Argentine Central Railway to Rosario, a beautiful city, with parks and wide avenues, familiar to her from those
long-ago days with her governess. *Rosario is more than ever a clean,*
orderly city. You could eat off the pavement, as Zita says. Neither of us
is discounting a permanent move to Buenos Aires.

She folded her mother's letter into its envelope and glanced
around the café. This was the best part: watching people. A woman
in a rose-colored slip of a dress, with her hair in kiss-curls across
her forehead, gazed into the distance with a melancholy look,
and then a man in plus fours joined her, and she began scold-
ing him for keeping her waiting, and he responded by laughing
uproariously, so that people turned to look. An elderly couple,
both thin to the point of emaciation, as if they lived on nothing
but air, cut iced cakes into small pieces and fed each other tastes
on their forks. At another table two priests were drinking coffee
and arguing, possibly over some doctrinal point.

Someone said her name. She looked up, and there was Herr
Becker. She recognized him at once. He beamed at her. "Is this
you?" he said. "Is this Fräulein Faber? But yes, it is you. I knew
it, you look so like your mother."

"Herr Becker," Natalia said. "How good to see you." He was
about to grab lunch, a solitary lunch, and then get back to his
office, he said. What could Natalia do but invite him to sit at
her table? She moved aside her papers. He thanked her and sat
down. He was now a junior member of a law firm with offices in
Potsdam. He often thought of her and Frau Faber, he said, when

she told him her mother was in Buenos Aires. He had wanted to get in touch with them, but always his natural reserve and respect for their privacy had held him back.

Was he still reading Spengler? Natalia asked. It was Chekhov now. Chekhov was his inspiration and moral guide in art and in life. The practice of law involved defending sometimes quite odious individuals, and he devoted whatever free time he had to literature, music, family, and friends; but his friends were few, and he had no family in Berlin. He talked while eating pickled herring on rye bread and gulping hot coffee, and when he was finished he wiped his mouth on a napkin and said again what a pleasure to see her looking so well. Would she give him permission to telephone her at home? Yes, that would be nice, she said.

In January the River Spree froze, and Natalia went ice-skating with Herr Becker, who insisted on holding her hand so they wouldn't get separated in the crowd. He skated with a fine, practiced efficiency, one hand in his coat pocket. The cold wind brought a high color to his cheeks. One day, after skating, Natalia invited him home for hot chocolate and a slice of Hildegard's warm spice cake with whipped cream. Hildegard approved of Herr Becker and praised his good manners. Natalia had to agree; it was difficult to find fault with Herr Becker.

When the weather warmed, and the ice thinned, she and Herr Becker skated indoors at the Sportpalast. They visited the library, walked in parks, decided it would be appropriate to address one another with the familiar *du* and to use first names, a significant change in their friendship that merited a celebratory lunch at a café. Natalia introduced Martin to Margot Brückner and her brother, Hermann. All four of them went to see an avant-garde film called *Ghosts before Breakfast*. It was only ten minutes long but seemed longer, each scene bizarre, disorienting. Hats floated in space, clocks dissolved, a man's head came off his shoulders and drifted around the screen. Natalia was enchanted and horrified, equally. "*Mein Gott*," Martin said, laughing. Hermann said it was an insult to the intelligence. It was French, he added: What did one expect?

➤∙∙◆

One afternoon in June, Miklós came to see her. He brought a basket of strawberries picked that morning by Katya, fragrant, warm from the journey, and nestled in a bed of straw. That morning Natalia had been sailing on the Wannsee with Margot and Hermann, and the bright sun or the wind, or both, had left her feeling languid, and she was unfazed about what he'd think of her sunburned nose or what she would say to him. He came in, and they sat talking in the living room. She asked how Rozalia was, and he said she'd been ill with a persistent summer cold but seemed to be on the mend. They went outside, so that she could show him the garden, and she invited him to stay to dinner. They had a simple meal of bread and cheese and cold cuts, and Hildegard served the strawberries with whipped cream in chilled cut-glass dishes. Miklós mentioned having received a postcard from Zita. Natalia said Zita was editing the German translation of a book by an Argentine writer.

"She is continuing to work, then, while she's away?" Miklós said.

"Yes, she is. I think that was her intention from the beginning. And there's good news. At last my mother has hired a new caretaker for the villa, but he can't take up his duties until the end of August, which means another delay in their return home."

"You must miss your mother."

"Yes," Natalia said. "Yes and no."

He smiled. As he was leaving, he glanced at the photograph in the front hall. "So this is the famous residence in Buenos Aires. This is where your mother and Zita are staying?"

"Yes," she said. "In Palermo. Near a golf club and a riding stables and a cemetery."

Two weeks later Miklós rang to say he was taking a day off and would she like to go with him to the Zoologischer Garten.

The zoo? A surprising invitation. She said she'd meet him at the Elephant Gate on Budapester Strasse. She was early and saw him before he saw her. He had his back to her. She should have gone over to him, but instead she stood watching him, thinking how handsome he looked. He was wearing a jersey, tan flannel slacks, and golf shoes, although he didn't play golf, as far as she knew. He turned and saw her and they walked together to the zoo entrance. She bought a bag of peanuts to feed the monkeys at the Affenpalmenhaus, where they made friends with a forlorn outcast cowering in a corner. Miklós knelt and put his fingers through the wire and said, "We understand each other, don't we, little fellow?" He disliked seeing animals in captivity, he said, but always ended up being entertained in spite of himself.

As they walked around the zoo, he told her that last year he'd been in Moscow, at the invitation of the commissar of education, for the centenary, on September 9, of Leo Tolstoy's birth. The Soviet government had earlier distributed leaflets explaining, or apologizing for, Tolstoy's religious philosophy, in many ways starkly inimical to Communist dogma. The opening ceremony, he told her, had been simultaneously overdone and restrained to the point of being incomprehensible. And it had lasted hours, until dawn the next day, when, without sleep, he and other visiting press people had boarded a train south to Tolstoy's estate,

Yasnaya Polyana, where Miklós ran into his friend, the Austrian author Stefan Zweig, and they had proceeded to depress each other by talking about the political situation in Germany. Zweig believed the National Socialist Workers' Party, with one percent of the vote in the May election, had been nullified as an electoral force. The fundamental decency of Germans would never allow Hitler to take power, he'd said. Miklós wanted to believe him. Earlier that month, however, he had seen Hitler's Storm Troopers marching in columns through Munich. Sixty-thousand strong. They inspired more terror in him than had Mussolini's Blackshirts.

Then, to Natalia, he said, "The penguins. We can't leave this zoo without seeing the penguins."

She did an imitation penguin walk, her arms held out stiffly, taking little shuffling steps. He laughed. The real penguins, dispirited in the heat, staggered wearily one after another around their pool. Poor things, she said. Miklós suggested lunch at the Wilhelmshallen, but the zoo's restaurant was full, and instead they went to a café on Kurfürstendamm. They parted at the train station, where Miklós said what people tend to say, out of politeness, thanking her for a lovely day. As she was boarding the train, he called out to her that he was going to see his mother; would she like to go with him. When? Soon, he said, gesturing that he'd phone.

At last, late in August, Beatriz and Zita returned from Buenos Aires. Their suitcases and trunks filled the house, and Beatriz dug around in them, spilling clothes across the floor, searching for Natalia's presents: an evening gown of green chiffon and lace, with an underdress of embossed gold silk. Zita had a gift for her, too: a tiny medallion in the shape of Argentina, on a fine gold chain, to wear around her neck. There were photographs taken by the ship's photographer: Beatriz and Zita dining at the captain's table; Zita on a deck chair, wrapped in blankets, recovering from a bout of seasickness. "I was never *not* seasick," Zita said, and Beatriz said, "But at least you didn't drown."

Beatriz showed Natalia photographs she'd taken of the interior of the villa in Palermo. "This was my bedroom when I was a child. Do you see my dolls, on the bed? I hated them; I had no use for dolls. And this is my parents' room, and here is the kitchen, where Zita and I did our own cooking. This bedroom is on the second floor. It will be yours, Natalia, when you come with me to Buenos Aires. Here, look at this photograph of the library, where my governess set up her laboratory and cut the hearts out of frogs and lizards. As soon as we walked into the house, I could sense the Fräulein's presence in every room. It was palpable and not very nice, to be honest. I became quite ill for a time, and I think she was responsible."

"You were ill?" Natalia said. "How do you mean, ill? You said nothing in your letters."

"I didn't want to worry you. The doctors said yellow fever or septicemia or consumption, then they gave up and just fed me quinine water. And laudanum, but it caused strange dreams. Strange obsessions. I was convinced a frog, a small, bright-green frog, which I believed was poisonous to the touch, had concealed itself under the bed, and I screamed at Zita to kill it. I resigned myself to dying in the house where I was born, and then Zita went to a herbalist in Palermo and bought dried herbs she made into a tisane. She added a little gin, and it was a miracle cure." She laughed. "Also, I remembered a quotation from Émile Coué:

When the will and the imagination are antagonistic, it is always the imagination that wins, without any exception. I thought, well, that's one thing—no one can accuse me of not having an imagination."

Anyway, she recovered, and now she felt wonderful. While in Buenos Aires she had kept an eye on the American stock market. She didn't like what it was doing. And the political climate in Germany was getting on her nerves. This Hitler, she said. Why can't he just do us all a favor and go back to Austria? Zita had told her that Hildegard had been to hear Hitler speak last November at the Sportpalast. She had talked to Hildegard about this. She was only curious, Hildegard had assured Beatriz, but she seemed to think Hitler had some good ideas, and she said he hypnotized everyone in the audience with his mustache and the way he flung his arms around.

Within a few weeks of being at home, Beatriz began talking of a trip to Paris with Natalia. Summer wasn't the best season in Paris, she knew; it would be hot, and everyone would be at the seaside, but they could do some shopping, see the sights.

Another time, Natalia said, she would like to go to Paris with her mother, but she had promised the countess she would visit her. It was already arranged that she would travel to Hungary with Miklós, in his car, and at this late date she didn't see how she could possibly change her plans.

In Prague, Miklós and Natalia stayed overnight at a hotel on Nerudova Street. The next morning they met downstairs in the hotel restaurant. Miklós wore a jacket with a belted waist, a blue shirt, a silk scarf knotted at his throat. And she had applied lipstick and powdered her nose, which was sunburned from riding in the open car. She knew, from the way the staff at the hotel welcomed Miklós, that he'd stayed there in the past. He had been with Zita, she supposed, but she was the one here now. She drank coffee from a translucent china cup and spread sweet, golden butter on a warm, floury scone. They walked up Nerudova Street toward the castle and then turned around and walked across the Charles Bridge. In the Old Town, Miklós photographed her in front of the cubist House of the Black Madonna, in Celetná Street. He kept looking at his watch and saying they should be on their way, and then he remembered another little street he wanted to walk up, another building he had to see, and then there was a bookshop he had to visit. At the Café Montmartre they drank cold lemonade and then walked on the Charles Bridge, where a little boy nearly ran into Natalia. She put a hand on his shoulder to steady him. He looked up at her, startled. Blue eyes beneath a fringe of blond hair. For a moment, she thought he was Franz, Dr. Schaefferová's son. He wasn't; his mother took his hand and said, "Jan, you must not run away from me like that."

CHAPTER TEN

Magdolna put down a long-handled spoon she was using to stir a galvanized pot of black dye in which floated one of the countess's gowns. Katya ran to summon the countess, who then appeared, leaning on Katya's arm. She looked at Natalia and said, "My God, you are here at last. Sit down, why don't you, and we can have a good talk." Magdolna left the dress to soak, and they sat at the kitchen table, the three of them, and Katya poured coffee into translucent white cups, and after a while Rozalia said it was a shame to be indoors, and she and Natalia moved to the garden. Rozalia walked without a cane or any assistance and sat very upright in the garden chair, bringing Natalia up to date on the life of the estate. She talked about the excellent crops of wheat and corn, the warm weather—God willing it would stay fine and not turn wet before the harvest was finished. She had hired Guido to make repairs to the school. A new stove had been put in, and the windows sealed to keep out drafts, a shelf's length of new books ordered from a bookshop in Budapest. Miklós had helped her select the books. He had hung the picture of the blessed King Karl of Hungary back up on the wall after he'd finished painting. Rozalia said she would take Natalia to see it after she had unpacked and settled in.

A few days later, Miklós drove to Budapest for a meeting with a German-language newspaper publisher. At about eight in the evening Natalia was reading in the library when she heard the Bugatti on the gravel drive. Time went by, then Miklós appeared at the door. "Come with me," he said. "There's someone in the kitchen I want you to meet."

This someone was a puppy, a puli, three months old, with a coat of corkscrew curls, white in color, coal-black eyes, a fat black nose. She knelt, and the puppy licked her face. "He knows you already," Miklós said. "He obeys you."

"He obeys no one," she said, wiping her mouth on the back of her hand. The puppy wiggled around ecstatically on the floor.

"Think of a name for him," Miklós said. "He's your dog."

"Mine?" she said. "How can he be mine? I will be leaving soon, and I can't take him with me, can I? Benno would never forgive me." But she gave him a name: Bashan, in honor of the dog in the story "A Man and His Dog," by Thomas Mann. "Hmm. A literary name, for such a small dog," Miklós said.

Bashan followed her everywhere and slept at the foot of her bed. Rozalia said she would catch a disease from him. He has no germs, Natalia insisted, although he had his fair share of fleas, which she had to comb out of his ringlets and drown one at a time in a bowl of soapy water. She hand-fed him bits of cooked meat from the dinner platter.

"For God's sake, he's only a dog," the countess said, but she too succumbed and praised Bashan immoderately and gave him bowls of warm milk.

On his walks, Bashan frolicked, barking his excited, high-pitched bark. Natalia took off his leash, and he immediately jumped into the river and refused to come out when she called.

"Does he know how to swim?" she said to Miklós.

"He's a dog," Miklós said.

She stepped on stones in the river, trying to reach Bashan, and slipped, soaking her shoes. Miklós put his hands on her waist and lifted her out of the water and set her down on the ground. There she was, in his arms, and he kissed her, they kissed. She picked up a stick and threw it into the trees. Bashan bounded to her side, shaking himself, showering her and Miklós with water.

The next day, she and Miklós went to Budapest, leaving Bashan in the care of Magdolna and Katya. They lunched at the Café Gerbeaud with friends of Miklós, newspaper people, writers, who wanted to know about her, how long she was staying in Hungary, what she did, and she felt intimidated by these brilliant people and answered their questions in a subdued voice. Miklós said she helped his mother with running the estate, did the accounting, taught at the school, where she was adored by the children.

On the drive home, they passed through a brief, although spectacular, thunderstorm—the opposite climatic conditions from that hot, starry night when the Bugatti had broken down, but still that night was in her mind when Miklós stopped to put up the top. And then, outside the castle, the sky clearing, the stars reappearing as the clouds dispersed, they sat in the Bugatti and talked and went from talking to kissing, and she thought: What is this mad behavior on your part, Natalia Faber? What are you setting yourself up for? They got out of the car, she linked her fingers with his, and he put his arms around her. It was opium, strong drink, this infatuation.

→··←

The agricultural accountant was due, and Natalia was going over the accounts for Rozalia. She sat on a stool at the long pine table in the room where Rozalia had read the tarot. As far as Natalia knew, the cards were still in the sandalwood box in the escritoire. "Ah, here you are," Miklós said. He bent and kissed her on the forehead. He had been looking for her. He had a question, a rather important question. "I'm interrupting you, aren't I," he said, gesturing at the ledger, the pen in her hand. "*Ich liebe dich, Natalia. Ich liebe dich.* Marry me."

She looked down at the ledger and at the ink on her fingers. Why had she thought life was possible for her? Why had she let things get to this point? If she did not speak, this silence would go on, and it would cause irreparable hurt, she knew that. She raised her eyes and began to say what she had to say, because she could not go on keeping secret from Miklós the truth about herself. But at that moment she heard the familiar, irregular tapping of Rozalia's walking stick at the door. She came into the room and said, "What's wrong with you two?" Natalia stared at her. Miklós turned on his heel and walked away. "What has he done?" Rozalia demanded. "What has he said to upset you?"

"He did nothing," Natalia said.

"A strange nothing, to make you look like that."

In the kitchen, Rozalia made tea and buttered a slice of bread; her sovereign remedy: drink and food. "I will have a word with my son," she stated.

"No, don't," Natalia said. "Everything is fine." Bashan kept touching her leg with his cold nose. She ran her fingers through his curls and stood up from the table and kissed him and fed him her buttered bread.

→··←

She and Miklós went horseback riding. On a forest path they dismounted and sat, one on either end, on a fallen log in a small clearing in the trees. The light, filtered through clouds of pollen and infinitesimal winged insects, was heavy, languid. At her request they had come here, to talk, where no one would overhear, and now he was waiting for her to say something, but the habit of years was to refrain from letting anything of the truth pass her lips. She drew in her breath. She felt light-headed, scared. "You will not like what I have to say," she began. Then, quickly, she told him that her parents had not been married. "Do you see now? My birth was never legitimate. It was kept secret from me until two years ago. The only person I've ever told was my friend Margot, and that was in a letter. I never said the words aloud. If you are angry, I understand. I know you can't marry me."

"If you think that, then you don't know me very well. It was your father's tragedy," he said, "not to know you."

Later, when they had taken the horses to the stables, he told her it was customary in Hungary for a formal marriage proposal to be made no fewer than five times. He had used up one, although it wasn't as formal as it should have been. Four proposals remained. He would keep asking until he got the answer he wanted.

After their marriage, Miklós and Natalia spent a week in Trieste. It was foggy, and it rained, and the streets shone with a gray light. Miklós was writing an article on James Joyce's years in Trieste. In the morning they went out, and he conjured James Joyce from the stones, looking just as he did in his photographs, tall and spare and literary, nearsighted and bespectacled. Miklós photographed the exterior of apartment buildings where Joyce had lived and street corners where, perhaps—who could say?—he might have stood. Miklós photographed the hospital where Nora Barnacle had given birth to a son in a charity ward. Miklós had Natalia stand in front of the hospital, in her black skirt and black stockings, pretending to be Nora Barnacle and smiling, which Natalia said Nora wouldn't do, not if she'd just given birth in a charity ward. But Miklós said the average newspaper reader liked to be reassured that life had its moments.

He read *Ulysses* to her from the first volume of the three-volume German translation he'd purchased at the bookshop in Pest. She loved listening, especially to the descriptions of food, everything fried in butter, seasoned with pepper. Greasy fingers, belches. Life was sensual. It was meant to be sensual and rich and verging on excess at all times. Miklós told her that James Joyce had said of Trieste, "It is the city that sheltered us." Trieste, little more than a day's drive from Hungary, had always seemed apart from the rest of the world's turmoil, he said. But that was Habsburg Trieste, whereas now Trieste was ruled by the Italian Fascists.

In 1930, Miklós rented an apartment in Berlin Mitte, the city's central district, convenient to everything. A pattern was established, in which six months of the year were spent in Hungary and six months in Berlin. The contrast between one life and the other was marked, and yet Natalia could not say which she liked better. The first winter in Berlin, she contacted Martin Becker. Days before her marriage, she had written to him and had received in reply a letter in which his congratulations were muted, but he had been explicit in describing his hurt that she had, as he put it, "unilaterally ended their relationship." When they met at the Café Kranzler one morning, he told her she had broken his heart. But he smiled as he spoke and eagerly imparted the news that he was soon to marry a young woman called Sophia, who lived in his hometown of Blankenburg.

In January 1933, von Hindenburg appointed Hitler chancellor of Germany. The Press Law of October 1933 stated that journalists had to be Aryan and could not be married to a non-Aryan and were required to belong to the Reich Press Association. Although these anti-Semitic laws did not directly affect Miklós, he was angered by them, as well as depressed, and resigned from Ullstein Verlag, which had been taken over by Eher Verlag, the Nazi-controlled publishing house. He did some work for newspapers in Budapest. He wrote a novel that was based on his brother's life and dealt with the war. Natalia thought it his best work.

In 1934, Zita was arrested and held at the Reich Main Security Office at 8 Prinz-Albrecht-Strasse, near Potsdamer Platz. She was released, but had been beaten, her arm broken. Beatriz would have taken Zita to safety in Buenos Aires, but if she lived that far away, she'd never see her grandson. Krisztián was two years old in 1934. Zita adored him. Four years later, in 1938, she and Zita did leave Germany and a year later Germany invaded Poland. Great Britain and then France declared war on Germany. At the castle, Rozalia turned the radio off when a newscast began and burned the newspapers in the library fireplace, sometimes before Natalia had a chance to read them.

PART
TWO

———

O century! O sciences! It is a delight to be alive,
even if not yet in tranquility.
Barbarity, take a rope and prepare yourself for banishment.
—ULRICH VON HUTTEN, 1518

CHAPTER ELEVEN

Anna was gathering chestnuts from the grass beneath the tree in the garden of her family's house in Malá Strana, the Lesser Quarter, in Prague. It was November; a light frost silvered the grass, and fog drifted up from the river, muting the sound of people walking past on the other side of the garden wall. Her father, Julius, had told her once that trees transmogrified, over time, into animals, rooted and sightless, yet sentient, in their way. If he believed this, then she did too. She sensed the chestnut tree gazing at her with its inner eyes. The chestnuts, with their burred outer skins, nipped at her fingers, like small forest animals. She filled the basket and took it upstairs to the kitchen. Sora, who before she came to them had worked in Italy and knew exactly what to do with sweet chestnuts, spread them out on newspaper and left them for a week to ripen, so that the starch in the fruit could develop into sugar. Then they painstakingly peeled away the outer casings, and the chestnuts were roasted in the oven and then ground into a coarse flour, which Sora used to bake a dense, moist Italian cake called *castagnaccio*.

The arrival of this cake at the table was an event in Anna's family. It marked the drawing in of the days, the approach of winter.

The last winter; the last taste of *castagnaccio*. That evening her father, who was an artist, pushed back his chair, picked up his sketch pad, and drew the scene, including the partly demolished Italian cake on a Bohemian-crystal plate. He drew Anna's mother, Magdalena, as she turned to say something to Franz, who had a fork in his hand. Anna's cousin Reina was about to pour coffee—or ersatz coffee, wartime coffee, occupation coffee, whatever it was—from a carafe into Franz's cup. Anna had rested her head on her mother's shoulder and was listening to her mother and Franz. Her father drew himself, sketch pad balanced on his knee. Candles burning, small pools of light, cake crumbs on the tablecloth.

Her father's paintings were in private collections in Prague, Vienna, London, Paris, and New York, and in art galleries in those cities and others. His portrait of President Tomáš Masaryk, while not as well known as the portrait by Oskar Kokoschka, had been a favorite of the president, who had hung it on his office wall.

Her mother was a specialist in diseases of the blood. Many of her patients were referred to her by doctors in other towns, in the countryside. Anna imagined these patients rising before daylight, traveling by train sometimes hundreds of kilometers. Often, they hung around on the pavement outside the house, delaying the moment when they would have to admit to the doctor that they were unwell, probably with nothing, a passing fatigue, trouble sleeping, no appetite. Anna had seen them lighting cigarettes, checking their watches. They came inside, meticulously wiped their feet on the doormat, hung coats and hats on the coatrack, glanced at the pendulum clock in the corner. They gazed for a moment at a painting on the wall by Anna's father, of three men fishing for carp on the banks of the Vltava. It was in a highly realistic style her father had since repudiated, but Anna liked it, and she'd heard her mother's patients remark that they could almost smell the river and feel the mist on their faces. Anna fancied herself invisible, watching the patients from the fourth step up on the staircase, where she believed she was hidden from sight. If her brother, Franz, saw her there, he asked what she was doing, sitting in a cold draft. She wanted to explain how happy she felt, part of the house's activities and close to her mother, yet separate, almost incorporeal. She wasn't always alone, either. Sometimes her friend Rosa sat with her, and they watched everything together.

→…←

Anna's father's father owned gypsum mines near the Neckar River. His parents had expected Julius to study chemistry and work in the family business, as his older brother, Anna's uncle Rupert, had done, but instead he came to Prague to study art with Alphonse Mucha and to see Prague's distinctive art nouveau and cubist architecture. In all of Europe, there were no other examples of cubist architecture. How, he had wondered, could he live anywhere else? Alphonse Mucha wasn't in Prague when he arrived; he was in the United States, and so Anna's father had studied at an art academy. He lodged at the home of Vivian and Tomáš Svetla and one day met their niece, Magdalena, a medical student at Charles University. Anna's father told her that as soon as he saw Magdalena, he fell in love with her. In 1921 they were married in the church of Saint Nicholas in Republic Square, and then they lived with Magdalena's father, in the house where Franz was born in 1923 and Anna in 1929. Anna's mother opened her surgery, and her father affixed a polished brass plaque, inscribed MAGDALENA SCHAEFFEROVÁ, DOCTOR OF MEDICINE, on the wall beside the entrance to the house. Anna had lived in this house since her birth, and she had decided, when she was quite young, that it was where she wanted to spend her life, every year watching as the chestnut tree flowered, produced succulent sweet chestnuts, and in autumn shed its beautiful leaves on the grass.

➤··◄

Anna was doing homework at the table in the dining room. Her cousin Reina, who was staying with them, had promised to help her, but she kept getting up and wandering around, opening drawers in the credenza, taking out a spoon, examining it for tarnish—not that she would bother to clean it—and putting it back. At the same time, she was telling Anna about a quarrel she'd had with the owner of the bookshop where she worked. Someone's order had been misplaced. She knew it wasn't her fault. The bookshop was busy; mistakes got made. Everyone was reading forbidden Czech literature, every book they could get their hands on, in defiance of the Nazis. The printing presses were running day and night to keep up with the demand. Anna had seen it herself: people read as they walked; they read in cafés, on trams, in queues at the shops. Here I am, they were saying, defiantly. Here I am, reading a book by a Czech author working in the Czech language. What are you going to do about it? Reina sat down and bit her fingernails and then got up again and went out of the room and came back with one of Franz's philosophy textbooks.

She flipped through the pages and said Franz was brilliant at philosophy, but it was her least favorite subject. "Nietzsche called other philosophers cabbage heads. He said the cabbage heads settled for a frog's-eye view of life. Cabbages don't have eyes, but it's a nice simile, isn't it? Or is it a metaphor? Or just an insult? A frog's-eye view is a term in art. Your father would know it. It means from a limited perspective, from near the ground, as if you were a frog sitting on a lily pad. I have no intention of settling for a frog's-eye view. As soon as this stupid war ends, I am going to America. Aunt Vivian says she'll give me the addresses of her relatives in Chicago, who'll be happy to put me up while I look for work. A lot of Czechs have emigrated to America. Half of Europe is there; the smart half, if you ask me."

She picked at the sleeve of her sweater, which was black and lacy, intricate as a spider's web, and then said she was going to take a bath, shampoo her hair, and do some sewing. "Listen," she said. "I think Franz is home." She went out, closing the door behind her.

Anna finished solving an algebraic equation and opened another book and began to take notes: *The boiling point of water is one hundred degrees Celsius, and the melting point of ice is zero degrees Celsius. As water heats, it expands. Solids and liquids expand when heated and contract as they cool. Even a mountain responds to heat and cold in this way, the rocks contracting and expanding along fault lines. A calorie measures the energy required to raise the temperature of a gram of liquid by one degree Celsius.* One fact led to another; one discovery opened the way to another. Anna's ambition was to become a scientist like her mother and her uncle Rupert in Heidelberg, who formulated new medicines from dyes at one company while also carrying out tests for the family's gypsum-mining business. There was another scientist in her family: her mother's stepmother, Eva Svetlová, had been a botanist, and Eva's brother, Maximilian Nagy, for whom Anna's uncle Max was named, had been an agronomist.

Once Anna had pricked her finger with a lancet, and her mother had squeezed a drop of blood onto a microscope slide so that Anna could see her blood magnified a hundred times. *Microscopy* was her favorite word, and she loved the microscope, with its polished lenses and fine calibrations. In a drop of rainwater legions of bugs thrived. Bits of earthworm appeared cratered and dimpled, like the face of the moon. Some microbes were benign, others capable of causing illness; and there existed microbes too small to be detected even under a microscope.

She could hear Reina and Franz in the hall. Something in their voices made her get up and open the door. They were standing on either side of Ivan Lazar. Anna almost didn't know him at first. He was bleeding from a deep gash beneath his left eye. Blood was running down his face and dripping on the floor. If Ivan didn't sit down, he would collapse, and since Franz and Reina seemed unable to move, she told them to take Ivan to the kitchen. She folded a clean kitchen towel to make a compress and asked Reina to press it to Ivan's face.

"You need stitches," Anna said.

"No, it will be all right," Ivan said.

"Without stitches it won't heal," Anna said. She was going to phone her mother, who had gone to the hospital to check on a patient, but as she went downstairs, her mother came in the front door. She ran upstairs with Anna and knelt beside Ivan and touched the area around his injury. He should be seen by a facial surgeon, she said. She would like an X-ray, to rule out a fracture to the cheekbone or orbital bone, and an ophthalmologist should examine him, to be on the safe side. Franz could drive him to the hospital in her car, she said; she would phone ahead and alert the staff.

No, out of the question, Franz said. They would be questioned; arrested. Anna's mother considered this. Gently, she again palpated Ivan's face around the wound and asked how it had happened. Franz said he would tell her later.

"Do what you can, please, Dr. Schaefferová," Ivan said. Marta Hempel, his fiancée, was on duty that afternoon at the hospital. He didn't want her to see him like this.

"Marta would want to know," Magdalena said, but then she relented. "All right. I will do my best for you, Ivan." But the light in the kitchen was insufficient, she said; she needed a lamp, a sterile surface, instruments, anesthetic. They went down to the ground floor, where she had her surgery. She set out instruments on a stainless-steel tray and swabbed Ivan's face with gauze soaked in an antiseptic. She prepared a syringe and injected anesthetic into Ivan's face, near the wound. Elli wasn't in the surgery that day, and Anna acted as her mother's assistant, holding a stainless-steel bowl to catch the blood and water as her mother irrigated the wound with a saline solution. Her mother talked as she worked. "The finest surgical thread in the world used to come from silkworms in the Cevannes, in France, but it became too costly, and now we use silk thread from China," she told Ivan. "The benefit of silk is that it leaves less of a scar than catgut." She pulled the needle through the skin with toothed forceps. "This is not so different from doing embroidery," she said.

Ivan said he would look a picture, then.

"For the next few hours, try not to move the muscles in your face," Anna's mother said. "When the anesthetic wears off, you'll feel pain. I can give you something for it. We'll leave the wound uncovered for now, and in the morning, I'll examine it and put on a dressing." Magdalena gave Ivan an anti-tetanus injection, and then Ivan got off the table. Anna and Reina made him a light lunch of buttered bread and a soft-boiled egg and carried a tray to the guest room, where Franz had taken Ivan to rest.

That evening, Franz described the assault to his parents. They were in the living room, Anna's mother and father, Franz, Anna, Reina, and Ivan Lazar. Franz said Ivan had been getting off the tram after finishing a shift at the armament factory where he worked. This wasn't by choice, Anna knew, but because everyone from the age of fifteen to sixty was compelled to contribute his or her labor to the German war effort. Franz went on to say he'd seen Ivan and had started to walk toward him, when a Gestapo officer pushed a woman hard enough to knock her down. She had got in his way or something. Franz had thought she was dead, but she began to move, and he got there in time to help her to her feet. Ivan was picking up the woman's groceries and putting them in her shopping bag. He said to the Gestapo guy, Why did you have to push her, why did you have to do that? In reply, the Gestapo officer took his rifle off his shoulder and smashed it against Ivan's face.

"So now," Franz said, "blood is pouring down Ivan's face, and the Gestapo officer is shouting at him to produce his identity card, and the woman is crying. And along comes another Gestapo, who wants to know what's going on. The first one gave Ivan's card back, and at the same time a car pulled up and they got in and drove away. I brought Ivan here, and Mother patched him up."

"The Gestapo took down Ivan's name and address?" Anna's father said.

They looked at Ivan's identity card, yes, Franz said. But they hadn't asked Franz for his identity card. They didn't know who he was or where he lived.

Ivan said he'd caused enough trouble; he would go home.

"Ivan, you should stay with us tonight," Anna's mother said. "In the morning I would like to examine your wound."

Ivan had started to get up. He sank back into the chair. He

was pale, and a violently purple bruise had spread across his cheek and nose. His eye was swollen shut. Ivan was a teacher at the Royal Gymnasium. He wrote poetry that was published in important literary journals. And there he sat, with that terrible wound to his face. Anna looked away. The evening sun, level in the sky, illuminated the room, with its comfortable blue velvet sofas and chairs and Bechstein piano and the credenza that had belonged to Anna's grandmother, Katharina Svetlová. But outside the house, out there in the streets of Prague, someone like Ivan could be grievously injured for no reason, for doing something any decent human would do. Understanding how this could be was beyond her.

The next day, Franz went to the school where Ivan taught and told the headmaster Ivan had been called home to Český Krumlov to be with his father, who was ill. Franz had no qualms about lying to protect his friend. He repeated the same story to Ivan's landlady when he stopped to feed Ivan's cat and water the plants. As far as he could make out, no one had been to the house in the past twenty-four hours asking questions. They were safe, he thought. But Ivan learned later that the Gestapo had questioned the headmaster at his school and had sent two men to interrogate Ivan's father, who unwittingly corroborated Franz's story. The elder Mr. Lazar had, in fact, been ill and was just beginning to recover when the Gestapo came to his door. Mr. Lazar, an engineer at the hydroelectric dam on the Elbe River near Český Krumlov, told Ivan he wasn't going to take any shit from the Gestapo. He had looked them in the eye and had said, yes, his son had been there to help him out when he was at death's door with 'flu. By now, his son would be back in Prague. Then he had a fit of coughing and didn't cover his mouth, and they had backed away, big men, big heroes, afraid of a few germs.

The Gestapo seemed to give up at that point, Franz said. But it illustrated the lengths they'd go to, to punish even a minor offense.

→·←

The occupation of Czechoslovakia by the German Reich had begun March 15, 1939, when the German army marched into Prague, and Hitler appeared at a window in Prague Castle. It was snowing that day, and it was Anna's tenth birthday. She hated that her birthday, for the rest of her life, would be linked to the day when Czechoslovakia ceased to be a sovereign nation and became the Protectorate of Bohemia and Moravia. She tried not to know what was happening, and for a time everything was unchanged, at least in her family. She knew, vaguely, that Hitler had appointed a German from Württemberg, Baron von Neurath, as Reich protector. Neurath immediately censored the free press and imposed the Nuremberg Laws, and that Anna could not pretend she didn't know. In June, two Schutzstaffel officers came into her classroom at school and removed her teacher, Miss Kleinová, who was Jewish. Anna's beloved Miss Kleinová's replacement was Fräulein Sauer, from Germany, who began by telling the class they were imbeciles. She punished Anna for speaking Czech instead of German and struck her across the shoulders with a stick. It hurt and left a bruise; she did not dare tell her mother.

Then all Jewish children, including Anna's friends Rosa Erhmann and Jacob Stein, were forbidden to attend school. The Reich Protectorate Office ordered Jews to leave the protectorate. Thirty thousand had to get out by the end of 1939, another seventy thousand in 1940. Rosa told Anna her parents did not know where they could go. France wouldn't accept Jews, and neither would Switzerland or Canada or the United States. South America was a possibility, but Rosa's parents knew no one in Argentina or Brazil or Paraguay. Her parents' bank accounts were frozen, and their house had been given to a Reich German family; there were now two classes of citizens in the protectorate. Reich Germans lived and worked in Czechoslovakia but as Germans received privileges denied to Czechs, who as Slavs were termed *Untermenschen* by the Nazis, which meant subhuman, a word no moral person would use.

Rosa's family moved into her grandmother's small apartment. Rosa's father was ordered to place a sign in the window of his pharmacy that said he could serve only Jewish customers. Jewish families were not allowed to keep pets, Rosa told Anna, and no one would love their cat as much as she did. They had never been religious, but now her family observed Shabbat and went to synagogue. Anna and Rosa had been sitting on the stairs in the entrance hall of Anna's house. Anna went upstairs and got her cat, Milo, and came down and put him on Rosa's lap. When they were younger, she and Rosa, and sometimes Jacob, had played a game in the hall that Anna had invented, in which they could step only on black floor tiles or only on white tiles. A misstep meant you had to walk backward up six stairs with your eyes closed. Another game involved the skeleton in her mother's office. They pretended he was chasing them down the hall, past the storage-room door and the door to Anna's father's workroom at the back of the house. The skeleton's bones clacked, his toes clicked; Anna and Rosa giggled and said if he touched them, they would die.

They should have more sense, Sora told them. In Germany, a long time ago, she said, people in a village saw skeletons tumbling out of a dark, threatening sky. It was a warning of bad things to come. "You need to think what you're playing with," she said. "Some things are better left undisturbed."

It was only a game, Anna had assured Sora. The skeleton would never hurt them. He was a three-dimensional lesson in anatomy, a useful reference, her mother had told her. Henri, which was the name Anna and Rosa had given the skeleton, had no malice in him. But maybe Sora had been right and those games of pretend with Henri had brought bad luck, not just to their house but to Prague.

If she closed her eyes, Anna could picture Rosa. She had small, perfect features, silky dark hair cut in a fringe, blue eyes, smoky black eyelashes. Rosa and her family had left Prague to travel to Palestine in August 1939. Rosa's mother had decided they would get there if they had to walk. In Palestine, they would have a house of their own again, and her father could open another pharmacy. Anna and her parents should come with them, she had said. They weren't Jewish, Anna had pointed out. But Anna's mother was a doctor, Rosa had said, and doctors were needed everywhere.

That same month Jacob and his family had emigrated to New York City, where Jacob's uncle lived. Jacob's father was a surgeon. The Nazis had revoked his hospital privileges and banned him from lecturing at the Charles University. Anna's mother had submitted a formal complaint to the hospital's administration. In response she had received a letter warning her that she was compromising her own professional standing and would be disciplined if she did not desist. She had ripped the letter in half and burned it in the fireplace.

→··←

They should have gone to Palestine, Anna thought later. Weeks before the occupation of Czechoslovakia began, Franz had tried to convince their parents to emigrate to England or Australia, New Zealand, South Africa. Anywhere out of harm's way. Their mother had said she couldn't abandon her patients. Their father had believed that if they remained quiet, reasonably obedient, never calling attention to themselves, they would be all right. And so they stayed. In 1940, Reina and Franz began volunteering to assist Jewish people with obtaining visas and exit permits from a new office overseen by an Austrian Nazi named Adolf Eichmann. Anna suspected Franz and Reina were helping in more illicit ways as well. They belonged to a Czech hikers' club that, as was generally known, functioned as a cover for partisans and secretly published anti-Nazi pamphlets and met at secret locations after dark to set up portable radio transmitters that beamed the BBC's Overseas Service to radios in Prague. Listening to these broadcasts was forbidden, punishable by execution, but how could the Nazis know what was going on in your living room, if you kept the shutters closed and the curtains drawn? Even Anna's parents listened, the radio turned down so low that exiled president Edvard Beneš spoke to them from London in the sibilant whispers of someone underwater.

Rosa left Prague in the same month that Anna's cousin Reina came to live in Prague to attend university. Reina had grown up on her parents' farm in Zürau. Her mother was Anna's aunt Gisele. Her half aunt, really, since her mother and Aunt Gisele were half sisters. Anna had adored her cousin, and when she visited the farm, she had followed Reina around, watching as she cleaned out barns and chicken coops, scythed grass, and helped her mother in the house and with the younger children. But the Reina who arrived in Prague had changed. She dressed in silk blouses and tailored skirts she had made herself from patterns Aunt Vivian Svetlová had mailed to her. Her curly auburn hair was in a smooth twist at the back of her head. Occasionally she smoked a cigarette. She got a part-time job at the bookshop where Franz worked. They went to coffeehouses together, met with fellow students and professors, discussed literature, philosophy, poetry—but politics, never. Not, Franz said, with SS officers at the next table listening. At least, one of them listened, a tall man no older than Franz, perhaps also a university student. He seemed conversant with Kant; perhaps he'd studied Kant before ditching any conception of a moral imperative. Perhaps he knew more on any given subject than Franz and his friends, but he was what he was, that SS officer; he had made his choice. For the first time, Franz said, he realized he could kill another man in defense of his family and his homeland. No, he could not, Anna's mother had said. And he must never repeat what he'd said to anyone, ever. A thoughtless word, a wrong look, would be interpreted by the Nazis as sedition, a crime punishable by death. Franz had said it himself, she pointed out: they lived in a police state. At the hospital she'd seen boys younger than Franz who had been beaten and tortured by the Gestapo. She saw their parents waiting in hospital corridors to learn whether their sons had any chance of recovering from their injuries, if they would ever be the same again.

At first, when Reina came to live with them, she and Anna shared Anna's bedroom, which was large enough for two beds, two wardrobes, a dressing table, and a desk for Reina. A muslin curtain on a rail separated Anna's side of the room from Reina's side. Immaculate in her appearance, Reina scattered clothes, shoes, books, and half-finished term papers everywhere on the floor. She read late at night, her lamp shining directly—deliberately?—in Anna's eyes. She walked in her sleep but denied having got out of bed during the night. One night, Anna woke and found Reina in the hall, at the top of the stairs, swaying unsteadily. Anna took her hand, and Reina turned and slapped her face. Reina let Anna guide her back to the bedroom and got back into bed, still asleep. Anna lay awake, her face stinging. In the morning, when she looked in the mirror, she saw a faint bruise on her cheek. At breakfast, her mother said, "Anna, let me look at you. Are you sleeping well?"

"Yes. No," Anna said.

"And you, Reina?" her mother asked. "How are you sleeping?"

"Why, what has Anna been telling you?"

"Nothing," Anna said.

"Aunt Magdalena," Reina said, "I am very grateful to be living here, but to be honest, sharing a bedroom with Anna is impossible. If I read at night, I disturb her. She hides my books, my clothes. I can't find anything. She's always watching me. I have no privacy whatsoever."

"That's not true," Anna said. "Anyway, if I didn't watch you, you would fall down the stairs and break your neck."

Later, her mother told Anna that sleepwalking wasn't all that unusual in young women Reina's age. "Could it be she's homesick, I wonder," her mother said. "Perhaps she misses her family more than she lets on. Be especially nice to her, won't you?"

She was nice to Reina, nicer than Reina deserved. In the morning, she brought her coffee in bed. She collected apple cores and used coffee cups from Reina's bedside table, picked her clothes up off the bedroom floor and took them to Sora to be laundered.

"Where's my sweater, the dark blue one with silver buttons?" Reina demanded, slamming a drawer shut.

"It's there, in the drawer. Look again."

"You have no business touching my things, Anna."

"Then pick up after yourself."

"Don't be rude, Mousekin," Reina said.

"My name is Anna."

"I know what your name is, Mousekin."

Anna's parents decided to let Reina move into the bedroom that had belonged to Anna's grandfather. "A year ago, even six months ago," Anna's mother said, "it would have been too soon, but it seems a shame not to use the room."

It should be her or Franz moving into that bedroom, Anna thought. Reina had never known their grandfather as well as they had. She had never fished with him from the riverbank or walked with him across the Charles Bridge to Wenceslas Square to have ice cream at a café. Their grandfather's name was František Jacobus Maria Svetla. He had thick silver hair and a mustache and wore high collars and three-piece suits. As a young lawyer, he had been employed in Vienna at the court of the Emperor Franz Joseph. He had told Anna that Franz Joseph began work every morning at five o'clock, and at the end of the day the emperor dusted off his own desk with a camel-hair brush he kept for that purpose. What a punctilious man he had been, her grandfather had said; what a shining example to his subjects.

When, in the last year of his life, illness had kept her grandfather confined to his bed, Anna would sit with him, and he would tell her about his land in Western Bohemia. His one regret was that he would never again see his fields of sugar beets. His orchards. The timber house he had built with his own hands for Katharina, his first wife, who had died of a hemorrhage of the brain when Anna's mother was six and her brother, Emil, was four. In the spring following their mother's death, Anna's grandfather had taken his children to Karlsbad. Every morning they bathed in the hot springs and in the afternoons strolled around the town, sometimes falling into step behind a young couple that kept stopping to poke around in flowerbeds, apparently hunting for insects, leaves, snails, moss growing on a stone. When he encountered them in the lobby of the hotel where they were all staying, he said good day and commented on the weather. One evening, he invited them (he had learned they were brother and sister) to join him and the children at their table.

Max and Eva Nagy were from Hungary. They lived and worked in Troja, near Prague. Eva had fair hair and blue-gray eyes and was soft-spoken and rather shy, but not as shy as her brother. Max had a square, ruddy face and tended toward stoutness; he was by profession a soil specialist. Eva had a degree in botany. She told Magdalena and Emil that trees, mosses, flowering plants, millipedes, and sparrows coexisted in a mutually beneficial environment, sharing sunlight and moisture and nutrients in the soil. She amused them with stories about timid field mice, pugnacious beetles, and frugal ants. On their walks, she held insects in her hand for Magdalena and Emil to see up close. She taught them more than their father felt entirely comfortable with about the mating habits of the voles that burrowed into gardens.

They hiked up a hill and stood gazing down at Karlsbad's festively colored buildings and at the Teplá River flowing past in the valley. Eva told the children the hot springs had been discovered when the emperor Charles V's hunting dog fell in the scalding water and had to be rescued. This story was almost certainly apocryphal, she added, and then had to explain to the children that the word meant something that might or might not be true. Magdalena asked whether the poor dog had drowned. No, Eva said, the dog was—he was a water spaniel. Eva had a dog called Bruno, a Russian wolfhound. She promised Magdalena she could meet Bruno someday. Magdalena invited Eva and Max to come home with them, and her father said, yes, they must visit his farm very soon. But it was a year later before Eva and Max came to the farm. They stayed for two weeks. The year after that, they stayed for a month and brought with them Bruno, the Russian wolfhound. And the year after that, František Svetla and Eva Nagy married. Max Nagy spent a few weeks every summer at the farm. He collected soil samples and later analyzed them at the Pomological Institute, mailing the results to his brother-in-law. One summer, he gave Magdalena and Emil two handsome Belgian rabbits with dusky-blue fur, liquid-brown eyes, and razor-sharp claws.

A son, Maximilian, was born to František and Eva, and two years later, a daughter, Gisele. But here Anna's grandfather faltered. Anna always wanted to say, "Don't tell me. Tell the story in a new way, with a better ending." But no one could undo the past. Three days after giving birth to her daughter, Eva became ill with a fever and died. She was buried in the churchyard beside Katharina Svetlová. Bruno quit eating, and he too died, and in the night, while the children were sleeping, František dug a grave for him not far from the churchyard fence.

Within the year, František sold his farm and moved to Prague with the four children. He had let Max know and had given him his new address. Max visited them in Prague once and later wrote to say he'd taken a job managing an estate in Pomerania. That was the last Anna's grandfather heard from him.

The house her grandfather bought in Prague, where Anna's

mother and her brother, Emil, and their half siblings, Maximilian and Gisele, had lived, was the house Anna's family lived in.

Did she know about the Belgian rabbits? Anna asked Reina one morning. Did she know about the rabbits her uncle Max brought to their grandfather's farm in Western Bohemia? Reina, filling the kettle at the kitchen sink, turned off the tap and said no, she knew nothing about Belgian rabbits and didn't especially want to. Her parents raised rabbits. They were pests, in her opinion, and had to be treated constantly for fleas and tapeworm. And she wasn't all that fond of rabbit meat, either.

"You have to understand what it was like for me," Reina said. "All my life, I had to share a bedroom with at least one of my sisters, and sometimes all three of us slept in the same room. On a farm you work all day, and yet the chores never get done."

She would never go back to the farm. She wasn't even sure she wanted to get married. Franz had given her Charlotte Garrigue Masaryková's Czech translation of John Stuart Mill's *Subjection of Women* to read. "I agree with him. With John Stuart Mill, I mean. Without female equality, no society can hope to succeed. Franz says that is a self-evident truth. I intend to have a profession, like Aunt Magdalena. Not in medicine, though, because I can't bear to be around sick people." She took the teacups to the sink and rinsed them. "Are we friends, then, Anna?"

"We are cousins," Anna said. "And, yes, friends too."

In January, a farmer—a neighbor of Reina's parents—came to Anna's house with a delivery of two dozen eggs and a large parcel of meat wrapped in butcher's paper and tied with string. He wore a long overcoat, the collar turned up, and a cap low on his forehead, very incognito. Anna had been too surprised to ask his name or even thank him. Franz carried the parcels, which were from Reina's parents, up to the kitchen, and Sora unwrapped them. Anna's father said they must share this unexpected bounty. He telephoned Magdalena's aunt and invited her and her husband to dinner. Then Franz invited Ivan and Marta. Sora, whose late husband had owned a greengrocery, still had friends in the trade who were more than willing to sell her certain commodities under the counter: a five-kilo bag of white sugar, a tin of baker's yeast, a slab of dark chocolate. Anna, Reina, and Franz ate the chocolate slowly, savoring it. Sora baked bread and vanilla cookies and used the last of the chestnut flour to bake the Italian cake *castagnaccio*.

Anna and Franz lit the candles in the candelabra on the dining room table. Anna slid into the chair beside Aunt Vivian, who told amusing anecdotes about the SS wives who came into her shop to buy hats. Reina said the same wives patronized the bookshop, stocking up on romance novels and snooping for banned titles they could report to their Nazi husbands. Some of her customers had chauffeurs to carry their purchases out to their cars, Aunt Vivian said. It made her want to slap their faces. "The wives or the chauffeurs?" Franz said. Aunt Vivian laughed and said, Both.

Franz put Mozart on the gramophone: *Eine kleine Nachtmusik*; Anna's father said the grace, giving thanks for the generosity of Reina's family and the fine meal they were about to enjoy. Then he uncorked the wine and poured a glass for everyone, even Anna.

On their way to dinner, Ivan said, a few flakes of snow had begun to fall.

"Didn't I tell you?" Uncle Tomáš said. "Didn't I predict snow?"

Anna's mother said, "Ivan, your face has healed nicely. The scar is almost invisible. Such a shame it happened. Most of those

SS men had the benefit of a good upbringing and should know better. But thank the Lord it turned out all right."

Sora said she must apologize for the dumplings, which she'd concocted of millet flour and starch, in lieu of potatoes. "The brown sauce is a disguise and a panacea rather than a sauce."

When Franz repeated what he'd heard on the BBC news—that in the Winter War, as it was known, Finns equipped with nothing more than snowshoes and rifles were decimating the heavily armed Soviet forces—Uncle Tomáš interrupted. He continued to be employed as an accountant in the Reich Protectorate Office at the Hradčany, he said, but as a Czech his position was precarious. He had learned it was wiser not to discuss politics or the war. There followed a silence, and Anna's father laughed and said, it would be a quiet evening then, since they'd lost the ability to talk about anything else.

Franz and Ivan began to discuss a play they had acted in, Karel Čapek's *R.U.R.: Rossum's Universal Robots.* They'd had minor roles, as two of the robots. Ivan's mother had kept his costume, he said. Franz said he'd returned his costume to the drama department at the university and regretted not having taken photographs. Anna remembered his costume of gold and silver foil, his face and his hands painted gold. The play was about a scientist, Dr. Rossum, who had engineered the production of robots from vats of blood cells and nerve fibers. The robots were biologically similar to humans and intended as an endless supply of cheap labor. The robots, however, continued to evolve, becoming in time ever more human, autonomous beings, who, in the end, killed their human masters and established a new society in which there were no masters and slaves, but only equal and free people.

A warning and a prophecy, Franz said. Čapek had written the play in 1920. Thirteen years later, the Nazis began imprisoning their own people in concentration camps at Dachau, Maut-hausen, Sachsenhausen. The Nazis did not hide what they were doing. The industrialists in Germany were pleased to have a source of free labor. Čapek had lived long enough to know what was going on.

"I think we are back to discussing politics," Magdalena said. "My favorite of Čapek's works is *Talks with T. G. Masaryk*. I would have liked more in those talks about his meeting with Charlotte Garrigue in Leipzig. It all happens in a few paragraphs, and then suddenly she returns home to America, and he sails after her. They are married and return to live in Prague. Dr. Masaryk said his wife was American, but she became 'morally and polit-ically Czech.'"

"It is the same for me," Aunt Vivian said. "I think of myself as completely Czech."

"Charlotte Masaryk is my hero," Reina said.

The play *R.U.R.* made him think, Anna's father said, of Heinrich von Kleist's essay on the marionette theater. "Didn't Kleist propose that puppets embodied more grace than humans?"

"Yes," Franz said. "Kleist suggested that since a puppet's grace is mechanical, not moral, puppets never experience self-doubt, while humans have to think before they act, and then it's too late, the appropriate moment for action has been lost. You know how it is. You lie awake at night worrying: Did I make the right deci-sion? And at three in the morning, you know it was completely the wrong decision. Marionettes are never indecisive; they simply exist, while our humanity undermines us, in a sense."

"I don't think you can talk about marionettes and robots in the same breath as human beings," Anna's mother said. "We have a choice; they don't. Listen to me—now I'm talking as if they were real."

"Yes, but in a way they are real," Franz said. "They are what we project on them, don't you think?"

"May I interrupt to ask a simple, not at all intellectual question?" Aunt Vivian said. "Marta, tell me, have you decided on an outfit for your wedding day?"

"Yes, I think so. A blue tweed suit and a cape in the same fabric, because it's cold in February."

"Don't you want a wedding dress?" Reina said. "With flowers and a veil? I would, if I were getting married."

"Yes, but this will be more practical, I think," Marta said. "Besides, the way things are these days . . ."

"Do you have a hat? I'll make you one," Aunt Vivian said. "Bring your wedding suit to my shop, so that I can match it with a nice fabric. Do you have pearls? Pearls look good with tweed. They set it off. I can lend you a pearl necklace and earrings."

"Your turn next," Ivan said to Franz.

"Oh, I don't think so. I'm not old like you, my friend," Franz said.

"Time goes quickly."

"Franz gave his heart away when he was a child," Anna's mother said, smiling.

"Not this old story again," Franz said.

"We were on the train from Berlin to Prague," Anna's mother said. "We had visited Julius's parents in Heidelberg, and I had been at a conference at the Berlin University. Anyway, on the train a passenger was taken ill, and while I couldn't have been the only medical doctor on board, I was the one who was asked to examine him. A young woman looked after Franz for me. Was her name Natasha, Franz? Do you remember?"

"Natalia, I think."

"He talked about her for weeks," Aunt Vivian said. "He would watch for her from the window."

"She talked about boats and fishing and cats," Franz said.

"Whoever she was, she'll be old and ugly by now and the mother of ten children," Reina said.

"Oh, I don't think so," Anna's mother said. "She'd be twenty-nine, or thirty at the most, which isn't old."

"It's not young," Reina said.

→··←

On Saint Valentine's Day, Ivan Lazar and Marta Hempel were married. After the ceremony, the wedding guests walked behind the bride and groom across the Charles Bridge to the apartment where Marta lived with her father. Sora had set out plates of bread and real butter, obtained on the black market, and sausages and cheese.

Reina read a few lines of a poem by Geoffrey Chaucer: "For this was Valentine's Day, when every bird cometh there to choose his mate." She said the poem had been written to commemorate the marriage of Anne, daughter of Charles IV, king of Bohemia, to Richard II of England. She held out her wineglass to be refilled.

"Are you drunk?" Franz said.

"On happiness only," Reina said sourly.

Ivan's mother had brought with her from Český Krumlov a china plate, which, at the appropriate moment, she smashed on the floor, and Marta had to kneel and pick up the pieces, to demonstrate her willingness to be an industrious and thrifty wife. Reina poured herself another glass of wine.

"You don't want to go back to work drunk, do you?" Franz said.

"Maybe," Reina said.

Everyone over the age of sixteen had to work sixty hours a week for the Nazi war effort. Franz worked at the armament factory on the other side of the Vltava, where, he said, the workers drew turtles on the walls in green ink, a reminder to go slow on the production line, as a way of sabotaging Germany's war machine. Reina had continued working at the bookshop until last summer, when the Nazis had assigned her to a printing press operated by the Ministry of Public Enlightenment and Propaganda. She said she'd drawn a turtle on the wall too. "I didn't care if I was caught, but I did mind that everyone said my turtle looked like an insect. 'Your bug is dead,' they kept saying. 'Your bug is dead.'"

After the reception, Anna and her father walked across the bridge to his atelier, which was on a narrow, curved street in Malá Strana. He lit a fire in the tiled stove. He showed her a portrait he was finishing of a brother and sister, three and five years old. The portrait had been commissioned by the children's father, a merchant who had moved with his family to Zürich to escape the Nazis. Anna's father didn't know whether the portrait and its owner would ever be united, he said, but he intended to get it completed, nevertheless.

While her father worked, Anna sketched the wedding guests with a stick of charcoal. She drew her mother and father arm in arm, and Franz and Reina, and Aunt Vivian and Uncle Tomáš. The farmer from Zürau, who'd delivered the farm goods to her house, was in her drawing too, if not in life, standing at the side of the bridge in his greatcoat; she labored over the folds of the coat, trying to suggest the straightness of the back, the length of arm. Ivan she sketched beside Marta. He was better-looking in real life, it was true. She drew a strand of pearls around Marta's neck. She drew herself, her braided hair, winter coat, stockings, and patent leather shoes.

Her father said that years from now, she would look at her drawing and remember the marriage, the reception, the taste of the food, bits of conversation. It would all come back to her; she would live it again, in her memory. Art, he said, made life not only more human but, in a sense, eternal.

->··<-

September of 1941 began hot and sultry; in the afternoons, clouds built up in the sky over Western Bohemia, and by evening, lightning flashed in the distance and the sound of thunder could be heard. But, as Sora said, it wasn't the weather that made everyone feel like quarreling with their own fingernails. It was seeing Gestapo and SS officers on the streets, swastika flags flying from Prague Castle, machine-gun emplacements on street corners, edicts from Reich protector Baron von Neurath's office on lamp-posts, in shop windows. The Reich protector had been recalled to Berlin, and another high-ranking Nazi was to take his place, but still for a time the edicts continued to be signed by Neurath. Lists of people who'd been arrested and those who'd been executed appeared in columns in newspapers or were read out on Radio Prague.

At the end of September, on the feast day of Saint Wenceslas, Anna attended Mass at Saint Vitus Cathedral with her parents. Then they stood on the street outside the cathedral and watched the ecclesiastical procession that conveyed the saint's relics over the Charles Bridge to Wenceslas Square. The Czech police ordered people to get back and stop talking, to shut up, but the crowd had started singing the Czech national anthem, which was forbidden by the Nazis. "This is a beautiful country, the Czech country, my homeland," they sang. The police formed a cordon and forced the crowd back against a wall. Anna nearly fell when someone pushed her, not intentionally, she was sure. Someone else was shoved to the pavement, a man, who immediately stood, embarrassed, and brushed off his jacket, retrieved his hat. She hated seeing people lose their dignity; it made her want to fight back, but that was impossible. Her mother took her arm, and they started walking home and met up with Anna's father and her uncle Emil, who had his two-year-old son, Jan, on his shoulders. Franz and Reina arrived almost at the same time, and Franz said he and Reina had seen a man accosted by the security police and beaten with batons and called a dirty Bolshevik, a filthy Jew. This happened, Reina said, in front of the man's wife and two children. She lit a cigarette and leaned against the trunk of the chestnut tree and wouldn't come into the house, where everyone gathered at the kitchen table and talked about the war.

"Will England bomb us?" Reina said. She stood for a moment in the door and then came in and sat beside Franz at the table.

"No, President Beneš is in London; the English are on our side," Emil said.

Anna's mother lifted Jan onto her knee and wiped his sticky hands and mouth with her handkerchief. Franz said he should have gone to England with Sora's son, Jiri, and joined the Czech army-in-exile. When the Czech army returned to Prague, as they would, Franz said, he would fight with them. He quoted Jan Masaryk, the former president's son and a minister in the Czech government-in-exile, who'd said it would be better for Czechs to be the hammer than the anvil.

"It's easier to advocate resistance when you are in England," Anna's father said.

"So for us, we play the anvil and get hammered, is that it?" Franz said.

"We endure," Anna's father said. "We wait them out."

"We let ourselves be enslaved, you mean."

Anna's mother set Jan down. He leaned on Anna's knee, and she picked him up and took him to the living room, and they played a tune on the piano. Rather, Jan banged his fists on the keys and laughed. Reina shouted from the living room door that no one appreciated the racket they were making, and Jan burst into tears. Uncle Emil came in and picked up his son and took him home.

That night, Anna dreamed her parents and Franz had been arrested and were imprisoned beneath the Petschek Palace, a former bank that had been taken over by the Gestapo. In the dream, she knew this. She knew the bank vaults in the basement were being used as cells. People were interrogated and tortured. The Gestapo had a guillotine. All this was true in life as well as in the nightmare. Her parents and her brother were themselves but not themselves, and when they looked at her from behind the bars of a cell, they seemed not to know her, and she kept saying, "I am your child, I am your daughter, Anna."

CHAPTER TWELVE

In February 1942, Anna's family traveled to Western Bohemia, where they went every year to ski. This was their first winter vacation since the occupation began. The previous owners of the inn were Czech and had been expelled by the Germans after the Munich Agreement, which had given the Sudetenland to Germany. The new owner met them at the train station. He called himself Herr Winter, he said, he who made *den Schnee und den Frost*. His name was not, in fact, Winter but Schulte. His leather coat creaked when he moved, like tree branches burdened with frost, and his breath, also rather creaky, clouded the air around his head, and so perhaps, in a way, he was Herr Winter. He drove them to the inn. On the way he said that they would find the inn unchanged; he and Frau Schulte had not made any alterations. As soon as he opened the door, though, Anna saw that the new owners had made a change. They had hung a large portrait of the Führer on the wall in the vestibule, so it was the first thing they saw. Herr Schulte took their coats and gave them sheepskin-lined knitted slippers to wear. He would bring in the luggage, he said, and told them to go and sit in the lounge, where there was a fire in the fireplace.

Anna's mother went to the Bechstein piano and ran her fingers over the keys and said, "Julius, do you remember when Mrs. Stanek and I played duets on this piano?"

Anna remembered lying on the rug on the floor in front of the fireplace with Martina Stanek, who was three years older than Anna was. She half expected Martina still to be there. Herr Winter, or Herr Schulte, or whoever he was, had got one thing right: nothing in this room had changed since the last time Anna and her parents—and Franz—had stayed there. The rose-colored sofas and maroon velvet armchairs stood where they always had, in front of the stone fireplace. Over the fireplace there was a stag's head. A chess set, the pieces carved from walrus tusk, was set out on a small table. Glass-fronted cabinets held Bohemian crystal and china, and one tall, narrow cabinet housed a collection of antique firearms.

"What would they think," Anna's mother said, "if they could see us here?"

"The Staneks? They would understand," her father said.

"They would despise us," her mother said. "We should not have come." She sat on the sofa beside Anna. Frau Schulte came in with a tray of coffee and cake. "We are quiet at the moment, as you can see," she said. "Several parties have canceled due to the weather."

"If there's no snow, they don't like it," said Herr Schulte, appearing from the hall, rubbing his hands together. "And if there's too much snow, they complain even louder. I took your suitcases upstairs to your rooms."

"The cake is best warm," Frau Schulte said. She poured the coffee. For Anna she had a cup of cocoa, frothy on top, with a tiny silver spoon left in the cup, to stir it with.

A girl with a high, round forehead and small glittering eyes like Herr Schulte's came into the sitting room. "Here is my Irmgard," Herr Schulte said.

Irmgard wore a cardigan over a checked dress, brown wool stockings. One of her shoes had a built-up sole, and she limped. Frau Schulte said she was to go upstairs and light the fires in the bedrooms for their guests.

Irmgard said she would finish setting the table first. "Did I say at your convenience?" Frau Schulte said.

"Listen to your mother, Irmgard," Herr Schulte said.

At seven that evening, dinner was served. The first course was chicken soup, followed by roasted pork and noodles, boiled carrots, and cabbage with sour cream and caraway seeds. The only other guests that evening were a couple from Berlin, Herr Doktor Voss and Frau Voss and their baby. Dr. Voss cut his food into small pieces and regarded it suspiciously before putting it in his mouth. Frau Voss mashed carrots and spoon-fed them to her baby, who promptly spit up on her. Frau Voss moistened an edge of her table napkin in her water glass and sponged at her dress.

"He's a lovely baby," Anna's mother said, smiling at Frau Voss.

"He is mischief incarnate," Dr. Voss said.

After dinner Herr Schulte carried a tray of brandy and coffee into the sitting room. For Anna, he had another cup of hot cocoa, which seemed to her like one cup too many. Frau Voss walked around the room with the baby, who began to scream and push at his mother's neck. Shush, shush, Frau Voss crooned. The baby was Friedrich, she said. "Our little Fritzi," Dr. Voss said, adding that little Fritzi was eight months old and cutting another tooth, which meant sleepless nights for his poor, beleaguered parents.

Usually they vacationed in Saxony, Frau Voss said, but what with the war and the baby, they had decided this would be quieter.

"And it is quiet, isn't it?" Dr. Voss said. "Another storm is on the way, I fear, because I have the most appalling headache."

Anna's father said he was sorry to hear that. Dr. Voss shrugged. "How are you in Prague?" he said. "In Berlin food rationing is a nuisance and the blackout even more so, and when you need a taxi, there are none. Damage has been inflicted by British planes, it is true, but nothing we can't cope with. You know, the English never wanted this war; Churchill pushed them into it. The Americans do not want war either, but President Roosevelt is determined to get involved." He tamped down the tobacco in the bowl of his pipe and took a book of matches out of his pocket.

Anna's father began to talk conversationally about skiing, when he was young, in Bavaria, with his brother and sister. His family did also, Dr. Voss said, every December. "My goodness, it just came to me," he said, slapping his forehead. "I know you, Frau Schaefferová, do I not? Frau Doktor Schaefferová, I should say. We met at a medical conference in Prague. In July 1937, I believe. Please tell me I am correct. Otherwise, I will have disgraced myself doubly. It is Dr. Schaefferová, isn't it?"

"Yes," Anna's mother said. "Yes, I remember the conference."

Dr. Voss stood and bowed and sat down again. "What a great pleasure this is. Just last month I read your monograph on the metabolism of iron and found it brilliant. Lise," he said, turning to his wife. "Isn't this wonderful? Dr. Schaefferová is a distinguished member of the medical community. Such a happy accident. A truly great pleasure."

A burning log rolled onto the tiled hearth and Frau Voss gave a small shriek. Herr Schulte ran to grab the poker. The clock struck nine. Irmgard came in and gathered up the brandy glasses and the coffee service. The baby began to cry. Frau Voss gave him to her husband and said she was going up to their room.

❧ ⸱⸱ ❧

In the morning, Anna and her mother and father went for a walk in the snow. Her mother said she could not remember meeting Herr Doktor Voss at any conference, in Prague or elsewhere.

"He is not a memorable character," Anna's father said.

"Julius, what are we doing here?"

"It's quiet, the air is fresh; it's good, Magdalena."

They were hiking up a mountain within spitting distance, as her father said, of the farm Anna's grandfather had once owned, the farm where her mother had lived as a child. Anna's grandmother, Katharina Svetlová, the first woman skier in Bohemia, had been the subject of a magazine story, and Anna's mother had kept the magazine, which featured a photograph of Katharina on her skis, ski poles in her hands, wearing a quilted swansdown jacket with a nipped-in waist and puffed sleeves, and an ankle-length skirt. The photograph was taken here, at Waldfrieden.

From a high, thin cloud, a small shower of dry snowflakes whirled down, ceased, mysteriously filled the air again. An owl flew out of a tree. Anna's father said they had to keep moving or they'd freeze and turn into statues. Magdalena stamped around, laughing. She said she was not going back to the *Gasthaus*. She was absolutely not going there. She wanted to know which way was south. Or west. Where was Switzerland from here? How far? "Come with me," she said, holding her hands out to Anna and Julius and saying they could stay or come with her, and she began walking away.

"Magdalena," called Anna's father. But Magdalena kept plowing her way through the snow. Anna's father ran after her and brought her back to where Anna was standing. Her mother was laughing.

"Oh well," she said. "Maybe tomorrow I'll try again. The thought of one more night *chez* Schulte with the Voss family is almost more than I can bear. What do you think we're having for supper?" she added. "Poison toadstools? Pan-fried newts?"

As they approached the *Gasthaus*, they saw that Herr Schulte was driving away in his Mercedes. He rolled down the car window and waved at them and then accelerated up the drive, the wheels slipping on ice and snow. Irmgard, sweeping snow off the front step, said her father was going to pick up new guests at the train station.

Later, Anna sat by the fireplace reading *War and Peace*, which she had taken from a shelf in the library across the hall. She used to read Martina's books in the *Nesthäkchen* series, by Else Ury, when she was here, but the books were no longer in the library. They were children's books, too young for her, really, but she wouldn't mind reading something undemanding. She had started *War and Peace* three times already. She remembered how she and Martina would curl up on the sofa happily reading about Else Ury's Annemarie Braun, the "nestling," the baby of the family, who, like Anna, had blond braids, and whose father, like Anna's mother, was a doctor.

She heard Herr Schulte's car returning from the train station, followed by the slamming of car doors and then voices in the hall. The new guests did not appear, however, until dinner that evening. They were two men in the field-gray uniform of the Waffen-SS. Herr Schulte introduced them. The tall blond man was *Hauptsturmführer* Karl Kessler. The other man was *Untersturmführer* Walther Krause. Captain Kessler did not eat but pushed his plate away and lit a cigarette. Frau Voss waved her hand at the captain's cigarette smoke. Her husband frowned at her. Attempts at conversation faltered, and as soon as the meal was over everyone moved to the living room for coffee. Second Lieutenant Krause asked for wine, and then he said he would maybe prefer a glass of schnapps, while Herr Schulte was at it. The captain went over to the gun cabinet. "Do you have ammunition for these firearms?" he asked. "If the enemy got their hands on these guns, they would shoot your head off your shoulders, Herr Schulte."

"The gun collection belonged to the Czechs, as I said. I doubt if those old firearms would work anymore, to be honest."

"They're valuable. They should be cleaned and polished."

The inn, Herr Schulte said, as he added wood to the fire, had once been a hunting lodge frequented by the nobility, hence the gun collection. So the stationmaster, who fancied himself an amateur historian, had told him. A Bavarian archduke had shot the stag mounted on the wall. Furthermore, according to the stationmaster, a niece of Marie-Antoinette of France had stayed at Waldfrieden after the queen's husband went to the guillotine in 1793 and had given birth to an infant that had survived only a day and was buried either near the chalet or in the dirt floor in the wine cellar.

"How ghastly," Frau Voss said, her hand at her throat. "I hope it's not true."

"Of course it's not true," Herr Doktor Voss said.

Anna took *War and Peace* upstairs to her room and read in bed, her feet on a hot-water bottle Irmgard had brought her. Prince Andrei marched to war; Napoleon Bonaparte entered Vienna. As she read she could hear Fritz crying in his parents' room and thought with a shudder of Marie-Antoinette's niece's baby buried in the cellar.

>··<

By morning, snow lay in drifts in the yard and against the doors. Herr Schulte went out early to shovel a path for Irmgard, so that she could feed the chickens and the cows. After breakfast, Anna's mother carried Frau Voss's baby around the sitting room while his mother slept in a chair. Anna and her father played chess with the carved walrus-tusk pieces. Anna put her father's king into checkmate. She asked if he had let her win. He said, no, she had played a better game. Then, as he set the pieces back on the board, he told her they were going home earlier than planned. "We are?" she said. He put a finger to his lips. "Yes," he said. He lowered his voice. "In the morning. If the road is cleared, and we don't have another snowstorm, God forbid." She nodded. In the morning they were going to leave, she kept repeating to herself. But that night it snowed heavily, and by morning the road to the station was, Herr Schulte reported, impassable. After breakfast, Anna put on her coat, hat, gloves, and boots, and went outside and tramped up and down on the path Herr Schulte had once again cleared between walls of snow. The cold penetrated her coat, and she started shivering, and when she turned to go back to the inn, she saw Captain Kessler at the window, watching her.

Dinner that night was roast pork, *Spätzle*, and sauerkraut, followed by a dessert of stewed winter apples sprinkled with brown sugar. Captain Kessler lit a cigarette and said that winter weather brought back good memories of when he went mountain climbing with his father, who was an Alpine guide. The Jungfrau, the Eiger, Mont Blanc. Up on the peaks, there was no room for a false step. The only sounds were made by ice shifting and cracking, wind scouring the peaks. The higher he climbed, the lonelier it got, and that suited him.

If his medical practice allowed him time, Dr. Voss said, he

would pursue mountain climbing. He skied, though, every winter. Except this one, he supposed.

The captain turned to Anna's father. "And what is it you do, Herr Schaeffer?"

"I am an artist. I teach art."

"Interesting. I studied architecture at university." He brushed a crumb off the tablecloth. "I had a professor who admired your work. You are Julius Schaeffer, is that right? You are a portraitist?"

"Portraits, yes, and landscapes. And graphic design."

"You have painted in the modernist style, I understand."

"Yes, some of my art is modernistic, as you say."

Two conversations were going on at once. Anna heard Frau Voss telling her mother that from the age of four months, little Fritz could grip her fingers and pull himself to a standing position. At the same time, Anna was listening to the SS captain telling her father that good art taught people to value their way of life. "Don't you think so yourself, Herr Schaeffer?" he said. "More and more, I think offensive artwork by Jews and Bolshevists, and those under their influence, is an attack on German morals and German values. I am referring to artists like Max Ernst, Otto Dix, Käthe Kollwitz, George Grosz. Modern German masters. They've had their day. They're finished."

He didn't know if they were finished or not, Anna's father said. They would always be an important—an essential—part of history.

"That kind of history is also finished," Captain Kessler said. "You know Elk Eber's painting *The Dispatch Courier*? That is a fine work."

"But perhaps it gives a romanticized view of war," Anna's father said. "Otto Dix's war paintings are painful to look at, but they are honest. I was there, in France, at the Somme, at Verdun,

as was Dix. War is destructive, a tragic waste of life. Young men
die, innocent noncombatants die. There's no point in pretending
otherwise, is there?"

"You know so much, Herr Schaeffer," the captain said coldly.
"But like so many, you know nothing."

Herr Schulte hovered uneasily with the coffeepot. The lights
flickered and went out. Herr Schulte recommended adjourning to
the sitting room. "Everyone together in one room," he said, "that's
the way. Frau Schulte will light candles. We will add wood to the
fire. We have no need to worry." Frau Schulte and Irmgard went
around lighting coal-oil lamps. Second Lieutenant Krause leaned
back in his chair and rested his right foot on his left knee. "You've
had it easy in Prague, haven't you?" he said to Anna's father.
"No bombing raids, no food shortages to speak of. No enemy air
attacks, full employment. Living in paradise, I'd say."

He began to sing:

When the Prussians they marched against Prague,
'Gainst Prague, the beauteous town,—
they took up in camp a position,
They brought with them much ammunition.

He said his grandfather had taught him that song. "The
Czechs lost the Battle of White Mountain; Prussia won. So history
repeats itself. When will the Slavs learn, I would like to know?"

"Now you have woken my son," Dr. Voss snapped.

"There's something wrong with that baby," Krause said. "He's
always bawling. Is he sick?"

"No, he is not sick. My son is in the pink of health."

"Children need a firm hand," Krause said. "When I was a
nipper my mother read me the poems of Heinrich Hoffmann.

Disobedient children get burned alive. Their hands are cut off. No, the thumbs are cut off, I believe. My mother said it could happen to me if I didn't behave. You Czechs will suffer the same fate, I'm telling you. Baron von Neurath isn't there now to coddle you. The acting Reich protector, Reinhard Heydrich, will keep you in line. He will cut off your thumbs, if you like." He stabbed the air with his pocketknife.

"For Christ's sake, would you shut up," the captain said.

"That's a hell of a storm out there," Krause said.

The captain shielded his eyes. "How long will this last?" he asked Herr Schulte, who said the electricity would get restored soon. Most of the generators were in the Sudetenland and any breakages in the system would get priority treatment.

The next day, Anna sat reading *War and Peace* by the light of a coal-oil lamp in the sitting room. Her mother and father were upstairs, getting ready for dinner, as were Herr Doktor Voss and Frau Voss. The baby must have been asleep, and the house was quiet. Captain Kessler came in and sat across from her. Irmgard walked in with a tray of coffee and bread and cheese. She had unpinned her hair and curled the ends and wore lipstick and rouge. The captain closed his eyes. Irmgard asked him: Would he like cream and sugar in his coffee? Yes, he said. He would do it himself. Irmgard put down the sugar tongs. The captain opened his eyes when she had gone. He asked, "How old are you, Anna?"

"Twelve," she said. "I will be thirteen in March."

"And my age is twenty-two."

The same age as Franz, she thought. She got up, holding her book to her chest. He told her to stay where she was and said she looked pretty in the lamplight. He enjoyed her company, in the midst of this tedium, being trapped indoors. The storm, being shut up with that idiot Krause. He was used to being out in the elements. As an Alpine guide, he said, his father spent winters away from home. When he was about Anna's age, his mother got bored, being left on her own with the children, and she moved to Berlin. "She took my brothers and sister with her, and I lived with my father until I went to university, where I studied, among other things, the writings of Friedrich Nietzsche, and I remember being very impressed with something he said. So impressed, in fact, that I committed his words to memory.

"'An atmosphere'—this is what Nietzsche wrote—'an atmosphere of inexhaustible meaningfulness emanates from architecture.' Perhaps those are not his exact words, but you get the idea, don't you, Anna? It is my belief our Führer has an innate understanding of this. He has a grand vision, a truly great vision, of Berlin as the world's preeminent metropolis. Germania, it is to be named. Germania: a city of inexhaustible meaningfulness. When the war ends, and it will, within months, I will go back to architecture school and finish my degree, and I will work on this project, the construction of Germania. First, it seems that I have to walk through a lot of shit. Excuse me, Fräulein. A lot of excrement, shall I say? I honestly can't think of another way of saying it. I was in Paris, you know, in 1940. Paris is a beautiful, civilized city, and Parisians, by and large, appreciate German culture. They are adaptable people; I got along with most of them. But then I was sent to Poland and the Baltic countries. There, it was swamps and more swamps, and atrocious weather and ruthless Jew partisans."

He got up and came around to the back of her chair and placed his hand on her neck. "A shot to the neck precisely here—where the spinal column enters the skull," he said. "*Genickschuss*. That is the word. An efficient execution, all down the line. You would think, wouldn't you, that someone would stop it. But no one does.

The orders are given—I give the orders, to be precise—and the action goes ahead, like an assembly line. Bang, bang, bang. But not quite. It is not quite like that. It is chaotic, unsightly. My ears ring from the gunshots. I will go deaf, I fear. And blind, from the things I am forced to witness. They say a woman will instinctively protect her child, but I can tell you that is not always so. People will do anything to survive. Half the time, you can't think why they bother. The problem is, one is human, after all, and it gets to you. But I tell myself, it is either them or me. They brought it on themselves, the Jews did."

He took the book from her hands. "Why are you reading a book by a Russian, when Russia is our enemy? You should know better, even at your age." He tossed the book on the fire. The pages flared in the heat, turned black on the edges, and then the book was consumed. When she got up to leave the room, he held her by the arm. He said she was not to tell anyone what he'd told her. Did she promise? "You don't want anything bad to happen to you or your parents, do you?" He let go of her arm. She ran through the door and felt her way up the stairs and down the hall to her room, where she lit a candle and held it up to be certain he had not crept in after her. She sat on the bed, trying to calm herself. *Genickschuss.* A word she thought she would hear in her head for the rest of her life.

Late the next day electrical power was restored, and the day after that the temperature rose, and icicles dripped from the roof. A plow was clearing the road, Herr Schulte reported. If Herr and Frau Doktor Schaeffer and their daughter wished to leave, he could get them to the train station. Irmgard made sandwiches for them to take on the train, rye bread and liverwurst, which, in the end, they couldn't eat, and her father gave them to two boys sitting near them on the train. In Prague, it was snowing. At the station, they were interrogated by the Gestapo, and then they met Uncle Emil, who drove them to his house for a supper of soup and bread and margarine. When they got home, Anna's mother spent an hour downstairs in the surgery reading messages Elli had left for her. Franz came home, took one look at his father, and said, "What is it? What's happened?"

"It was like this," Anna's father said. "We spent four days snowbound in a house with two Waffen-SS men and a doctor who was a doppelgänger for Joseph Goebbels. We could not ski, the skis having been requisitioned by the Germans. There was a storm, and no one could get out, and the train wasn't running."

Anna's mother came in and said it was worse than that. They had broken bread with the enemy, and now their names were known.

"They already know your names," Franz said. "In a police state, everything is known."

For days Anna distrusted her own eyes. She had to touch things—tables, chairs, the piano—to assure herself of their solidity. Often she sat by herself on the staircase with her shoulders hunched and her arms around her knees. If the doors to the surgery were left open, she could see Elli at the reception desk. Light from the window near the door fell on the marble tiles. A trapezoid of light. In the hand there was a bone called the trapezium. In this world there were such things: circuses, people laughing. There were girls like her who went to school and studied and went to movies with their friends. But not here, not here.

In March her father's atelier was searched by two SS officers or Gestapo—he wasn't sure which, as both men wore plain clothes. They went through his filing cabinets and took away many of his paintings, including a portrait of Anna's mother and another portrait, of Anna and Franz when they were about fourteen and seven, and the portrait of the merchants' children her father had completed just after Ivan and Marta's wedding.

Anna's father said the SS officers had questioned him about his technique, his use of color, and so on. Franz thought the men were quite possibly attached to the Einsatzstab Reichsleiter Rosenberg, the task force headed by Alfred Rosenberg, with the authority to find and confiscate art, primarily from the art collections of wealthy Jews but also from other sources, including museums and national galleries in occupied countries: Czechoslovakia, Poland, France, Belgium, the Netherlands. The organization had been renamed, he thought, but the theft of art continued.

The men did not return, and her father was not arrested, but for a time he avoided returning to his atelier, and instead worked sitting in an armchair at home, a sketch pad on his knee, drawing in pencil a series of figures with misshapen, tuberous heads, ribs like spokes, twisted hands, huge eyes, dilated pupils. The drawings, which her father sometimes went over in pen and ink, reminded Anna of Robert Hooke's etchings in *Micrographia*, except these were not magnified images of microbes or fleas; they were human, their humanity apparent in the eyes and the contorted ligaments of the neck. Not a blade of grass or a wisp of cloud anchored them to the world. She thought the drawings allowed her father to work without actually working; they were a way of seeing without seeing. But she hated those drawings, and when her father left them lying around, she gathered them up and hid them in a drawer in the credenza, underneath lace tablecloths. As far as she knew, her father never missed the drawings or searched for them.

CHAPTER THIRTEEN

Natalia left the castle early, at dawn, leaving a note propped up on the kitchen table for Rozalia. It was very brief, that note, and said only that she'd be away for a few days. The less Rozalia knew, obviously, the safer she would be. Or so Natalia hoped. The Bugatti made its usual horrendous racket as she backed it out of the garage, but no one was awake, with the possible exception of Vladimír, and he would not hear anything from the stables. For the first part of the drive she worried that a breakdown, a punctured tire, would stop her, or soldiers at a military checkpoint would force her to turn around, but she got to Budapest without incident. At the garage where Miklós had always taken the Bugatti for repairs, she paid the owner, Mr. Barta, in cash, in advance, to store the Bugatti for three weeks, which should, she said, give her lots of time. If anything happened and she didn't come back, he could either keep the car or sell it. Mr. Barta said he would never sell Count Andorján's Bugatti. He drove her to the train station, where she saw men in the uniform of the Royal Hungarian Army and other men, not in uniform, wearing yellow armbands identifying them as Jews, who had been conscripted to the labor battalions and would be sent to the front. In winter they would not have warm clothing. They were not given helmets or weapons.

Hungary was at war with Russia. And with Yugoslavia. Hungary had declared war on the United States of America. Hungary was at war with everyone except Hitler and the Third Reich. The Hungarian parliament had brought in anti-Semitic laws based on Germany's Nuremberg Laws, and these laws made it illegal for Jews to own property and banned Jewish students from attending university and barred Jews from the professions and forbade marriage between Jews and Christians. The regent, Vice-Admiral Horthy, a self-declared anti-Semite, a man for whom Natalia had never had much respect, had, out of expediency, advocated caution in appropriating Jewish businesses and industries, so as not to damage to Hungary's economy. Such hypocrisy, such opportunism. She was ashamed of her adopted country and ashamed of her German birth. ·

The Sinti men living on her land—it was hers too now; she thought of it as hers—had been sent to labor camps in the Carpathians or ordered to clear land mines in war zones: a death sentence. The women and children were transported to collection centers near the Austrian border and from there to concentration camps in Germany. Rozalia had taken a gun to the Sinti encampment on the estate and had threatened to shoot the soldiers ordering the Sinti people into trucks. I will shoot, she had shouted at them. They had aimed their rifles at her; they had called her a crazy old bird. Natalia had made her promise she wouldn't try anything like that again, in anyone's defense. It wouldn't help if she got herself killed. Ah, but think of the satisfaction I would have, said Rozalia, who had to get in the last word.

➤·◄

Natalia checked into a hotel on Celetná Street in Prague. She used the name Faber, Frau Faber. She and Miklós would be reunited within days, she thought, but this did not happen. She had brought very little with her and had to rinse her clothes in the bathroom sink, just as she used to do for Beatriz, and place them on the radiator, in the sun, to dry. There was a vase of highly scented purple lilacs on the dresser, and in this heady atmosphere she emptied her purse on the bed and counted her money and kept arriving at a different total, but she could see just by looking at it that it wouldn't last for long. She had registered at the hotel without producing a passport or other document, saying it was in a piece of luggage the train had misplaced. A not very believable excuse, and yet the woman at the front desk had accepted it, for now. She knew that without identification papers she ran the risk of being questioned by the Gestapo.

Rather than eating at a restaurant, she bought food from a small shop, where the proprietor, a Turkish man named Danyal Aslan, always gave her sesame-seed cookies and chatted with her about the fine weather and the ducks he'd seen on the river or the glorious full moon the night before. He kept day-old newspapers for her. Gratefully, she read them in her hotel room, at first searching for her husband's byline, for reports from the Eastern Front that could have been written by him, but then she realized the newspaper was an official Nazi Party organ. But the smell of the ink, the smudges on her hands reminded her of Miklós, and she could almost see him sitting at a table with a cup of coffee, writing or reading a newspaper. Mr. Aslan's wife, Milena, was Czech; they lived in an apartment behind their shop and had two children, a boy and a girl. Natalia mentioned to Mr. Aslan that she had to find somewhere cheaper than a hotel to live, and he said, as it happened, he had a house for rent, if she was interested. She told him the truth: she couldn't afford much in the way of rent. He called his wife to mind the shop and took Natalia to his house, which was on Zlatá Ulička, the Golden Lane, near the Hradčany (the castle district). Since 1939, Prague Castle had housed the Reich's administrative headquarters. The presence of SS and Gestapo so close to Mr. Aslan's house was a serious detriment, but the low rent compensated for this. Besides, Franz Kafka had lived here for a year with his sister, and Miklós had been here, and those things would surely be a protective influence.

She moved in the next day. On the table she placed her breviary and Rozalia's tarot cards, which she had put in her suitcase, thinking, perhaps, that they might serve as a disguise, a prop, a talisman. She placed her hand on the cards and thought of Rozalia and felt tearful, and then she thought of returning home with Miklós, driving up to the castle, the sun bright on its butter-colored walls. This small house on Zlatá Ulička she shared with mice and rats, nocturnal in their habits, and spiders that showed up at any hour, day or night. There was a smell of mildew, ashes, rust.

At night she lay awake on a narrow, hard bed, wondering where Miklós was sleeping and whether he had dry, warm clothes and enough to eat, and whether he was on his way to Prague. She thought of their last day together, before he'd left for the Russian front. It was October then, the birch trees turning from green to gold, a blue haze from wood fires lying along the hills. She begged him not to go. Winter in Russia, she had thought. Winter with the Red Army and German warplanes strafing them and cannon fire and grenades exploding and snipers with rifles. How skilled men were at devising ways to kill one another, she said, and when he merely smiled, she got angry and swore at him, and then she threw her arms around his neck. He wiped her tears away with his hand and repeated what he always said: he was a journalist; a journalist had a responsibility to bear witness; he had to go to the front lines and speak to the soldiers, the ordinary fighting men; otherwise people would read only the official lies, the official bullshit, the propaganda that came from the Reich press chief's office.

He had done enough already, she kept saying. In 1939, he'd been in Warsaw, under German aerial bombardment. In 1937, he'd gone to Spain to report on the fighting between the Republicans and General Franco's Nationalists. In Berlin, in 1939, he'd been arrested, beaten, hospitalized. She knew of this only when he came home and she saw the scar above his eye. But, as he said, he had survived. In Russia, though, in a war like this, what kind of chance would he have? Tell me that, she had said.

Someone he knew, a journalist, would meet him in Budapest and would drive him through Romania to the Black Sea, where he would be taken by boat to Sevastopol and from there across the Sea of Azov to Rostov. So he had told her. From Rostov he would take a train—if trains were running—to Kursk and from there to Moscow. He would travel with fake credentials, his bona fide papers and press card concealed in the lining of his great-coat. If necessary, he would get permission to travel with the Red Army from Stalin himself. Stalin, whom he detested. But he had friends in Moscow who would be willing to act as inter-mediaries.

"Stalin has thrown those friends of yours in prison," she said.

"Not all," he said. He promised to be back in a year. He would write to her. If the war dragged on, if things looked bad, they could meet in Prague, he said, and go to Spain and from Spain to Portugal, and they would book passage on a boat to Argentina, where Beatriz and Zita would give them sanctuary.

On their last night, she lay in his arms and watched the moon sail behind a thin, opalescent cloud. She heard the wind in the trees. A night bird singing. Wolves howling, clocks ticking. Near dawn she fell asleep, and when she woke, he was gone.

At the convent school the nuns had taught her: conjugal love is a totality—all the elements of the person enter this totality. It is a unity that involves body, heart, and soul.

She missed Rozalia. She could see her, the way she would sit in a high-backed chair, small, bent, huddled darkly in sweaters and shawls, clutching her glass of pálinka, singing her mournful songs. *The black coach of sorrow*, she sang. *Angels have taken you, and never will they return you*. Natalia had asked her not to sing that song, it was too sad, and Rozalia had raised her eyes and gathered her shawl around her and said, But it is true, it is out there, the black coach of sorrow, waiting.

In the last letter from Miklós, dated February 12, 1942, sent from Moscow, he had reminisced about being with her in Prague during "that beautiful May of 1942." He must have meant 1932—she imagined him writing by the light of a kerosene lamp, shells exploding, artillery fire, the wind howling around an army tent, if he had the shelter of a tent. But he was a newspaperman, precise with dates; he would never make such an error. He was sending her a message in code: she was to meet him in Prague this year, this spring. And she was here, looking for him in bookshops, tobacconists, barbershops. She returned many times to the Café Imperial and the Café Arco, on Hybernská, just to look in the door, but the only patrons seemed to be SS men too involved with devouring shanks of lamb and meat-filled pastries to notice her. She spent more than she could afford on a meal of noodles and spiced beef at the Café Europa in Wenceslas Square. It was so good; she enjoyed every bite and felt the muscles in her neck and back begin to relax for the first time since she had arrived in Prague. She fell into a pleasant fantasy, picturing Miklós coming in, sitting down, and lighting a cigarette. Smiling at her, saying darling to her, and telling her they were soon going home. Or to Portugal, to South America. And they would begin again, he said, reaching for her hand. She saw it all clearly. And then a darker image intruded, would not be pushed away. Her husband lying on a Russian battlefield, with blood on his coat, his arms flung wide, frost on his hair and face, on his eyelids.

Throughout the city she saw men who, at first glance, from a distance, could have been Miklós. A bespectacled man in a rumpled khaki jacket reading a newspaper, his dark hair silvered at the temples. A man on the street in front of her giving his pocket an abstracted pat, a gesture so reminiscent of Miklós she quickened her step—but it was not him, it was never him.

Life was so tenuous! How long was a life? Forty years, sixty? Less than five years? She had a malady of the spirit: *tristezza*. In three days it would be her son's birthday, his ninth birthday. László Krisztián. Krisztián, they called him. His hair was blond, like hers; he had his father's dark eyes, and he was, as Natalia and Miklós said, either full steam ahead or fast asleep in his bed. We can't keep up with him, he's wearing us out, they said. He was nearly four years old, never sick a day in his life. Then came late March 1936, a cold month, blustery, raining constantly, the ice breaking up on the river, cracking like thunder, the fields sodden. Rozalia said it was dangerous weather; germs got carried on the wind, and you breathed them in. Krisztián wanted to know: Am I breathing them in now? An old wives' tale, Natalia told him. What was an old wives' tale? A story, she said. A story that is not based on fact and is very often wrong. Krisztián had nodded, satisfied. At the school they shut the door on the bad weather, the malign March air. The children took off their wet boots and put on slippers. Krisztián sat beside Katya's daughter, Alena. They were so small, so eager to learn; they could read everything, and had memorized the words to all the songs. They spoke Hungarian and German. They played together; they fell asleep in the kitchen, in Rozalia's rocking chair, curled up like kittens.

That March morning, in the schoolroom, Natalia was reading to the class, and Alena began complaining that her head hurt, her throat was sore. She said she was going to throw up, and she did, she was sick on the floor, and Krisztián stared at her and said, *Ugh*. Natalia felt Alena's forehead; she was burning up. Rozalia told Natalia to take Krisztián home and send Katya for Alena. Natalia was to bathe Krisztián and change his clothes, and she did, even though he protested that no one had a bath twice in one day. Yes, sometimes they did, she assured him. She scrubbed him all over and washed his hair and dressed him in clean clothes from the inside out and sent him down to Magdolna, in the kitchen, while she washed her own face and changed her dress. She held her son on her knee and let him have whatever he liked for lunch, but he must eat it all, so that he could grow big and strong. And when he had finished even his liver dumplings, about which he was decidedly ambivalent, Magdolna gave him a big portion of dark, sweet chocolate. He put his arm around Natalia's neck and pressed bits of the chocolate into her mouth and asked if Alena would be better in the morning, and Natalia said yes, she would be better.

Katya's daughter recovered in time, but the illness left her profoundly deaf. Natalia bargained with God: deafness, yes; a long convalescence, yes, she would accept that. She remembered the fear surrounding a case of meningitis at the convent. She would not let Dr. Urbán diagnose that sickness. A mother should not let her child die. If a mother lost her child, then the mother should also die; she believed that. Miklós had rushed home from Berlin; he was there with her, sitting beside their child's bed. At the last, Miklós was the one who had to take their lifeless son from her arms; she would not give him up, he would get cold, she said, colder than he was.

The doctor gave her an injection; she tried to remain in a place where food, oxygen, and love were unnecessary. Miklós spoke to her from a great distance, from an unearthly place, and when she opened her eyes and saw how thin he was, how swollen and bruised his eyes, she got up, an automaton, a shell, and resumed some kind of life for his sake. He said, "There is no easy way out, my love, and no remedy for the pain."

In the weeks that followed, they sat in the library, in the desolate light of evening. Miklós drank whiskey; he kept getting up to pour more into his glass. He drank, and he smoked one cigarette after another. She worried about his health and his agnosticism. Her faith was battered and poor, but it was there, somewhere. She could not bear to think of him deprived of the grace and consolation of Heaven, of the clemency of saints, or of the hope that such things could be. She brought him coffee and sat beside him and then jumped up to open a window and then again to let the dog in when he scratched at the hall door and then to put a piece of wood on the fire. She made him seasick, Miklós said, reaching for her hand, pulling her down beside him on the sofa. A midnight lethargy kept them there, two spirits in an empty castle that breathed around them like something sentient, unquiet.

Remembering, she felt tearful, shaky; everything looked gray to her. Was it despair or hunger? The meal at the Café Europa had been days ago. At Mr. Aslan's shop she bought a half loaf of rye bread, using cash, paying under the counter. He asked her to wait and disappeared through the door to his apartment. When he returned, he handed her a brown paper parcel. No charge, he said. He took risks for her; he was a good friend.

On the streets of Prague fear hung in the air like smog. It seemed to her that a false, forced energy animated the Wehrmacht soldiers, the SS, the Gestapo—a dull, mean light flicking off them like phosphorus. She kept out of their way. But she heard them accosting people, cursing, ridiculing, lashing out. Sometimes they seemed to be following her. She kept an even step, looked neither left nor right, didn't cease her vigilance until she entered a leafy park, where she sat on a bench and unwrapped the parcel Mr. Aslan had given her. A hard-boiled egg in its shell and six sugared dates. She ate two of the dates. She talked to Krisztián. Tell me, she said, should I go home? No, stay, wait for Papa, her son replied. She heard him; sometimes she could hear him.

When she got back to her little house, she set out the tarot cards. The Empress resembled Beatriz in a Grecian robe designed by Coco Chanel. Here was Zita Kuznetsova, Queen of Wands, signifying adventure, ambition; but when reversed she became a saboteur exacting vengeance: a clever adversary. Here was the Magician, haloed with the symbol for infinity, an uroboros knotted around his waist. Infinite recurrence; inescapable fate. The Wheel of Fortune, and the Chariot of Fire: together meaning an unforeseen event? The Star card could connote a loss of direction.

Superstitious nonsense, wholly, utterly, Natalia thought, and yet, and yet.

→·←

One day she found a dead man lying on the ground in the park. He was nothing but skin and bones—his face pale, mottled, his lips dry and slack. His coat was dirty, and he did not smell very nice. No one else saw; she could walk away. But as she knelt to feel for a pulse in his neck, he moaned, his eyelids fluttered. She helped this dead-and-then-alive man to his feet. She picked up his knapsack and led him over to a bench. She said he should have something to eat. "*Nein,*" he protested. "It would do you good," she said. "*Nein,*" he repeated.

She brought him back with her to her rented house and brewed a pot of tea and gave him bread and cheese and the remaining sugared dates. He chewed slowly, a hand in front of his mouth. She hoped to God he didn't have fleas. She let him have the bed in the bedroom and tried to sleep on the sofa. The man she had resuscitated? revived?—whose name she did not even know—coughed all night. In the morning, she put out the remainder of the bread and the cheese, which had gone hard, for breakfast. She sliced the hard-boiled egg in half and shared it with him. Feeding two people on nothing—how was that to be accomplished? She boiled water and poured it into the metal washtub in the washroom and gave him one of the towels supplied by Mrs. Aslan. He reappeared some time later, with his coat buttoned up to the chin, and thanked her for her hospitality and said he would be on his way. For today, she said, he should stay.

She told him her name was Faber, Natalia Faber. He gave his name as Max Nagy. He was on his way to Budapest, where he had been born. Over the next few days, he told her how he came to be lying on the ground in a park.

For twenty-five years Max Nagy had been employed as head gardener on an estate in Pomerania, where he'd had his own cottage, a cat, a songbird in a cage. And the soil! The soil would grow anything. He was trained as an agronomist, a profession that suited him—he smiled—down to the ground. He would have stayed happily in Pomerania for the rest of his life, but what a person wanted was of no consequence in this world. Two years ago SS officers had come and ordered him to leave with them for Poland, where he was to work at an agricultural facility being built by a Nazi, Heinrich Himmler. Himmler, a chicken farmer before his current role as a top Nazi, intended to establish the world's most advanced agricultural research station. This was near the Polish town of Oświęcum; in German, Auschwitz. Himmler lost interest in the agricultural project, and when Germany invaded Russia in June 1941, the facility became a prisoner-of-war camp. The prisoners, Polish and Russian soldiers, were beaten, starved, left to die of exposure and thirst, so many crammed into a few meters of space they could not sit or even crouch down to rest.

Since he had seen all this, Max Nagy said, he'd thought the Nazis would never let him get away alive, but they had reassigned him to an estate in Brandenburg owned by a Junker family, where his job was to oversee Polish slave laborers. He had to fill production quotas. The German army needed to be fed. Germany needed food. On the estate they grew barley, wheat, and potatoes. Among the workers there was a lot of sickness. People died and were replaced by more slave laborers from the east, who in turn succumbed to overwork, malnutrition, and disease. It was not in his nature, nor should it be in anyone's nature, to order people to labor from dawn to nightfall when they were ill and weak. One day he was sent to the train station to pick up a shipment of seed potatoes. He watered the horse and gave it a bag of oats, and he walked away. He slept in fields and in forests. He stole fruit and vegetables. Sometimes a farmer gave him a meal and a dry place to sleep or a ride in a hay wagon or a truck.

"You walked from Brandenburg to Prague?" Natalia said.

"Yes, I walked," he said, and began to cough and could not stop.

⇥⇤

She found a piece of cardboard in the street and brought it back to Zlatá Ulička. She wrote on it: PERSONAL FORTUNES TOLD and a price in crowns—a small amount, anyone could afford it. She placed it in the window. Mr. Nagy raised his eyebrows at her. We have to eat, she said. She told Mr. Nagy that if someone came to have their fortune told, he was to go immediately to the bedroom, close the door, and not make a sound. To her surprise, clients soon arrived at her door. Almost always they were women, and they were pleased to receive predictions of good health, pleasant journeys, fortuitous meetings, romances. One or two readings a day gave her a small income, with which she bought food for herself and Mr. Nagy, as well as candles and a cheap pottery candlestick holder to lend a more convincing atmosphere.

One afternoon two German women, wives of SS officers, came for a reading. They giggled and said they'd had too much wine with lunch. She lit the candle and shuffled the tarot cards. They said she did not look like a fortune-teller. What was her name? Frau Faber, Natalia said.

The women were both named Frau Ursler; their husbands were brothers, officers of such distinction within the Schutzstaffel that even though they were close relatives, they were posted to the same unit in the same city. A rare privilege, the younger Frau Ursler said, giggling behind her hand.

"And where is your husband, Frau?" the younger Frau Ursler asked. She had the bright, inquisitive eyes of a sparrow. Natalia said her husband was in the Wehrmacht, on the Eastern Front.

"My father and brother, too," said the older Frau Ursler. "It is nerve-racking, isn't it?"

"Yes, it is," Natalia said.

The sparrow wore a tailored two-piece dress, and her hands were beautifully manicured, while the other Frau Ursler had a raw-looking scratch on the back of her hand, perhaps made by a pet cat, or by a brooch pin as she rushed to attend to her children or husband. Her pale eyes swam behind the lenses of her glasses. Natalia touched a card and said, You must take care of your health. Yes, she hadn't been sleeping well, the woman confided.

A constellation of favorable cards on either side of the Ace of Wands suggested an addition to the sparrow's family, to her delight. Commendations for the SS husbands, travel, new acquaintances, an increase in wealth. The sparrow wanted something more specific. Natalia turned up three cards in succession: the Emperor, Ezekiel's Chariot, and the Devil. *Der Teufel.* A violent death. Catastrophe, ruination. Quickly she reshuffled the cards and said the reading was finished. Her clients, unaware that the final spread of cards did not predict anything good, rose, laughing at their unsteadiness, and opened their handbags and added a generous tip to her fee.

She could not go through an ordeal like that again. A repulsive thing to do, invading someone's thoughts, pretending lies were real. Mr. Nagy crept out of the bedroom, his face ashen, damp with sweat, and sat at the table, across from her. He had a fit of coughing. She gave him a glass of water and said she was sorry he'd had to stay for such a long time in that little room.

He said, "They were German, weren't they, those women? Their husbands were SS men?"

"Yes," she said.

It was untenable, he said, this situation. He thought she was mad to invite them in and also mad to believe in tarot cards. He thought she would know better than that, he said sternly. He could never thank her enough for all she had done, but he had to prepare himself to leave. Quite soon, he expected, he would be fit enough to continue his journey to Budapest.

CHAPTER FOURTEEN

Anna's father had known Dr. Cornelius Shapiro since coming to Prague in 1919. Dr. Shapiro was a professor at the Charles University, a patron of the arts; he had been an enthusiastic supporter of Julius's career. When Dr. Shapiro came to the house one day in April, however, he said it was merely to say goodbye and to ask a small favor of Julius. That morning he had received an order to report to the train station at seven a.m. tomorrow, to be transported to the ghetto at Theresienstadt. His wife was not coping well with this, Dr. Shapiro said. She was Lutheran, Danish, and would have to continue alone in the effort to gain exemptions for their sons, who, having one Jewish and one Christian parent, were classified as *Mischlinge* and might be left with their mother in relative safety or might be sent to a camp. He had a favor to ask: Would Julius keep the manuscript of a story he had written? He had hoped to commission Julius to do the illustrations, but now, of course, that was impossible. Anna's father sent her to put the kettle on. She made tea and brought teacups and the teapot on a tray to the living room. Her father poured a cup for Dr. Shapiro, who sat smoking a cigarette and drinking his tea, with one hand on the envelope that held his manuscript. He had ideas in mind for his book's illustrations, he said, and talked about the merits of linocuts or woodcuts as opposed to pen-and-ink drawings with watercolor washes, in the style of Arthur Rackham, whose illustrations for *Alice in Wonderland* delighted him even more than those of John Tenniel. Having produced Arthur Rackham, John Tenniel, and Lewis Carroll, England could never produce a Hitler, he said. Not even France, with its history of anti-Semitism and xenophobia, could have produced Hitler. Prague had not been free of anti-Semitism, no place was, it seemed, but it had been a good home to him and his parents before him.

His little tale was not *Alice in Wonderland*, he said; it was merely a retelling of a very old Slovenian folktale called "Salt over Gold," collected in the nineteenth century by the Czech writer Božena Němcová.

"Three sisters are asked to tell their father, the king, how much they love him," he begins. "The youngest, like King Lear's daughter Cordelia, cannot 'heave her heart into her throat,' and finally says that she loves her father more than salt. Which enrages him, just as Cordelia's silence enraged Lear. Freud proposes that the youngest daughter's silence represents death, but in my story, as in Němcová's version, the youngest daughter triumphs over death. She embodies, indeed, a life-affirming principle. In fact, I began to worry as I studied various versions of the folktale that I had missed a crucial and darker interpretation. Now I understand all too well; the darkness was there all the time. When, like the young girl in the story, you have lost your family and home, and in my case also the right to practice the profession you love, to walk in a park, to read a newspaper at a café—all of your gold, in other words—when all of that is gone, only salt remains, an essential compound without which there cannot be life. That is the evil genius of the Nazis: to take away even the salt of life."

Anna's father said he would like to offer Dr. Shapiro sanctuary in their home. Dr. Shapiro would have his own room, a typewriter, books; he could work undisturbed; his family could visit in secret. If necessary, he could go up to the attic, which was quite habitable; they would put a mattress up there and bring him his meals, and when it was safe to do so, he could come downstairs. Dr. Shapiro said, Julius, one prison is much like another. When he was leaving, he said, "If you want to see what the heroine of my little tale looks like, you have only to look at Anna. She is exactly as I picture Marica."

Early the next morning, Anna's father went to the train station, but the police kept him from approaching the boarding area, and he was unable to find Dr. Shapiro.

Theresienstadt was sixty kilometers north of Prague, near the Elbe River. A former military garrison, it had been built by Emperor Joseph II and named in honor of his mother, the archduchess, Empress Maria Theresa. Gavrilo Princip, the young man who belonged to Free Bosnia and assassinated the archduke Franz Ferdinand and his wife, Sophie, precipitating the 1914 war, had been imprisoned there. Acting Reich protector Reinhard Heydrich had designated Theresienstadt a ghetto for Czech Jews over the age of sixty-five and for those who were war veterans or had been distinguished or influential in some sphere of life. Anna remembered Franz saying that this attempt by the Nazis to present a prison as some sort of retirement home or holiday camp fooled no one.

There is too much cruelty, Anna thought. Her head ached, her eyes bothered her. Her mother took her to an optician for an eye examination and to another doctor, who drew blood from her arm, listened to her heart, and tested her reflexes. She was in good health, the doctor said. A little nervous, maybe. She should try to get more sleep.

Fear kept her from sleeping. Fear and a feeling that at the back of her neck she had a small wound where the SS captain had placed his hand. He had not really shot her, but sometimes she felt as if he had, as if fear could inflict as mortal a wound as a bullet. If so, she surely had a dangerous injury. She looked at Dr. Shapiro's manuscript on the coffee table in the living room. Franz had read it, her father had read it. Anna ran her fingers over the title page. She hesitated, retreated, came back, and then one day she sat down and began to read:

Long ago, there was a king who ruled over a vast and prosperous kingdom. This kingdom was richly endowed with mountains, rivers, fertile plains, a wealth of precious minerals beneath the ground. In season the land produced barley, corn, and wheat. The orchards and vineyards flourished. The king was respected by his subjects; his soldiers ardently pledged their loyalty to him; his retainers and servants, down to the merest scullery maid in the royal kitchens, obeyed his every wish, often before the king himself was entirely aware of what he wished for.

But it was a king's nature never to feel entirely satisfied, never to accept that he had a sufficiency of anything. Especially love.

And so the king summoned his three daughters into his presence and commanded them to tell him how much they loved him.

The king was resplendent in a scarlet tunic and silk hose of forest green, a cape lined with ermine over his broad shoul-

ders, a sword in a jeweled scabbard buckled around his waist. On his plump white hands he wore rings set with diamonds and lapis lazuli and bloodred rubies. He regarded the three royal princesses, whose names were Branimira, Danjana, and Marica, and he said, "Tell me, each in your own way, how much you love me."

The oldest daughter, Princess Branimira, curtsied and smiled her bewitching smile. Simply put, she loved the king more than gold, she said. More than all the gold in the kingdom.

The king beamed. To be loved more than gold meant something to him.

The second daughter, Princess Danjana, knelt before her father, her long chestnut-brown hair spilling over her shoulders, and said she loved him more than the sun and the earth and the stars. More than Heaven! More than God!

Really? said the king, with a wry smile. More than God?

Yes, Princess Danjana said. Yes, she did love him more than God. She loved him more than gold and more than the flowers she would pick on her wedding day for her bridal wreath: rosemary for remembrance, cowslip for grace, and violets for steadfastness.

Graciously, the king inclined his head. Her reply, he said, was poetic; it pleased him.

He beckoned to his youngest daughter. "What about you, my child? What do you say?"

A father should not have favorites among his children. A king learned impartiality, or he should learn it. But he was human, after all. He loved Marica not more than gold, since gold was essential to the administration and success of his kingdom, and he would be lost without it, but he loved her *as much as gold. He had told her so, he was sure, on many occasions. Gently, he chided his youngest daughter to speak up. And yet she remained silent, her eyes downcast.*

At last, her head meekly bowed, she spoke:

"I love you, sir, more than salt," said Princess Marica.

"Salt!" repeated the king, his eyes narrowing. Her answer was like a knife thrust between his ribs, directly into his heart. His little Marica, his darling, his treasure, had betrayed him. He trembled with rage. His cooks, he said angrily, seasoned his soup with salt, and sometimes they used too heavy a hand and ruined his meal. Fishermen salted their catch to keep it fresh for the royal table. His groomsman put out salt for his horses and for the wild deer he hunted. Salt was everywhere; it was—it was as common as salt. It was nothing.

He swept his arm through the air. "Go," he thundered at Marica. "Your sisters have answered as royal daughters ought to answer. But you! Ingrate! Traitor! Viper! I never want to see your face again."

The Princess Branimira knelt before the king and begged him to forgive Marica. "She is young," Branimira said. "She didn't know what she was saying." Princess Danjana wept. But the king was adamant. He forbade Marica to take anything with her. "Get out of my sight," he thundered.

Marica curtsied to her father, the king. She looked up at him, her eyes swimming in tears. But she obeyed his command. Clad in only a simple gown and a plain wool cloak, with sandals on her bare feet, she walked to the castle's outer doors. She walked across the drawbridge over the moat and kept going until she passed the border of her father's kingdom. She was in a land she had never seen before. As night fell, she became lost in a dark forest, where she took shelter beneath a tree. In the morning she woke and looked up at the sky between the fir branches. Why hadn't she answered her father's question as her sisters had? Why hadn't she prevaricated? Because, she thought, she knew her answer was the only one she could give.

She brushed fir needles and leaves from her dress. She ate berries from a bush and drank from a stream. Days passed, and sometimes she couldn't find anything to eat, and she became weaker and felt her life ebbing away. At last, she lay on the forest floor, clasped her hands on her breast, closed her eyes, and said a prayer, thinking she would not wake again. But at dawn she heard birds singing in the trees, and everything was as it had been, except that a woman appeared and knelt beside her and took her hand. This woman wore a plain gown of homespun gray wool; her snow-white hair curled around her head like an aura.

"Get up," she said gently. "Get up off the cold ground and come with me."

And Marica did as the woman said. They came to a cottage in the woods that seemed to grow out of the trunk of a tree and had a twisting chimney with smoke curling up out of it. The woman took Marica into the cottage and bathed her hands and feet in scented water and gave her bread and honey and a fragrant tisane to drink. The woman's name was Apolonia.

Marica could not discern whether she was in the company of an angel or a sorceress.

In the weeks and months that followed, Marica learned from Apolonia how to spin wool and dye it with colors made from flowers and roots and the bark of trees and weave garments with it. She learned how to prepare a rich, nourishing stew from herbs and various vegetables and how to candle eggs. Apolonia taught her to collect honeycombs from beehives without suffering a single sting and how to milk nanny goats and how to plant beans and corn in long, straight rows facing east and west. And when the fruit in the orchard ripened, Marica learned to put up preserves. She did not know how long she lived in the little cottage with Apolonia. Three years? Four? Then Apolonia said she had no more to teach her; Marica was ready to make her own way in the world. Hearing this, Marica wept and said she would rather die than leave Apolonia.

"It is the way it must be," Apolonia said, placing her hand on Marica's head. She gave Marica a bag of salt, a feather, and a wand cut from a willow branch. "Whatever you do, keep these things safe," she said, helping Marica to wrap herself in a beautiful cloak she had woven for her. "Use these gifts only when necessary, or their magic will not keep, and be sure to take care of the salt."

Weeks of rain and flooding in the kingdom, she said, had caused all the salt there to go black with mold or to melt away into the ground, and now there wasn't a single grain of it to be found anywhere in the land. With the exception, that was, of the small store of salt Apolonia kept in a warm, dry corner of her cottage, and from which she had taken enough to fill the bag Marica now held.

Marica made her way back to the palace, hid her true identity, and begged for work in the kitchen. Her diligence and skill encouraged the head cook to heap more and more responsibilities on her shoulders, so that she worked from dawn until nightfall, carrying buckets of water, scrubbing stone and marble floors, and replenishing supplies of coal and wood for the stoves and fireplaces. When those tasks were completed, she mended clothes and dyed wool and wove it into garments for the royal household.

Every now and then, she would catch a glimpse of her father, the king, accompanied by his retinue of courtiers and physicians and alchemists. She saw her sisters, Branimira and Danjana, dancing to the music of lutes and pipes in the great hall with their dancing tutor. They didn't see Marica; she was just a servant in an apron and cap and wooden shoes—and no one saw servants. She ran back to the kitchen, where the cooks were consulting their recipe books, attempting to prepare tasty meals without salt. They seasoned the roasted meat with rosemary and thyme, with basil and finely ground black pepper. They added thick cream to the potatoes and sprinkled dried oregano and thyme in sauces. When the butler and the footmen served these dishes at the royal table, the king scowled. "Eggs without salt! Fish without salt! Knaves! Miscreants! I will have you flayed alive! I will have your heads on pikestaffs!" he roared.

The head cook lamented: "What are we do to? His majesty will have our heads chopped off. We must have salt, and there is no salt anywhere in the kingdom or beyond."

Marica thought, The truth is, the king deserves to suffer a little. He needs to learn humility and kindness. A king should not misuse his authority. But she loved him, in spite of his rages and his vanity. Moreover, it was obvious that he was growing weaker. Even Marica's sisters began to droop. People needed salt to stay healthy. A small amount of salt every day was crucial, Apolonia had taught her.

Marica gave Apolonia's pouch of salt to the cook, warning him to use it sparingly, so that it would last. Then she wrapped herself in the cloak Apolonia had woven for her and, taking with her the feather and the willow wand, walked away from the castle for the second time in her life. Many days later she reached the mountains and began the ascent, climbing up a narrow path. On her right were sheer cliffs and on her left jagged, cloud-covered peaks. She came to a place where the path divided. Which route was she to follow? She threw Apolonia's feather into the air. The wind caught it and sent it whirling higher and higher toward the heavens, and it was transformed into a magnificent hawk with a speckled breast and golden talons. The hawk flew ahead of her, showing her the way. When it settled on the branch of a tall tree, she stopped and touched the willow wand to the ground. At once the earth opened, revealing steps that led down to a salt mine. The air in the mine smelled of the salt sea and burned her lips with its astringency. Statues carved of salt stood in niches in the walls: kings and queens, saints and angels. She came to a lake rippling with light from a thousand blazing torches. All around, miners wearing hats with candles were chipping away at walls of salt. The vaulted roof of the salt mine rang with the sound of their industry. Salt was shoveled into carts and the carts were drawn up to the surface by teams of sturdy little horses with shaggy manes. Marica promised the miners they would be richly rewarded if they delivered a cartload of salt to her father's castle, which they agreed to do.

The cooks ran out to greet the miners. The bags of salt were carried into the kitchen, and the miners were paid with gold coins.

The king's physicians helped him up from his sickbed and wrapped him in a cloak of ermine and velvet, and, supporting him on either side, they assisted him to the kitchens, where the bags of salt were opened for his inspection. The cook told him that, to be perfectly honest, one of the servant girls, the most junior girl, in fact, was responsible for this miracle. The king demanded to see this servant. He wished to thank her, he said. When the servant was brought before him, he stared at her. In an unsteady voice he said, "Is it you? Is this you, Marica?"

The king got down on his knees and begged her forgiveness, which she at once joyfully gave. She helped him to his feet. She said his majesty should never again kneel to her or to anyone. Her sisters embraced her. With the king's blessing, Marica ordered the table set for a banquet. She invited the miners who had delivered the bags of salt to join the festivities, which lasted long into the night. The king proclaimed Marica his heir. She, wisest and most practical of daughters, would inherit his kingdom and his throne, he said. He understood now: she loved him more than salt, and salt was indeed more precious than gold.

And when the king had grown old and had passed into eternal rest, Marica ascended the throne. She governed with compassion and wisdom, and her loyal subjects knew her as the most generous and practical monarch in all the world. It was said she often worked in the kitchens with the cooks and every spring she planted rows of beans and, in winter, she wove garments at her loom for her husband and children. Her husband ruled at her side as her consort, and they and their children and their children's children lived very happily for a very long time. And so it was. So it was.

CHAPTER FIFTEEN

Natalia wrote to Miklós. She dated the letter May 22, 1942, Prague, and began by describing her circumstances and the house where she was staying, in the same street where Franz Kafka had lived.

Maybe, she wrote, *this is the same house.*

I have with me your mother's tarot cards. I am pretending to be a tarot card reader. It is not that suddenly I believe in the occult. It is just that I need the money. One evening two young women came to my door. They are cousins, Anna and Reina. They entered my house, those two girls, like beams of light, unstoppable. A journey by water, I said. A fortuitous meeting. Anna, the younger girl, gave me a look. "Well," I told her, "That's what I see. That's what the cards see. You have a special fondness for animals," I said. "You like knowing why things are as they are." She conceded that this was true. Reina wanted to pay me. I said, No, I haven't told you anything, the cards were not cooperative today.

A day later they were back, and this time they brought food. And what food! Bread baked fresh, with white flour. Strawberries that glowed like cabochon rubies. Cheese made at a farm near Zürau, where Reina's parents live. Kafka again. The Zürau Aphorisms.

Reina asked for a reading, I said, No, I'm not very good at it. No, you are crap at it, she said, and we laughed. I set out the cards. I moved them here and there. I said, "The Twins are a positive sign. And here's Temperance. Do you see how she has one foot in water and one on land? This suggests accord, balance, compromise. And happiness."

Three times lately, Miklós, I have set out the cards and turned up the Emperor, Ezekiel's Chariot, and the Devil. This is a sign of loss, misfortune, violence.

My hands tremble. I am always cold. I suffer tristezza. *Beloved, are you well? Do you have a safe place to lay your head at night, are you taking care of yourself? Where are you? I remember ordinary things, everyday life. Driving to Budapest in the open Bugatti, driving to Berlin, attending the Press Ball at the Hotel Adlon. Our apartment in Mitte, where we were so happy. The warmth of your smile, the touch of your hand on mine. The way you impatiently searched your pockets and briefcase for your reading glasses. That ever-growing stack of newspapers on your desk. The clatter of your typewriter keys when you were working.*

→··←

She missed Rozalia. That was one thing. Then there was the other: she was so hungry her stomach felt as if rats were gnawing it. She wanted a real bath, with hot water up to her chin. Another thing:

Mr. Nagy had not left Prague for Budapest. His health was deteriorating. He was short of breath; he described a sensation as if a weight was sitting on his chest, and this woke him in the night and he could not get a good breath. Natalia stood up. She paced one way and then another in the confined space. She said they were going to the hospital. He would see a doctor in Budapest, he said. Yes, in Budapest, of course, she said. But here too, right now, he had to see a doctor.

"No, please leave me alone," he said.

"You are like a child," she told him.

She went to Mr. Aslan's shop and used his telephone, asking the operator for the number and address of Dr. Schaefferová. As soon as she had that information, she located the doctor's house. It was a fine, tall edifice with plaster walls and an iron balcony and a white front door. Crossing the street, she was nearly struck by a black limousine flying the SS standard. The driver stopped and shouted at her. A man got out of the back seat and asked if she was hurt. No, she was fine, she said. He asked if she was on her way to see Dr. Schaefferová. This man, the passenger, was, she realized, Dr. Schaefferová's husband. He was carrying a sort of portmanteau splotched with paint and a collapsible artist's easel. He walked beside her to the door. He put down the portmanteau and opened the door for her. On the wall beside the door, she noticed there was a small brass plaque inscribed with the doctor's name.

→‣←

After leaving Magdalena's patient at the door to the surgery, Julius went upstairs and poured himself a glass of wine and stood at the door to the balcony. Every day he was driven to Schloss Jungfern, the acting Reich protector's residence, to paint a portrait of the man. It was not a commission he had sought or wanted. Today Frau Heydrich had told him the acting Reich protector would be late arriving for the sitting. He was at Wallenstein Palace, finalizing preparations for a concert in honor of his late father, the composer Richard Bruno Heydrich, whose Concerto in C-minor was to be the program's centerpiece. She said someone would bring him coffee. They were near a window, and Julius could see prisoners working in the garden. They were guarded by Gestapo with dogs. One of those men so cruelly stripped of individuality, clad in ill-fitting prison garb, subjected to constant surveillance and mistreatment, could be his friend Dr. Shapiro. The thought caused him to flinch. He turned back to a scene that seemed almost as improbable as the one outside the window. Coffee was being served to him in fine china on a silver tray by a pretty young Czech girl in a maid's black dress and white apron, with a fluted white cap on her blond hair. The men who had driven him to the *Schloss* stood outside on the terrace smoking. He set out his brushes and tubes of paint. Madder Rose, Venetian Red, Manganese Blue, Lapis Lazuli. Malachite. He squeezed Cobalt Blue onto his palette. It was made from minerals mined in Bohemia and—this was an odd story, odd enough to have some basis in fact, he supposed—the mines were said to be inhabited by ghosts. He believed it. He thought the ghosts were in the tubes of Cobalt Blue as well. He used the paint sparingly to give the Reich Protector's ice-cold gray eyes a touch of blue, so that, as requested, they conformed more closely to the Germanic ideal.

He worked for an hour, and then Heydrich came into the room, accompanied by his secretary, a plump young man in an SS uniform clutching a sheaf of telegrams and correspondence. They raised their arms in a Nazi salute and snapped out, *Heil Hitler*. He was occupied with tubes of paints and brushes and did not return the salute. Heydrich went to stand beside a lacquered occasional table. On the table there was a glass bowl filled with white rhododendron flowers. It was a terrible thing, to paint the portrait of a man you detested. Julius was forty-two. Heydrich was thirty-eight. He wore a *Totenkopf* ring on his right hand. The death's-head ring; the SS sword; the Iron Cross, first class; the silver oak leaves on the collar. Flemish White to highlight the high cheekbones, the bridge of the thin nose. A tincture of blackness had seeped into the palette, something he, the artist, had no power to control. Inspired by Hans Holbein's painting *The Ambassadors*, in which, depending on the angle from which it was viewed, a skull appeared, Julius painted a tiny skeleton in the folds of the window draperies. It grinned at him as he worked. Unless you knew where to look, you'd never see it.

There were days when he got home from Schloss Jungfern so depressed, he considered ending it all. The relief of giving up! Diogenes had killed himself by simply refusing to breathe. If it was that easy, would he do it? Probably not. How could he leave Magdalena alone?

He went out onto the balcony and looked down at the street. The woman the Nazi driver had nearly struck was walking in one direction just as Sora and Anna appeared from another. He waved to them. Then, in the kitchen, he rinsed his wineglass and put it on the counter.

Magdalena came upstairs and said, "Do you remember, Julius, the girl I told you about, who looked after Franz on the train? The most extraordinary thing: she was my last patient of the day. Can you imagine? 'Natalia?' I said. 'Dr. Schaefferová,' she said, 'I knew I would see you again one day.' She is now Frau Natalia Faber; her husband is somewhere on the Eastern Front.

At least, that is what she told me, but from the expression in her eyes, I think perhaps it was not quite the truth. She consulted me about an elderly friend of hers. I told her I could do nothing without examining him in person."

→·←

Why did people always believe in the wrong things? Anna wondered. They looked past the truth and went straight for what was not real and would never be real. Imagine someone like Albert Einstein or Louis Pasteur or Marie Curie believing in tarot cards. But then she remembered that Madame Curie had attended séances in the hope of contacting her husband, Pierre, after his death in a road accident. Anna remembered also that her mother, a medical doctor and scientist, believed spilled salt meant bad luck and a broken mirror foretold disaster. Franz sometimes teased Magdalena for being superstitious. *There are more things in heaven and earth, Horatio, than are dreamt of in your philosophy*, her mother quoted to him. That was Shakespeare, and Shakespeare was full of ghosts. Even if you did not believe in ghosts, they were there, in the dark, sometimes just visible in the corner of your eye. All the houses in the Golden Lane were said to be haunted. When she and Reina had walked into the fortune-teller's house, Reina had tripped over a pair of shoes by the door. The fortune-teller had put them away under a couch. Later, when she and Reina were leaving, Reina said, "Did you see the pillow and blanket on the couch? And that scrap of bread on a plate on the dresser? Someone else is there, in hiding. Perhaps a lover? I'm sure of it. And yet she is an enigma, isn't she, and so thin and pale, like one of Aunt Magdalena's patients. We should take her some food, don't you think, Anna?"

->··<-

On May 27, 1942, the acting Reich protector's car was hit by a grenade in an assassination attempt. The assassins had been trained in England and parachuted into a village outside Prague and were concealed in the homes of partisans in the country-side and in Prague. The assassination attempt went wrong. A gun jammed and failed to fire. The grenade missed Heydrich and damaged the car. But debris from the explosion, splin-ters of metal, fragments of the car's upholstery, had penetrated Heydrich's side. Emergency surgery was performed that day and his spleen was removed. Hitler sent doctors from Berlin to take over Heydrich's care, and it was expected Heydrich would recover. But he developed septicemia, which his doctors tried to treat with blood transfusions and high doses of Prontosil, a drug Anna's mother said had limited efficacy treating bacterial infec-tions. The antibiotic drug penicillin could perhaps have cured Heydrich, but while a small quantity was available in England, Germany of course had no access to it. The acting Reich protector fell into a coma and died on June 4, 1942.

From Berlin, Hitler ordered severe reprisals. Prague was sealed off; no one could get in or out. Prime Minister Emil Hácha was arrested and imprisoned. The former prime minister, General Alois Eliáš, was executed.

The parachutists who carried out the assassination took refuge in the church of Saints Cyril and Methodius. One of their comrades turned informant and gave the Gestapo information that led to the storming of the church. The two parachutists, from the Czech army-in-exile, escaped, in the end, by shooting themselves.

Franz said the parachutists, Jan Kubiš and Jozef Gačbík, would be honored and remembered long after Heydrich was forgotten.

The reprisals for Heydrich's killing continued. The village of Lidice, twenty kilometers west of Prague, was wrongly believed to have sheltered the assassins. As a consequence, all the men over the age of sixteen were shot, and the women and children were transported to concentration camps in Germany and Poland. Many of Franz's friends—students at the university, some of his professors—were arrested and executed. Workers at a Skoda automobile factory were shot to death in front of the other workers. In less than four months, two thousand people in the protectorate were executed. Anyone suspected of approving of the assassination—of even *thinking* of approving—was arrested and sent to the Mauthausen concentration camp in Austria.

Anna's father was questioned by the Gestapo at Petschek Palace, but he was released. Uncle Tomaš was arrested and detained. As an accountant who was employed in the Reich's administration offices at the Hradčany he was suspected of having supplied details of the Reich protector's itinerary on May 27, specifically the time he was to have been driven to the airport to fly to Berlin. Anna's aunt Vivian went to Gestapo headquarters every day, but she was told, pardon her, the same bullshit over and over: there was no information. Go away, Frau, she was told. She continued to work at her millinery shop, making hats for people who were, she said, without compunction or shame.

Why does God allow these things? Anna asked her mother.

I think God is not here now, her mother said. He had to turn away, out of sorrow, I think. It's up to us to help each other. She cupped Anna's chin in her hand and kissed her forehead.

If a stranger is harmed, her mother said, we are all harmed. If a man is persecuted, so are we all. You can pray for us, Anna, and for the victims of this brutality. But for the murderers, you don't have to pray. They don't deserve forgiveness. Forgiveness is not possible. We can't pretend life will ever be the same. The scars might fade but will never go away. For this, you must prepare yourself.

For Anna's mother there were two truths in the world. There was prayer, and there was science. Anna thought sometimes one took precedence for her mother and sometimes the other. Or rather, faith and science were two sides of one greater truth. One day not long after the reprisals had begun, Magdalena came home with three vials of typhus vaccine from the hospital and vaccinated Anna and Franz and Reina. Not because she believed they were in danger of being sent to a concentration camp, but as a precaution. Just in case. The vaccinations gave Anna and Franz sore arms for a few days, and Reina developed a fever. A slight fever was normal, Magdalena said. A little soreness in the arm was to be expected.

It wasn't often that Franz and Reina had a break from work at the same time, but two days after Magdalena had administered the typhus vaccines, they were both at home. Reina was still complaining of feeling unwell; she said she thought she had typhus. Franz said her forehead was cool, she didn't have a fever. He made her a cup of tea. Anna poured one for herself and sat at the table with them. Franz and Reina didn't seem even to know she was there. She saw Franz take Reina's hand and kiss her fingertips, slowly, one at a time. Better? he said. Reina smiled.

Anna got up from the table and took her tea to her room and drank it while she read *Madame Bovary*. She wished she could tell Dr. Bovary to worry less about Madame Bovary and more about his profession. Madame Bovary she couldn't comprehend at all. She put the book down and thought of Franz kissing Reina's fingers. It hadn't seemed very cousinly. It had seemed like something Madame Bovary's lover would do. A few days ago, she had

233

seen Reina standing behind Franz's chair in the living room, and Reina had bent over him to say something, and he had reached up and put his hand on her neck and he had gently pulled her closer. Anna had stared at them for a moment and then had gone away. She told herself it meant nothing. Franz and Reina had always been good friends as well as cousins. But she was the only one unsurprised a few weeks later when Franz announced that he and Reina intended to get married. He was standing near the balcony door in the living room and Reina was on the other side of the room. Anna was at the piano, practicing Czerny studies. Franz asked her to stop. Why should she, she said. He gently lifted her hands off the keys and held them, both of her hands in his. His hands were cold. He said it again: he and Reina planned on marrying as soon as possible.

Anna heard her mother's quick intake of breath. "May I remind you, Franz, that you and Reina are cousins. As you both well know, the church forbids marriage between first-degree cousins, for good reason. From any perspective, legal, medical, ethical, that is a preposterous idea."

Reina went to stand beside Franz. "We are not actually first cousins, Aunt Magdalena," she said. "My grandmother Eva was not related to you by blood."

"You are first cousins, Reina. You can't pretend otherwise. And in any case, you're too young to marry."

"How much time do any of us have? No one can answer that, can they?" Franz said impatiently. "Listen. I applied weeks ago for permission to marry from the Reich office. An application is usually rubber-stamped if at least one applicant is German." Magdalena said Franz was never to speak of this again. Anna stared at the black notes of the Czerny study, a cascade of black sixteenth notes that were to race down the keyboard, a phrase played *diminuendo* and then *crescendo*, and a final chord, an act of completion. No one, she thought, could keep Franz from doing as he pleased in this matter.

➤··❖

Franz and Reina were married on a June morning, at the church of Saint Lawrence of Rome on Petřín Hill. The air at that hour was unsullied, infused with light as the sun rose behind a thin veil of mist. Reina wore a blue dress, a hat with a narrow, upturned brim and a little dotted veil, and a double strand of pearls. She carried a bouquet of roses from Magdalena's rose garden. Before entering the church, Uncle Maximilian had asked Anna's aunt Vivian if she'd had any news of Tomaš. She said no and gripped Uncle Maximilian's hand tightly. She was very brave, Anna thought. When people told her how strong she was, she said she was hanging on by the skin of her teeth.

Reina's family had been unable to travel to Prague for the wedding, due to restrictions on travel imposed following the assassination. But Ivan and Marta were there, as were the owner of the bookshop where Franz and Reina had worked and some of Franz and Reina's friends from university, the same group that used to meet at coffeehouses to discuss poetry and philosophy.

Anna noticed her father glancing at the painting to the right of the altar, of Saint Lawrence of Rome being tortured to death on a hot gridiron. Being tortured for using the church's treasure to feed the poor. It was more difficult in this world, she thought, to be kind than to be cruel.

The priest presented Franz and Reina to the congregation, transformed by the sacrament into one flesh.

The sacristan opened the church doors and sunlight poured

in, and the organist began playing the recessional, the glorious, irresistibly frenetic music of Bach's *Der Himmel lacht! Die Erde jubilieret*. Heaven laughs! The Earth rejoices.

→··←

When Anna was younger, she had believed her grandfather's spirit lived in the sweet chestnut tree in the garden in front of their house, and Eva Svetlová's spirit in another tree, and in the tallest tree of all dwelled God the Father, God the Son, and God the Holy Ghost. In a dream she climbed the tree, and Reina stood looking up at her; she shook one of the branches. Come down, she called, or Franz and I will leave without you. We're taking a steamboat ride on the Vltava, and then we're going to Kampa Island for a picnic. It will be good, a good time, and you will miss out on it. Anna, listen, don't make me cross with you.

Reina said, "Anna, Anna, you have to get up now."

"Go away," Anna said, brushing a hand across her eyes.

"You were having a dream," Reina said.

"No," Anna said. "I was awake."

CHAPTER SIXTEEN

Mr. Aslan came to the house in Zlatá Ulička with some food and a newspaper for Natalia. He wanted to let her know of a new law requiring everyone who was not a Reich German to apply for a new identity card. The law gave her an opportunity to legitimize her presence in Prague, he said. It would allow her to obtain a ration card, and then she could buy food without placing herself, and him, in danger of arrest. She thanked him and said she'd think about applying, but she admitted to herself that the Nazis were never going to give her an identity card. If she went anywhere near them, they'd throw her in prison. She looked at the newspaper Mr. Aslan had left. *Der Neue Tag*, the official Nazi newspaper in Prague. *The New Day* was fit only for burning. Its main function was to publish lists of names, the same lists that were posted on street corners and in shop windows. The names of people accused of a crime against the protectorate. She always looked away from those signs, and now she commanded herself not to read the names printed in the paper. Do not read the names, she repeated, but she did read the names and she saw this: Franz Schaeffer, age twenty-two, occupation, factory worker; executed. His address was given; there was no possibility of doubt. She stood, she walked haltingly around the table, bent over, arms folded, thinking she was going to be sick. She told herself she had no right to feel such pain. He did not belong to her, that boy.

She walked to the river and thought how simple an act, to go into the water and drown. The water dazzled her; her eyes burned; her foot inched closer to the stone edge of the embankment. Then she thought of Miklós. She could hear him telling her not to do it. That's not the answer, he said firmly.

Franz was a partisan, a member of the home-front resistance, Reina told her. He had set up portable radio transmitters used by the parachutists to maintain contact with headquarters in London. He learned the codes, knew how to unscramble messages. He kept the machine operational. The partisans had no real training in counterintelligence or espionage; not one of them knew how robust the Reich's surveillance system was. How could they know the Gestapo drove around in vans equipped with radio-signal detectors? Even if they did know, they would have carried on with the resistance. And then, in a sudden Gestapo sweep, most of the partisans were arrested. "Franz was at work at the munitions factory when they came for him," Reina said. "They took him to the Petschek Palace prison. He was given a mock trial at a summary court and taken from there to the Kobylisy rifle range and shot. I wish they would get on with it and arrest me too. We thought fighting fascism in here," she said, tapping her head, "would constitute a form of resistance, a noble form, because then you don't get covered in their filth, you don't have blood on your hands, but we were wrong. We should have fought back with everything we had."

Reina pulled her scarf roughly off her hair, shook out the hairpins, combed her hand through her hair. She lit a cigarette.

At the time of his arrest, she and Franz had been married for two weeks. Now she was a widow. And Dr. Schaefferová and her husband had been taken to Petschek Palace for questioning. She kept reminding herself that her uncle Julius had been questioned once before and released. He and her aunt would be released this time, too, she said. She was all right as long as no one asked her how she was holding up, but it was very hard on Anna.

"Frau Faber," she said, "you look exhausted. I'll show you where you are to sleep."

She stubbed her cigarette out in an ashtray and took Natalia to a room at the end of the hall. She gave her a nightgown and a robe, and when she'd said good night and had gone, Natalia undressed and got into bed. Her head was full of images: Reina coming into the house in Zlatá Ulička and telling her she had to pack up and come with her. Her own hands shaking as she threw things into the suitcase she'd brought from home. Reina taking the suitcase and leading her through lightless streets to the tall house with its plaque that said MAGDALENA SCHAEFFEROVÁ. And then, as she remembered Reina unlocking the front door, she must have fallen into a deep sleep.

In the morning Natalia had the incomprehensible luxury of getting into a bathtub and using a bar of scented soap. She washed her hair and dried it with a towel and got dressed. How wonderful to feel clean again. But when she looked in the bathroom mirror, she saw a woman with a gaunt face, dark shadows under her eyes, thin colorless lips. On the outside, she looked just the way she felt inside. She went back to the bedroom where she'd slept. There was a bird singing in a tree outside the window. On the walls, which were white, there were watercolor paintings of Prague scenes. A white translucent vase was on the dressing table. She sat on the bed and closed her eyes, thinking of Dr. Schaefferová and remembering the first time she saw her, on the train to Prague. For that brief moment, her life and Dr. Schaefferová's life had intersected. And now she was in the doctor's home, and the doctor was in prison. She opened her eyes. Franz had arranged for Max Nagy to travel on a transport truck headed for Budapest to pick up a shipment of food to feed the German Wehrmacht. Perhaps it was Reina who had asked Franz to do this. In any case, Max Nagy had to travel incognito, hidden under burlap sacks in the back of the truck. By now, he would be in Budapest. He would be safe. Had this act of mercy condemned Franz? Had the Gestapo found out, and was that why they'd arrested Franz?

Reina said Natalia couldn't go back to Zlatá Ulička, But, Natalia protested, she was another mouth to feed, and Reina said, So what? Natalia tried to help in the kitchen, but soon realized that she and Sora were like two crows with one nest between them. She would start filling the kettle and Sora would take it from her and put it on the stove. When she tried to slice bread, Sora would remove the bread knife from her hand, saying Anna liked it cut thinner. "Show me how thin," she said. Sora's eyes were brown, her lashes thick and black, and her chin sharp. In her dark hair, there was a dramatic strand of white. Natalia saw how good she was with Anna. She chatted away to her about ordinary things without looking at Anna and without expecting her to respond. She promised Anna she was going to get honey for her, from a man who kept bees. "You know who I mean, Anna? He has that little Pekingese dog you can hear snuffling all the way down the street. His beehives are out in the country, where there are lots of wildflowers."

The days passed, and Dr. Schaefferová and her husband were still being held in detention. But at least there was hope. Anna kept watch, sitting on the stairs where she could see the front door. Then one morning, when Natalia and Sora were in the kitchen, trying to keep out of each other's way, they heard a commotion from the hall downstairs. Sora went to the kitchen door and listened. Then they heard Anna cry out, and Natalia followed Sora down to the entrance hall. Elli was there; she had her arm around Anna's shoulders. Anna was crying and trembling. Two Gestapo agents had delivered envelopes to Anna. Before Elli could take them from her, she'd ripped one open. It had contained her parents' weddings rings and wristwatches and her mother's gold crucifix on a chain.

"Anna, let me put them somewhere safe," Elli said.

"My mother would never remove her wedding band," Anna said. She ran upstairs. Elli, Natalia, and Sora followed her. Anna was crying and calling for her parents. Natalia went to the kitchen. She put her hands over her ears and kept saying, in her head, not this, please, not this.

Elli brought Anna in and got her to sit down, and then she went down to the doctor's surgery and returned with a vial of powdered medicine; she measured a few grains into a glass of water and held the glass to Anna's lips. Anna drank but fought the drug's effects, until at last she had to lie down on the sofa in the living room. Sora sat beside her. Elli opened the second envelope and took out the documents, death certificates for Julius Schaeffer and Magdalena Schaeffer, who were executed on the fifteenth day of August, 1942, at the Mauthausen concentration camp in Austria.

→··←

A colleague of Dr. Schaefferová's came to see Anna. He sat with her in the living room. He took her pulse and said she must rest and most importantly she must eat, even if it was only a piece of toast. He looked at the bottle of Veronal and said to Elli she could give Anna five grains, no more than twice in twenty-four hours, for no longer than necessary.

Not long after the doctor left, Anna's uncles, Emil Svetla and Maximilian Svetla, arrived. Maximilian said he wanted Anna to go home with him or Emil. Emil said he believed Anna would be happier with him and his wife, because she was fond of her young cousins, and then, too, there was the matter of his brother's atheism. What did religion matter? Maximilian interrupted. His wife, Teresa, loved Anna. Moreover, his house had the advantage of being secluded, set back from the street behind a hedge. Did Maximilian believe a hedge would deter the Gestapo? Emil asked. No, Maximilian said; he merely thought that Anna would benefit from a sense of privacy, and she could walk in the garden and feel safe.

"Listen to us. Are we quarreling? We must not quarrel," Emil said. He wiped his eyes. "Should we let Anna decide for herself, perhaps?"

Anna said she wanted to stay with Reina and Sora. And with Natalia. For one thing, how would her parents find her, if she left? Emil and Maximilian exchanged a glance. Emil said the decision could be made another day.

That night Natalia was in Anna's room—she and Sora took turns sitting with the girl while she slept—when Anna sat up in bed, and asked, "When someone dies violently, does the violence remain in their souls and keep them from going to Heaven? Does God forgive them? Are they innocent in His eyes?"

"Yes, they are completely innocent," Natalia said. "They are the ones God loves the most."

Anna said it was her fault. At the inn in the mountains, in

winter, a man told her how he killed people. Even children. "He said if I told anyone, he would harm my family. If I had been braver, I would have told my parents, and they would have listened to me. We would have emigrated to England or somewhere, and my parents and my brother would be alive."

"No, Anna. Listen to me. It is not your fault." Natalia held Anna's hand. She stayed with her until Sora came, and then she went and sat in the dark in the living room. The next day, Anna wanted to see her mother's rose garden. Natalia went outside with her. Anna picked dead leaves off the rose bushes and crushed them in her hands. Natalia watered the roses, and she and Anna began pulling weeds out from around the roots of the rose bushes. Anna knocked over the pail of water, and it soaked Natalia's shoes, and seeing this, Anna sank to the ground and buried her face in her arms and sobbed. But it's nothing, Natalia said, kneeling beside her. Anna got up and ran to the house. Natalia followed, carrying her wet shoes inside. Sora loaned her a pair of shoes, brown, with thick rubber soles, like the serviceable shoes Rozalia had the cobbler make for her. Natalia looked at her skinny bare legs and her feet in these shoes, and she and Sora laughed and then stared at each other in dismay, horrified at their levity.

Reina had placed votive candles on the credenza, in front of a photograph of her and Franz on their wedding day. Beside it, there was a studio portrait of Franz on his eighteenth birthday. Another photograph, of Magdalena and Julius, had been taken on the Ringstrasse in Vienna. There was a photograph of a young woman in a long pinafore dress standing in a garden. Natalia thought it was Reina. Sora told her the woman in the photograph was Dr. Schaefferová's stepmother, Eva Svetlová. Doesn't Reina look like her, though? Sora said. Eva died when Reina's mother was born. Dr. Schaefferová had lost her own mother, and it was hard on her to lose Eva too.

"She has a beautiful smile," Natalia said.

"Dr. Schaefferová thought the world of her. She was a botanist. Before she married Mr. Svetla, she worked at the horticultural institute in Troya with her brother, who was also a scientist, an agronomist, I think Magdalena said."

Natalia became very still. "Do you know his name?" she asked.

"Eva's brother? Let me think. Yes, his name was Nagy. Maximilian Nagy. Dr. Schaefferová's uncle Max."

Why had Mr. Nagy not said anything? Silence, these days, was a protective strategy. Protective on both sides. She knew that. Even now, she did not reveal to Sora that she and Mr. Nagy were acquainted. But what a secret! Then she thought about how Franz had helped Max Nagy without knowing the man was his mother's uncle. And yet, in their brief meeting, they had right away liked each other and Max, who was so wary of everyone, had put his trust completely in Franz.

In the evening, Reina fiddled with the radio dial, tuning in the BBC's Overseas Service broadcasting in Czech. They sat very close to the set, with the sound down low, crackly with static. The Red Army was retreating from German forces in the Crimea; the German U-boat offensive against British and American ships in the Atlantic continued unchecked; the Luftwaffe had attacked the Black Sea Fleet. The Wehrmacht had taken Sevastopol; Germany's Panzer army was advancing on Stalingrad; in the Pacific the Allies were sustaining heavy losses. *Generalfeldmarschall* Erwin Rommel had captured Tobruk and was in striking distance of

Alexandria. None of the news was good, although there were carefully worded reports of Allied bombing raids on the German cities of Cologne, Essen, and Bremen, and on the cities of Lübeck and Rostock in the north.

Reina said the Allies would win the war. It couldn't be any other way; their suffering, the suffering of the world, had to mean something, didn't it? Franz used to quote Schopenhauer: *For the power of truth is incredibly great and of unspeakable endurance.*

Natalia wondered how much truth could be endured. A little? This much? And then this additional notch, another turn of the screw?

→··←

One evening Emil Svetla stood in the Schaeffers' living room and, first touching his handkerchief to his upper lip, said he had something very unpleasant to say and they must prepare themselves. This house, their house, had been confiscated by the Reich and was to become the property of an SS officer. An hour ago, he had received this information.

"No one is taking my home from me," Reina said. Franz's home; her husband's home.

"Reina and I won't go," Anna said.

"When?" Reina said.

"Soon. You have five days." Emil said he would leave now and give Anna and Reina time to come to terms with the situation.

"Now he will wash his hands, like Pontius Pilate," Reina said.

"It's not his fault," Anna said.

Natalia could see that Anna was fighting to control herself, her hands tightly clutched together, her thumbnail gouging at the skin on her finger. Reina said, Not this, not this, and she said she hated God, she hated everyone. Sora went to put on the kettle. Natalia saw her stirring Veronal into Anna's tea, and then she stirred a few grains into the other cups as well.

At six the next morning, Reina left for work at the printing press. Later, Anna went downstairs to her father's studio and came back with an art portfolio of gray cardboard. She knelt on the living room floor, opened the portfolio, and took out a typed manuscript, which she gave to Natalia. It belonged to a man who had been sent to Theresienstadt, Anna said. Her father had been working on illustrations for the manuscript. "Read it," Anna said. "Then I'll show you the paintings."

The story was a moral fable, familiar to Natalia from her childhood. Salt had more worth than gold; love exceeded both in value. Generations of children cut their teeth on this fable, believed in its lesson, and yet spent their lives acting as if the opposite were true.

The portfolio held the watercolor sketches Anna's father had been doing to illustrate the story; Anna had posed for him as the Princess Marica. In the paintings, she was wearing the white dress she'd worn when she'd come to Zlatá Ulička with Reina for a tarot card reading. Her hair was loose and crinkled from her braids. She wore sandals on her bare feet. The paintings were beautiful, but Natalia hated to see Anna depicted lost in a forest, cast out of her home, foraging for food as the shadowy forms of wolves and bears lurked in the trees. The paintings were a father's last images of his beloved daughter and simultaneously a daughter's last memories of her beloved father.

Anna took the paintings from Natalia and placed them with the manuscript in the portfolio, which she closed and tied shut with red strings. She had started assembling in the entrance hall downstairs a collection of items: her mother's framed medical degrees and her microscope and stethoscope, her grandfather's onyx pen stand and his Bible. An illustrated magazine from before the turn of the century featuring an article on Anna's grandmother, "the first expert woman skier in Western Bohemia." A tortoiseshell box her mother had used for her hairpins and her gold hair combs. Her parents' rings and watches. Several half-completed canvases, notebooks, sketch pads. Franz's philosophy books. A play by Karel Čapek, heavily marked up by Franz in red ink.

Anna asked her uncle Emil whether the piano could be moved to his house. "My darling child, it is not possible," Emil said.

"We can't leave my mother's piano for *them* to play. I won't leave the piano." She turned and fled upstairs.

"None of us will get over this," Emil said to Natalia. "Little Jan has nightmares; my daughter, Elena, refuses to go to Mass. How do you respond to a child of ten who says she will believe in God when God believes in her?"

He picked up Vicki Baum's novel *Grand Hotel* and said now anything written before 1939 was like a message from a vanished civilization. He wondered how his sister's library had escaped confiscation by the Nazis. His voice broke. How could he go on living without Magdalena and Julius and Franz?

That night Natalia wrote to Miklós. *Dearest, when you read this, you will be at home. If it happens that we don't find each other again, will you, for my sake, remember how happy we were, how happy you made me? I have many memories and they are all of you, of your smile, your tenderness. My darling, you are my life.* Ich liebe dich.

She wrote a note to Rozalia and placed it with the letter in an envelope and addressed it.

In the living room, Reina raised a wineglass to her. "Don't look at me like that, Frau Faber," she said. "They're not getting the liquor. When this is gone, there's beer in the pantry. There's sherry, liqueurs, cognac in the credenza. Let me get you a glass of something. Wine? Red or white?"

"Red, please," Natalia said. Reina poured the wine, gave Natalia a glass, and sat on the sofa with her feet up on the coffee table. She abhorred her own instinct for survival, she said. The way she kept breathing, eating, sleeping disgusted her. She was no different from the sheep on her parents' farm.

"Didn't you say you had a farm, Frau Faber?" she asked. "I know so little about you. Only that you tell fortunes that miss the mark. Franz and Magdalena talked about meeting you on a train. I was quite jealous of you. I told Franz and Aunt Magdalena you'd be old and ugly by now, but you are beautiful, just as they said."

She got up and tried to uncork another bottle of wine and dropped the corkscrew on the floor.

Natalia picked it up and uncorked the wine bottle, saying that her mother-in-law had taught her the knack.

"I propose a toast to your mother-in-law. Here's to her good health." Reina took a drink.

She talked about the summers when Franz had stayed at the farm in Zürau. They would go outside at night and lie on the grass looking up at the sky. Franz knew the names of the constellations. When she was fifteen, she told him they would marry one day. It is written in the stars, she said. Oh, is it? he had said, laughing at her.

"*Le cousinage est un dangereux voisinage.* So I read in a Tolstoy novel." She spilled her glass of Cointreau on the rug. "I'm not cleaning it up," she said. "And neither are you. Anyway, I don't think I like Cointreau."

"My mother-in-law is fond of an herbal liqueur that tastes of wet moss and aniseed," Natalia said. "She claims it's medicinal."

"Do you have a husband, Frau Faber, as well as a mother-in-law?"

"Yes," Natalia said.

"Where is he? Not in Prague, I assume. In Russia? A German soldier? I hope not, Frau Faber."

"My husband is a journalist. He went to Russia to talk to the soldiers on the front lines."

Reina stared at her. She filled two clean wineglasses and gave one to Natalia.

Sora made scones for breakfast. Reina took an analgesic tablet for the headache she had from drinking too much the night before. Natalia helped Sora pack food from the refrigerator and cupboards into a hamper, and they went around the house looking for things to take with them. They lined up suitcases in front of the door. Anna picked hers up and started going upstairs with it.

"Anna, this is a time for pragmatism," Reina said as she left for work. "You are just going to have to do what we think is best for you." She bent to kiss Anna's cheek.

"Your breath stinks," Anna said.

Vivian Svetlová arrived and said they were coming with her, to her apartment. Emil had telephoned to tell her his wife, Adriana, was ill, not seriously, but she needed quiet, apparently, and he'd asked that Anna and Reina stay overnight with her, which, to her, was a pleasure, she said. Natalia and Sora, too; they were very welcome.

The SS officer arrived. He took the door key from Sora. He looked at the portfolio in Anna's arms and said it seemed a large object for a small girl "What is it you have there?"

"My drawings, from school," Anna said, not raising her eyes.

"I have a sister about your age. She, too, likes to draw and paint."

Natalia's eyelid twitched. My God, we look guilty, she thought. The door opened and a woman she presumed was the SS officer's wife came in. She stared at Natalia with her little bright sparrow's eyes and said, "Oh, look, Karl-Heinz, it is the fortune-teller." Karl-Heinz and the sparrow would live in the Schaeffers' house, Natalia realized. They would use the furniture and the utensils and sleep in the beds, and even though it was an atrocity and a blasphemy, nothing would stop them from doing this. You will receive good news, the tarot had predicted, Natalia remembered. Not the tarot; she was the one who had thoughtlessly made that prediction, she told herself, and felt hot blood rush to her face. Aunt Vivian took the portfolio from Anna and held it under her arm and said good day to the SS officer and his wife, who had gone past them up the stairs and could be heard in the kitchen, clattering around in her high-heeled shoes. Aunt Vivian had the bearing of an empress. She stood very straight and smiled at the SS officer as if they were meeting at a social event, a garden party, maybe, and at the same time she conveyed her disgust, as if the SS officer, with his scrubbed-clean face and immaculate uniform, stank, as if he were a pile of fresh manure deposited on the street by a cart horse.

At Vivian Svetlová's apartment, they drank tea, ate biscuits, and chose neutral topics of conversation, such as Vivian's hat designs, the fabric she had managed to buy in spite of shortages, and, of course, the weather, which they observed from the windows. Natalia felt safe there. Then, after a few days, she remembered that she had left Zlatá Ulička without telling Mr. Aslan, and she owed him the last month's rent. She couldn't pay him, but she could at least explain. On her way to his shop, a car pulled over; a man in a civilian suit and another in a Gestapo uniform got out, and the Gestapo officer took hold of her arm and opened the car and said, "Get in, Frau Andorján."

-><-

They brought her to the old bank vaults in the cellars of Petschek Palace. A Gestapo agent tapped his pen on a manila folder. He glanced at her and opened the folder and went through a few pages of a report she supposed was on her. She was told to sit on a chair in front of this man's desk, and a lamp was positioned to shine in her eyes. The man at the desk blew cigarette smoke in her face. There was a kind of humming noise in the air, possibly from a ventilation system. Another man came in, letting a door swing shut with a clang behind him.

This second man placed a hand on the back of the chair she was seated in and leaned over her. "Well, Countess Andorján," he said. "We are interested in why you are here in Prague instead of in Hungary. Why are you telling fortunes? Isn't that an odd occupation for a countess? But then, you aren't just a countess, are you? You are the wife of a traitor. Isn't that so? We know that Count Andorján is a Communist. We know he is a traitor to Germany."

"My husband is not a Communist. He never was."

They knew her name, her date of birth, her birthplace, the date of her marriage. It wasn't *information* they wanted, she knew that. They liked to break people, destroy their minds first and then their bodies. She was taken to a cell and left for several days. Then she was taken out and interrogated again. They kept repeating that her husband was a spy. A Communist, a Bolshevik, a traitor. Karl-Heinz came in and sat across from her at a plain wooden table. The other man came back. Or was this someone new? This is the fortune-teller, Karl-Heinz said. This is the woman who sits in the Golden Lane and tells lies for money, so don't expect to get the truth from her. The other man said, let me see your hands, Countess Andorján. Or should I say Frau Faber?

Do you prefer one name over another? He held her by the wrist. "Open your fingers," he said.

This was what she learned about pain: it made you unknowable to yourself. The soul receded, grew less, gazed dismissively on the body. She saw the fever in the torturer's eyes; the longing, almost erotic. Another SS officer came in. An appreciative audience, she could see. The second man spoke with Karl-Heinz at the far end of the room. A uniformed Gestapo agent took her out of the room, to the prison, where she remained for several weeks. The cuts on her hands healed at different rates, leaving scars. Then she was transferred to a prison camp in Germany, a camp for women, not far from Berlin. When she got to the camp, she was classified as a political prisoner and had to stitch a red triangle to her sleeve.

CHAPTER SEVENTEEN

It was night and dark and Anna thought the train was taking her to Theresienstadt, where she would be a prisoner and she would die, there or at another camp. But the journey continued to the border with Germany and then went on to Dresden and finally to Berlin. She was one of many Czech girls and young women being sent to Germany, at the end of 1942, as domestic servants or to live with German families, who would instruct Slav girls who had what the Nazis called Aryan racial characteristics to behave and think like true Germans. At the Potsdamer Bahnhof, in Berlin, a man came forward and introduced himself as Dr. Haffner. He was slight, wearing a tightly belted greatcoat, a fedora. He sneezed and apologized, saying he had a cold. By a small miracle, he said, he had managed to buy enough petrol for the drive to his home. It had started snowing again. He lived on the banks of the Kleiner Wannsee. He told her the villa had belonged to his wife's parents. Anna watched the wipers clearing snow off the windows. She had nothing to say. When Dr. Haffner reached his house, he got out to open the gates to the drive. The snow made it bright enough to see the villa's asymmetrical façade, a sort of curlicue roofline. Dr. Haffner closed the gates and drove to the front of the villa, and they got out.

Frau Haffner scolded her husband for being late. "You're letting in cold air," she said, at the door, and then, accusingly, "You're sick."

Dr. Haffner rubbed his hands together to warm them. "This is Fräulein Schaeffer," he said.

The Haffner family ate in the dining room; Anna had a bowl of soup in the kitchen. Dr. and Frau Haffner were the parents of six children, she learned. Like Joseph and Magda Goebbels, Frau Haffner proudly pointed out. The eldest Haffner son, Baldur, was fifteen and wore a Hitlerjugend uniform and bragged that he had been trained as a sharpshooter and owned a pistol. He did not see how Anna could be "Germanized," since she was a Slav, and it was not possible even to domesticate a Slav. Weren't they basically Picts? he said. The Picts were ancient Scots, not Slavs, Anna said, and he said, Well wasn't she the genius, and it amounted to the same thing.

The daughters were twins, thirteen years old, and played with dolls and laughed at Anna behind their hands. Their names were Bettina and Vera; they had small, sharp features, like ferrets. Heinrich was eight, Josef was four, and the baby, Paul, was ten months old. The children caught their father's cold, and Frau Haffner asked Anna to take their meals to them in their bedrooms and to rub liniment on the younger children's chests. Where are your own mother and father? the twins asked. Why don't you live with them?

Frau Haffner did not disguise her preference for her oldest child, calling him "her handsome boy," her "little man," although he was taller than she was, a broad, muscular youth with a thatch of light brown hair. His mother never reprimanded him when he bullied his sisters or pinched the baby hard enough to make him cry. She instructed Anna to polish Baldur's shoes, sew missing buttons on his uniform, and help him with his schoolwork. Anna saw his school reports; he received good marks, particularly in mathematics and science, and Anna suggested he'd benefit more from doing his own schoolwork. Frau Haffner slapped her face and told her not to talk back. "I can send you away like this," she said, snapping her fingers. Anna did help Baldur with his schoolwork, after that, and to show his appreciation, he yanked her braids hard, nearly ripping hair out of her scalp, and tripped her as she walked past him. He left a dead mouse in a fruit bowl on the sideboard in the dining room. She picked it up by the tail and carried it outside, to the garbage can. Baldur put wet ashes from the stove in her bed, which was in a small narrow room in the basement, beneath the kitchen.

At night, when she was alone, Franz sometimes appeared to her. He knew everything that had happened to her before she was sent here. The physical examination, the X-rays; having her head measured with calipers, her eye, hair, and skin color compared to crude charts. Then—and this Franz knew as well—she was given a card that stated she was suitable for "Germanization," and he knew she'd had to leave Reina and her aunts and uncles against her will and that she was in Berlin, in a suburb just outside Berlin, living with the Haffner family, who fulfilled the requirements of having many children, six of them, like Goebbels and his wife, and of having a firm grasp of the nation's ideology. Franz knew, also, that while she might look like Anna, walk around in Anna's body, speak with Anna's voice, the essential Anna-ness was gone and what remained was a stranger to her.

→··←

Dr. Haffner was not a medical doctor; he held a doctorate of philosophy in literature and had lectured at the Berlin University before taking work as an editor with the Reich's domestic press division. Anna served him his breakfast in the dining room, when the children had finished eating. He spent a long time polishing his spectacles and then squinting at the lenses and polishing them again. It wouldn't surprise him, he said, if the smudges were actually on his eyes, since his father had lost his sight to an inherited condition. And blind, of what use would he be to the Third Reich?

Every morning he ate one slice of toast and an egg in an egg-cup shaped like a hen, standing on clawed chicken's feet. He grimaced at his first taste of chicory coffee. He swallowed a small white tablet that gave him, he said, "some pep." In the past year he had lost five kilograms, he said, tugging at his shirt collar to show her how loose it was. He used to do calisthenics and run in the park near his house, but his long hours at the office made such activities impossible.

"Do you know what it's like in that cauldron?" he said. "No, of course you don't. How could you?" Every hour, he said, fresh directives came from the press chief, Otto Dietrich, and each one had to be studied, made sense of, and obeyed, which meant a volley of telegraphed memos, often contradicting previous memos, had to be sent posthaste to newspaper editors all over Germany and the occupied territories in the east and in Belgium, Holland, and France. As a young man, he'd imagined writing something Proustian, on a vast and sublime scale, but the lightness of spirit essential to creation had been truly knocked out of him. Self-pity, however, was inexcusable, he said.

He could not pretend he knew nothing. He moved the salt-cellar a millimeter on the tablecloth. "Sit down, Fräulein," he said. "You make me nervous." He said, one morning, that he didn't feel good about some of the things that were going on. He tried to convey a sense of what it was he didn't "feel good" about, without being specific. He put his hands flat on the table. Frau Haffner had joined the Nazi Party ten years earlier, he said, and her brother, Ernst, was in the SS, so he had to keep quiet. He had a brother-in-law who'd been in prison for months after voicing his criticism.

On the last day of January 1943, General Paulus and the Sixth Army of the Wehrmacht surrendered to the Red Army at Stalingrad. Out of a force of three hundred thousand men, only ninety thousand had survived, Dr. Haffner told Anna, and they were prisoners of the Red Army. He called it a devastating defeat, but Dr. Goebbels termed it a "misfortune." After General Paulus had surrendered, Goebbels gave a speech to an invited audience at the Sportpalast and said, "Let the storm break loose." He urged "total war," which would of necessity be a long war but at the same time the shortest war, the shortest path to victory over Bolshevism. These were his words, which Anna heard in a radio broadcast she listened to with the Haffner children while their parents were at the Sportpalast. Baldur stood at attention in front of the radio. His brother Josef and his sisters marched around the room. They knocked over a table. Josef jumped on the sofa beside Anna, and the baby, on her knee, began to scream. The parents returned home. Dr. Haffner slapped Josef and told him to settle down and took the baby from Anna. Frau Haffner, her eyes glassy and her cheeks flushed with excitement, kept saying what an honor it was, what a privilege, to hear Dr. Goebbels. Where there was no hope, he had given hope. "Didn't he, Andreas?" she said, turning to her husband for confirmation.

Baldur should have been there, she said, to see the young men who had been wounded in the war. Some were in wheelchairs, attended by nurses, but as soon as they'd convalesced, they would return to the fighting. "Their courage moved me to tears," she said. "From now on, we must all be as courageous. Total war means total victory. Isn't that so?"

Dr. Haffner was of the opinion that Anna should be going to school. Frau Haffner disagreed, but Dr. Haffner enrolled Anna at his daughters' school. Anna thanked Dr. Haffner, and his wife said it was Germany she should thank.

Frau Haffner volunteered at a hospital for convalescent soldiers. She sacrificed some of her cast-iron cooking pots to be melted down for weapons. When the Reich government recommended foraging in the woods for wild plants to augment the reduced food rations, Frau Haffner took Anna with her to a park, where they gathered figwort and dandelion greens and dug wild garlic out of the ground. None of the Haffner children liked eating these plants, and Heinrich gagged and threw up at the table, and Frau Haffner went into hysterics, thinking she had poisoned him.

A foreign laborer, a young man from France, was sent to the Haffner house to dig and plant a victory garden. The young man's name was Jean-Marc; he was eighteen. He had been studying at the Sorbonne, but then came the invasion and occupation of Paris in June 1940. His brother had been killed in the fighting. And now Jean-Marc was a prisoner, a laborer for the Germans.

Frau Haffner let Anna take Jean-Marc sandwiches and a flask of water at midday. When his hands blistered, she brought him into the house and washed off the dirt and applied ointment and bandages. He told her he had never in his life gardened or, for that matter, done any form of physical labor, nor did he particularly want to. His smile was gentle, rueful. Like her, Jean-Marc hoped to become a scientist, a chemist. She told him she had an uncle who was a chemist. She too wanted to be a scientist, she said, and Jean-Marc said, yes, that's good, that's wonderful, and they smiled at one another.

In the Haffners' pretty garden they saw a family of quail crossing the grass in single file, and a scarlet tanager in a tree. The trees and shrubberies in the garden were lush and refulgent, and then in contrast there was this patch of dark, newly dug-over ground. Anna scooped up some dirt and showed Jean-Marc its denizens: earthworms, millipedes, snails. She picked out a beetle dazed by the light; it crawled around in her palm, its wings trembling. Being so close to the lake, she said to Jean Marc, the ground was fertile, rich.

It was true: the garden Jean-Marc planted produced an exuberant crop of beans, beets, carrots, garlic, onions, turnips. These vegetables had a subtle, indefinable flavor, because, Anna believed, they had taken in something of Jean-Marc's goodness. She had committed to memory his parents' address in Paris, and he had memorized her uncle Emil's address in Prague, so that one day, *when they got through this*, they would meet under better circumstances. He had at first assumed she was a daughter of the Haffner family; she had quickly set him straight. She was Czech, she said. He asked about her family, and she wanted to tell him, but the words would not come, the words were forbidden to her. Anna, he said, gently. He bent and kissed her, lightly, on the parting in her hair.

→··←

In November 1944, the Royal Air Force intensified bombing raids on Berlin. Liquid incendiary bombs containing asphalt, magnesium, and rubber fell on Berlin, and the city burned. Phosphorus bombs ignited fires that could be extinguished only with sand, and there was never enough sand. People running from burning buildings fell victim to a second wave of bombers dropping incendiary bombs. In air-raid shelters that escaped a direct hit, there existed the very real danger of suffocation or fire, and Anna heard of people's lungs bursting from shock waves when a bomb exploded. There were days when the trains stopped running, and Dr. Haffner had to stay in the city. Then, when the air raids began, Frau Haffner refused to go to their shelter. She grabbed a knife from a kitchen drawer and waved it at Anna. She dropped the knife, and Anna picked it up and put it back in the drawer. Without her husband there to reassure her, Frau Haffner became terrified of not being able to breathe in the confined space, and wanted the shelter's steel doors left open. Anna closed the doors. They had a flashlight and some candles. Paul sat on Anna's lap, an arm tight around her neck, and Vera and Bettina huddled against her. They begged to hear once again, from the beginning, the story of the princess who loved her father more than salt.

The ground shook, the sounds of sirens and ack-ack fire penetrated the shelter. Every bomb made a different sound as it fell through the air, and then there were shock waves, and the air trembled, and in the shelter it seemed that the candlelight wavered and the torch Anna held grew dim. But in the morning, Anna opened the shelter doors and saw that nothing in the immediate vicinity had been damaged in the air raid, and they went back to the house.

In the summer of 1944, a Polish prisoner was sent in Jean-Marc's place to do the gardening. Anna heard from Baldur that the trees in the Tiergarten were being cut down to make space for food crops—corn and potatoes and beans—and she wondered whether Jean-Marc was working there.

Baldur was away for two weeks in Bavaria, training as a *Luftwaffenhelfer*, an assistant to the soldiers in the air forces. Then he came back to Berlin and was stationed at the flak tower in the Tiergarten. His mother was terrified that he would be killed, and out of fear and maybe penitence she tried to ensure his survival by fasting for entire days. She walked around with her elbows tucked in, a flightless bird, her lips moving without sound. She ignored her other children. Anna did everything for them. She combed the twins' hair and chose the clothes they put on in the morning. She had been with the Haffner family for two years and the baby, Paul, was walking. He followed her around; he wanted her to stay with him at bedtime. Josef had nightmares and wet the bed. She had to change his pajamas when she woke him up to go to the shelter. The British air force bombed at night, and the Americans bombed day and night. When the weather got cold there was no coal—not that coal did not exist, but the railroads between the coal mines in the Ruhr Valley and Berlin had been bombed. By the late winter of 1944, food in the Reich was scarce. Frau Haffner stood for hours in a queue to receive what was always an insufficient amount to feed a large family. At the table, she made sure her children got larger portions than Anna. Some days, Anna got nothing to eat. Did she think Anna cared? She said she wasn't hungry. Frau Haffner stared coldly at her.

Baldur, stationed at the flak tower in the Tier Garten, was at least fed. The flak tower was not what Anna pictured: a thin needle piercing the night sky, emitting flashes of citron light as its bullets raced toward the enemy aircraft. It was a substantial building with suites of offices and sleeping quarters and a medical facility. The antiaircraft gun was, Baldur said, the biggest in Europe. He was immensely proud of it. He didn't want to come home; he wanted to remain on duty. Civilians were dragooned into service to defend Berlin. No one had seen Hitler for weeks.

Frau Haffner kept saying the bombs were unnecessary because they were going to starve to death. She measured, weighed, counted cans of meat, ordered her daughters not to share even a taste of food with Anna. Her family, she said, was her only concern. She had spoken to the authorities, she told Anna, and it was arranged that she would be moved. Someone else would have to take on the responsibility of feeding and housing her.

"Find her a warm coat," Dr. Haffner said. "Give her at least a sweater and some wool stockings and boots."

"She has a coat. She'll wear what they give her," Frau Haffner said. "When she gets there."

A car came for Anna. She was driven to a building in Berlin, an office, where documents were produced, and a woman sitting at a desk entered her name on the documents and stamped each page with the date and added her signature and Anna was taken outside, and she waited on the pavement with a woman in uniform until a car pulled up, and then she was driven to a camp near Hanover. Not far from the camp there were homes with nice gardens and fenced fields, and it all looked tranquil and untouched by the war, and she thought—this odd idea came to her—that she was being taken out of the war and sent to a distant country she had not known existed. Then she saw the concentration camp. Barbed wire, dark earth. Low, mean-looking buildings. Huts with small windows. And the people she saw moving between the huts were SS or Gestapo guards. Or they were prisoners.

She saw corpses heaped up outside the huts. They were just bones with some skin on them. Anna looked away, but everywhere it was the same, and inside the hut it was almost the same, except that some of the corpses were still living. The hut was overcrowded, and yet every day more prisoners were forced in the door. These people, the newcomers, were being moved from camps in the east, just ahead of the advancing Russian army. Anna saw sickness in the feverish, sunken faces around her. The floor was covered in mud and excrement. Some women sat in it or even lay down in it, having no strength to do anything else. Anna stood, her back to the wall, arms behind her, fingernails digging into the damp wood. In this hut a baby was born. It made no sound; someone took it away. Later, Anna climbed into an empty bunk. When she woke, a woman took her to a place where they were handing out food, partly cooked potatoes, one half to each prisoner, and she took her half and ate it, shoving it into her mouth, trying not to gag.

→·←

In April 1945 the British army came and liberated the camp. Anna heard the soldiers shouting: *Sie sind frei. Sie sind frei.* You are free.

When the soldiers entered the camp, they said no one should be afraid, everyone was going to be helped. Anna heard the soldiers also saying to each other, Fuck it. Fucking hell.

The worst jobs, cleaning out the huts, for example, the British ordered the SS guards to do, without gloves, without overalls. The British stood over the SS guards with guns and said, Work harder, put your back into it. They made the SS guards carry the dead to a huge grave dug with tractors.

The British gave the prisoners army rations. Some of the prisoners ate ravenously and got sicker, and some died because their bodies were too frail and desiccated to take that kind of nourishment. Many were ill with dysentery and typhus. Medical personnel arrived, British doctors and nurses. They prescribed special diets, invalid food. Anna understood English, and some of the doctors spoke a little German. To her, they looked like angels. She didn't want to know what she looked like to them. Her head was shaved because of the lice. She had sores on her mouth, and she hadn't eaten for days, but she wasn't sick; she had been vaccinated against typhus, she told the soldiers. One of the soldiers spoke Czech. She repeated to him that she had been vaccinated against typhus. My mother was a doctor, she said. She liked the British nurses and watched with interest as they tended to people. They asked if she would like to help them. They sent her from one ward to another in search of a roll of bandages or a tube of ointment. The camp's hospital had been built by the Nazis specifically for men in the Panzer brigades who'd been wounded in battle. It provided the British medical staff with modern equipment, surgical instruments, beds, everything needed to care for the liberated prisoners.

Sometimes she looked at these people, these survivors of atrocities, almost with antipathy. They were so sick, so pathetic, so noisy in their suffering, some of them. She felt impatient and tried to atone by saying, Let me find you another pillow. Let me help you to sit up.

There was one patient in the hospital who never complained but just lay there in her bed. The quiet ones were the sickest, the nurses said. Anna helped her to raise her head, to sip from the glass. Take just a sip or it will make you gag, she warned.

This patient pushed her hand away. "Anna," the patient said.

Anna looked at her. "Frau Faber?" she said.

Frau Faber had no hair, and her blue eyes were bloodshot, the lids inflamed. There was nothing to her. Perhaps enough of her remained to reconstitute a viable person, perhaps not.

"Natalia," Anna said, and they smiled at each other.

In the weeks that followed the camp's liberation, the British army went house to house in the neighboring towns and demanded donations of clothes and shoes for the internees. Everything they brought back got heaped on the floor in one of the huts at Camp Two. Anna picked out a print dress and a sweater. A woman tried to pull the sweater out of her hands, but Anna refused to let go, and the woman gave up. You had to be like that in the melee, to get anything. She searched in a pile of shoes and couldn't find a single matched pair. People clomped around in mismatched shoes. They spoke in Czech, Dutch, Hungarian, Polish, German. A woman found Anna mismatched shoes, and she put them on at once. One fit, the other was a little too big. There was room for at least two Annas inside her new dress. Her hair was shorn, and her face had erupted in a rash from the DDT delousing powder. She imagined her mother could see her and was consoling her, saying it was all right, her hair would grow, and she must let the nurses put ointment on the rash, which would soon heal.

Every day, she silently spoke to her mother. The dead get buried, she said, and there are prayers at the grave, and the Kaddish is said, and everyone cries, even the British doctors and nurses cry. Today, however, for the first time, no one has died.

Natalia looked pale and thin, lying there on her pillow. But she would get well. Anna wouldn't let her not get well. She bathed Natalia's face and arms with a cool cloth to bring down her fever. Natalia's scalp itched, and she was afraid she had lice again. But Anna told her that no one had lice anymore—bad reactions to insecticidal powder, yes, but no lice. She changed Natalia's bedsheets and washed her nightgown in the bathroom sink, and helped her to eat. At first it took half an hour for Natalia to finish a small bowl of broth, but at least she kept the soup down.

Are the thermometers disinfected? Anna would ask the nurses. Are you sure this hypodermic needle is sterile? Where is the adhesive tape? Don't you think this patient needs a chest X-ray? She preferred being at the hospital to the hut where she slept, even though it had been thoroughly cleaned and supplied with blankets and mattresses.

A social worker with the United Nations Relief and Rehabilitation Administration interviewed her in an office at the hospital and let her know that she couldn't stay at the camp; everyone was being transferred to more suitable places. If possible, they were being returned to their countries of origin and reunited with their families.

Anna said she couldn't leave without Frau Faber. Frau Andorján, she corrected herself. But you must understand, Anna, that no one is staying here, he said. Some are, she said stubbornly. She happened to know that a school was being started for the Jewish children who had to wait for the British government to arrange for them to go to Palestine. If the Jewish children were allowed to stay, why couldn't she, also, attend the school and perhaps also go to Palestine, where she had a friend called Rosa. She could live with Rosa's family, and she could go to school with Rosa. It seems like a very practical solution to me, she said, looking out the window. Then she turned to face the social worker, who wore pinned to his uniform jacket a badge with his name on it: JAMES GRANT. He told her he was from Seattle, Washington. She pretended she knew Seattle, who didn't? She took the chocolate bars he gave her. American chocolate, she said disdainfully, and told him her grandmother, whose name was Katharina, had made the best chocolate in Prussia at their chocolate factory in Halle an der Saale.

The room where James Grant interviewed her was above the

kitchens, which were staffed by British soldiers, who cooked and baked from early morning to night, so that the smell of boiled meat and potatoes and freshly baked bread wafted through the building. It was the kind of smell that induced acquiescence, she thought, and she tried not to think of being hungry. James Grant moved his chair out from behind the desk and wrote in a file folder balanced on his knee. Three times he asked her age, and three times she gave a different answer. "Fifteen," she said at last. Her real age.

He tried to get her to talk by talking about himself. He told her he had a degree in sociology. His parents owned a department store. His older brother, Owen, was a captain in the U.S. Army. He had a pet dog. What about you, Anna? Any pets at home? She didn't answer. What a stupid question, she thought.

Did she have relatives in France? A number of the camp children were going to live with French families. "I've never been to France," she said.

"Any family in England?" he said. "Sweden?"

"Why would I want to go to Sweden?"

"One of the nurses told me your mother was a doctor."

"Yes," she said. "Yes, my mother was a doctor." She looked away. She let herself float out the open window into the June sunshine and over the fields until she became a mere speck in the sky. She thought: What a relief it would be, to be done with the me that is me.

->··<-

On a warm summer morning, James Grant removed his uniform jacket and hung it on the back of his chair. His hair was thick and straight, light brown with streaks of blond, and his features were neat, well organized. He had a lot of straight, very white teeth. He looked not quite real. If anyone qualified as a displaced person, it was him, not her, Anna thought.

"How would you feel about going to the United States?" he said. "An air force flight leaves from Bremen in five days. I think we could get you aboard. You'd be staying with a family I have in mind. A nice family. I know they'd look after you very well. What do you think?"

"I am not leaving here," she said. "I told you before; you can send me to Palestine if you want. I am willing to go there."

"Anna, you are not Jewish."

"Don't you ever listen to me? I have a friend in Palestine," she repeated, this time in English. "Her name is Rosa."

"But still, you cannot go to Palestine." He sighed. "Anna, you can't stay here. You'll understand when I tell you there are active cases of tuberculosis here. For that reason alone, we'd like to get you away. Germany is not the place for you right now. Do you really want to go to another refugee camp, a displaced persons camp? I don't want that to happen."

"Why do you care?"

"I just do, Anna."

"I can't go because of Natalia," Anna said. "We're going to stay together."

"I'll talk to her, then," James Grant said.

"She won't want to talk to you."

"We'll see," he said.

The next time she saw James Grant, he presented her with a pair of shoes that matched, a new pair of shoes. She took them out of the white cardboard shoebox and held them. "Do you like them?" he said. "Try them on. Let's see how they look."

She studied her feet in the mismatched shoes, one black with perforated holes in a swirly pattern, the other brown and too big, and thought she'd become accustomed to them. She bent and undid the buckle on the black shoe and the laces on the brown shoe and stepped out of them. Then, after a moment's hesitation, she slipped her feet into the new shoes. Never had she worn such beautiful shoes, not even from the Bata shoe store in Prague. She remembered that when James Grant had traced her foot on a piece of white paper, she had actually thought it was nothing unusual, that it was part of the UNRRA bureaucracy, another means of identifying her as a refugee, another paper to go into that file folder James Grant carried around. Nothing seemed too strange to believe. He told her now that he'd sent the outline of her foot to Seattle, and his parents had chosen the shoes in the shoe department at their store. She nodded, picturing this American couple she didn't know opening shoe boxes and examining shoes, trying to decide which pair would be suitable for a girl like her. A girl with nothing.

She got up and walked around, a little shocked at the sight of her stick-thin legs ending in these pretty shoes. "Thank you," she managed to say. She took the shoes off and tried to give them back to him, but he wouldn't take him, so she put them on again and walked out of the room, the old shoes in her arms.

"Natalia, you have to get out of that bed," Anna said. "If you lie there one more day, your muscles will waste away. You have to learn to walk again, Natalia," Anna said, "or you'll be in a wheel-chair or leaning on two canes, like an old woman."

"Thank you for your candor, Anna," Natalia said. She got her legs over the side of the bed and, with Anna holding her hands,

269

stood up. "Well," she said, after a moment. "How strange the world looks vertical."

⇒··⇐

James Grant gave Anna another chocolate bar. Dark chocolate, with bits of some kind of nut in it. She shared it with Natalia, sitting on a bench in the sun. "Is that it?" Natalia said, shaking the empty foil wrapper. "Is it all gone?"

Nearby, a man played a violin, and when he took a break he came over to where Anna and Natalia were seated and said this was his farewell performance. He was leaving in the morning for a displaced persons camp. "Do I congratulate you?" Natalia said.

He laughed. His name was Zoltan; he was Hungarian. He was from Keszthely.

"Oh God, I know that town," Natalia said, shading her eyes from the sun with her hand. "I met my husband there. Or near there."

"I'm not going back," said Zoltan. "Budapest is in ruins from the siege. What the Germans and Russians did to Budapest is an atrocity, I am told. I have friends who emigrated to Los Angeles years ago. They're in the film industry, and they're going to see what they can do for me."

"You're a filmmaker?"

"A playwright. That is, I'm an architect. I was an architect, and I got inspired to write one play, a smidgeon of a one-act play, two actors, lots of high-flown rhetoric, but eventually it got produced at a theater in Budapest."

"My husband is a writer," Natalia said.

"What is his name?"

Natalia told him her husband's name.

"Are you kidding?" He held out his arms, the violin in his hand. "I knew him, for God's sake. A long time ago, in Budapest. There was a group of writers, architects, musicians, composers, who called themselves the Elastics, and I hung around with them, and so did your husband, sometimes, occasionally, when he was in Budapest. By the way," he said to Anna, "do you know why we called ourselves the Elastics?"

"The shoes," Natalia said.

"Exactly. The shoes we wore, with elastic sides, no laces." After a moment he said, "I want to ask, and I'm afraid to ask. Where is your husband? Is he well?"

"You mean is he alive? I don't know. I'm going to find him."

"Yes, of course you will. I wish you luck," the man said.

Anna listened to Natalia and this man called Zoltan and leaned forward, her elbows on her knees, so that she could admire her shoes, which did not, thank goodness, have elastic sides. Every night she polished them with her skirt. She slept with them under the pillow.

A British soldier was playing soccer with some of the boys. They were all different ages and spoke many languages, but they all knew how to play soccer. People walked past where she and Natalia were sitting. Six weeks ago, they were in Hell and now they were strolling in the sun. How did it happen? People were remarkably durable and resilient. Maybe too resilient. It shocked her a little. She didn't know what to make of it. Perhaps on the inside, in the soul, in the heart, it was a different matter. She felt happy, and yet she also felt angry, all the time.

Once, in a group of doctors walking past, Anna saw her mother. Her crown of braided hair shone in the sun. She was wearing a gray wool-flannel skirt, a blouse she liked, and over this a doctor's white coat. Look, Anna nearly said to Natalia.

Look, my mother is here. But she knew that her mother was not, in fact, there.

→··←

"Would I be allowed to ask a question?"

"Of course you can ask a question," James Grant said.

"This is my question. I want to know, what happened to the guards?" Anna said.

"The guards?"

"The SS guards. The British army came. The SS guards waved white cloths at them, and they were made to work. They were made to see and touch what they had done. I would like to know what happened after they were taken away from here."

"Why do you ask?"

"I saw one of them shoot a woman."

"Oh, Anna," said James Grant.

"She was digging with her hands in the dirt, trying to find a potato or a turnip. We all were. There were no turnips, no potatoes left in the dirt; dig as hard as you could, you couldn't find a thing. One of the guards came over to us, and he shot a woman. I crawled away in the dirt."

She didn't tell James Grant what she had thought when she saw that woman die. She had thought: Now I know what it's like, when someone is shot dead in cold blood. Executed. This is how my mother died, she had thought. This is how my father died. And Franz, he died like this.

"Anna, what is important now is your future. Soon you'll be on your way to the airfield at Bremen," James Grant said. "I'm going to drive you to Bremen myself. I'm going to see you get on the plane safely."

"I can't go. No one can force me to go," she said.

He left and came back with tea and biscuits and a clean hand-kerchief, which he handed to her. He showed her a photograph. He was in the photograph, standing on a beach, his hair ruffled by the wind. He was with his brother, Owen, his parents, his sister, his dog.

She glanced at the photograph. So he had a family, she thought. Big deal.

"I have to stay and look after Natalia," she said.

James Grant said he would see that Natalia was looked after. He would help Natalia to reach her home in Hungary. Anna did not have to worry about Natalia.

A week later, James Grant drove her in a jeep to Bremen. She wore her new shoes and carried a new canvas rucksack, in which she had an apple and bread, a change of clothes. James Grant waited with her until it was time to board the plane. She was frightened. Her heart was racing; her mouth was so dry she couldn't speak. She got on the plane; this was the first time in her life she had ever flown.

PART
THREE

—

In my heart I was opposed to war as to any
other kind of murder. . . .
—SOPHIE ANDREEVNA TOLSTOY

CHAPTER EIGHTEEN

On the road from Hanover to Berlin, James Grant pulled the jeep over to let a convoy of American and British military trucks pass. The trucks carried food, medicine, drums of gasoline, carpentry tools, lumber: everything needed to carry out the occupation and rebuilding of a ruined country. After delivering their cargo they would return to port cities—Ghent and Antwerp—to take on fresh supplies. It would go on like this for months, for years, James said. For as long as it took.

The dust and heat made Natalia feel feverish. Had her fever returned? The nurses said she was well. They had packed a few clothes and toiletries for her in a cardboard box meticulously tied with a length of white string. They walked with her to the hospital door. The door was open, and she'd had no choice but to walk through it.

Hundreds, thousands of people were traveling on foot, on the road and in the fields beside the road. An inchoate dark line against the bright summer sky. At first the scene made no sense to her, or, what was worse, it made the most awful kind of sense, as if the barbarity of the last six years had been distilled in this last moment. Some of the people carried infants in their arms. Some pulled carts or pushed baby carriages or wheelbarrows piled with cook pots, clocks, violins, radios, blankets, a birdcage, and even, in one case, a rocking chair—everything left to them, the meager scrapings. The elderly leaned on their middle-aged daughters' arms. Small boys ran after the military transport trucks, hands out to catch candy and chewing gum tossed to them by the soldiers.

There were concentration camp survivors, slave laborers, prisoners of war, all going home to Belgium or France or wherever home had been the last time they'd seen it. Some, undoubtedly, said James Grant, were German citizens fleeing west to escape the Red Army. Many of the refugees were ethnic Germans expelled from the east, where they'd been settled by the Nazis. About these people, the Germans, Natalia didn't know how to think.

They came to Magdeburg. How many bombs, Natalia wondered, did it take to reduce a city to this state? All but one of the bridges across the Elbe had been destroyed; the traffic had backed up, and the long lines of waiting vehicles and people on foot, pushing or pulling various crude conveyances, began to look to her utterly static and remote, a painted scene from a chaotic, troubled past or a future gone terribly wrong. At one point, when the line began slowly moving, the jeep stalled, and they had to wait for the engine to cool down before James Grant could start it again. They drank the last of the water from their canteens and James unwrapped cheese sandwiches that had been supplied by the kitchen at the hospital.

Once they crossed the bridge, it took only a short time to reach Dahlem, on the outskirts of Berlin. They passed the pretty little train station, which had not been damaged and looked just as it had when she'd lived near Dahlem, she told James Grant.

American military personnel strolled in the shade of leafy trees. Everything seemed familiar to her and yet remote.

They stopped at a mansion on Dahlem's Cäcilienallee that had been requisitioned by the American army. A white villa, with a garage and outbuildings, a stone wall around the garden. A woman in uniform greeted them at the door. *Willkommen*, she said. Her name was Daphne. She was a British UNRRA welfare officer. In the kitchen she introduced Natalia and James to Gudrun, the cook. Gudrun had set the kitchen table with what she called an English tea: sausage rolls, buns, sliced tomatoes, corned beef sandwiches. Someone was playing a jazzy tune on a piano somewhere. Natalia sat with her little cardboard box at her feet. Later, after she'd had something to eat, Gudrun took her upstairs and showed her the room where she'd sleep. On the bed were a nightgown and a flannel housecoat.

James said she could stay in this house. She would be expected to help Gudrun with the cooking and laundry, and she'd receive a small wage. German women didn't always get paid for working for the Americans, he said, but here, at least, they were trying to be fair.

"Do you think you can manage the work?" he said. "Do you feel up to it?"

The laundry room, down a short flight of stone steps behind the kitchen, was equipped with a stone sink and an electric washing machine that needed only to be plugged in and filled with water. Gudrun found another dress for Natalia to wear, and Natalia washed the one she'd been given at the camp. When she did the laundry, Natalia wore a bibbed apron that wrapped around her waist and tied in the front. One of the Americans came to the door of the laundry room and talked to her, not that she could understand every word he said. His name was Mike

Rose. He was married; his wife's name was Gloria; they had two kids; he taught music at a high school in Milwaukee, Wisconsin. He played in a band and collected records and sang. She had heard him earlier that morning, in the kitchen, humming and singing. He sang:

> *Mairzy doats and dozy doats and liddle lamzy divey,*
> *A kiddley divey too, wouldn't you?*
> *If the words sound queer and funny to your ear, a little bit*
>   *jumbled and jivey*
> *Sing "Mares eat oats and does eat oats and little lambs eat ivy."*

One morning she got up too fast from a chair and fainted. An American doctor took her blood pressure and said it was low. He shone a light in her eyes and examined her hands. He didn't comment on the scars, for which she was grateful. She was anemic, he said, and advised her to eat red meat. Eat lots of everything, he said, and asked her whether the meals were adequate. Yes, more than adequate, she said. At the table the Americans told her to dig in. Obediently, Natalia picked up her fork. *Mares eat oats and does eat oats and little lambs eat ivy.*

James drove her into Berlin.

She saw men returning from the war, many severely injured. She saw small children running in packs, like wild dogs. She saw a dead horse that had been butchered for its meat, the carcass heaving with huge, fat flies. Beneath the rubble, bodies were interred; the stench of decay was unendurable. She saw buildings on Friedrichstrasse and Leipziger Strasse bombed nearly flat. She saw Russian soldiers. She saw German women made to clear the rubble. They wore dresses, high heels, some of them. They wore scarves to keep the dust out of their hair. They were guarded by American soldiers with guns, and yet the women could smile; there were signs of camaraderie.

Nowhere in the city was there a place for the eye to rest. No clean, straight lines, no right angles. Berlin had been gutted, pulverized. This was *Stunde Null*. Zero hour. That was the term she heard. There couldn't be anywhere to go from here but up, could there? Already the Americans had restored water and electricity to Berlin. The tramlines and the U-Bahn were operating; cabarets and restaurants and shops were reopening.

Messages were chalked on brick walls, scrawled on windows; notes were nailed to posts: *Have you seen my mother? Have you seen my parents? Where are my parents?*

"If you could drop me off," she said to James, "I could look on my own."

No, he said. She must not be alone in Berlin. There was a lot of crime in the city. Red Army soldiers stole from everyone. They stole watches, wine. They swaggered through Berlin, intoxicated, undisciplined and behaved without decency toward German women. It wasn't only the Russians, either. Mostly the Russians but not exclusively the Russians, James said.

Gudrun, too, had told Natalia about the rape of women in Berlin. In eastern cities, in Danzig, the Russians spared no woman, not the very young or the very old. The women were raped and killed, the men tortured and killed. That, she thought, was how it went: the conquerors took what they wanted from the conquered.

→··←

President Truman came to Berlin for a conference in Potsdam. Truman, Churchill, and Stalin were meeting at the Cecilienhof, once the palace of the Prussian crown prince, to work out the conditions of the peace. Mike Rose told Natalia and Gudrun he'd spent the day chauffeuring Potsdam Conference delegates around Berlin. He said he'd heard two generals saying that at the conference Truman and Stalin sparred with each other through their translators, while Molotov stood at Stalin's right arm like a well-trained dog. Mike had been there when Churchill toured the Reich Chancellery. Churchill had placed his hand on a globe of the world in what had been the Führer's office. Then he sat in Hitler's personal chair, after a British soldier had tested it to make sure it was safe. Wherever he went in Berlin, Churchill attracted crowds; people tried to shake his hand, touch his coat. These were Germans, Mike said.

Mike said being that close to Nazi rule, the actual place where they'd planned and carried out the worst evil the world had ever seen, gave him the creeps.

Gudrun and Natalia were sitting on the steps at the back of the house, and Mike was standing, smoking a cigarette. Gudrun had snipped a few sprigs of parsley and held them in her hands. In 1939, before the war started, she said, she and her husband had sent their children to England. Her husband was Jewish, and she was Lutheran, but they weren't religious. There was anti-Semitism in Germany before 1938, but with the Nuremberg Laws the Nazis institutionalized racial hatred; they made it an obligation. Even if Jews had been born in Germany and their families had lived in Germany for generations and had established businesses in Germany, or were doctors or lawyers or had sacrificed their sons in war for Germany, as her husband's family had, the Nazis said they had no right to live and work in Germany. Hitler said they had no right to exist. In August 1939, Gudrun and her husband got their children to England on a *Kindertransport*. Her little boy was only three then, and he was eight, nearly nine now, and her daughter would soon be fifteen. Gudrun feared she would be a stranger to her children, a stranger who had to tell them their father had died in a concentration camp. According to his death certificate he had died of heart failure, but Gudrun knew it wasn't like that. Her husband had been thirty-eight and in excellent health.

"I'm Jewish," Mike Rose said. "In the States, we didn't do enough. We didn't see it coming. We should have, we have no excuses, but we didn't see it. In 1939 a boat carrying a thousand Jewish refugees from Europe was turned away by the U.S. and Britain and Canada. That's something we should never forget."

Gudrun took a photograph out of her apron pocket. "Look," she said. "It's from England. The Red Cross sent it with a letter."

"These are your children?" Natalia wiped her hands and took the photograph.

Mike Rose said, "Your kids are almost the same ages as mine. They look like you, Gudrun."

"Elise, my daughter, looks like her father," she said. "She has his smile. My little boy's name is Henry. In the letter it says they're thriving, but of course it would say that, wouldn't it? They should be wearing coats in that wind."

Mike stood. He started to go into the house and then turned and asked if Gudrun and Natalia had heard the news. President Truman had delivered an ultimatum to Japan: unconditional surrender or an escalation in the bombing campaign. Hiroshi Ōshima, the Japanese ambassador to Berlin, had been flown to New York. It was believed he would recommend to Tokyo an acceptance of the terms of surrender, as drawn up at the conference.

"And the war in the Pacific will end, maybe," Natalia said. "And there will be peace."

She and Gudrun went inside and started getting supper ready. Gudrun drained steaming water from a pot of boiled potatoes and then sat with Natalia at the table, where she was shelling peas.

"When you see your children, it won't seem like you were apart that long," Natalia said.

Gudrun said that at times she wanted only to give up. Two years earlier, when she got kicked out of her apartment in Charlottenburg by the Nazis, she went to stay with a cousin in Berlin Mitte. She helped with the housework and looked after her cousin's twin daughters. Then, this April, as the Russians were entering Berlin, Gudrun went out to shop for food. She waited hours in a queue for a loaf of bread and some tinned beans and when she returned to the apartment, she found her cousin and her family dead. Her cousin's husband had shot the little girls and his wife and then himself. The gun was still in his hand. He had, Gudrun knew, been taking an amphetamine called Pervitin to keep himself awake at night, in case the Russians came. People did that. There was a big demand for that drug. She believed in his case the drug had caused a mental breakdown, because otherwise he would never have harmed his family. In Berlin there were suicides every day. People knew what the Russians had done in Pomerania, as they marched west. They had heard of the rapes and torture and murders. Gudrun covered her cousin's body, and those of the children and the husband, with bedsheets, and locked the apartment door, put the key under the doormat, and walked away. She should have taken her cousin's gun with her.

"At night I hid in the ruins. For a few days friends let me stay with them, until the Russians got too close, and I left.

"In the Tiergarten," she said, "there were dead SS men lying on the ground. It looked like Hell, like a vision of Hell, everything black and dead, the trees gone, dead animals in the zoo. Imagine being an animal in a cage with bombs falling and antiaircraft guns firing. Imagine. There was a boy. He had been dead for some time. A child, no older than fourteen, a cheap celluloid swastika pinned to his coat, no doubt conscripted to man the flak tower in the Tiergarten.

"Often I feel such shame. Many things have happened that I feel shame over. The Russians caught up to me. Even though it wasn't my fault, I felt like it was. I thought of throwing myself into the canal. But my kids shouldn't lose both parents, I told myself. It's strange, isn't it? When you want to die, you don't. Somehow you go on living."

"Yes," Natalia said. "Somehow you do."

"In England there's a nursing home for elderly Jewish refugees. Daphne told me about it. She said I could get a job there, as a cleaner, or helping in the kitchen maybe, or as a cook, and if it works out, I'll stay. I won't come back to Germany."

The living room of the house on Cäcilienallee had thick, richly patterned carpets on polished oak floors, elegant plaster cornices around the ceiling, brass wall sconces beside the fireplace. There was a Bechstein grand piano with a bust of Beethoven on it, a gramophone, a tall pendulum clock that showed the phases of the moon, and on a shelf above a cabinet, a glass skull. Beside the skull were opera glasses and a stuffed songbird on a ceramic stand. A bookcase held books by Heinrich von Kleist, Friedrich Schiller, newer authors such as Vicki Baum and Ernst Jünger and Thomas Mann, and, she noticed, a novel by Arthur Schnitzler—all writers that had been banned by the Nazis. There were the two volumes of Oswald Spengler's *Der Untergang des Abendlandes*, which of course brought to her mind Martin Becker on the train to Prague all those years before. Had he survived? She hoped so. On a lower shelf of the bookcase were gramophone recordings of Schubert, Beethoven, Wagner. *Götterdämmerung. Der fliegende Holländer.*

So this family listened to Wagner, hung romantic, sentimental oil paintings of peasants toiling in fields on their walls, read Schiller and Goethe, but also had a collection of modern novels, books that had been banned by the Nazis, right there on their bookshelves. Perhaps they'd supported the Nazis and perhaps not. Perhaps they deserved to have their house taken over by the Americans and perhaps not.

She got a cold stare from the glass skull. Once a curio, now—overtaken by the war—a horror.

A car turned into the drive, stopped, and two men in U.S. Army uniform got out. She drew back from the window and went to the kitchen and scrubbed potatoes and cut up carrots, and then, when she and Gudrun were having a cup of tea, Mike Rose came in to tell them that Lieutenant General George Tanner would be staying at the house. "Come and meet him when you've finished your tea," he said.

There were suitcases in the hall. In the living room the lieutenant general had spread a red swastika flag on the sofa and was sitting on it, smoking a pipe and drinking cognac. He stood, his pipe in his hand, and shook hands with Natalia and Gudrun and asked if they would like a drink.

"No, thank you," Natalia said.

"Yes, that would be nice," Gudrun said.

The lieutenant general's aide-de-camp, Major Stevens, handed Gudrun a drink. The lieutenant general sat on the sofa. Fair hair, a narrow, intelligent face, narrow eyes. A very direct gaze. "Your name, again?" he asked Natalia.

"Natalia Andorján," she said.

"Hungarian?" the lieutenant general asked.

"My husband is Hungarian," she said.

"Frau Andorján was a prisoner in a concentration camp near

Hanover," Mike Rose said. "I believe she's recovering well, now, though, sir. Isn't that so, Frau Andorján?"

"Yes," she said. "Yes, thank you."

"Good, that's good," Lieutenant General Tanner said, taking a lighter out of his uniform pocket and relighting his pipe.

Within a few days, typewriters and filing cabinets had been moved into the sitting room. Telephone lines were installed. In Bavaria, Natalia learned, Lieutenant General Tanner had been in charge of a German-language newspaper published by the U.S. Army, the *Bayerischer Tag*. Now he was assembling the equipment and resources to publish a similar newspaper in Berlin, a German-language newspaper aimed, it was said, at the intelligent reader who needed a little encouragement, a nudge in the direction of accepting a free, democratic Germany with strong economic and political ties to the United States. An American information control office was being set up on Milinowskistrasse, in Zehlendorf. At the former Ullstein Verlag building in Tempelhof, a printing press had been recovered and repaired.

The lieutenant general employed the glass skull as a paperweight. He played Wagner on the record player. He often reclined on the sofa, his feet up on the swastika flag—the modest spoils of war, he said—while writing rapidly in a stenographer's notebook. At first he intimidated her. She felt more at ease with him when she learned he was, in civilian life, a journalist, like Miklós. They were all journalists or newspapermen in some capacity, these Americans assigned to publishing a newspaper. She wondered whether anyone at the American information office knew anything of her husband, she said to James Grant, and one afternoon he took her to the house on Milinowskistrasse. A Polish newspaperman there said in German that Miklós Andorján had filed reports with the Associated Press from Stalingrad and Moscow and, more recently, from western Poland. Count Andorján had been with the Russian Forty-Seventh Guards Tank Division. In January, he'd been in Warsaw. Then he'd been in Łódź. In February, he filed a story from Poznań. That was six months ago, Natalia thought. "If you see him, if you hear news, any word, would you please let me know?" She wrote her name and the telephone number of the house on Cäcilienallee on a slip of paper and gave it to the person who seemed to be in charge.

While they were in Zehlendorf, Natalia showed James her mother's villa. It seemed strange, to be standing there, in the garden of what had been her home. She remembered the day in 1934 when they came to see Zita, just after the Gestapo had released her and she was recovering from her injuries. James Grant was watching her and she turned and told him how Zita had been imprisoned and beaten by the Gestapo.

"She had a compound fracture of the arm; her face was bruised. When Miklós and I saw her, she had a plaster cast on her arm and she was drowsy from the Luminal her doctor had given her for pain. My husband talked to her about hiring a lawyer. 'The lawyers are all Nazis now,' she said. 'Well, that's not true,' she added. 'But these days you almost feel left out if you aren't picked up and interrogated.'"

Natalia remembered Hildegard carrying a tea tray into the room, and then Beatriz pouring the tea and announcing quite casually that she and Zita were thinking again of leaving Germany to live in Buenos Aires. "You and Natalia can't stay here, either," she said to Miklós. "Not with the child."

"This is where my work is," Miklós said.

"You think you can file stories from a prison cell?" Beatriz said.

"I can't leave my mother alone in Hungary," he said.

"Bring her too," Beatriz said. "Bring her to Buenos Aires. The climate would do her good."

Natalia remembered she'd been listening to this exchange while she knelt on the floor, playing toy soldiers with Krisztián: Napoleon at Austerlitz, the French general and his troops fighting the armies of the tsar of Russia and the Habsburg emperor. She combed her son's fine, blond hair with her fingers. Firmly he pushed her hand away. Her beautiful Krisztián, with his translucent skin and blond curls, his stubborn willful mouth. The way he would laugh, his head back, his eyes crinkling. She could never punish him; if he did anything wrong, he made her laugh. Before he was two years old, he knew who he was. He looked sometimes disapprovingly at his parents and grandmothers; even Rozalia couldn't get away with a thing around Krisztián.

That day, at Beatriz's house, he plucked a French cavalry officer from the fray and carried it to his father. Then he leaned against Zita's knee and touched the cast on her arm.

"You must be gentle with Zita's sore arm, that's a darling," his grandmother said.

"As if this little lamb could hurt me," Zita said.

"It's time for his nap," Natalia had said.

They should have gone to Argentina that year. But Beatriz and Zita had kept delaying their departure and then when they did sail to Argentina, in 1938, it was too late for Natalia and Miklós. They couldn't leave Rozalia. They couldn't leave the castle, which held so many memories of their son. It pained her, to think that if they had left, maybe Krisztián would not have contracted a fatal illness. And Miklós would not have gone into a war zone. She would not have been sent to a concentration camp, and right now, at this moment, she and her husband would not be separated.

James asked her if she was all right. He got her to move into the shade of a tree. He gave her his parents' address in Seattle. "If you would like to write to Anna," he said.

"Yes, I would like to do that," she said, putting the folded slip of paper in her dress pocket.

"There's something I should tell you," she said, as they walked back to his car. "Perhaps you know already that Anna has family in Prague? I believe she has grandparents in Heidelberg as well. Her father's parents; they're German. And there was an uncle and his family, also in Heidelberg. Did Anna tell you about them?"

"No," James said. He stopped. "I'm shocked. As far as we knew, she had no relatives living. I don't know what to say. It's my fault. I feel horribly negligent."

"Anna went through too much and doesn't know who to trust. If I'm in Prague again, I could give Anna's relatives your address, if that's all right."

"Yes, please, give them my address. I'll try to get in touch with Anna's family in Heidelberg."

Something else James Grant did, to help in her search for her husband, was to take her to visit hospital wards set up in requisitioned private homes in Spandau, in Charlottenburg, but she did not see her husband's name on any hospital lists or in any of the wards. At the Haus des Rundfunks, the broadcasting center on Masurenallee, on the day of a conference held by the *Kulturbund zur demokratischen Erneuerung Deutschlands*, an alliance formed to encourage a cultural revival and a free press in a democratic Germany, she stood near the door and watched. Everyone was there: writers, journalists, playwrights, actors, artists, many of whom had returned from years of self-imposed exile in Switzerland or Britain or the United States. Everyone except Miklós. Her searches seemed futile, but she was not going to give up. She had tried to phone Rozalia, but the phone lines in Hungary were only slowly being repaired, after having been destroyed in the war. Finally, she got through to the postmaster in the village. Yes, he said, yes, of course he remembered her. The army had only a few days earlier got the telephone lines to the village in place; he had just got service back. How are you, Countess? he said. He would be happy to give her message to the dowager countess. No, he had not seen Count Andorján. She gave him the number where she could be reached, so that he could call her if he had any kind of news.

James Grant called his parents in Seattle. He spoke to them and then handed the phone to Natalia. Anna came on the line.

"Are you doing well, Natalia? Are you getting stronger now?" Anna said.

"Yes, thank you," she said. "How are you, Anna? How is America?" She held the receiver tightly; how good it was to hear Anna's voice.

"America is okay," Anna said. "I've really only seen Seattle, but it's nice." She had a new bike, red, with white handle-grips and a basket she could carry her books in. But she thought she was obviously too old for a bike like that. She would prefer to walk or take a bus. In America, she would be starting school. They wanted to put her with kids a year younger until her English improved and she got used to doing schoolwork again. She was afraid the other kids would laugh at her, and anyway, she hadn't forgotten what she'd learned and would just have to show them she belonged in her proper year, with kids her age. After she said goodbye to Anna, Natalia handed the phone to James. She went to the kitchen and begged a cigarette from Gudrun and sat down with a cup of coffee.

→··←

Gudrun opened the doors to a wardrobe in the bedroom where she was sleeping and took out a blue silk dress. She held it against herself, smoothing the folds of the skirt.

"Go on, take it," Gudrun urged Natalia. "It's good quality. She had taste, whoever she was." Gudrun put the dress on the bed and tried on a skirt and a blouse and then a jacket. "Does this jacket go with the skirt?" she asked, doing up the buttons. "Maybe not. Still, I can wear it when I go to England. What do you think, Natalia?"

"Yes, the color suits you," Natalia said.

"It smells of camphor, but never mind," Gudrun said. "I'll wear it tonight. We're going out to a nightclub."

"I'm not going," Natalia said. "What would I do at a nightclub?"

"Yes, you are. Here's a dress that should fit you. I'm not going alone."

Mike Rose drove them in the lieutenant general's new car, a supercharged Mercedes coupe "borrowed" from a former Nazi. The nightclub, run by the Americans and called the Rio Grande, was in the cellar of a building that had suffered a lot of bomb damage. It was hot down there and noisy and smoke-filled, and they shared a long table with three GIs. There was a saxophonist and a piano player and a drummer. The lieutenant general offered Gudrun and Natalia cigarettes. Major Stevens brought a plate of food to the table, flat bread, little dry-looking sausages.

"Horse meat," one of the Americans said.

"How do you know that?" someone asked.

The American shrugged and said, What the hell, and took two sausages. A friend of his came to their table and asked Gudrun for a dance. "Yes, okay," she said.

292

Soon the others got up to dance. George Tanner asked Natalia if he could get her a drink. "No, thank you," she said. "I'm fine." He went to the bar and came back with a beer for himself and a glass of white wine for her. She felt annoyed and grateful at the same time. She let the glass sit there, untouched.

"When my brother and I were young," he said, "our parents brought us to Europe on vacation. This would have been the summer of 1921 and again in 1923. The first trip, I was thirteen—an impressionable age—and everything I saw impressed me deeply. We stayed in Paris for three weeks and then visited Belgium, Germany, and Switzerland. When I finished university, I lived for a year in Paris. I wanted to see Budapest but never got there. Tell me about your life in Hungary."

"Well, we live in a castle. Picture a French château. That's what it looks like. It has a cellar full of bones. Skeletons."

"What?" George said, laughing.

"We grow grapes and wheat and barley and raise horses that are directly descended from the horses of Andalusia kept in the private stables of the Habsburgs in Vienna, according to my mother-in-law. In the spring, when a foal is born, my mother-in-law takes a bottle of plum wine to the stables, and she and the groomsman and the stable hands toast the health of the foal. We have a school on the estate. A kindergarten, really."

A fight had broken out on the dance floor. A soldier had punched another soldier in the nose, and there was a lot of blood. A crowd gathered, and men separated the combatants. A janitor with a bucket and mop was summoned to scrub the floor. The dancing went on, and the saxophonist played a solo, something dolorous, smoky, like the atmosphere. Americans held German women in their arms and drew them closer, and they kissed. It was like a film, Natalia thought. One of those Dadaist films she

293

and Martin Becker used to like so well. Soon the camera would follow the couples out into the night. They would find a place, a room somewhere or a sheltered spot beneath a tree, to make love. All over Berlin it was like that.

"Go on, have a dance," Gudrun said, leaning over to touch Natalia's arm. Gudrun was drinking crème de menthe; her mouth was green.

->··<-

Natalia got permission from the lieutenant general to telephone Beatriz in Buenos Aires. She listened as a Spanish-speaking operator spoke to a woman Natalia didn't know, a servant, perhaps. She had a call for Beatriz Faber, the operator said to this woman, and then Beatriz was on the line.

"Can you hear me, Mother? It's Natalia. This is Natalia. Can you hear me?"

"Don't shout, please," her mother said briskly. "Who did you say you were? You aren't Natalia. My daughter is dead. She's been dead for three years."

"Mother," Natalia said. "I'm in Dahlem."

"Hold on a moment."

Natalia heard her mother speaking to someone.

"Mother, for God's sake. It's me, Natalia."

"Natalia? Is it you? We thought you were dead. I had Masses said for you. Wait a minute. Zita wants to know if Miklós is with you."

"No, he's not here," Natalia said. "Mother, I need your help. Can you send me some money? I have nothing, only what I get doing laundry for the Americans."

"Listen, you and Miklós must get on a ship to Buenos Aires. Every day Nazis are coming to South America. Did you know that?

They get as far as Spain, and someone takes their money and gets them passage on a steamer. The Rat Line. That's what the newspapers call it."

"I can't leave Berlin, not yet," Natalia said. "But I still need money."

She'd ask at her bank, Beatriz said. The bank would know what to do. She took the address and the telephone number where she could reach Natalia.

"Is our house still there, in Zehlendorf? Have you seen it?"

"Yes," Natalia said. "It's still there."

"Now listen to me. I will send money, but you must use it to come here. You and Miklós. You have to promise me, right now."

"Yes, I promise."

Beatriz kept her word. She telephoned to let Natalia know she had to open an account at the Deutsche Bank. The Deutsche Bank operated under the authority of the United States Department of the Treasury, and George vouched for her, providing proof of her identity, her address, and employment. When the funds were deposited in the new account, he drove her to the bank and stood at her side as she completed the paperwork.

She withdrew some cash and later gave some of it, nearly half, to the priest at a bombed church in Berlin.

—❖—

Natalia was in the laundry room, measuring bleach into the washing machine, her face turned away to avoid the fumes, when Lieutenant General Tanner appeared at the door and said he'd like to speak to her. George, she meant. They had graduated to first-name terms.

"Yes?" she said.

"Not here. In my office," he said. He held the door open, waiting. She screwed the top back on the bleach bottle and put it on a shelf. She removed her apron and hung it on a hook near the sink. In his office, the lieutenant general sat on the edge of his desk. He fiddled with the glass skull and then put it down on the papers. Another man came in and was introduced to her as Nigel Thorpe, a British newspaperman with the *Manchester Guardian*. What is going on here? Natalia thought. She watched as Nigel Thorpe placed a satchel on the floor near the hearth.

George Tanner cleared his throat. "Frau Andorján," he said. "Frau Andorján, your husband, Count Andorján, died on or about April 5, as a result of a motor vehicle accident, on a road near a village on the Polish side of the Oder River."

Nigel Thorpe picked up his satchel and withdrew from it a bulky envelope. He came over to Natalia and gave it to her. She opened the envelope, which was unsealed. Inside there was a wallet, which she took out and opened. It contained two items: her husband's press card and a photograph of Natalia.

Two GIs were clattering down the hall. One said, "Man, it cost me forty bucks and two packs of cigarettes for a bottle of whiskey, can you believe it?"

Major Stevens closed the door.

Nigel Thorpe said he'd met a Russian journalist at a café in Berlin. The Russian told him of being in a village in Poland near the Oder River. He'd witnessed an accident. The Soviet Marshal Georgy Zhukov, had moved in with his unit, and there was a lot of activity. The weather was bad, and a truck skidded on a patch of snow and ice and hit a man walking on the road. He died instantly. He was identified by the press card in his wallet. Some of the villagers buried him. They gave his coat and wallet to a priest, and the priest gave the wallet to the Russian journalist, who was on his way to Berlin, thinking he might meet someone there who knew the owner of the press card.

Natalia slipped the photograph into her pocket. She left the wallet and the envelope on the desk and walked out of the room. She went through the kitchen and out to the garden. She took the photograph out of her pocket. She was nineteen, in a beaded shawl and long skirt, in Trieste. *The city that sheltered us.* She refused to cry; the wallet in itself was hardly conclusive. For fifteen years she had been married to a newspaperman. She knew what gave a report veracity, and this report of an accident involving her husband had, she told herself, no veracity.

Between us and heaven or hell there is only life, which is the frailest thing in the world. That was Pascal, she thought.

She wouldn't let Gudrun or anyone else offer sympathy. She was okay, she kept repeating, until she was sick of the words. She just wanted to get on with the laundry.

When he got home to the States, Mike Rose said, he was going to tune up his Chevrolet and trade it in for a new car, a Buick. Not new, but newer than the Chevy. He talked about his kids, the one who did well in the school, and the one who liked sports better than studying. She knew he was trying to distract her, and she was grateful, because sometimes it worked. They were all very kind to her. George told her they were hiring someone to take over the laundry. She admitted that, yes, she got tired, and she had burned her hand once, clumsily, on the iron, but she would rather do the laundry than sit alone with her thoughts. Did they want her to leave? she asked.

"No, we don't want you to leave," George said. "Of course not.

Why would we?" As it happened, he said, he needed an assistant in his office. Would she be interested? He needed someone to proofread and type up articles that were to be translated from English to German, for publication in the U.S. Army's German-language newspaper, *Neue Zeitung*. Yes, she would like to type up those articles, she said; she would like to give it a try at least. George smiled and said, when she was ready, they would get started, then.

→··←

The new laundress was Martha, a seventeen-year-old with a pallid face and gray eyes, hostile eyes; she never smiled. Martha didn't like Natalia, and Natalia didn't care for Martha, but it was almost refreshing to encounter something no more lethal than ordinary human antipathy. The new cook, Helga, was brisk and efficient. Helga's twenty-year-old son had been killed at Stalingrad in 1943. Her husband had been blinded by a shell explosion at Verdun in 1918.

Natalia was beginning to learn of events in Hungary during the last year of the war. In October the regent, Miklós Horthy, had tried to negotiate an armistice with the Allies. The Nazis then kidnapped his son, locked Horthy up in Bavaria, where he remained imprisoned, and placed the fascist Arrow Cross Party in control of Hungary. This gave Hitler what he was desperate to get hold of: the oil fields near Lake Balaton. It allowed Eichmann to begin the brutal mass transportation of Hungarian Jews to concentration camps. She heard from the Americans about the siege of Budapest. The Hungarians and the Russians fought the Waffen-SS on the streets of Budapest and the Luftwaffe and the Soviet air force carried on relentless bombing campaigns.

The civilian population sought refuge in the caves beneath Buda Castle, which had been equipped with a functional hospital staffed with doctors and nurses. Food became scarce, down there in the caves, by the end, and people were starving. God knows how many died during the siege. She remembered Max Nagy and wondered whether he'd survived.

She rinsed her teacup in the sink and went to the sitting room, where George was at his desk. He lit a cigarette and handed her a folder full of newspaper articles.

She sat at the typewriter and got to work, proofreading stories that had been translated from English to German. She recognized propaganda when she read it. George said it was called reeducation, not propaganda. Newspapers, Miklós always said, had an obligation to use their power responsibly, because truth and lies could be equally persuasive in print, if presented with authority. The same message repeated in the newspaper, in the editorial column, and on the front page began to seem true, even if untrue and completely without merit.

"Germany was a liberal democracy before Hitler, you know," she said to George Greaves. "Even before the Weimar Republic, Bismarck brought in accident insurance, medical insurance, laws protecting workers' rights. People here aren't as uninformed as you think."

"They aren't uninformed, but they're traumatized," he said.

"Not so traumatized they won't sneer at propaganda," she said.

He raised an eyebrow at her.

On one side there was democracy and on the other communism, he said. Truman and Stalin each had a corner of Germany in his hands, and they were pulling hard in opposing directions.

"The Americans should feed people, then, instead of starving them," Natalia said. "The Russians are shipping food to Berlin, meat and grain and vegetables. They bake fresh bread every day and give it out free. Eisenhower is saying Germans should be punished by going hungry. Do you see the difference? You know what Stalin says? He says dictators like Hitler come and go, but the German people will remain forever. That, frankly, is what people want to hear."

Silence from George. And then he said, mildly, "I expect you're right."

She bent over her work. The typewriter was a Mercedes. Miklós owned both a Mercedes typewriter and a Mercedes car, not quite as grand or as new as the one the lieutenant general drove. She liked the Bugatti, but it was old, an old car. It ran sometimes, and sometimes the motor seized up. She was a sedate driver, very cautious. She had to be, because her husband wasn't a good passenger. Keep your hands on the steering wheel, he kept saying. Don't go so fast, he said. I'm not, she said. It had been what now, three years since she had driven a car, and that was on the day she left the castle to meet Miklós in Prague. She rested her hands in her lap, remembering.

"Are you all right?" George said.

Why did he and everyone else assume she was in mourning? Anxiety, she felt. Worry wore away at her nerves, it was true, but it was not the same as grief. She had no reason to grieve. Every day in Berlin, in Germany, everywhere in Europe, people were climbing out of cellars and attics after years of hiding. Soldiers walked for miles across muddy, ravaged fields, crossing borders obliterated by war. Somehow they survived, and at length, per-haps at the exact moment they were giving up—at that moment—they encountered a cousin, perhaps even a wife, a husband, or their own beloved child among hundreds of children at a refugee camp. The newspaper the Americans published was full of such inspirational accounts. James Grant, who went to the camps, said he'd witnessed these reunions himself.

George picked up his attaché case. He was going to the officers' mess at the Grosser Wannsee, he said, and would see her later.

Natalia proofread and then typed up a story about General Patton, the military governor of Bavaria, going horseback riding with friends. She typed up a story on the appointment of a college professor from New York to oversee industrial development in the American zone of occupied Germany. She corrected a pronoun problem in a report on a fashion show in New York: the little black dress in which no one could go wrong was back in style; skirts were longer; sleeves were elbow-length, worn pushed up. She worked for a while and then heard Mike Rose talking to Helga in the kitchen. Yesterday Mike had brought a dog back to the house with him. Its hair was sparse and rough, its ribs visible. He washed it and fed it, and it had slept in the laundry room. Mike named it Truman—no surprise there, Natalia thought. He got an army doctor to give him a salve for the dog's skin and something to kill the fleas. Helga complained that the salve smelled terrible and the dog kept getting under her feet. As if to prove her point, she stepped on Truman's paw and he yelped. Mike cut a small slice of meat from a roast on a platter.

"Don't feed that to the dog," Helga said.

"I had a dog once," Natalia said, kneeling beside Mike and petting Truman. She said, "My dog was a Hungarian puli. His name was Bashan."

CHAPTER NINETEEN

Natalia was in her room reading the novel by Arthur Schnitzler she had found in the living room when someone rapped lightly on the door. She got up. James Grant asked her to get her coat and hat. They were going somewhere. He would explain on the way. "Do you have rain boots?" he said, looking at her feet, and she said, no, she did not have rain boots. "It's raining," he said. "I know it's raining," she said. He looked at his watch. She made him wait in the hall while she brushed her hair and put on some lipstick.

She and James went downstairs, and James opened the front door. The air was mild; the damp grass smelled sweet. George was at the wheel of the Mercedes. She sat in the back. They drove to Steglitz, to a Red Army military hospital located on Unter den Eichen. Within a few weeks, George said, the hospital, which was in the American zone, would be handed over to the U.S. Army.

"You know Steglitz quite well, I imagine, Natalia," James Grant said. "Yes," she said. Margot and Hermann Brückner had belonged to a youth club in Steglitz, she remembered. She'd gone to the dances there with them.

The inane words of one of Mike Rose's songs came to her mind:

I could swear that she was padded from her shoulder to her heel.
But then she started dancing, and her dancing made me feel
That everything she had was absolutely real!

Absolutely real. She was learning English from these silly little tunes. It wasn't even a nice song, she thought.

At the military hospital they got out of the car, and George held an umbrella over her head as they walked to the main entrance. She was starting to feel afraid. Were they going to leave her here? Was she being handed over to the Russians?

"I'm not going in," she said. "Not unless you tell me what's going on."

"Natalia, a patient in this hospital says his name is Miklós Andorján."

The foyer of the hospital was brightly lit, and as they entered, a nurse walked past them, pushing a patient in a wheelchair. Natalia stared at the patient, a young man with blond hair, his right arm bandaged, amputated at the elbow. Near an elevator two doctors conferred in Russian. A Red Army officer appeared and introduced himself to George. He took them to an office at the end of the corridor. He offered them chairs in front of a desk. He switched on a desk lamp, sat down, picked up a telephone, and spoke into it in Russian. Not once did he look at Natalia. She heard footsteps outside in the corridor. The Russian officer stood, went to the door, opened it, and three men came in, a doctor, an army officer, and a patient in a dressing gown and pajamas. This patient was tall and thin; his head was shaved, and he looked very ill. She took a step toward him. Her heart was hammering against her ribs, and she kept thinking she was going to pass out. "Natalia," the patient said. He held out his arms, and she walked into his embrace. He placed his hand gently on the side of her face. He had tears in his eyes. They said one another's names; they breathed the names, as if in naming they could make it true, that they had found each other.

He had been with General Zhukov's army, that was true enough, Miklós told Natalia, when they were left alone in the office for a few minutes. She held Miklós's hand. He told her his jacket had been stolen in Łódź, and whoever was wearing the jacket, that was the man who had been struck by an army vehicle and buried in an unmarked grave near the Oder River. Miklós had been told that a priest at the church near the graveyard had taken his wallet out of the coat when the body was brought to his church. He had given it to a Russian journalist.

"Yes, and the Russian gave it to an English journalist, and he brought it to me," Natalia said.

It was winter, Miklós said, and he'd removed a greatcoat from a German soldier's corpse and was wearing it when he reached Germany. The Americans refused to listen when he said he was not an SS officer and threw him into a prisoner-of-war camp near Munich. The American guards waited with a rather uncivil degree of impatience for him and the other prisoners, German Wehrmacht soldiers, to die of starvation. One of the prisoners, a genuine SS officer, cut a hole in the wire fence, and he and Miklós crawled out and walked away. Near Leipzig they parted company, and Miklós made his way to Berlin. In the Russian sector he met people he'd known at the newspaper before the war. They took him to a canteen called the Seagull, where the Soviets provided coffee and hot food. He had blackouts. He had a fever, an infection in his leg, in a wound caused by the barbed wire at the prisoner-of-war camp when he escaped. The Russians put him in the hospital in Steglitz. The hospital required information: name, date of birth, where he lived. He filled out the forms; they told him he was using a false name. The name you're using, they said, is the name of a dead man.

What were they to do now, he asked her. He didn't know if he was ready to leave Berlin yet. Natalia thought longingly of going home to the castle, where, in her mind, nothing had changed since 1942, and she could feed Miklós fresh eggs and cream and butter.

Gently he traced the scars on her hands. She had been a prisoner too, she said, and please, don't ask her why, because she didn't know why. Then, and later, she told Miklós very little of the previous three years, when she'd been at what became known as one of the worst of the German concentration camps. Anyway, any reference to her arrest and the internment camp, and he became very quiet, very still, and asked her why in God's name she had left home in the first place. Because you weren't there, she said.

When, three weeks later, Miklós was discharged from the hospital, he stayed with Natalia at the Americans' house, and his health improved a little, day by day. He talked to Zita Kuznetsova on the telephone. She and Beatriz continued to encourage them to book passage on a ship to Buenos Aires. Zita said she would help Miklós find work at a newspaper. "I don't speak Spanish," he said. "How could I function as a journalist in a country where I don't speak the language?" Zita told him he could learn Spanish, and he must be aware there were German-language newspapers in Buenos Aires. They had been in circulation since the nineteenth century. After the call, he repeated Zita's words to Natalia and said it was too early to make any kind of plans, and if they went anywhere, he said, he thought it should be to England. He spoke English; he respected Clement Attlee, the new prime minister; he could live in Clement Attlee's England. England, Natalia said, would not be practical, and Miklós said, no, it was not, and they began to plan their return home, to the castle.

➤··◄

In October they traveled to Prague on a night train. She was terrified, at the last minute, of boarding the train, of being enclosed, held captive. Miklós took her hand and on the train she rested her head on his shoulder, on the rough fabric of his coat, and listened to the other passengers shuffling around, coughing, settling down for the journey. It was past midnight when the train arrived at the Prague station. They checked into the hotel on Nerudova Street, where the concierge recognized Miklós and embraced him and kept calling him Count Andorján and beaming at Natalia. In the morning, she and Miklós walked around the city, marveling that it had been so little touched by the last six years of war. And yet the city, beautiful, shining in the pale autumn light, had transparencies, veils that parted, wavered, and she saw herself alone, stranded in a city under occupation by a brutal, murderous regime. She had to discipline her mind to remain in the present, in this moment. She and Miklós went shopping for warm coats and sweaters, because the weather had turned unseasonably cold. Miklós bought a car, a 1930 Škoda with a cracked windshield and a missing headlight. While he stayed at the hotel to read and rest, Natalia walked to Mr. Aslan's shop. "It really is you, isn't it?" Mr. Aslan said. She told him she had found her husband, and they were going home.

Mr. Aslan was well, he said; his wife was well, and his children were, thank God, healthy, growing, both at school. He told her about the end of the war, the Russians coming in, the Germans defeated, and President Edvard Beneš returning from exile in England. And Beneš wanted all Germans out of Czechoslovakia. Germans who had lived and worked in Prague or anywhere in Czechoslovakia were ordered to leave. Those who failed to get out fast enough were shot. People who had become Reich Germans to protect themselves during the Nazi occupation now had to wear white badges that signified they were German, not Czech. It was a horrible thing to see, after what had happened under the Nazis. Some Germans were, believe it or not, Mr. Aslan said, sent to Theresienstadt, or to use the Czech name, Terezín. After the war, no one had room in their hearts for compassion. But Mr. Aslan believed it would come, things would return to normal. The important thing, he said, was that the brutality of the Nazis was never forgotten.

He gave her sesame-seed cakes. He wished her well.

After saying goodbye to Mr. Aslan, Natalia went to the millinery shop of Anna's aunt Vivian. Aunt Vivian was sitting at a worktable, stretching dark red felt on a hat form. She kept moving her fingers over the fabric as she looked at Natalia. Natalia gave her Anna's address in Seattle. "Anna is fine," Natalia said. "She lives with a nice family over there, in the States. I know their son; he's with the United Nations Relief and Rehabilitation Administration. It's his parents who are taking care of Anna."

Aunt Vivian knew Seattle; she'd visited there once, when she was a girl.

She wore a pincushion on her wrist; the glass heads on the pins shone as she moved her hands. She took off the pincushion and got up and went to a cupboard and took out the gray cardboard portfolio that contained the story of the princess who knew the worth of salt over gold. She gave it to Natalia, to send to Anna.

Natalia and Miklós stayed overnight at Aunt Vivian's apartment. She insisted on it. She wanted Natalia to see Emil and Maximilian and tell them about Anna. Miklós was happy to meet them. They talked for hours, about the war and about what was going to happen in Czechoslovakia.

→··←

As they reached the castle, snow began to fall, and when Natalia and Miklós got out of the car, the clouds parted, and moonlight glinted on the copper roof of the tower. She had pictured returning home in summer, the horses in the paddock, cows and sheep grazing in the fields. Fields of lavender and poppies. But there were no animals in the fields, and the fields were white with snow, and there was no sign of Rozalia. The doors were bolted, the windows shuttered; no smoke came from the chimneys. And such silence, broken only by the cry of an owl and then a dog barking. Miklós had to break in through a window in the room where the agricultural accountant used to manage the estate's accounts. Then he opened the kitchen door to let Natalia in. She lit a candle. They went up to the second floor and found Rozalia in her bedroom, in bed, beneath a pile of blankets and quilts. "Rozalia?" Natalia said. "It's us, it's Natalia and Miklós. Are you awake? Rozalia, can you hear me?"

She took Rozalia's wrist and felt for a pulse. Rozalia's eyes flew open, and she swore at Natalia. She struggled to sit up in the bed. She brought a knife out from under her pillow. Miklós took it from her. Natalia found a chair and sat beside the bed. She felt the countess's forehead. "When did you last eat?" she said.

"God knows. Every now and then Katya brings me something."

Miklós lit a fire in the kitchen stove, and Natalia heated a can of soup. She toasted some bread they had brought with them from Prague.

They ate on trays in the countess's bedroom, with a small fire burning in the grate and the wind blowing dry snow against the window. Natalia thought that in the morning she would get to work and scrub the place clean or at least clean the rooms they used. What had happened here? she wondered. Later, Rozalia told them that in October of 1944, the Germans had arrived and moved into the castle. To begin with, she said, there must have been ten or eleven of them. "Only one had any manners; he was a gentleman, but the others I think were from the lowest levels of society, even if they called themselves officers." They emptied her storehouse of food. Finally, only two were left, and they showed no sign of leaving. "In the end," Rozalia said, "I had to get rid of them."

"You got rid of them?" Miklós said.

"Do you see them, Miklós? Do *you*?" she said to Natalia. "Look behind the doors; look in the cupboards. You won't find them."

"Where did they go?" Miklós said warily.

"They're buried behind the horse barn," Rozalia said. "They stole my rifles, so that I couldn't shoot even a rabbit or a sparrow for food, and they slashed the tapestries out of their frames and stole my jewelry, even the diamond and ruby necklace I inherited from my mother. I had hidden László's pistol, his Steyr automatic from the other war, down in the cellars. And the clips, I had kept them, too. After all that time, I was astonished when the Steyr fired. But I was always a good shot, wasn't I, Miklós? I wish I'd thought to shoot the Russians who came here and took my horses. They sent my horses to Russia, the bastards."

She and two men from the workers' cottages buried the Germans, she said.

"How many, did you say? How many Germans?" Miklós asked.

"Only those two. The others left earlier, as I said. I imagine the Russians finished them off. Not that the Russians are any better, but at least I didn't have to look at their ugly faces over my breakfast table."

When spring came, Miklós dug up the ground. He found two corpses. Two corpses in SS uniforms. He covered them over again.

Their rifles, Rozalia said, were with the skulls in the ossuary.

In 1945 the coalition government in Hungary appropriated large private landholdings, dividing them into parcels of land that were given to the tenant farmers or to people who had never in their lives owned land. Once, Miklós had considered his estate a burden; now he said he felt unjustly robbed of his property. He smiled as he said this. Most of the people around here didn't want the land, he said; they wanted industrial jobs in Budapest. Steady work, regular pay, that was what they wanted, Miklós said. But the Germans had dismantled the factories in Budapest and had trucked the components to their own country, so everyone would have a long wait for those jobs. Natalia saw that the peasants, a term she'd never heard Miklós use before, were quite happy to move onto the estate. They put up houses; their woodsmoke seasoned the night air, and their lighted windows made a kind of community. The Hungarian republic was declared on February 1, 1946. That spring, Miklós and Natalia plowed a patch of ground and planted vegetable seeds. They cut firewood; they cleaned out the henhouse, and Miklós brought home a rooster and a dozen speckled hens. So they had fresh eggs, wild strawberries, fresh milk, from Magdolna's farm, and bread Natalia baked every morning.

Rozalia had good days, when she got up from her bed and sat in the kitchen, or wandered around the garden, her braid hanging down from under her headscarf. Then there were days when she did not get up but stayed huddled in bed with a hot-water bottle to ease the pain in her back. The doctor who came to see her told Natalia she had a compression fracture of the spine. She was also suffering congestive heart failure, he said. The doctor's name was Benedek Imre. He had taken over Dr. Urbán's practice. The Germans had sent Dr. Urbán to a Wehrmacht field hospital, and he had not come home. Dr. Imre told Natalia he had graduated from medical school in Budapest in 1941.

While he was talking to her, at the castle, they heard Miklós coughing. "My husband has been ill," said Natalia. Dr. Imre, preparing to leave, had picked up his medical bag. Now he put it down on the hall table and said perhaps he should examine her husband.

"I don't think he'll let you," she said. Dr. Imre said, perhaps another time then, and went away in his old two-seater car.

Natalia saw that Miklós was losing weight and had a fever that waxed and waned, but anything, she told herself, could cause a fever: a touch of flu, a chest cold. It could be anything. She wasn't feeling well either.

Miklós wrote an article on the Soviet Cominform, an organization that, as far as Natalia could understand, united Communist parties in Eastern Europe, France, and Italy. What did she think of his article, he asked, and she said it was very good: thoughtful, not provocative, very balanced.

How it pleased her, to see Miklós working at his desk in his tower room. Sometimes while she was hand-washing clothes or stirring soup made with potatoes and onions they had grown themselves, she remembered the first time she climbed the stairs to the tower room and how there, in the windows, like a vast tapestry, had been the Hungarian landscape and the wide Hungarian sky. She remembered the sense it had given her of flying, and that reminded her of Zita's story of the monk who escaped his mortal body and ascended to the stratosphere and looked down at the forests and rivers. Then she thought of her dog, Bashan. She remembered throwing sticks into the river for him and the way he bounded into the water, his long curls swirling around him, and that she and Miklós had kissed beside the river. It seemed long ago; it seemed like no time at all had passed.

→··←

Natalia and Miklós talked about going back to Berlin to live. Miklós was eager to begin working for a newspaper again. And he could foresee the day when leaving Hungary would be difficult, if not impossible. The Communists were likely to take over the government in Hungary. The world was dividing itself into East and West, into them against us, once again. So it would be wise to get out while they could.

In Berlin, Miklós said, they could rent a house with enough room for Rozalia to live with them.

Rozalia said she wasn't deaf; she could hear what her son was plotting.

Miklós hired men from the village to do heavy work in the garden he had planted. Natalia fed the chickens and gathered eggs. Katya came every day to help Natalia with the cooking and cleaning, the laundry. Sometimes her daughter, Alena, was with her. Katya taught Natalia some sign language so that she could communicate with Alena. Natalia loved Alena; she was a graceful child, her smile was heart-melting, and every time Natalia looked at her, she saw her son, Krisztián, beside her.

Miklós had a setback; the fever returned, he woke drenched in sweat, he coughed up blood. Natalia, terrified, sent for Dr. Imre. He told her that her husband had pulmonary tuberculosis. Your husband needs immediate treatment, the doctor said. Complete rest, three meals a day, sunshine and fresh air.

"Are you all right?" the doctor asked her. She said she felt a little faint. She didn't know what was wrong with her; she was tired all the time. He insisted on examining her. He took blood and urine samples. When he came back to the castle, he said she was anemic. He gave her a bottle of iron pills. Then he told her that fatigue was not an uncommon symptom of pregnancy. "You didn't know?" he said.

How was she to know? Natalia thought. Nothing was regular with her body, not after the camps, being starved, being sick with typhus. Like most doctors, she thought, he believed every symptom a woman had indicated pregnancy. How could she look after a child? And a sick husband. And a sick mother-in-law. And she wasn't young anymore.

→··←

In Budapest, Natalia walked around the streets near the hospital where Miklós had been admitted for tests. When she saw Russian soldiers, she tried to avoid them. She had heard how, during and after the siege, they had committed acts of brutality and rape, as they had in Berlin. She didn't know where Max Nagy lived in

Budapest or even if he had been alive in 1944 or how he could have survived. When she was in a shop or at a café or at the hospital, she would ask people if they knew Max Nagy. Some people did know a Max Nagy but not the one she was looking for.

At the hospital she sat in a waiting room furnished with three straight-backed chairs and a small statue of the Virgin Mary on a table. Miklós came in and took her hand and pulled her up, out of the chair, and said, "Let's get the hell out of here." On their way to the car, he saw a stationery store that was open, and they went in, so that Miklós could choose a new fountain pen. It took a long time. He compared the filling mechanisms of various pens and considered the merits of iridium nibs over gold nibs. The store's proprietor offered his opinion, and Miklós said his wife would make the decision. "Why?" she said laughing. "Go on, you pick," Miklós said. Natalia decided on a dark blue Pelikan fountain pen with a fourteen-karat-gold nib. It looked like a jewel; it looked like the most civilized thing in the world. It came in a silver and gold box. They left the store. They were optimistic, suddenly, about Miklós's health. Surely, after all they'd been through, they deserved good news.

When they got back to the castle, they sat in the car for a few minutes, dazed, exhausted. Should it be now? Natalia thought. How much longer could she keep such a secret? Dr. Imre had not been wrong when he'd told her she was pregnant. She started to open the car door. "What is it?" Miklós said. "It can wait," she said. "No, tell me," he said. She closed the door. She told him.

He didn't say anything for a long time. He stared out the cracked windshield. Then he asked her when this would be. In the fall, she said. November, maybe late October.

"How long have you known?"

"I didn't know. I was tired, I wanted to sleep all the time."

"Well," he said. "I don't know what to say." He kissed her. "This changes things, doesn't it," he said.

❖

Perhaps, Miklós said later, he should think about doing what the doctor advised. "Good," Natalia said. "I think you're right." But she was afraid too. Still, she telephoned Dr. Imre, and he arranged with the doctors in Budapest for Miklós to begin treatment. The specialist was Dr. Ferenczi. He ordered more tests, more X-rays. He talked with Miklós and Natalia in his office. He wanted to know everything: when the cough had begun and when the fever had started. He wrote and then placed his pen on the desk. He sighed and rubbed the bridge of his nose and at length gave his opinion, which did not, to Natalia, sound like something she wanted to hear. He suggested what he called a relatively simple pneumothorax procedure. It involved collapsing a lung, which would, for one thing, he explained, reduce the ability of the tuberculosis bacterium to replicate and spread the disease. She knew about this procedure from when she'd visited Julia Brüning at a hospital in Moabit, in Berlin. Julia was there for months.

The next time they saw Dr. Ferenczi, he had reconsidered the operation. He said they would continue for a while longer with bed rest.

Miklós was admitted to a tuberculosis hospital in Budapest. Dr. Ferenczi introduced him to a tuberculosis specialist from Sweden, Dr. Janssen. The Swedish presence in Budapest, which dated from 1943, interested Miklós. He and Dr. Janssen talked about the disappearance of the Swedish envoy to Hungary, Raoul Wallenberg, and his efforts to help the Jews of Budapest escape Adolf Eichmann, who had remained in Budapest transporting

Jews to the death camps even as the Russians were approaching. Miklós wanted paper and a pen, but Dr. Janssen said no writing, no intellectual activity for now. Rest, he said. Miklós asked Natalia to bring him the things he had asked for. She said she would see what she could do, but she had no intention of going against the doctors' orders. It scared her, seeing Miklós in that hospital bed. She forgot sometimes, or didn't want to remember, that he was fifty-four years old. She didn't want to hear, either, what the doctor told her: that tuberculosis was a more serious disease in people over the age of fifty. She didn't want to know that.

In the early hours of the morning, while Natalia slept at her hotel, Miklós experienced a serious hemorrhage of the lungs. A nurse met her at the door to his room and said she must wait to speak with the doctor. How serious, she wanted to know, when Dr. Ferenczi came down the hall to see her. Dr. Ferenczi studied her over his glasses for a moment, and said they were not by any means giving up on the treatment. When he was studying medicine in Vienna, at the end of the Great War, he said, he had developed tuberculosis. Within a year it had cleared up spontaneously.

"So it can happen?" she said.

"In the early stages."

Like God, he gave and he took away, that doctor.

She began to hate the hospital. It smelled of carbolic soap, boiled potatoes, medicine, the same as all hospitals. People came here to be cured or they died, it was that simple, and these days, after six years of war, and the deprivations that went with war, they mostly died. The nurses, when they had time, encouraged her to sit quietly in the hospital chapel. Pray, they told her, guiding her to the chapel door. Natalia did what she was told to do. She dipped her fingers in the font, genuflected, prayed wordlessly, having nothing to say. She was afraid of calling attention to herself, of forcing God to notice her, and thinking, Why should this one be all right, when so many are suffering? She prayed to Dr. Schaefferová. Magdalena, she said, I know you're here with me.

Her child, this child, must not grow up without a father. It was a terrible thing, not to know your own father. She would not allow it.

At the hotel where she was staying, the staff and the other residents were nice to her, but their smiles irritated her, their inquiries about her husband's health made her want to scream. She always said the same things: Thank you, he's doing well. The nurses are wonderful. The hospital staff are wonderful. Thank you for asking. Yes, I am on my way to the hospital now.

She slept; she hated herself for sleeping, but the pregnancy made her want to do nothing except sleep. She fell asleep sitting up at the hospital; in the chapel; she woke and sat up, dazed, and went back to the hotel and tried to eat a piece of toast; she drank a cup of tea, which gave her heartburn. She walked back to the hospital. The sun shone, and there was a mild wind; the air smelled cleaner, less smoky, and the sound of hammers echoed throughout the city as buildings were being repaired. The Chain Bridge had been bombed and was going to be rebuilt. Budapest was being rebuilt. Even this soon after the end of fighting, it was being reconstructed. Was that a hidden function of these terrible wars, she wondered, to destroy and destroy, in the manner of a child kicking aside beloved toys he'd grown tired of, in favor of new bricks and mortar, a new way of living in this difficult world?

→·←

Dr. Ferenczi stood waiting for her at the end of the corridor. The nurses had told her he wanted to talk to her. Countess Andorján, he said, and his tone alarmed her. She knew what he was going to say. *There was a deterioration in Miklós's condition. There was nothing else they could do.* At first Dr. Ferenczi's actual words didn't get through to her. He said, "Countess Andorján, we have been giving your husband two new drugs. He seems to be responding well."

These were very new, very promising drug therapies to treat tuberculosis, he said. The newer drug, streptomycin, had entered human clinical trials in the United States only a year previously. It was not yet approved for use, and it wasn't being manufactured. It was in the nature of a miracle that he had received a small supply of streptomycin. Another drug was para-aminosalicylic acid. In Sweden, this drug had cured a female patient in the final stages of tuberculosis. Cured her, Dr. Ferenczi repeated. The two drugs, used in combination, appeared to be highly efficacious. His colleague Dr. Janssen had obtained the second drug from his brother, a doctor in Stockholm. The streptomycin had come from a friend of Dr. Ferenczi in London. The treatment would take fifty days, and Miklós would have to remain in the hospital for some time. There could be serious side effects, but in his opinion, the risks were worth it. Overall, Dr. Ferenczi said, there was reason for optimism.

Hungary at the end of the war was not a good place for them. They knew this, they had discussed it, but even after Miklós was able to leave the hospital, they did not make any definite plans. She was going to have a child. Rozalia was unwell. In addition, they had unfinished business at the castle. When the ground thawed, in the early spring of 1948, Miklós and Vladimír exhumed the German soldiers' corpses and doused them with kerosene and burned them. Later they moved what was left of the bones down to the ossuary. Natalia went with them, to say a prayer, because somewhere these men had had families, parents, perhaps wives, children. Vladimír's flashlight illuminated the Greek lettering on the wall. She stared at it. *The gods cannot count and know nothing of arithmetic.* A cold little observation, she thought, and seemingly irrefutable. She shuddered. Miklós put his arm around her. They went up out of the cellar to the kitchen, and Miklós and Vladimír drank vodka. No one must ever know, they said, and Rozalia, hearing them, said she would do it again, if necessary, and think nothing of it.

Natalia, washing dishes at the sink, thought of Gudrun. She wondered whether Gudrun was still in England, and if she and her children were doing well in their new life. She had a sudden, vivid picture of Gudrun in the garden outside the house in Dahlem, with her small bunch of parsley, speaking haltingly of what had happened to her when the Russian army had occupied Berlin, in May 1945. Natalia could still hear the terror and shame in Gudrun's voice as she recounted the things she had gone through, the terrible things she had seen.

Natalia wiped and put away the dishes, moving slowly between the worktable and the cupboard. She remembered the hours of work she and Gudrun had put in, in the kitchen of the house requisitioned by the Americans. How many meals had they cooked and served? She remembered filling endless tureens with vegetables, roasting meat, mashing potatoes. That such mundane tasks had to be done with such wearying regularity had sometimes annoyed her, but she had also believed that the work was, in a way, sacramental. To feed the hungry, give shelter to the homeless, was a holy act. It was just that there were so many hungry people. Displaced people. While everyone in that house had been well fed, outside its doors people had nothing. It troubled her to remember this.

But she was selfish. She wanted peace, sanctuary, untroubled days slipping past like rosary beads. She had a debilitating fear that somewhere, not far away, the war was still being fought. Phantom armies were massed at borders, waiting for the order to begin an assault. Or real armies. A seemingly insignificant diplomatic incident, and it could begin. Right now, at this moment, in some country that hadn't yet been named, a tyrant could be taking office. If it had happened once, it could happen again. Who could assure her that the death camps, the forced-labor camps, now belonged to history?

Every morning she woke with a sense of panic. At first, she wasn't even sure where she was. Then the room took on its familiar shapes, and light appeared at the window, and she knew she was in bed, in the castle, and her husband was better and had come home, and they were going to have a child.

Was this too much good fortune for one woman? What if the gods became jealous? She said this once to Rozalia, who told her: "Look, if you are going to be constantly afraid that something bad will happen, then do this: break a dish, break a matchstick. The bad luck will have had its moment, and you will feel better. If you can't let go and trust life, what is the point, Natalia?"

For the child's sake, she had to be cheerful, Rozalia said. The baby would not arrive in a perfect world, but Natalia had to make it seem nearly perfect, a good place, with music, games, sunlight, people who loved him. They all had to keep this in mind, Rozalia said, but especially Natalia, because she was the mother, and it was her responsibility, and besides, it would make her happy too.

But it was Rozalia who decided they had to leave Hungary. As soon as Miklós was well and after the baby was born, they were going somewhere else to live. She pored over an atlas. It had to be a country where she could speak the language. It had to be in Europe. Germany, she said; the west of Germany. She had no intention of subjecting herself to Communist rule, not in Hungary and certainly not in East Germany.

Only a few days later Natalia got a letter from Beatriz, who exultantly passed on the news that her house in Zehlendorf remained legally her property. Rozalia said, "That's settled, then. We will live in your mother's house. Do you see how everything comes together, Natalia, when you have a little faith in life?"

CHAPTER TWENTY

Franz slips an arm around her neck. She leans slightly, adjusting his weight on her hip. He's warm from running around and pedaling a shiny red toy car, a gift from Beatriz. Natalia kisses him, kisses his damp hair; he pushes her away and protests, Mama, don't.

Franz, where are we? she asks. Buenos Aires, he says. And where is Buenos Aires? Argentina. And whose house is this? Oma's house, Franz replies, and wriggles down out of her arms and runs to the open French doors to find Oma, who never insists he's sleepy and needs a nap. Natalia plucks a peach from an espaliered tree that Beatriz swears is the same one that grew here when she was a girl. Are the trees in this garden immortal? Beatriz is as pretty and youthful as when she left Berlin fourteen years ago, in 1938. Prettier, even, with a luster, a glow bestowed on her by the southern sun. Her blond hair shines, her skin seems transparent; her eyes are the same intensely clear blue, and she pays great attention to fashion and wears the latest styles, dresses with three-quarter-length sleeves, tiny waists, full skirts nearly to the ankle. Scarlet lipstick, heels, a clutch purse. What have you done to yourself? Beatriz asked, frowning, when she met them at the airport in Buenos Aires. She arranged appointments for Natalia with hairdressers, cosmeticians, manicurists. Beatriz knew that even people like her daughter had suffered in the war, but the way suffering went deep into the body, into the soul, that had obviously shocked her.

Beatriz's former caretaker, Dom, is now her gardener. He lives in Buenos Aires with his wife, Maria, who is Beatriz's cook. Maria's sister, Desirée, is the housekeeper. Five mornings a week they travel together on a tram to Beatriz's villa in Palermo. On Fridays, Desirée slips though an iron gate in the garden wall and cleans house for a neighbor, Professor Lucien Dray, whose entire family, including his elderly parents, were deported from France by the Nazis to Auschwitz and were killed. Every Sunday the professor is Beatriz's guest at brunch. He and Miklós talk about books and the weather, annual rainfall in Buenos Aires. This quiet man with blue shadows under his eyes is in danger of being dismissed from his position. The Argentine president distrusts university teachers and despises higher education. *Shoes, yes, books, no*, is a popular government slogan, Zita tells them.

Before eating, Professor Dray wipes his fork on his table napkin. He drinks water but not coffee or wine.

After lunch, Miklós goes through the iron gate with Professor Dray, and they continue their conversation in the professor's library.

Everything in the garden shimmers with an extraordinarily clear, luminous light: the sky, the magenta bougainvillea, the floribunda roses. Plants with leathery, spotted leaves, vining plants with orange flowers like small ecstatic trumpets. It doesn't matter what you've been through, Natalia thinks, such profusion gives you hope. She's forgotten her dark glasses in the house, and the bright sun hurts her eyes. Her eyesight is poor, from those years of malnutrition, of starving, of sickness. She has regular prescription glasses too, but there's something appealing, salutary, about seeing the indistinct, hazy otherness of objects and landscapes.

This morning Zita took Miklós to her office at a publishing house and to have lunch with friends of hers: journalists and newspapermen and other writers. Natalia worries that Miklós will overtire himself. He needs to conserve his strength, and to do that, she thinks, he should not immerse himself in the political discussions Zita and her colleagues engage in for hours at a time. Natalia knows; she's been to one of these lunches. She understands, sympathizes with people who feel they're under siege. In fact, they are under siege, as Perón attacks newspapers, publishing houses.

"It doesn't matter what hemisphere you're in, what country," Zita says, "it begins with censorship of the press, doesn't it?" Perón admired Mussolini and Hitler and had allowed Nazi war criminals to find refuge in Argentina. Sometimes, in a shop or on the street, Natalia hears someone speaking German and stares, wondering whether the man buying a bag of apples or walking with his wife is one of them. Whether he held a gun, ordered men, women, children into cattle cars, slammed and bolted doors, authorized executions, beat people to death. It sickens her. But that's how it is. That's the world she lives in. All she wants to do is go home. She misses Rozalia, and so does her son, who a few days ago collapsed in a tearful rage on the living room floor and cried, *"Wo ist meine Oma Rozzi?"* Where is she? he kept saying. He can't pronounce Rozalia; it comes out "Rozzi," and so that's what Natalia and Miklós call his mother too.

Franz's tears upset Beatriz, who likes to think she's his favorite grandmother. He has no trouble saying my name, she says. She comforts him with a dish of ice cream, bribes him with promises of playgrounds, shopping, the cinema. Stay a while longer, she says to Natalia and Miklós.

One day, at the lunch table, Beatriz says, "Zita and I are thinking of going back to Germany. We have a good life here, but times change, don't they? Then there's inflation. Land values go up and down, mostly down; you can't possibly second-guess Argentina's economy. Or any economy," she added, helping herself to a triangular crabmeat sandwich from a plate Desirée places in front of her. "The villa needs repairs," Beatriz says. "It's falling down around us."

"It will last for centuries," Zita says.

"Why not stay an extra week or two?" Zita says to Miklós.

Miklós thanks her and says they'd like to, very much, but can't leave his mother alone any longer.

"She has Hildegard," Beatriz says.

Hildegard survived the Allied bombing of Hamburg and came back to Zehlendorf to help Natalia with Franz, and now it's Rozalia she's looking after. Trudy is in Poland with her husband and children. During the war, Erich Saltzman went into hiding in the home of a wealthy widow, and now he and the widow are married.

Natalia sees that her mother is on the edge of tears.

"We'll come to see you soon, then," Beatriz says, wiping her nose on her table napkin. "Zita still has a phobia about crossing the Atlantic by ship, but she enjoyed our flight to New York last year, didn't you, Zita? I think it's irrational to feel safer flying than on a ship. If a ship goes down, there are at least lifeboats."

Natalia thought being in the Americas would mean she could fly to Seattle, but a travel agent told her the distance is six thousand nautical miles, over eleven thousand kilometers, and would take almost two days each way. It would be better to fly to New York from Berlin and then fly to Seattle, the way Anna did in 1945. She would love to see Anna. She mailed her father's art portfolio to her. She remembers the house in the Golden Lane, the tarot cards; every day, and this is true, every day she remembers Dr. Schaefferová.

"Come, sit with Tante Zita," Zita says, holding out her arms. This is after lunch. Beatriz is in the kitchen, talking to Maria about dinner. Zita sits Franz on her knee and reads Curious George books to him.

A few days ago, Zita said to Natalia, "Franz looks so much like Krisztián. The resemblance startles me sometimes."

Her words hurt Natalia, who had looked away. "Yes," she had said. She got up and walked out into the garden, where Desirée was just coming back through the iron gate in the garden wall, carrying a tray covered with a napkin, the remains of Professor Dray's midday meal.

Franz has his father's dark hair and gold-flecked brown eyes. He has her pale skin and dislikes the sun hat she makes him wear. She keeps squashing it down firmly on his head, and he keeps pulling it off and throwing it on the ground. Only if she tells him it makes him look like an explorer will he acquiesce and then only for a limited time. He is interested in insects and in the solar system. When they first arrived in Buenos Aires, Miklós showed him the Río de la Plata, the widest river in the world. "It shines like silver," Miklós said, "and that is why it is named the Río de la Plata." Franz was interested to know that his Oma's cook, Maria, sometimes cooks for them fish that used to swim in the Río de la Plata. Natalia tells him about the carp his namesake, Franz Schaeffer, caught in the Vltava. And how Magdolna cooked trout caught fresh daily in Lake Balaton. She tells him the Danube is the longest river in Europe, flowing from its source in Bavaria through Hungary to the Black Sea. A tributary of the Danube runs past the house where he was born. She tells him how mountain streams in the Erzgebirge can turn into dangerous torrents and how his father once saved Tante Zita's life when she almost drowned.

"Zita drowned?" Franz says.

"No. Your papa saved her," Natalia says.

On that day, Natalia thinks but does not say, on that same day, Franz's grandfather died on the train to Prague. Miklós says she must tell Franz; she owes it to her son not to conceal the truth. The truth, strangely, is that here in Argentina she often thinks of Alfred Faber. In the bedroom where she and Miklós are sleeping, she woke and saw someone standing beside the bed, staring at her. She gasped and sat up, waking Miklós, who said no one was there, she was dreaming.

In bright sun the villa casts a deep, precisely outlined shadow over the garden. As Natalia walks into this shadow to get out of the bright sun, a figure seems to appear on the balcony above her. Slim, delicate, inquisitive Fräulein Hoffman. Natalia feels as if she knew her, grew up with her, listened to her lessons on anatomy and taxonomy. In the library, Beatriz showed her the governess's writing table, collecting jars, scalpels, spirit lamp. The governess's resentment at this intrusion casts a small fiery light on the wall, stirs cold ashes in the fireplace.

Beatriz is sitting on the edge of the fountain, watching Franz sail a toy boat. Beatriz gave him the boat. She spoils him and says she is really spoiling herself, because she loves buying him things. Toys, clothes, anything, everything. "Franz," she says, holding out her arms. "Give Oma a kiss." The boat bumps against the fountain's stone rim, and Franz gives it a gentle push to safety. The water splashes; the toy boat rocks unsteadily, nearly capsizes, but settles on the water as if it were sailing on the broad surface of the Río de la Plata.

CHAPTER TWENTY-ONE

What Anna learned was this: her memories were part of her, rooted and immutable, like her eye color, the shape of her hands, her predilection for dark chocolate and piano music. It would happen like this: at a grocery store while picking up a quart of milk and a loaf of bread, in the lab preparing plant material for microscopy, on a corner waiting for a bus, she would see a face, an apparition startling in its clarity, all sharp angles, skin paper-thin, parchment-colored, and she'd think: I know you. I am you.

Sometimes she dreamed she was at home, in Malá Strana, and the fortune-teller appeared, her pale hair shining in the moonlight. Rain glistened on the cobblestones. A cat ran past, a rat in its jaws. Lines of washing hung, damp, motionless, already grimy with coal dust. Broken windows, shards of glass on the street. Ragged children tossed a ball back and forth.

Life begins and ends in rivers, the fortune-teller said. There are gods that do not love us, she said.

Anna remembers those dreams. When she first came to Seattle to live with the Grants, she had the same dream night after night, and often she would wake feeling lethargic, numb. She forgot where she was and walked into walls, tripped, dropped glasses on the kitchen floor, and Mrs. Grant said not to worry and cleaned up the pieces. She would go to her room and shut the door, to avoid Mr. and Mrs. Grant's concern, their desire to help. She must talk, they said, she mustn't keep things bottled up inside. Would she consider seeing a doctor? A psychiatrist, they meant. But she didn't want to talk if it meant relinquishing her memories, because without them, she was nothing.

She remembers her mother playing the piano and singing. *V černym lese ptaček zpiva.* "In the black wood a little bird is singing." Anna loved that song and always asked for another one. She asked her mother to sing "The Maiden and the Grass." A maiden is gathering grass in a field. She fills her arms with grass because it is so fresh and green and sweet-smelling. *I can't stop myself,* she cries, half laughing, to her lover.

In her head, Anna hears Dvořák's *Mně zdálo se, zes umřela.* "I dreamed last night that you were dead." The song goes on, in her mother's beautiful, soft voice. *In my dreams you were dead, and I heard the death bells.* Anna wants to listen, but she is going to die from this song. In the last verse, she remembers, a stone speaks from a grave.

Saxa loquuntur: the stones speak. The stones speak, but Anna is silent.

➤·◄

After the war, Anna's aunt Vivian wrote to her in America. She saved the letters, a year's worth, and when she felt she could at last reply without being overwhelmed by her emotions, she wrote back. She apologized for not replying sooner and said the letters were wonderful, they were a lifeline. She meant it. She tried to give the impression she was not unhappy, which was true. In time, she found the courage to ask whether her house had survived the war and what it looked like now. Aunt Vivian replied that, yes, her house was there, although following the election of the Communists in 1948, it had been divided into apartments. A factory foreman and his wife and their two children lived there, and a young couple, both teachers in the music faculty at the university. A Communist Party functionary occupied a suite of rooms on the second floor. A librarian lived on the third floor with two dachshunds left behind by their former owner, a German dentist, when he'd fled Prague.

On her way home from her millinery shop, Aunt Vivian wrote, she often met the librarian out walking the dentist's sausage dogs. The librarian, who looked scarcely out of her teens, wore a shapeless wool coat and lace-up shoes. Her eyes were red-rimmed from the cold weather. Or from loneliness. Who didn't suffer from it these days? The librarian had a litany of complaints: the music teachers played their piano late at night, with no consideration for anyone; the factory foreman let his children rampage on the staircase; a smell of cooking came from an open window: boiled fish, scorched potatoes; and worst of all, the party functionary, the official, whatever he was, had a grudge against her because dachshunds were a German breed of dog. Wasn't that crazy? What did a little dog know of war?

The lovely old chestnut tree in the front garden had been cut down, Aunt Vivian regretted having to say, leaving a strange, empty place without shadows, without softness, if Anna knew what she meant.

The onionskin paper her aunt wrote on carried the scent of Prague: lilacs, factory smoke, river water in summer. *If only you were here*, Aunt Vivian wrote, *I would be happy*.

Come to America, Anna suggested in a letter to Aunt Vivian, who was not her aunt but her great-aunt and had been born in Chicago; why shouldn't she come back?

Dearest child, Aunt Vivian replied, her life was in Prague. All her memories were there and her friends and her shop. Besides, at her age, how could she start over?

Even now, in her seventies, Aunt Vivian kept her millinery shop open. Under Communism, she said, she designed plainer, more serviceable hats of fabric tough as asbestos, and they sold surprisingly well to the wives of Soviet officials.

Anna, who rarely wore a hat, wished she owned at least one of her aunt's creations. Something dashing, pre-Communist, in velvet, with a little dotted veil.

Why had the tree been cut down? She had loved that tree. Every autumn she had gathered the chestnuts that fell to the ground and carried a basketful to the kitchen, and Sora made the Italian cake and sometimes *marron glacé*, which Anna's mother loved.

Anna considered writing to Natalia, but she didn't have an address, and so she bought school exercise books at a drugstore and wrote in those. When she'd filled every page of one book, she began another. They were for her, these books; more than for Natalia, even if it was Natalia she addressed. She wrote:

Are you "happy," Natalia? I hope you are. I think I am, some-times. In America, happiness exists; it is a constitutional right or perhaps more of an obligation.

I study, read, take piano lessons from Mr. Grant's sister, who teaches piano in her living room. I'm learning to roller-skate.

334

Natalia, when I left that camp near Hanover, I flew on a USAF plane to New York City, and from there I flew across the continent to Seattle. It was July 9, 1945, and in America on that day there was a solar eclipse. It became cold and dark; I waited for bombs to explode, for the sound of antiaircraft fire, for a rocket to strike the plane. The stewardess cautioned me against looking directly at the sun, but I did look, and I saw the corona like a crown of thorns. Then the plane flew on into a second, dazzling awakening.

She can write to Natalia now at a new address Aunt Vivian sent. The sight of the address in West Berlin reminds her of the months she lived beside the Kleiner Wannsee with Dr. Haffner, who wasn't a bad person, and Frau Haffner, who was. She remembers the children. She pictures Jean-Marc in the garden, laboring in the hot sun on a wartime garden so that the Haffner family could enjoy fresh vegetables.

Next year, she will be there, in Germany, when James takes her to see her father's parents, her Oma and Opa in Heidelberg. She is a little afraid of the feelings the reunion will evoke, on both sides. But she has a while to prepare herself.

A letter came from Natalia. She and her husband are well; they have a son named Franz. It gave Anna a painful start, when she saw the name. Then she thought her brother would have liked to know a child was named in his honor.

Natalia sent Anna a parcel. Like her great-aunt's letters, she keeps it but doesn't open it. She knows it contains Dr. Shapiro's manuscript and her father's paintings of her as Marica, the resourceful princess who understood that salt could at times be valued higher than gold.

She and Natalia continue to correspond. You'll be interested to know, Anna tells her, in a letter, that Reina lives in Waukegan,

Illinois, is studying to be a teacher, and is now an American citizen. Her friends from Prague, Ivan and Marta Lazar, live in Chicago. Ivan is working at a restaurant and taking courses at the university, in order to qualify as a teacher there. He and Marta have two children, a boy and a girl. Anna continues:

Last summer I saw Reina, when she and Ivan and Marta drove all the way to Seattle. I hadn't seen her since 1942 and that was more than ten years ago. She hasn't changed, or she has, she has achieved what she wanted, a new life in the United States, and it gives her a look of serenity, of completeness, although she says she is only partly herself without Franz. To be honest, I wanted Reina to be less happy than she was. But why should I begrudge her some happiness? While they were here, James's parents put on a barbecue for them. We stayed out after dark, with electric lights in paper lanterns and the air scented with those night-blooming flowers, phlox, I think they're called, and always beneath the lighthearted conversations about books, movies, football, the weather, are the unsaid words of grief, the unspoken names. You know, Natalia. The names you can't say except when you're alone, and then only silently, and sparingly, as if you're taking a tincture of something that could be either healing or harmful in larger doses, and you're afraid to find out which it is.

She almost crosses that out but leaves it.

On the street, after walking to the mailbox, Anna is caught in a brief downpour. Almost as quickly as the rain begins the clouds part, the sun shines, mist rises from the wet street, droplets of rainwater glisten on rhododendron leaves. Her heart lifts. The world is, she thinks. The world is beautiful and good. For this time, this moment, this seems to her a reliable truth. As she reaches the Grants' house, she sees James parking his car in the driveway. He gets out and sees her. She waves, he waves back, smiling, and then he stands there, waiting.

ACKNOWLEDGMENTS

I would like to thank Iris Tupholme, my editor, whose insight, warmth, and wisdom guided this book to completion. Thank you to Patrick Crean. Thank you, Julia McDowell, Noelle Zitzer, and the entire team at HarperCollins Canada.

Heartfelt thanks to Amy Hundley at Grove Atlantic. To Savannah Johnston and Corinna Barsan, my appreciation and thanks. Thank you to the copyeditors, for their empathy and skill.

Thank you, Tara, Mac, Darius, and Naveen, and especially thank you to my partner, Robert, for always being there, without complaint, with fresh coffee, patience, and love.

I will never forget Ginger Barber's enthusiasm and encouragement, or her delightful telephone calls, during the early stages of this project. I miss her. I hope that somewhere she knows the novel is, at last, finished.